GRAVESEND

ALSO BY J. L. ABRAMO

The Jake Diamond Series

Catching Water in a Net
Clutching at Straws
Counting to Infinity

J. L. ABRAMO

GRAVESEND

Down and Out Books, LLC
3959 Van Dyke Rd, Ste. 265
Lutz, FL 33558
www.DownAndOutBooks.com

Cover design by JT Lindroos

ISBN: 1937495345

ISBN-13: 978-1-937495-34-3

To Brooklyn

We shall not cease from exploration
and the end of all our exploring
will be to arrive where we started
and know the place for the first time.

T. S. Eliot

GRAVESEND

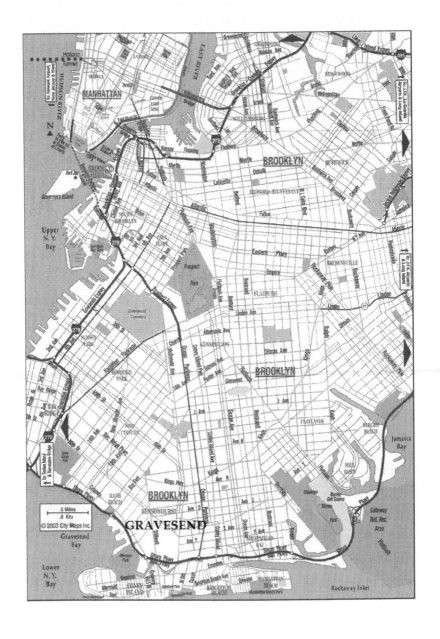

CAST OF CHARACTERS

JAMES SAMSON.............Detective Lieutenant, NYPD, 61st Precinct
ALICIA SAMSON...his wife
JIMMY, KAYLA and LUCY.............................the Samson children
LOU VOTA........................Detective Sergeant, NYPD, 61st Precinct
JOE CAMPO...a grocer
BILLY VENTURA..a victim
PAUL and MARY VENTURA...his parents
REY MENDEZ..................a uniformed officer, NYPD, 61st Precinct
STAN LANDIS..................a uniformed officer, NYPD, 61st Precinct
THOMAS MURPHY........................Detective, NYPD, 61st Precinct
DR. BRUCE WAYNE.............Medical Examiner, City of New York
MARINA IVANOV..........................Detective, NYPD, 60th Precinct
LORRAINE DiMARCO........................a criminal defense attorney
VICTORIA ANDERSON..........a law student, Assistant to Lorraine
BOBBY HOYLE.........................a murder suspect, Lorraine's client
KELLY.....................................Desk Sergeant, 61st Precinct
SALVATORE DiMARCO.....................................Lorraine's father
FRANCES DiMARCO..Lorraine's mother
TONY TERRITO.....................................a dealer in automobiles
VINCENT TERRITO..Tony's father
BRENDA TERRITO...Tony's daughter
DOMINIC COLLETTI...a Mafia boss
SAMMY LEONE...Colletti's bodyguard
SONNY COLLETTI.......................................Colletti's older son
RICHIE COLLETTI.......................................Colletti's younger son
ANNIE...a homeless woman
FRANK SULLIVAN...a homeless man
SUSAN GRAHAM...an innocent bystander

MITCH DUNNE..a proprietor
GABRIEL CAINE...........................a patron of Mitch's Coffee Shop
KEVIN ADDAMS..a victim
GEORGE ADDAMS..his father
SANDRA ROSEN...........................Detective, NYPD, 63rd Precinct
MICHAEL MURPHY..............Detective Murphy's younger brother
MARGARET MURPHY......................................Murphy's mother
SERENA HUANG...a journalist
STANLEY TRENTON.............Brooklyn Chief of Detectives, NYPD
ANDREW CHEN............................Detective, NYPD, 68th Precinct
ROBIN HARDING...Dr. Wayne's assistant
RIPLEY.....................a senior FBI agent, New York City Field Office
WINONA STONE...a junior FBI agent, New York City Field Office
KYLE and MICKEY RIPLEY...................................Ripley's children
VICTOR SANDERS.....................a dealer in stolen pharmaceuticals
EDDIE CONROY..a maintenance man, Our Lady of Angels Church
FATHER DONOVAN...............Pastor, Our Lady of Angels Church
AUGIE SENA...a barkeep
STEVIE TERRITO...Tony's cousin
THERESA FAZIO..............................a receptionist at Titan Imports
DR. ROWDY BARNWELL...a neurosurgeon
DWAYNE HARRIS...a dealer in narcotics
ANDRE HARRIS..his brother
STUMP..an informant
MICHAEL DAVIS......................a uniformed rookie officer, NYPD
HARRY JACOBS.......................Internal Affairs Bureau, NYPD
MARTY RICHARDS.......................Internal Affairs Bureau, NYPD
RALPH...Murphy's best friend

PROLOGUE

THE TRANSGRESSIONS

And they went off the road there with the purpose of stopping for the night in Gibeah and he went into the town, seating himself in the street, for no one took him into his house for the night.

Judges, 19:15

1

Mid-January. Well past midnight.

He moans in his sleep.

His wife tries to wake him gently; using soft, steady pressure to his shoulder.

Her efforts interrupt a bad dream.

Another terrible dream.

The dreams have been recurring more frequently as more time passes since the day he lost his job.

Bad dreams.

Nightmares, manifesting the fear, have crowded his waking hours as well; the terror of not being able to provide for and protect his family.

He wakes gasping for breath, for words.

"What's wrong?" he asks, choking on the question.

"It's Derek. He's been vomiting all night and he's burning up with fever," his wife answers. "I called the doctor. He said we should rush Derek to the emergency room. He said that he would meet us there."

"Get the boy ready. I'll take him over myself," he says, throwing off the bed sheet and blanket. "You need to stay here with the baby."

2

Coney Island Hospital is a fifteen-minute drive; there will be little traffic on the Belt Parkway at this hour.

His wife straps the five-year-old boy into the child seat in back as he climbs behind the steering wheel of the relic they call an automobile.

"Call me."

"I will," he promises, and pulls away from the curb toward the parkway entrance at 65th Street. He gazes across the underside of the Verrazano Bridge as he races past the Fourth Avenue exit. The boy has cleverly managed to free himself from the restraining belt of the child carrier.

The other car comes from out of nowhere, barreling into the right lane from the Bay Parkway entrance, smashing into his right quarter-panel. His car spins a hard ninety degrees. He desperately tries to brake, but he is unable to avoid crashing head-on into the chain-link fence separating the parkway from the service road. The impact bounces his forehead off the steering wheel.

The boy lies on the seat beside him after hitting the dashboard on the passenger side.

The boy is bleeding from a wide gash above the eye.

The small body looks terribly broken.

He tries to start the car with no success. He tries to locate the other vehicle. The other driver has stepped out of the second car and is slowly walking toward them. The man suddenly stops and quickly turns away. He watches in stunned silence as the other driver climbs back into the second car, rolls slowly past them and then speeds off.

The license plate on the BMW reads *TITAN1*.

He is terrified at the thought of leaving the boy there alone, but he is afraid to move the battered body. He removes his own coat and uses it to cover and protect the boy from the bitter cold.

He viciously tears a sleeve from his own shirt and wraps it around the boy's head, trying to slow the bleeding. He jumps from the car, runs to the exit and up to the service road. The area is dark and isolated. There are only retail businesses here, shut down for the night. He turns onto 26th Avenue and runs under the parkway toward the nearest house.

It is nearly three in the morning; he has not shaved for two days. His shirt is roughly torn. He beats on a door for help, crying that his son is hurt badly, and he needs to use a telephone. The woman on the other side of the door will not let him in. She is alone she says, her husband out of town. He pleads until he can hear footsteps moving her back into the depths of the house. He cries out after her, begging her to call for an ambulance to the scene of the accident. He looks at the house address and then turns from the door not knowing what to do, where to go.

A yellow taxicab approaches, heading in the direction of the parkway. He waves his arms wildly, like a madman. He is becoming a madman. An off-duty sign quickly lights on the roof of the taxi as the cab speeds past him.

The number on the rear of the cab is 4354.

His head is filling with numbers.

He runs back to the car. The boy is still breathing. He finds an old blanket in the trunk. He carefully wraps the boy, lifts the body out of the car and begins walking blindly in the direction of the hospital.

A panel truck approaches from behind, slows briefly and then drives on. The lettering on the side of the truck reads *Addams Dairy*. There is a white bumper sticker on the rear with two words in bold black lettering.

Got Milk?

His head is filling with words.

He turns to the sound of another approaching vehicle. A tow truck has stopped at his abandoned car. He reverses direction and hurries back, the boy limp in his arms.

3

The tow truck driver drops him and the boy at the emergency room entrance off Ocean Parkway.

A nurse rushes up and grabs the boy from his arms as she shouts for a room and a doctor.

He tries to follow, but he is held back by another nurse.

He asks for the boy's physician, insisting that the pediatrician was to meet them there.

He is told that the boy's doctor never arrived.

Ten minutes later he is informed that his son is gone. His firstborn has died.

"We did all that we could do," says a nurse. "The boy lost so much blood. It was too late."

His legs go out from under him; he is helped to his feet by the nurse and a security guard. They sit him in a chair, a glass of water appears and a young doctor quickly checks his blood pressure.

"Just sit for a few minutes," the doctor says. "You're going to be alright."

"Never," he replies.

Everything, everyone, every thought is blurred.

"Is there someone we can phone?" asks the nurse.

He looks up at the woman, trying to regain focus.

"My wife," he says weakly. "I need a telephone. I promised her I would call."

PART ONE

UNFORTUNATE PEDESTRIANS

Hast thou that holy feeling in thy soul to counsel me to make my peace with God, and art thou yet to thy own soul so blind, that thou wilt war with God by murdering me? Ah, consider, that he who set you on to do this deed will hate you for the deed.

William Shakespeare

ONE

It is a cold and cloudy afternoon, the first Friday in February.

The wind chill factor races across the rooftop.

Joe Campo turns away from Detectives Vota and Samson and the small body lying on the tar surface behind them. Campo gazes down at the street corner, directly across the avenue, where his wife stands at the door of their family-owned and operated food market. A pair of teenage boys take turns slapping a rubber ball against the west brick wall of the grocery.

Campo's Food Market is the only grocery, delicatessen, newsstand and produce shop remaining in the neighborhood that is not owned and operated twenty-four hours a day by Korean immigrants or owned by Boston or Canadian entrepreneurs and operated by Indian or Pakistani clerks. Not necessarily a bad thing. Just not the way things used to be.

Little was as it used to be in Gravesend.

Lieutenant Samson stares at Joe Campo's back and waits patiently.

Only Detective Vota looks down at the body, and then only for a moment before looking away again. He nervously works at the buttons of his coat.

"I could use my jacket," Vota says, "to cover the body. He looks so cold laying there."

"We'll wait for the medical examiner," Samson says softly, "and Landis will be back with a blanket."

Lou Vota moves over to the northwest corner of the roof and looks down to the street entrance of the building. The small crowd they had encountered at their arrival is steadily growing.

Officer Mendez is down in the street, energetically trying to keep people back.

11

Joe Campo remains at the ledge, silently.

"Mr. Campo," says Samson, just above a whisper.

"When we were his age," Campo says, referring to the boy on the roof, "we would sneak up here to fly a kite; my friends Eddie and Carlo and me. The kite set us back ten cents at old man Baker's Candy Store across the avenue. We would pick up a bag of penny candies while we were there, when penny candies actually cost a penny, or two for a penny. Tiny wax Coca-Cola bottles filled with brown-colored sugar water. Giant fireballs. Pink and white sugar tabs stuck on strips of waxed paper. Chocolate-covered marshmallow twists. And then we'd pick up hero sandwiches at Nick's salumeria, before it was Angelo's and then Vito's and then ours. Ham, hard salami, Swiss cheese and gobs of yellow mustard on half a loaf of seeded Italian bread still warm from Sabatino's Bakery on Avenue S. Twenty-five cents each."

Vota is about to interrupt; Samson stops him with a hand gesture.

Joe Campo looks out toward Coney Island, at the 250-foot tall steel framed Parachute Jump ride that had been moved from the 1939 World's Fair to Steeplechase Park in the forties. The landmark attraction has not carried a passenger for more than thirty years.

"This apartment house was one of the tallest buildings in the neighborhood. Still is at that," Campo goes on. "We thought if we started up here we'd be closer to the sky. One of us would have to run down to Baker's every ten minutes or so for another ball of string, 250 more feet for a nickel. We would watch the paper kite sail toward the ocean, followed by a long tail we had made out of strips torn from one my father's old handkerchiefs. We were sure we could fly the thing all the way to Europe, wherever we thought that was. When the long pieced-together string inevitably snapped we were positive that the kite would eventually come down to land somewhere in France or Germany."

Detective Vota catches sight of Officer Landis waving him over.

"The street is getting very crowded. Mendez is having a time keeping everyone out," Landis says as Vota reaches him.

Landis hands Lou Vota a blanket.

Landis stands just inside the metal door that gives access to the roof from the stairwell. The four-story apartment building has no elevator.

"Get down and give Mendez a hand," says Vota. "When help arrives, move everyone back at least fifty feet from the entrance. No one comes up until after Dr. Wayne gets here."

Landis heads back down the stairs and Vota carries the blanket back to where Samson is silently letting Campo say whatever the man needs to say. Vota glances out toward the Narrows, looks up further to where the Statue of Liberty sits in the harbor and over to where the Twin Towers once stood.

"I grew up in the last tall stucco house," Campo says, pointing up West 10th Street across Avenue S. "My uncle and aunt still live there. My uncle is ninety-five and walks two miles every day. It was the last house on that side of the street for a number of years after my grandfather had it built. It was all farmlands from there on. Across the road there was a large lumber mill. Eddie lived next door. He plowed his Chevrolet Impala into a telephone pole on Stillwell Avenue on the night we graduated from Lafayette High School. Died instantly they said. Carlo lived across the street; he was an All-City sprinting champion. He came back from Vietnam with no feeling from his waist down and now spends most of his time in some tribal casino up in Connecticut."

Campo pulls a package of Camel nonfiltered cigarettes from his coat pocket and holds it out to Detectives Samson and Vota.

Both decline.

Vota is looking for somewhere to place the blanket, not ready to use it for its intended purpose. He strays back to the west ledge and looks down. Reinforcements have arrived to assist in keeping the curious neighbors at a distance.

Campo lights a cigarette. He takes a deep pull and finally comes back to the matter at hand.

"When I was this boy's age, the Brooklyn Dodgers finally beat the Yankees in the World Series and this whole neighborhood was like a carnival."

Campo stops and at last looks back to the small body lying

near Samson's feet on the roof.

Samson takes it as a cue to begin work.

"How did you discover the boy's body, Mr. Campo?" Detective Lieutenant Samson asks.

Thirty minutes earlier, a woman, who Campo could only identify as Irina since her last name was unpronounceable to him, had rushed out of the apartment building and had miraculously negotiated her way across Avenue S with merely one close call. That being with a Pontiac Firebird shouting rap music so loudly into the street that the driver would have never heard the contact had he knocked the woman all the way to West 13ᵗʰ Street.

She ran into the grocery store crying out in Russian, the only language she knew. Joe Campo was no linguist, but changes in demographics over the past ten years had necessitated the recognition of basic words relating to food and credit. In this instance, the woman's body language alone was enough to convince Campo he was being urged to follow her back to the apartment building across the avenue.

Campo had left his wife behind the counter and rushed off to follow the Russian woman.

She had led him up to the roof.

Vota pulls out his cellular phone and calls Detective Murphy at the Precinct.

"Anything on a missing eight-year-old boy, Tommy?" asks Vota, after the desk sergeant transfers the call to Murphy up in Homicide.

"Not yet. Missing Persons is going through their log," says Murphy. "Batman just called in. He was at a meeting in Manhattan and he got stuck crawling in traffic on the Gowanus. He's just now coming off the Belt at Bay Parkway. He should be over to you in five minutes."

"Do we have anyone handy who speaks and understands Russian?" Vota asks.

"I'll check around. Need me down there?"

"No, we need you where you are."

"I'll be here," says Murphy and rings off.

Detective Vota looks down again to the street. The uniforms seem to have the crowd under control. An ambulance has pulled up in front of the building; Officer Rey Mendez is exchanging words with the driver. The attendants will sit tight until the medical examiner arrives and then they will wait until he releases the body.

Vota calls down to Landis and signals for him and Mendez to come up.

Campo has fallen silent again. Lieutenant Samson waits a few moments before gently nudging him on.

"And?" Samson says as Detective Vota joins them again.

"And after seeing the body, I followed Irina back down to her apartment and called it in. Your men were out here in less than ten minutes."

"You obviously didn't call 911," says Vota.

Campo nearly allows himself a smile.

"I called Stan," he says.

Vota and Samson exchange looks.

"Stan?" says Samson.

"Stan Trenton, your chief. Stan and I played football together at Lafayette High. Stan dropped what would have been a game-winning touchdown toss in the final seconds of a contest against Erasmus and decided on a change in career plans. Stan went to Queens College and eventually into the law school there. I broke my ankle in the season closer at Lincoln, took a job working for Vito in the grocery after graduation, and ten years later, I had enough saved to buy the place from his wife when these things killed him."

Campo takes out his package of Camel straights and lights another.

"Recognize the boy?" Samson asks.

"No. Irina said he didn't live in the building. At least that's what I think she was saying. My son lives in the house where I grew up," Joe Campo says, gazing back up West 10th Street. "My grandson is the same age as this boy was. If he was from the neighborhood, I'd have known him."

Officers Landis and Mendez have come onto the roof.

15

Detective Vota walks over to meet them.

"Dr. Wayne just pulled up," says Landis.

"Canvass the apartments," says Vota, "top to bottom. Maybe we'll get lucky for a change. Skip 3-B, that's the woman who found the boy. Sam and I will see her. Murphy is scouting out a Russian translator. Make note of where else we may need one."

"Might need someone who knows Mandarin or Hindi," says Mendez.

"We can only hope," says Vota. "Dr. Wayne have anyone with him?"

"He's alone," says Landis. "The city still has him waiting for a new assistant."

"Okay, go," says Vota.

Officers Mendez and Landis head down, squeezing past the medical examiner, Dr. Bruce Wayne a.k.a. Batman, as the doctor walks up the narrow stairway.

Wayne moves briskly over to where Samson and Campo stand near the body, Vota tagging along.

"Sam," says Wayne.

"Bruce," says Samson.

"Why don't you guys give me ten minutes alone up here, go do what you guys do," says Batman.

Wayne immediately directs his attention to the boy on the ground. Vota places the blanket down near the body.

"Can I go back to my wife?" asks Joe Campo.

"Sure," says Samson, leading the man away from the examiner. "I may want to talk with you again, later on. Thanks for your help."

"I'll be at the store until seven. I'll buy you a Coca-Cola," Campo says.

"Ten minutes, Sam," Wayne calls as Campo and the two detectives reach the doorway to the stairs, "then send up the stretcher."

Samson and Vota follow Campo down, catching sight of Landis and Mendez rapping on doors on the third floor. Campo goes on. Vota and Samson stop for a quick report from the uniforms before continuing down to check the situation on the street.

When Vota and Samson exit the building, they see Campo enter his grocery across the avenue.

"What do you think of him?" asks Vota.

"Just another hardworking guy who would prefer not knowing that these things happen, but can't stay out of the way."

An unmarked car rolls up. It stops on the avenue just past the southeast corner, unable to turn onto 10th Street, which is blocked by three marked police vehicles. A young woman, smartly dressed in pleated slacks and a gray blazer, slides out from behind the wheel. She wears her long black hair in a ponytail.

She quickly crosses to Samson and Vota.

"Lieutenant Samson?" she asks.

"That would be me."

She looks up at the huge black man, who stands at least a foot taller and outweighs her by a hundred pounds.

"Nickname?" she asks.

"Not exactly, and you?"

"Marina Ivanov, 60th Precinct Detective Squad. We got word that you were looking for someone who speaks Russian."

"This is Sergeant Vota, Detective. Let's go up," says Samson, turning back to enter the building. Vota follows. Detective Ivanov hesitates at the bank of mailboxes.

"Which apartment?" she asks.

"3-B," answers Lou Vota, turning back to Detective Ivanov.

Ivanov reads the name on the box.

"Kyznetsov," she says. The t is soft."

"That helps," says Detective Vota. "Is that a rare moniker?"

"I would guess it's something like Johnson or Williams over here, two million or so. Ivanov, on the other hand, is twice as prevalent as Smith."

"And there are eighty-eight million Wangs," says Samson from halfway up the first flight. "Let's move."

They run into Landis and Mendez between the second and third floors. The two uniformed officers are coming down.

"Nada," says Mendez before Samson can ask.

The lieutenant glances at his wristwatch.

"Start hitting the second floor," Samson says. "Rey, run down and tell the ambulance guys that they can come up."

Officers Stan Landis and Rey Mendez continue down, Landis stopping on two and Mendez hurrying down to the street. Vota, Samson and Ivanov come off the stairway onto the third floor and find the door to apartment 3-B. Ivanov taps on the door and a few seconds later it is opened by a woman in her early thirties. A girl, four years old, hangs on to the woman's dress. The woman looks from face to face at the three detectives, finally stopping at Samson's.

One glance into the woman's eyes made it an easy call for the lieutenant.

"Maybe you should speak with her alone, Detective Ivanov," he suggests. "We'll meet you back out front."

Marina says a few words to Mrs. Kyznetsov in Russian and the two women disappear into the apartment. Samson and Vota hear steps coming down from above and wait at the landing to be joined by Batman. At the same time, the two ambulance men arrive at the landing with a folded gurney, followed by a two-man forensics evidence team, causing a serious traffic jam on the stairway. The detectives and the medical examiner make way by stepping into the third-floor corridor while the others pass.

"The boy was killed somewhere else and then brought up here," says the M.E. "There was physical trauma to the head involved, but there may be more. I didn't see signs of anything sexual. That's all I can tell you until we get him down to the lab, so don't bother asking."

"Can you tell me anything about the marks on his face, Bruce?" asks Samson, unable to resist.

Samson *has* resisted asking about the boy's hand; he is unprepared to accept even the most clinical hypothesis as to how that could have happened. And Dr. Wayne is on the same page.

"I'm not sure. Looks like the cuts on his face were made with an X-Acto knife, maybe a box cutter, but very precise. If it's what I think it is," says Wayne, "well, I'd rather not think about it."

"Having a bad day, Doc?" asks Vota.

"Did you happen to look into that boy's eyes?"

"*I* did," says Samson.

"There's your answer," says Batman, and the medical examiner moves quickly down the stairway without another word.

"What is it, Joseph?" asks Roseanna Campo, seeing the expression on her husband's face as he joins her behind the counter of the grocery.

It is an expression of disillusionment.

The two teens who had been playing handball against the building are rifling through the cooler, seeking out the coldest root beers.

"A dead boy, around little Frankie's age," says Campo solemnly.

"My God, Joe."

"Yes."

Reluctantly, Roseanna Campo asks the question. "Is it someone we know?"

"I didn't recognize him."

The boy's own mother won't recognize him, Joe Campo sadly thinks.

Detective Ivanov has joined Vota and Samson in front of the apartment building.

"Her husband is the building superintendent," Ivanov says, filling them in on her talk with Irina Kyznetsov. "He's out working a second job. He had called asking her to check the roof antenna; they were getting complaints about TV reception. She went up and found the body. She says that she didn't know the boy. Says that she didn't see or hear anything."

"Why am I not surprised," says Vota.

"We may need you again, Ivanov," says Samson, "if you wouldn't mind."

"I'd love it. It's been a little slow at the 60th."

"Consider yourself fortunate," says Samson. "Thanks for your help."

Detective Ivanov returns to her car as Officers Landis and Mendez come out of the building.

The steeple bell at Most Precious Blood Church peals four times.

"No luck, Lieutenant," says Officer Landis. "Not many people are back home from work yet. The few we found at home had nothing to contribute. A few apartments had kids back from school waiting for their parents and smart enough not to open the door to us. We'll have to return later to do the rest."

"Okay, let's leave four officers here to clear the street. Why don't you guys get some dinner and start up again in an hour or so."

"The body is on the way down," says Rey Mendez. "The forensic team is going to stay up there and get whatever they can while there's still daylight."

"Good. Lou and I are going back to the Precinct to see if Murphy has come up with any missing kids," says Samson. "Call me after you canvass and feel free to call me at home."

Officers Landis and Mendez walk off to instruct the other uniforms, still struggling with the crowd, as the ambulance men come out with the gurney. They hurry the small body into the vehicle and drive quickly away from the scene. The uniformed officers are trying to dodge questions and get the people on the street to return to their homes.

"What do you think, Sam?" asks Lou Vota.

"My daughter Kayla is that boy's age. What am I supposed to think? And when we learn who the child was, we have notifying his parents to look forward to. What do you think?"

All Vota can think about is the finger.

TWO

Lorraine DiMarco sits restlessly at the defense table of Courtroom D in the Kings County Criminal Courthouse on Court Street in downtown Brooklyn. It is late in the day on the first Friday in February and there is no one in the large, cold room who would not prefer being almost anywhere else. Except the prosecutor, perhaps, who has a visit to his dentist scheduled for later that evening.

To Lorraine's right, her assistant Victoria Anderson is staring at the large clock behind and above the judge's podium, rapping a Krupa beat on an 8½-by-14 inch yellow legal pad with a No. 2 lead pencil. Anderson is a third-year law student attending New York University, working the summer in the Law Office of DiMarco and McWayne on Remson Street in Brooklyn Heights. Lorraine slaps Anderson's knee under the table, and Victoria drops the pencil and clasps her hands in front of her like a kid in Sunday school.

On Lorraine's left sits the defendant, Bobby Hoyle. Lorraine would not allow a pencil anywhere near Bobby. The kid is so nervous he would probably stab himself to death with one. Hoyle is charged with first-degree murder and is, of course, innocent.

The defense is self-defense.

According to Hoyle, he had run out of the house in the wee hours to grab a pack of cigarettes from an all-night deli at Bay Parkway and 85th Street. Bobby had borrowed his brother's 1965 Mustang convertible, without permission. Hoyle left the car idling in front of the small deli and started toward the entrance. Before entering, Bobby saw a stranger at the passenger door of the Ford, ready to climb behind the

21

wheel. More concerned about having to face his brother with news of a stolen vehicle than about his own safety, Bobby accosted the intruder. A struggle ensued, a gun appeared, a gunshot was discharged and Bobby jumped into the Mustang and sped away. Discovering that the gun had found its way into his hand, Bobby dropped it to the floor. Hoyle was stopped by a police cruiser after running a red light at 20th Avenue. Bobby insisted he was rushing to the 62nd Precinct on Bath Avenue to report the shooting. An officer found the weapon at Bobby's feet and Bobby found himself cuffed in the back seat of the police car.

Back at the scene of the shooting, a second patrol car had responded to a 911 call. The victim was DOA. The shop clerk, who had been stocking canned goods in the rear of the store, could not verify that Bobby had left the vehicle before the shooting occurred. When he ran to the door to investigate, the clerk saw the Mustang speeding away and the body of the victim in the street. He went back to the telephone to call the police. A second witness looked out the window of her apartment across the avenue after hearing a gunshot and also saw the Mustang speed off and the body on the ground. She left her vantage point to call 911.

The accounts of both witnesses sounded very much like the description of a drive-by shooting.

The victim was later identified as Johnny Colletti. The store clerk was able to aid in the identification, recognizing Colletti as a local troublemaker, which was helpful since no wallet or other ID was found on the body.

To compound Bobby Hoyle's dilemma, the only prints found on the weapon were his own. The defense contended that sometime while the witnesses were making their phone calls to the police, someone had come along and grabbed Colletti's wallet and the pair of gloves he must certainly have been wearing during the attempted carjacking.

Lorraine DiMarco had three motions before the judge for this late Friday afternoon hearing. First, she moved that all charges be dropped since the victim had a criminal record, Bobby had no such record, and he was pointed in the general direction of the 62nd Precinct when he was stopped. Everyone involved, Lorraine included, saw the chances of the judge granting the motion as slim at best.

Everyone was correct. The motion was quickly denied.

The second motion was for a reduction in bail, which was currently set at $200,000. Hoyle's brother was having difficulty raising the ten percent needed for a bondsman. The fact that Ron Hoyle was trying so diligently was almost surprising, since he wanted to strangle his kid brother for running off with the Mustang in the first place. The kid had been behind bars for three days already and Bobby Hoyle wasn't well equipped for the experience. The judge agreed to a bail reduction to $100,000; but it would still take some doing for Ron Hoyle to scrape up the ten grand.

Lastly, Lorraine asked for a delay to the start of the trial. She argued that the defense needed sufficient time to try locating the person who had lifted Johnny Colletti's wallet and gloves. The thief may have been witness to the actual shooting. The prosecution argued there was nothing to substantiate that Colletti had gloves on his person, or even a wallet for that matter, at the time of the shooting. Since the start of the trial was more than four weeks away, the judge ruled to let the date stand and invited Defense Attorney DiMarco to resubmit the motion if more time was necessary as the date became imminent.

All in all it was not a great day for Bobby Hoyle.

Lorraine had known Ron and Bobby Hoyle their entire lives. She had babysat Bobby when she was a teen. Hoyle's father, who lost a battle with lung cancer the previous summer, had played pinochle with Lorraine's father every Friday night for many years. Hoyle senior, who also played the horses at Aqueduct, Belmont and OTB without restraint, left little for his sons beyond a heavily mortgaged house on West 12th Street, a few doors from Lorraine's parents.

Coming up with $10,000 to free Bobby on bail was going to be tricky.

Bobby Hoyle rises to join his escort back to Rikers.

"How did we do?" he timidly asks Lorraine.

"I guess it could have been worse," she answers, not too convincingly. "Stay away from the other inmates. Get through the weekend; I'll get you out by Monday."

"Promise?"

"Hang in there, kid," Ron Hoyle says, coming up from his seat in the gallery. "*I* promise you'll be home Monday."

The bailiff walks Bobby Hoyle out of the courtroom; Lorraine turns to his older brother.

"Will you be able to swing it?"

"I hope so. I think I have someone interested in going ten thousand for the Mustang," Ron says. "Perfect irony."

He thanks Lorraine and heads out of the courtroom.

"Is everything alright, Victoria?" Lorraine asks as they collect their paperwork.

"Last time I checked, why?"

"The way you were drumming on your pad, I thought you were late for a date."

"The only date I have is with my bar exam study books, and I'm totally monogamous. And you? Big Friday night plans?"

"Detective Vota is coming over to my parents' house for dinner. We'll eat lots of delicious and unhealthy food and then I'll look through old photo albums with Mom while Dad and Lou glue themselves to the hockey game."

"Bobby didn't look very good," says Victoria.

"Not surprising, the kid is terrified. We have to get him out of there, and soon. Have a good weekend. I'll see you Monday morning."

Vota and Samson were back at the 61st Precinct at four-thirty. The three-story brick building sat back off Coney Island Avenue at Avenue W.

For all appearances, the building could have been a city public school. Only the marked police cars filling the parking area gave away its identity.

Desk Sergeant Kelly calls down from his throne as they head for the stairs to the third-floor Homicide detectives' squad room, stopping Vota in his tracks.

"Got a minute, Lou?"

"I'll go up and see if Murphy has found anything," says Samson.

"What are you reading now?" asks Vota, referring to the book sitting open in front of the desk sergeant.

"*One Flew over the Cuckoo's Nest*, as part of my continuing attempt to somehow understand the nature of this precinct. I just got a call from old man Levine at the liquor store on 86th Street."

"Oh?"

"He wants to talk with you, about the shooting on Bay Parkway. The carjack incident your lovely attorney friend is working on. Isn't that case with the 62nd?"

"Yes."

"You don't want to step on their toes, Lou. That's a treacherous bunch over on Bath Avenue."

"I was only asking a few questions. I'm not looking to rain on anyone's parade. But I do appreciate the concern. I didn't know you cared."

"There's a lot about me you don't know," says Kelly. "For example, I came in second in the Brooklyn Borough Spelling Bee finals when I was fourteen years old. I missed the word *decorum*."

"Figures. What did Levine have to say?"

"Levine said that some street guy who comes into the store to buy a bottle of Ripple or Boone's Farm, whenever he can scrape together enough pennies and empty soda cans to afford one, walked in two nights ago and purchased a bottle of expensive Irish whiskey with a crisp new C-note and then tried to sell Levine a pair of genuine calfskin driving gloves. Levine thought you might be interested."

"I am."

"Levine said he'd be at the liquor store until nine."

"Okay, thanks Kelly, I'll give him a call," Vota says and heads for the climb to the squad room.

"How do you like the new addition?" Detective Murphy asks when Samson walks into the Homicide squad room.

Murphy is pointing at the photograph which had found its place hung between pictures of Dennis Franz and Clint Eastwood on the wall behind his desk. It was Murphy's Wall of Fame, his shrine to the great homicide cops of film and television.

"Is that my man Pembleton?"

"None other. Andre Braugher circa 1993."

"Any luck with missing kids?" Samson asks.

"I don't know if luck is quite the word for it. We have eight girls: 6, 9, 10, 11, 13, 14 and two 16-year-olds. Three Caucasian, three African-American, one Korean and one Hispanic. And four boys: 3, 8, 12 and 13. What the hell is going on, Sam?"

"I wish I knew, Tommy. Or maybe I'd rather not. What about the eight-year-old?"

"Jamaican," says Murphy.

"Any luck?" says Vota, walking into the room. "Is that Andre Braugher?"

"No and yes," says Murphy.

"Do me a favor, Tommy," Samson says. "I realize that it is Friday night, but I could use you over at the scene to see how Landis and Mendez are doing with the apartment canvass. Residents should be starting to arrive home from work. I'd go myself, but it's Lucy's birthday. I promised Alicia that I wouldn't be late and I'm having strong feelings about wanting to spend time with my children. I'll have Kelly forward any calls about missing kids over to me at home."

"Sure, Sam, no problem."

"Call me if you need any help, Tommy," Vota offers, handing Murphy a telephone number. "I'll be at Lorraine's parents' house watching the Islanders pummel the Rangers."

"Fat chance," says Murphy, wondering afterward where the expression came from.

Vota goes over to his desk to call Levine at the liquor store.

"What do you have in the Prince of Pizza box, Tommy?" Samson asks.

With Thomas Edward Murphy, nothing was obvious.

"A meatball calzone for Ralph. I refuse to cook for him on

Friday nights."

Before heading over to join Mendez and Landis at the crime scene, Murphy goes over to his apartment to share the meatball calzone with Ralph and run Ralph over to John Paul Jones Park. Murphy parks his Chevrolet in front of a fire hydrant a few hundred feet from his building. Finding a legal parking space that was closer than a taxi ride to his place would be impossible at that time of day. He plants a city parking permit on his dashboard.

Murphy takes the stairs up to the fourth floor, calling it his daily aerobics. He had missed his usual three-mile run that morning and was feeling the worse for it. He knew that Ralph had surely had a bad day, pacing the apartment, rearing to sprint. Thomas Murphy struggles with his Irish-Catholic guilt over denying Ralph his morning exercise as he takes the stairs two at a time. The calzone is Murphy's attempt at atoning for his sin.

Ralph's joy at Murphy's return is manifested by barks and attempted embraces that have Murphy juggling the pizza box for control. He manages to fake left, do an end run to the kitchen and safely place the box on the kitchen table. It takes Murphy several minutes to calm the large German shepherd. Deciding that a trip over to the park is more critical than diving into dinner for the moment, Murphy grabs the leash from the front door knob, for appearances only, and leads Ralph out of the apartment and quickly down the three flights. The two trot up Marine Avenue toward 4th Avenue and Shore Road.

Lou Vota drives from the 61st to his house in Red Hook via Ocean Parkway into the Gowanus and then onto the Brooklyn-Queens Expressway. At that hour, the great majority of traffic is headed in the opposite direction, coming from Manhattan into Brooklyn.

Vota lives in the house he inherited from his parents. Vota's two sisters had long ago followed their husbands to places west, gladly leaving the Borough of Churches behind. Lou, on the other hand, loved Brooklyn and had lived there all of his life. When his mother passed away, after losing a battle with leukemia, Lou Vota moved back into the house where he grew up, to provide companionship for his father. John Vota had spent fifty years in the plumbing business, doing most of his work there in the neighborhood. When a massive heart attack took John's life at age seventy, Lou remained in the residence.

Red Hook had been a predominantly Italian-American stronghold for many years. A slow steady migration to Bensonhurst, Bay Ridge and Staten Island, by families who saw such moves as upward mobility, set the area into a progression of changes. The neighborhood saw worse times before seeing better. In recent years, the so-called gentrification of Brooklyn Heights, Carroll Gardens and Cobble Hill had finally spilled further south into Red Hook. Now Red Hook, as those other neighborhoods before it, had become the next up-and-coming place to live.

Vota had started remodeling the house, as time and resources allowed, after his father's death. He had redone the second floor and created a two-bedroom, one-and-a-half-bath apartment which brought in a substantial monthly rent. Vota had also built a deck on the roof of the two-story brownstone, which offered a spectacular view of the Harbor.

Vota stops for a box of pastries from Attanasio's Bakery on President Street, a few doors down from where Joey Gallo was born and raised, before continuing to his house on Verona Street near the corner of Van Brunt.

Vota quickly checks his mail, shaves, showers and dresses in preparation for his dinner engagement.

Checking his father's prized grandfather clock, Vota finds that he has some time to spare before he needs to be at the DiMarco home. He takes the less trafficked Prospect Expressway into Ocean Parkway toward Bensonhurst to pick up a few bottles of Cabernet and find out what he could learn from old man Levine at the liquor store on 86th Street.

. . .

Lorraine DiMarco goes straight from the courthouse to her parents'home.

Lorraine has decided that she can shower and find a change of clothing there and help her mother prepare the meal.

The DiMarcos live in a two-family house on West 12th Street between Avenues T and U in Gravesend, a few doors down from the Hoyle residence. Lorraine finds a parking space directly behind Ron Hoyle's now infamous 1965 Mustang convertible. The DiMarco house is only three short blocks from where the boy's body had been found on the roof.

Salvatore DiMarco is a retired Transit Authority cop, who had always wanted to be a lawyer. He had instilled the love of the law in his three children and was extremely proud when Lorraine graduated Queens College Law School and passed the New York bar exam. Lorraine's mother, Fran, is a retired schoolteacher, having taught third grade at P.S. 97 on West 13th Street for more than thirty years, and Lorraine experienced both the advantages and disadvantages of having a mom who taught at the elementary school where Lorraine herself had attended for seven of those years.

Lorraine's older sister, Linda, never caught the law bug from her father. Instead she followed her mother's footsteps into the admirable profession of educating young children and taught elementary school in Denver, where her husband was a surgeon at the Colorado Health and Sciences Center. Sal and Fran DiMarco's first child, Salvatore Jr., who was smart enough and talented enough to become anything he wanted to become, was killed by a sniper in South Vietnam when Lorraine was three years old.

After a quick shower, Lorraine throws on a T-shirt and sweatpants and joins her mother in the kitchen.

Fran DiMarco immediately puts her daughter to work breading the veal cutlets.

Samson stops at the Reliable Bakery on Sheepshead Bay Road to pick up the birthday cake before heading out Avenue

U toward Flatbush. Samson has decided to avoid the rush-hour traffic on the Belt Parkway by taking Flatlands to Pennsylvania Avenue, hopping onto the Jackie Robinson Parkway and then to the Van Wyck Expressway up to Northern Boulevard. The twenty-one-mile trip from the 61st to his three-bedroom ranch house in Douglaston is a thirty-five-minute commute under the best of circumstances. As he passes Flushing Meadows Park and the ball field, Samson gives thanks that the start of the baseball season is less than seven weeks away.

Douglaston is located in that hazy area that was either Queens or Long Island depending on a resident's disposition. For those who had migrated from Woodside, Astoria, Elmhurst and Flushing, it was called Long Island, with all of the prestige the title could muster. But for Samson, who was born and raised in Bedford-Stuyvesant in Brooklyn, it was Queens. For Samson it was important to be living in one of the five boroughs.

The move to the suburbs had great advantages. A private residence with front and back yards and safe streets for the kids. Alicia's family nearby. Peace of mind. But it came at a price. A long, nerve-wracking commute. A sense of isolation from his fellow detectives. And a feeling of having abandoned a neighborhood in need of help. It provided Samson with enough guilt to have him working after-school athletic programs in Bushwick and Bed-Sty at least two evenings every month.

Samson comes off Douglaston Parkway onto 235th Street and drives toward 41st Avenue and Alley Pond Park. When he pulls into the driveway, his five-year-old birthday girl runs out to meet him at the door.

THREE

Vota places the two bottles of Cabernet on the liquor store counter and reaches for his wallet.

"Please tell me about the man who came in with the calfskin gloves, Mr. Levine," Vota says.

"He comes in quite often, but I can't tell you his name. He's known on the street as Sully. I haven't seen him since he was in with the gloves and the hundred-dollar bill. That was Wednesday night."

"Any idea where this Sully lives?"

"As I told the desk sergeant, I'm sure he lives on the streets. In the warmer weather I've seen him a few times sleeping in vestibules along 86th Street," says Levine. "At this time of year, I imagine that he has found a place more protected. It's my understanding that some of the homeless use the train station at 25th Avenue, but they wouldn't show up until the clerk at the token booth goes off at ten."

"Thanks for your help," says Vota, taking his change and lifting the bagged wine bottles from the counter. "If Sully comes in again, please call the Precinct. See if you can keep him here, or persuade him to talk to us. Tell him there's a reward involved."

Murphy arrives at the apartment building on Avenue S after polishing off the entire meatball calzone with Ralph and regretting the accomplishment. There is more activity than he had expected. A uniformed officer at the building entrance directs Murphy to apartment 2-D.

Officers Landis and Mendez are there, along with the forensic team called down from the roof. The apartment is void of furniture and looks freshly painted. A small, wood step stool sits in the middle of the front room.

"What's going on?" asks Murphy.

"Looks like this is where the boy was killed," says Mendez. "Looks like the killer carried him in through the window."

"From the fire escape in broad daylight?"

"Seems so. From the back of the building," says Landis, "and no one we've spoken with saw a thing."

"Has this place been rented?" asks Murphy.

"Not yet," says a woman coming out of one of the bedrooms, "but a few people have come to look at it."

Murphy looks to Officer Landis for a clue.

"Detective Marina Ivanov from the 60th," Landis says as she walks over to them. "Ivanov, meet Detective Murphy. Ivanov was here earlier with Sam and Vota to talk with the woman who discovered the body, and we called her back."

"I tried to get descriptions of the three people who came to look at the place," says Ivanov, "but they're all pretty sketchy. The woman is still very upset."

"Did she get any names? Anyone fill out papers? Don't you need a credit check to rent an apartment?"

"This is Gravesend, Murphy," says Landis. "Credit here is what you owe at the grocery across the street."

"So, the boy is brought in here, maybe killed here and then carried up to the roof. Is that the going theory?" asks Murphy.

"At the moment," says Landis.

"Why take the chance of being seen carrying the body?"

"Couldn't say," says Landis, "unless he wanted the body to be found sooner."

"Or later," says Mendez.

"So, what do we have here?" asks Murphy.

"We have a hypodermic needle for starters," says Mendez.

"This guy shot up while he was here with the kid?"

No one had an answer.

"Then there was this," says Mendez, leading Murphy into the kitchen.

The numbers were written on the wall opposite the open refrigerator in what appeared to be red crayon. One of the forensic investigators was scraping a sample from the top of the large five.

"71915? What the fuck is that supposed to be, a date? A zip code? A fucking lottery number? What?"

Landis follows as Murphy storms back out into the front room. A second investigator is dusting the door for fingerprints. The calzone is hurling itself against the walls of Murphy's stomach. He wants to sit. He walks over to the wooden step stool and sees the blood.

"And this?" asks Murphy.

"Has to be where he cut the boy," says Mendez.

"Did what?"

"Didn't Samson or Vota tell you about the boy's finger?"

"What finger?"

"The small finger of the right hand. The missing finger," says Landis.

Lucy Samson has just blown out the five candles on her birthday cake and Samson is ready to cut into it when the telephone rings. He hands the knife to his wife Alicia, and walks over to take the call.

"Sorry to bother you at home, Lieutenant," says Kelly.

"No problem, Kelly, what have you got?"

"We got a call on a missing kid, a boy, eight years old," says the desk sergeant. "It sounds like it might be the one you're looking for."

"Who called it in and when?"

"The mother, ten minutes ago."

Samson looks at the kitchen wall clock.

"What took her so long?" he asks.

"She says she had to work late. She has another kid, four-year-old girl, who stays with a neighbor. The boy was supposed to go over there after school, but never showed up. There was some cross-up in communication and the neighbor wasn't expecting him. When the mother arrived to pick up her children and discovered that the boy wasn't there, she called it in."

"Does she know about the kid on the roof?"

"No."

"What about the father?"

"He doesn't live with them. They're separated. We got an address on him from the mother."

"Damn it, I was hoping I'd know more from the medical examiner about what happened up there before I had to deal with parents," says Samson.

"There is more. Murphy just got back. I'll let him fill you in."

Kelly transfers the call and Murphy tells Samson about the empty apartment and what was found there.

"What are you doing now?" asks Samson.

"I'm writing it up."

"I mean, do you have plans?"

"I know better than to make plans on a Friday night, Sam. What do you need?"

"Can you try to locate the father of the boy?"

"Sure."

"I'm coming back in. I'll see the mother. Check in with Batman to find out if he has anything from the medical exam and ask him to get the boy ready for a possible ID. Call me on my cell phone after you speak to him."

"Copy that."

"Thanks, Tommy."

"Like I have a choice," says Murphy.

"Of course you have a choice," says Samson.

"A fine dinner, Mrs. DiMarco, thank you."

"You're very welcome, Lou, it's my pleasure."

"We heard about the boy they found over on 10th Street, Lou," says Sal DiMarco. "Were you there?"

"Unfortunately, yes, but I can't say much about it yet."

"How about coffee?" says Fran DiMarco, changing the subject.

"Sounds great," says Vota, and changing the subject again he turns to Lorraine. "I may have a lead on the man who lifted Johnny Colletti's wallet the night your client Bobby Hoyle was picked up."

Vota tells her about his talk with Levine at the liquor store.

"Can we go look for the homeless man tonight?" asks Lorraine. "We have to get Bobby Hoyle out of Rikers before things get worse for him. The kid is a mess."

"Sure, we can go over to the train station after ten, see who's camping out."

"What a terrible thought," says Fran DiMarco, bringing the espresso pot and pastries to the table.

No one disagrees.

Samson is using the Belt Parkway for the trip back into Brooklyn. The evening is cold and damp; the traffic heading toward Manhattan is mild. As he speeds past the Flatbush Avenue exit his cell phone chirps. He would rather not answer the call.

Samson is expecting Murphy on the other end of the line, but is not entirely surprised to find Batman there.

"I'll make it quick, I have two more to do tonight," says the medical examiner. "The boy was struck severely on the back of the head. If it didn't kill him, it definitely would have left him unconscious. The hypodermic needle that was sent to me from the scene contained pancuronium bromide. It's a serious muscle relaxant; you may have heard it referred to as Pavulon. It's often employed in hospitals to facilitate the use of artificial respiratory devices during surgery. It shuts down the patient's normal breathing mechanisms. In this case, administered in large dose by injection, it would make it impossible for the victim to breathe."

"The boy suffocated?"

"By all appearances. You saw his eyes."

"Was it painful?"

"It would be something close to drowning; the trauma would be more mental than physical."

"How accessible is the drug?"

"Today, Sam, there is nothing you can't get if you look for it. This Pavulon, by the way, is used in lethal injections in most prisons for capital offense executions. It's what makes the victims appear so calm and remain silent while they are strapped onto the gurney. The drug renders the victim literally speechless."

"Tell me about his hand."

"The boy's finger was removed postmortem, if it's any consolation. I'm guessing a pair of shears. Something was used to cauterize the wound, to stop the bleeding."

Samson has heard more than enough, but he needs more.

"What about the boy's cheek?" he asks.

"The cuts were deliberate. As I said earlier at the scene, I'm guessing a sharp razor knife, the kind used for layout and design. Maybe a scalpel, but less likely."

Samson waits for the bad news, though he suspects that he knows already.

"It's a message of some kind. Two letters, J and G."

Samson feels a chill run through his entire body; he recalls the disappointment in the eyes of his two young daughters as he left the birthday celebration to attend to this thankless business.

"I'm on my way to see a woman who may be this boy's mother and may be bringing her over for identification," says Samson. "Somehow, we miraculously avoided the press this afternoon. I don't want anyone getting wind of the missing finger or the cuts on the face. I hate the idea, but we need to hide it from the mother."

"I'll take care of it," says Wayne.

Joe Campo has decided to treat his wife to a movie. It is a damp, chilly evening, but they agree to walk the five blocks to the Marlboro Theater on Bay Parkway from their home on West 9th Street.

Holding hands.

As they walk, Joe Campo thinks back to his childhood. When he and Carlo and Eddie walked West 10th Street to the same movie theater for Saturday matinees. When there was only one screen, not four. When the boys went equipped with hot, homemade hero sandwiches of veal and eggplant parmigiana. When the price of admission was twenty-five cents. When they watched the now classic Universal horror films like *Creature from the Black Lagoon* and an audience packed with preteens screamed in unison every time the Creature raised his huge claw from the dark depths.

The films today were far more terrifying, telling unfathomable tales of current-day creatures who committed unthinkable atrocities. And still more horrifying were the creatures of the real world that these contemporary movies attempted to represent and failed to explain. Tonight, the Campos have chosen a romantic comedy. Lighter fare. But even modern comedy had an uneasy edge that has Joe Campo pining for Tracy and Hepburn.

Tony Territo pulls up in front of the Velvet Lounge on New Utrecht Avenue in Borough Park. Sammy Leone moves toward the Jeep Cherokee from his post in front of the busy nightclub. Territo climbs out of the car and meets Sammy halfway.

"Where's the Beemer?"

"In the shop. I'm already very late," says Territo, "and my wife is waiting to serve dinner. What do you need?"

"The old man is inside. He wants to talk."

"About what?"

"About how you managed to get his nephew killed."

"I had nothing to do with what happened to Johnny."

"The kid was trying to pinch a vintage Mustang; the old man seems to think the kid was working for you."

"I don't deal with antiques. And Colletti knows it. And no disrespect, but I wouldn't let that kid wash a car for me, let alone steal one."

"Tell it to the old man," says Leone. "Wait here."

Leone walks over to the entrance and opens the door. As he goes in, the deafening sound of a band covering an old Rolling Stones song spills out into the street.

Territo lights a cigarette and looks at his watch. He knows he's going to catch hell from his wife. After a few minutes, Dominic Colletti walks out of the lounge. The old man tells Territo what he expects and how much he would hate to be disappointed.

Territo knows enough to hold his tongue.

Ten minutes later, Tony Territo is tearing up 65th Street. Racing home to placate his wife and to call his father.

Murphy has located the apartment building on Ocean Parkway where Paul Ventura is said to reside. He parks at a fire hydrant in front and enters the lobby. He finds the buzzer for apartment 6-R and pushes twice. He listens for a sound from the intercom speaker, wondering how he is going to tell the man that a dead boy on a roof may have been his son. After thirty seconds, Murphy presses the buzzer again, three times. He returns to his car and calls Samson.

Samson takes the Bay Parkway exit and finds the house on 81st Street, just across Stillwell Avenue from the public school. He pulls into a parking space a few doors down and switches on the dome light. Samson looks down at the notes he took from Sergeant Kelly on Mary Ventura, whose missing son may have been the boy on the roof.

Twenty seven years old. Two children. William, eight. Wendy, four. Separated from her husband, three months. Mary sells and rents co-op apartments out of a real estate office on Third Avenue in Bay Ridge.

She answers the door holding the young girl in her arms. Her face is streaked with tears.

"Mrs. Ventura," he says, softly. "I'm Detective Samson from the 61st Precinct."

"Have they found Billy?" she asks.

"May I come in?"

He follows her into the house and then into the kitchen.

She offers him a seat at the table. She offers coffee. He accepts both. She places the girl down; the child hangs on to her dress. She pours two cups and sits across from Samson, taking the child into her lap.

"May I ask you a few questions?"

"You haven't answered mine," she says.

She reaches to a wallet on the table, opens it and removes a photograph. She hands it across to Samson.

"Billy," she says.

He glances at the photograph and somehow manages to look back up into her eyes.

"I'm deeply sorry."

Murphy has been sitting in his car, the engine running to fuel the heater, Cat Stevens on the stereo. He calls Samson's cell number.

"Nothing yet, Sam, want me to hang?"

"I'll send a couple of uniforms over. Wait for them and then go home."

"Was it the Ventura kid?"

"Yes. The mother insisted she drive herself. She's following me now to Coney Island Hospital. She doesn't believe that her husband would harm the child, but we need to find out where he's been."

"I don't mind staying," says Murphy.

"That's okay, just wait there for the uniforms, I know it's your weekend off, but I'll probably need you tomorrow morning. Sorry."

"Sure. Just call me."

The Territos finally sit down to dinner. Barbara Territo is complaining about the roast drying up in the oven. Thirteen-year-old Anthony Jr. is complaining about how hungry he is. Brenda, sixteen, would rather skip the whole thing altogether and get over to the party at her friend Diane's house. All Tony Territo can think about is what old man Colletti had the fucking balls to say to him outside the Velvet Lounge. And about how his father, Vincent Territo, was making Tony wait until morning to discuss the situation.

Mary Ventura looks at the body of her son from the other side of a large glass pane. It is very much like the one she looked through when he was a newborn infant in the nursery in this same hospital.

Batman has done a fine job. He has covered the facial cuts with makeup and turned the carved side of the face away from the window. Dr. Wayne has covered the boy's body with a stark, white sheet to hide the small hands.

She begs to be allowed into the room to hold her boy. Samson has to choke out the refusal.

Finally he manages to tear her away from the window, reminding her that her little girl is waiting for her at the nurses' station above.

As he drives back to Douglaston, Samson realizes that he is very angry.

Vota and Lorraine arrive at the 25th Avenue train station shortly after ten and climb the stairs to the platform. A woman sits on a bench, positioning a small cloth bag she will use as a pillow. There is a large suitcase tied with a short piece of clothesline to her wrist. She wears a pair of work boots, at least two sizes too big for her feet, the laces wrapped around the legs of her pants at least three times and tied in front.

She is about to lie down when they walk up to her.

"Don't hurt me," she says.

"We're looking for Sully," Vota says.

"Are you his brother?"

"No."

"He's always talking about his brother, you know, how his brother is going to come for him and take him home."

Lorraine cannot help staring at this woman. The woman is very close to Lorraine's own age.

"Can you tell us where Sully is?" asks Vota.

"Are you buying?"

Lorraine reaches into her purse and removes a twenty-dollar bill. She hands it to the woman.

"Wow, you must want him bad. What's he done?"

"Nothing," says Detective Vota. "We just need to talk with him."

"He should be back Sunday night. He went up to the Bronx to visit a friend for the weekend."

"Do you know the address?"

40

"Sure. The Kingsbridge Road train station near the end of the D Line."

"Okay, thanks for your help," says Vota, as he takes Lorraine's arm to turn and leave.

Lorraine pulls up short and turns to the woman.

"What's your name?" Lorraine asks.

"Annie. Annie from Bay 38th."

Back down on the street, Vota starts the car and then turns to Lorraine beside him.

"I'll just be a minute," he says.

He goes to the trunk and pulls out a heavy green wool blanket and walks back up the stairs of the train station.

When he drapes the blanket over the woman's body, she is already asleep.

When he had left the roof that afternoon, after he had carried the dead boy's body up to the top of the building, he had walked calmly down the four flights of stairs and out of the front door of the apartment house. He had been in the building for close to forty-five minutes and had seen no one.

No one, it seems, had seen him.

He crossed West 10th Street and walked the one block to West 11th, where his car was parked at the end of the street facing Avenue S. He pulled away from the curb, turned right onto S and headed east. He slowed the car briefly to take a last look up at the apartment building as he passed.

As he turned onto the street where he lived, he saw a car up ahead crossing the avenue. It was the skis on the roof rack of the vehicle that caught his eye. He continued past his house to the corner at 6th Avenue.

He stopped at the intersection and watched the other car double-park in front of a small house. A male driver left the vehicle running and walked up to the door. A moment later, a woman came out carrying a suitcase and a pair of ski boots. He drove across the avenue and passed the double-parked car as the man loaded the luggage into the trunk. The woman climbed into the passenger seat.

He drove back around to his house and pulled into the

driveway. He took a cloth tool satchel from the car seat and entered his house. He removed a small plastic bag from the satchel and placed it into the refrigerator's freezer compartment.

He poured himself a tall glass of Scotch and set to work at the kitchen sink, washing the small pruning shears and dropping the empty drug vial and what was left of the red crayon into the garbage disposal.

He took his drink and went to his son's room.

Later that night, he walks to the house on the next street where he had seen the couple leave earlier for what he felt confident was a weekend on a ski slope upstate or in Vermont. It was exactly what he needed, a place that would be empty until at least Sunday morning.

He carries the tool satchel and hides a long pry bar under his coat.

The night is damp and foggy, creating eerie haloes around the lamps of the light poles on both sides of 69th Street.

Tall trees also line the street. Oak. Maple. Apple. Cherry. Elm. Nearly every kind of hardwood tree grows in Brooklyn. Aside from a few lonely evergreens, the trees are bare, leafless. Through the fog, the branches appear to be long, menacing arms and tentacles, reminding him of creatures in the picture books scattered across the floor of his son's room. He wonders about the fascination that children have with monsters, about the strange attraction adults have to fear.

He walks silently up the dark alley between Bay Ridge Avenue and 68th Street to the rear of the empty house. He passes through the gate of a tall cedar fence, crosses the small back yard and reaches the door that comes off the kitchen. He quickly pries open the lock and finds the door held by a short chain. He uses the pry bar to break the chain, closes the unlocked door, leaves the satchel behind a small hedgerow under the window and walks back home.

He walks into his son's room and sets the alarm clock.

He sits on the floor and reaches for a coloring book.

A tree branch taps against the window.

. . .

Detective Murphy sits in his three-room apartment on Marine Avenue in Bay Ridge, not far from the Fort Hamilton Army Base at the Brooklyn foot of the Verrazano Bridge. The fort was built to protect the Narrows, the long waterway connecting the Atlantic Ocean to the New York City Harbor.

Murphy swallows the last of his fourth bottle of Samuel Adams lager while the beat-up sofa tries to swallow him. He is half-watching Jay Leno interviewing someone Murphy can't quite place.

It is past two in the morning.

Murphy wonders what kind of losers are up at this hour watching the repeat of a TV program that wasn't worth the time or effort when it aired three hours earlier the same evening. Realizing that he is doing just that, Murphy turns his attention to Ralph.

"I should be out with a redhead on my arm," Murphy says, "painting the town the color of her hair. Instead, I'm sucking down beer that tastes as if it was in and out of the cooler at Maury's Deli at least three times, being slowly devoured by this fucking sorry excuse for a piece of furniture and complaining to you."

Ralph has no comment.

Three weeks earlier, Murphy had spent his birthday in much the same way.

On that mid-January evening he had made it to Joe's Bar and Grill on Avenue U just in time to be on hand when Augie Sena dropped a full keg of beer on his own leg, breaking Augie's limb in two places.

At just about this time on his thirty-fourth birthday, Murphy had been sitting in a hospital emergency room while doctors worked on Augie's leg.

Looking into the vacant eyes of a man who had just lost his child.

Hell of a way to celebrate.

. . .

Murphy extracts himself from the spongy sofa with the intention of collecting another bottle of the ruined beer from his refrigerator.

One look at Ralph lets him know that his best friend needs a walk in the park.

Murphy and his dog walk past John Paul Jones Park toward the Shore Road promenade. A heavy fog engulfs the ancient cannon and the stack of cannonballs left over from another revolution.

They walk down to the water's edge.

Murphy can hear the scurrying of small animals in the dense bushes.

Ralph is all ears.

Murphy stands at the railing, gazing out at the bridge while Ralph chases shadows.

The massive, concrete piling is the tomb of a luckless construction worker who fell and disappeared into a molten grave. Another immigrant who came to build a new world.

Murphy looks out across to Staten Island, once only accessible by ferry. Beyond the island, New Jersey and California and all of those unknown places in between.

And beyond, the Pacific and all of those unknowable places that Murphy has only read about.

Murphy takes an unsung pride in the fact that people from nearly every foreign land beyond both seas have come here, have carried their children, their hopes and their dreams to Brooklyn.

The Narrows beats up against the rocky shoreline below.

The alarm wakes him at two-thirty in the morning. He finds himself on the floor of his son's room. Surrounded by toys.

He tries not to think about the other boy, the boy he had to kill and leave up on the cold roof.

He washes his face with cool water from the kitchen sink and goes out to his car.

44

He reaches the dairy on Ralph Avenue as the young man is leaving to begin his route. He follows, always staying at least a block behind and waiting out of sight each time the truck makes a stop for deliveries.

He knows this route very well by now.

He wants to be sure he has chosen the best spot to do what he needs to do the following night.

FOUR

The following day. Break of dawn. Detective Murphy is coordinating a house-to-house canvass that will cover West 10th Street between Avenue T and Highlawn Avenue and Avenue S between West 9th and West 11th. Landis and Mendez are there in addition to four uniforms borrowed from traffic control. Fewer parking tickets will be issued this morning. Fewer residents will sleep as late as they planned to sleep on a Saturday morning.

Did anyone see a man at or near the apartment building early yesterday afternoon? Alone, or with a young boy, or carrying a child? Anyone acting suspicious, any person or persons unknown? Any unfamiliar vehicle, alongside or near the building? Anyone? Anything?

Nothing.

The two-man forensic team is back on the roof, picking up where they left off before losing daylight after being called down to the apartment where the boy was apparently held. Nothing more was found in the rooms, nothing further discovered on the roof, nothing at all to help identify the perpetrator.

Murphy stops into the grocery store across from the apartment building for coffee and a buttered hard roll.

"It's almost impossible to believe that this guy drives up, carries the boy up the fire escape, then up to the roof, comes out again, and drives away with not a single witness," says Murphy, stirring far too much sugar into the light coffee.

"When I was a kid, growing up here," says Joe Campo, "a stranger couldn't walk down West 10th Street without having twenty pairs of eyes glued on him every moment he was on the block."

. . .

Brooklyn neighborhoods are much like small, individual towns and villages. Varying degrees of acquaintance and recognition. Family. Friends. Neighbors. People known to each other by name, or only by sight. The other patrons of the coffee shop, the grocery, the bank, the pizzeria. Familiar faces on the bus, the subway station. Shopkeepers and regulars. Bank tellers and patrons. Bus drivers and commuters. Fellow pedestrians. *Good morning, John. How are you, Millie.* Or just *hello* to the woman recently met at the checkout in the local pharmacy, the man who stood in line at the local movie theater.

"Good morning, gents," says Bill Meyers, bouncing into Mitch's Coffee Shop and taking a seat at the counter. "Long time, no see, Gabriel."

"Been very busy, Bill," says Gabriel Caine, working on a plate of eggs and home fries at the adjacent stool.

"I'll have the special, Mitch," says Bill, "scrambled well and with a little less hair."

"I add the hair for the extra protein," says Mitch, breaking two eggs onto the griddle.

"Drop a few fingernail clippings into my coffee cup," says Meyers. "That should take care of my minimum daily requirement. Been working, Gabriel?"

"Yes. And you?"

"I just started a major renovation over on Ovington Place," says Meyers. "Remodeling the kitchen and bathroom and finishing a basement. Should keep me in groceries for the rest of the month."

"How well done do you want these eggs, Bill?"

"Burn them. Are you taking a vacation this winter, Mitch?"

"You bet. A week from today. Thirteen days in sunny San Juan," says Mitch Dunne. "Which reminds me, I'd better get a sign up on the door saying that we'll be closed."

"Closed?" says Harry Johannsen, walking into the shop.

"Vacation," says Mitch, plating the eggs.

"Where am I going to get stale rye toast while you're gone?" asks Harry, grabbing a seat next to Gabriel.

"I'll fix you a few orders to go before I leave," says Mitch, placing the plate on the counter.

"Where's the hair?" asks Harry, checking Bill's food.

"Mitch used it all up in my omelet," says Gabriel.

"Pass the ketchup," says Bill.

Detective Marina Ivanov has returned to the apartment building where the Ventura boy was found. She is sitting with Irina Kyznetsov and a police artist in the woman's kitchen. They are trying to put together likenesses of the three men who had come at different times during the week to view the apartment where the boy had been held. Later, in spite of strong opposition from her husband Mikhail, the building superintendent, Irina would accompany Ivanov to the 60th Precinct to look at photographs.

The night before, Paul Ventura arrived back at his apartment on Ocean Parkway at three in the morning. The two uniformed officers approached him with the news of his son's death. Ventura had just come off a ten-hour shift driving a cab for the Empire Taxi Company out of a garage on Fourth Avenue and Warren Street, following eight hours at the counter of a Pep Boys store on 86th Street. After being questioned, Ventura called his estranged wife and then drove over to the house on 81st Street to be with Mary and their daughter.

Early Saturday morning, Samson is making visits to the taxi garage and the auto parts store to check that all of Ventura's time the previous afternoon is accounted for.

When Tony Territo arrives at Angelo's Coffee Shop on 18th Avenue he finds his father, Vincent, sitting at the counter. Angelo pours a second cup and, after a few quick words of greeting, Vincent leads his son to a booth in the rear of the shop.

"Tell me what Colletti said, Anthony, word for word."

"He fucking threatened my family," says Tony, loud enough to attract attention from nearby tables.

"Calm down, tell me *exactly* what Colletti said."

"He said that I was responsible for the death of his worthless nephew, Johnny. He said that whether or not the kid was working for me, it's clear that Johnny intended to come to me with the vehicle since I'm running the South Brooklyn business. What kind of fucking logic is that?"

"Control yourself, Anthony. Please don't make me have to say it again. What else did Colletti say?"

"He reminded me that I couldn't sell a hot dog let alone a hot vehicle if it weren't for his blessings."

"And that's true, Anthony," says the older man. "Tell me how he threatened you."

"That's the thing. The old fuck didn't threaten me, he threatened Brenda."

"Please. What did he say precisely?"

"He tells me what I need to do to make him happy and begs me not to let him down. Then he says, in the same fucking breath, *and how is your lovely daughter?*"

"Perhaps it was an innocent inquiry."

"You weren't there, Pop. You didn't hear the way he said it. If that fuck comes anywhere near Barbara or the kids, I'll tear his heart out."

"Anthony, you are talking about Dominic Colletti. Be very careful. What does he want you to do?"

"He wants me to kill the kid who shot his nephew."

Vincent Territo sighs deeply and places his hand on his son's arm.

"You will do nothing and you will say nothing. You will stay clear of Colletti and you will not speak disrespectfully of him to anyone."

"Pop."

"Do you understand me, Anthony?"

"Okay, yes, I understand."

"I will talk with Dominic. Wait to hear from me."

· · ·

Lou Vota has had the luxury of sleeping in late this Saturday morning at Lorraine's apartment in Park Slope. He is thankful for the weekend off, but he understands that Murphy also had the weekend off and Murphy is beating the streets in Gravesend. Detective Vota is next in line if something should come up.

And something always did.

Vota opens his eyes to a new day. He doesn't know precisely what he is wishing for, but he hopes it will be different.

Lorraine DiMarco is already out of bed. She stands in front of the bathroom mirror struggling to remove the cap from a large plastic bottle of Excedrin. The pain behind her eyes that violently woke her is exactly the same as the pain behind her eyes that she went to sleep with the night before. And the night before that.

Only worse.

She might have complained about the stabbing pain to Vota, but she couldn't bring herself to say the words.

Not tonight, Lou, I have a terrible headache.

Vota calls to her from outside the bathroom door.

"How about one of my famous potato, egg and onion frittatas?" he asks.

"Sounds great," she answers.

Barely able to hear the words above the thunderous roaring inside her head.

Samson has had a busy morning. His visits to the taxi garage and the auto parts store confirmed very quickly that Paul Ventura had absolutely no opportunity to get anywhere near his son the previous afternoon. Samson had to use most of his time at each workplace vigorously assuring Ventura's employers that the man had done nothing wrong.

Samson then did what he could to determine when the boy had last been seen alive. Samson learned that Billy Ventura left his school building with two schoolmates a few minutes before two. The other boys lived on the same street as Billy, just across Stillwell Avenue. The three used the West 13th

Street school exit, walked to Highlawn Avenue and turned to the crossing at Stillwell.

At the corner of Highlawn and Stillwell, Billy decided to enter the Avenue Hobby Shop. He wanted another look at the Union Pacific locomotive that his father had promised for his birthday. The other boys went ahead, crossing the avenue and continuing to their homes on 81st Street.

According to the store owner, the boy remained in the shop for ten or fifteen minutes, politely thanked the man and left. The next confirmed sighting of the boy was on the roof of the apartment building four blocks away, less than ninety minutes later.

Samson and Murphy sit at a rear table in the New Times Restaurant across Coney Island Avenue from the 61st Precinct just after one in the afternoon. They each ordered the daily special. Meatloaf and mashed potatoes smothered in brown gravy, a side of kernel corn bathed in butter, salad with blue cheese dressing. Murphy attacks his lunch with fervor. Samson approaches his lunch with guilt, Alicia's warnings about cholesterol buzzing in his ear.

After filling Murphy in on his progress, Samson listens as Murphy does the same for him.

"We found only one guy who had anything to contribute, if you can call it that. A Korean gentleman. He was driving past the apartment building on the way to his house further up 10th and saw a man he didn't recognize leave the building with a cloth satchel. He didn't pay attention to where the man went from there. I put him with the sketch artist," says Murphy, shoveling a forkful of potatoes into his mouth before he continues. "What the artist managed to come up with vaguely resembled one of the sketches he had done with the woman who found the boy's body. And both sketches vaguely resembled Jerry Seinfeld. Which can mean one of three things."

"Okay," says Samson.

"That all white males look like Jerry Seinfeld to Koreans, that the perp looks like Seinfeld, or that the artist can only draw likenesses of Seinfeld."

"How about the perp being Jerry Seinfeld?"

"I ruled it out," says Murphy. "We came across a woman who claimed to have seen a car she didn't recognize. From the description she gave, I'm surprised she even knew it was a car. American make. Chevy, Pontiac or Oldsmobile. Old and beat up. Two-door, maybe four. Gray or green. It sounds familiar. I put out an APB."

"So, we have nothing," says Samson.

"Nothing may be too generous a term. I saw the grocer this morning, Joe Campo. He's quite a guy. He put his son through medical school selling milk, eggs, Genoa salami, cigarettes and lottery tickets out of that hole-in-the-wall corner store. He talked on and on about the way the neighborhood used to be. How everyone looked out for one another. The block parties. The slapball and stickball games in the street. The forts the kids built from fallen trees after a hurricane or from snow and ice after a winter storm. He says that everything has changed, even the climate. He made the old days sound idyllic. It had me thinking that I was born twenty years too late."

"No one is born too late, Tommy," says Samson. "Some die too soon."

He sits on the floor, in the middle of the boy's room, surrounded by toys no longer used.

The silence in the house is deafening and has been since his wife took the younger child and ran off to her mother. Carried what was left of his family on a plane to sunny Florida.

"I can work with my father down there," she had said. "My mother can care for the baby. We need the money, until you can find another job."

"Don't go," he had said.

"I can't be here right now," she said. "I can't bear to look at the door of his room."

The room he sits in now.

Surrounded by toys.

Two weeks since driving them to the airport. Dropping them off in front of the terminal and seeing the taxi.

4354.

He reaches for the box of crayons.

He chooses orange. The red was the boy's favorite, but the red is gone. He tears the cover from a coloring book, turns it to its blank side and writes the note.

Samson and Murphy leave the New Times Restaurant, cross Coney Island Avenue and return to the 61st detectives' squad room. Murphy left the tip; Samson left most of the meatloaf. Back at their desks they take to the phones. They are trying to track down sales of pancuronium bromide.

Before long, it is clear that the drug wasn't purchased over the counter. So, now the tedious job of plowing through computer files and databases to identify known local dealers in illegal pharmaceuticals.

The possibilities seem endless.

The body of Billy Ventura has been moved to Graziano Funeral Home on 24th Avenue and 86th Street, directly across from Levine's Liquor Store. The wake is scheduled to start the following afternoon. Samson leaves Murphy at a computer monitor and drives over to the mortuary.

There are reasons to keep certain details about the boy's death out of the public eye. Samson meets with the funeral director to make these reasons unambiguous. The man seems to understand. In this part of Bensonhurst, Graziano has had to deal with similar concerns before.

Many times.

This was the easy part. Now, Samson would have to be as successful with the boy's parents.

The Ventura home is only five blocks away. Samson has made an appointment to meet Mary and Paul Ventura there at three.

It is time to tell them the whole story.

How do you tell a mother, *someone has used a razor blade on the face of your eight-year-old son.* How do you tell a father, *the small finger of your son's right hand has been amputated.*

There is no way.

Only to tell it.

And then there is moaning and wailing and inconsolable grief and it is as if the boy has died again, this time more terribly, and Samson is trying to explain MOs and copycats and the small daughter is crying for her mother from the bedroom and the woman escapes from Samson's voice and goes to the child and the man sits stunned, unable to move to show Samson to the door.

Samson sees himself out.

Before he reaches his car, Samson hears Ventura's voice calling from the front door and waits as the man comes down to meet him.

"Something happened," says Ventura, moving up to the car, "a week or so ago. I didn't give it much thought at the time."

"Okay," says Samson.

"A man got into my cab, hailed me as I left the garage at the beginning of my shift. Asked to go to Fourth and 36th, about two miles up the avenue. It was a cold day; it had snowed earlier. He was bundled in clothing, stocking cap, scarf across his lower face. And sunglasses."

Ventura pauses, he places his arm on the hood of Samson's car as if needing support.

"Go on," Samson says.

"He asked me if I knew the story of Abraham and Isaac. About the sacrifice asked of Abraham to prove his fear of God. I said I knew the story and then he asked me if I would be willing to make the same sacrifice. I told him that I didn't think I could."

Ventura pauses again, collecting his thoughts.

Samson doesn't interrupt.

"Now don't get me wrong," Ventura continues, "it wasn't all that unusual. I get that kind of talk from passengers all the time. But here's what *is* strange. I drove around the block after dropping him off, over to Third and then back up to Fourth to go downtown and I think I saw the same man get on to a Fourth Avenue bus heading back in the direction of the garage."

"Can you do better describing the man?"

"Not really, most of his face was covered. Do you think it has anything to do with what happened to Billy?"

"Can you think of any reason why someone would want to do harm to you or your family?"

"Nothing."

"Then it's probably nothing. Will your wife be alright? Can you see to it that she understands the importance of what I was trying to explain in there?"

"Is there anything you're not telling us?"

"No," says Samson.

"I'll do my best," says Ventura and moves to return to the house.

Return to his wife.

And Samson watches the man go and climbs heavily into his car. And all Samson can think about at this moment is the horrible circumstance that has brought these two people back together.

Lorraine DiMarco drives over to her parents' house late Saturday afternoon. At dinner the previous evening, Fran DiMarco had mentioned to her daughter that she could use help going through some old clothing and packing it up into boxes for Goodwill or the Salvation Army to pick up. That is if Lorraine has the time.

Lorraine doesn't really have the time, but she knows that her father will be playing pinochle at the Italian-American Social Club on Highlawn Avenue and it will be a good opportunity to speak with her mother alone.

Lorraine waves a quick hello to Ron Hoyle before going into the house. Hoyle is out at the Mustang, looking under the hood of the car with a younger man who Lorraine guesses is the prospective buyer. The other man is poker-faced, fighting to hide his excitement.

The look on Hoyle's face, on the other hand, describes his own sentiments exactly.

Lorraine pulls an old winter coat off the heap of clothing

her mother has piled in the middle of the living room floor and places it aside. It looks like something her sister Linda wore in high school.

"I met a woman last night who may be able to use it," Lorraine explains without being asked.

"Okay," says her mother, not asking.

They fold pants and shirts and sweaters and place them into cardboard boxes that Sal DiMarco carried home from Joe Campo's grocery that morning. Lorraine spots a pair of men's dress shoes and lifts them up, toying with the idea of placing them aside with the winter coat. Lorraine is thinking of the man called Sully, of what they might find if they ever find him, of what it might take to make him at least *look* like a credible witness, if he had seen anything that could help Bobby Hoyle, and if they could even persuade Sully to go before a judge.

Lorraine shakes her head and drops the shoes into one of the boxes.

"Are you alright, sweetheart?" her mother asks.

Lorraine brings her fingers up to her face and is surprised to discover that her cheeks are wet. She turns to her mother and says, "I guess not."

And then she tells her mother about the headaches.

And about the rendezvous with the MRI table scheduled for the following Wednesday morning.

FIVE

Samson returns to the Precinct and finds Murphy just as he left him, staring at a computer monitor.

"Get anything?" he asks.

"A neck ache. I tried running some queries in an Access database from tables of known dealers in controlled pharmaceuticals with the intention of isolating drugs used particularly for presurgical anesthesia."

"How did that go?"

"Sort of like trying to solve a Rubik's Cube blindfolded," says Murphy.

"That well."

"I e-mailed the Access files to the central computer lab; they've got people down there that can work on it all night. They'll also be looking for any known felons with the initials J and G—maybe the sick bastard monogrammed his work— and looking for any similar mutilations in the five boroughs, though I doubt we'll find anything quite like this one. I just hope that we never see another. I put in a request to the phone bank to contact all of the Brooklyn hospitals to inquire if any of this Pavulon has gone missing recently."

"How about the number written on the wall?"

"Lou called after you left and made the mistake of asking if there was anything he could do to help. He said he'd work on it."

"Good. Why don't you call it a day? It's Saturday evening, I'm sure there's something you'd rather be doing."

"You bet there is. Ralph and I have to get the chips and guacamole ready for the HBO Saturday night premiere and *Boxing After Dark*. How did it go with the Venturas?"

"Rough. Give me a quick take on this, Tommy. Ventura tells me he picked up a guy in his cab a week or so back who engaged him in a conversation about biblical references to human sacrifice. Then Ventura thinks he saw the same man hop a bus back toward where he picked the guy up originally."

"Sounds like any one of the three head cases I come across on the street every day. Ventura say if anyone has it in for him or his family?"

"He said no."

"I guess we could put in a request to the dispatcher. Have local patrols run by both residences occasionally with an eye out."

"Okay, let's do it."

"What did you tell them about how the boy died?"

"I feel guilty as hell about it. I didn't mention the needle, only the blow on the head. I felt that I had to hold something back, I'm not sure why. I guess it's just become a habit when these kinds of crimes come up," says Samson. "The kind with no apparent motive. What's the HBO movie tonight?"

"Nice segue," says Murphy. "Some Steven Seagal flick where he's a cop in yet another urban jungle. Detroit this time, I believe."

"I've always wondered why you don't have Seagal up there in your collection."

"I could never find a spot on the wall large enough for his ego. I'll check in with the troops tomorrow to see if anything popped up."

"Thanks. I'm heading home. Try to make up for missing most of the birthday party last night. Give me a call if you need me."

After cooking up potatoes and eggs at Lorraine's late that morning, Lou Vota had returned to his house in Red Hook to deal with a slow-draining sink. As he tried to squeeze his arms into the small bathroom vanity he thought about all the times he had watched his father work when he was growing up. About how all he wanted to be when he grew up was a plumber like his dad. When the large pipe wrench slipped as he was trying to loosen the U-trap and smashed his hand into the wall, he appreciated the relative safety of his current profession.

Later that Saturday afternoon, Vota sits in front of a computer in the main branch of the Brooklyn Public Library at Grand Army Plaza. He is looking for any clues that the number 71915 might reveal, the number written on the wall of the empty apartment where the Ventura boy may have spent the last minutes of his life.

He quickly ascertains that it isn't a postal zip code and begins to treat it as a date.

July 19, 1915.

Vota rules out the possibility that it was the perp's birthday. He couldn't picture a man in his nineties carrying the boy up a fire escape.

He plugs the date into a number of Internet search engines, using words in his search criteria like *Today in History*. Most of the hits have to do with World War I events and are of little help. Vota does learn that the Brooklyn Dodgers had defeated the Pittsburgh Pirates, 3–0, at Ebbets Field on that date. He jots the information down to have handy for the next time Murphy claims to be the undisputed king of baseball trivia.

Vota considers the possibility that it could be a parent's birth date, the father or mother of the killer. Since he doesn't have access to that kind of data from the library, he decides to call it into the central NYPD data center. Since no relationship between the numbers on the wall and the letters cut into the boy's face has yet been established, Vota also recommends that combinations of the two be looked at as a possible telephone number.

Finally, Vota simply plugs the number itself into a mega search. What comes up is a wide assortment of retail items with a 71915 product code. A Dell computer universal floppy drive cable. A wooden box for carrying artists' paints manufactured in Düsseldorf, Germany. An Edelbrock nitrous oxide kit for boosting horsepower on motorcycles. A painted Christmas angel lightbulb. A twenty-five-thousand-gallon Mueller tank for storing hazardous liquids. A twenty-one-foot run of plastic tents and tunnels called the Playhut MegaPalace for kids three years old and up, which sounds to Vota much more appealing than the storage tank.

71915 is also the identifying number of a weather buoy off Coral Harbour in Nunavut, Canada, a computer bug known as Bugzilla that creates problems when cutting and pasting URLs into e-mail and the Rhino Records catalog number for *The Very Best of John Lee Hooker.*

Vota decides that he has learned enough for one day. He leaves the library and heads home to nurse his scraped knuckles.

Lorraine DiMarco left her mother after helping carry boxes out to the garage and before her father returned from his afternoon card game at the club. Now at dinner, which Fran and Sal take at the kitchen table when they are alone, Fran is somewhere else. She is in a frightening place where medical specialists sit around a table looking at X-rays and discuss options. And the pictures they are gathered around are pictures of her daughter's brain.

Fran is pushing the food around in her plate and has not taken a bite.

"What's wrong?" asks her husband.

"Nothing."

She is making a feeble attempt at coming back from that scary place and at looking interested in her food.

"I know you better than that, Frances."

"It's something I'm not ready to talk about right now. Are you going to press it?"

"No, I won't press it," says Sal DiMarco. "I know better than that, also."

After dinner, Samson is helping Alicia dry the supper dishes. At the dinner table, he had been very quiet.

"Okay, what is it Sam?" his wife asks.

"What's what?"

"Give me a break, what's bothering you?"

"Why do I have to ask why Jimmy wasn't at dinner?"

"Because I thought you already knew, since I told you this

morning that he was having dinner at a friend's house. I guess you weren't listening."

"What else did you tell me?"

"I also told you that he and his friend were going to a movie after dinner and that he'd be home at eleven."

"What friend?"

"Nicky Diaz, a friend from school. He lives over on 40th Avenue. I've met him and he seems like a good kid. I'm guessing he doesn't have a rap sheet," says Alicia.

"We found a dead eight-year-old boy on a roof in Brooklyn yesterday; so forgive me if I'm interested in where my son is and who he's with."

"That's understandable, but Jimmy is seventeen and he has a good head on his shoulders. Which, I might add, he inherited from his father."

"I think about myself at that age and all the crazy things I got myself into."

"That was the old neighborhood, Sam. And you turned out alright and you teach your children well. Relax, Jimmy is fine."

Samson walks over to peek in on his two girls. They sit on the living room sofa staring straight ahead at a blank television screen.

"They look like two little zombies in there," he says.

"They're waiting for you to start the movie. And you're stalling."

"How many times are they going to watch *The Little Mermaid*?"

"Half as many times as you've seen *Do the Right Thing*. And they haven't watched it for a while because they like watching it with you. They enjoy your imitation of Sebastian the Crab more than they do the movie. Although I've always thought you sounded more like Desi Arnaz."

"How did you get to be such a comedian?"

"It's easy when you have such a great straight man. Now get in there, I'll make the popcorn."

. . .

Vincent Territo enters the Torres Restaurant on Bay Parkway. Across the avenue, pairs of Saturday night moviegoers are leaving the Marlboro Theater. Territo removes his fedora as he walks in.

Dominic Colletti sits at a table in the rear of the dining room. At his side sits Sammy Leone, 220 pounds of paid muscle. Colletti smiles as Territo approaches the table.

"*Paesano, buona sera.* It is good to see you. Sit. Have some espresso, *per favore,*" Colletti says offering a hand, but not rising from his chair.

Territo accepts the handshake and sits opposite Colletti.

"Sammy, bring a demitasse for Mr. Territo," says Colletti, "and a bottle of anisette with two glasses."

"Dominic, I wanted to pay my respects. I was very sorry to hear about your nephew," Territo says after Leone leaves the table.

"My nephew, Johnny, was a foolish and reckless boy," says Colletti. "I am thankful that my brother is not alive to see how he turned out. The boy's mother, however, *is* alive, and as every mother she believes that her son could do no wrong and in her anger has demanded action. And I cannot deny my brother's widow in her time of grief."

Leone returns with a small coffee cup, a bottle of liqueur and two short glasses. Colletti pours espresso from the small pot on the table and moves the cup across to Territo. He then pours the anisette.

"I spoke with my son, Anthony, this morning," says Territo. "He told me that he was disturbed by the talk he had with you last evening."

"Sammy, please leave us for a moment," Colletti says.

Leone walks off to sit at the bar.

"Vincenzo, with all respect, your son does not show proper appreciation for all that I do to allow his business to thrive."

"It is my understanding that Anthony provides your family with a fair percentage of every transaction."

"Yes, as is required," agrees Colletti. "But what I speak of here goes beyond the business arrangement. All I ask of your son is that he show a willingness to volunteer personal services when necessary."

"Forgive me, Dominic, I want to clearly understand what was said last evening. From what Anthony told me this morning, it did not exactly sound voluntary. And he seemed to have the idea that you were threatening his family."

"He said this?"

"He said that you inquired about his daughter, Brenda."

"And why would I not—his daughter is a lovely girl and a friend to my granddaughter. Your son misunderstood, which concerns me greatly. Anthony should know that my dealings with him would not involve innocent members of his family. I have a problem. I need to satisfy my brother's wife. I simply asked your son to assist me and I expect him to do so. The consequences of not complying with my wishes will affect him and him alone. Please make him understand this."

"Are you now threatening *my* child."

"Vincent, please. Be careful how you speak. Put yourself in my place. My arrangement with Tony has nothing to do with what is between you and me. Anthony knew about the requirements of the life he chose. Times have changed, but some unpleasant duties do arise. I would think your son would be honored to be given an opportunity to show his loyalty and his courage. Please, do not make the mistake of taking this as a mark against our own long friendship. Have Anthony come to see me and stop worrying. I am certain that Tony will do the right thing."

Territo has nothing more to say. He drinks what remains in his glass of anisette and rises to leave.

"Thank you for your time," he says.

"You must bring your lovely wife to our home for dinner soon," says Colletti. "It has been too long since you last visited."

"We will do that," says Territo, taking Colletti's hand in farewell.

As Vincent Territo exits the restaurant, Sammy Leone returns to the table.

"Trouble, Don Colletti?" asks Leone.

"Tony Territo cannot be depended on for this thing. He sends his father to speak for him, like a child. Call my sons; I want to see them in the morning. We will take care of this problem ourselves, before my brother's widow drives me insane."

"So, you're letting Territo off the hook?" asks Leone, sounding a little disappointed.

"I am not done with Tony Territo," says Dominic Colletti. "He still needs a lesson in responsibility and respect."

Murphy sits on the sofa and drains the last of his fourth bottle of Samuel Adams lager. He is staring at the television screen, thinking that Steven Seagal is looking old. Too old to be running around the streets of a big city chasing the bad guys.

Ralph is nudging Murphy's leg, hoping for another fistful of tortilla chips. Murphy is oblivious. He is wondering if, at the tender age of thirty-four, he is also too old to be running around the streets of the big city chasing bad guys. But even in his beer-induced stupor, Murphy is conscious enough to realize that there is nothing else he knows how to do. Nothing he would rather do.

Ralph has finally managed to get Murphy's attention. Murphy drops some chips at his feet and makes an attempt to go after another beer. Before he can wrestle himself from of the grip of the sofa, he is dead asleep.

Kevin Addams pulls up in front of his girlfriend's house to drop her off for the night. It is just past one in the morning. They are both freshmen at Kingsborough Community College in Manhattan Beach, Brooklyn's answer to Isla Vista. They have dated since high school. They have come from a popular club over on 3rd Avenue in Bay Ridge and, though it is a very cold night, they are still warm from the lights and the movement on the dance floor.

Very early Saturday and Sunday mornings, Kevin covers his father's delivery route. He has been doing the weekend run since graduation, earning pocket money and giving his father a few nights off. He leans over to kiss the girl goodnight.

"I wish you didn't have to go to work," she says.

"Tell me about it," he says, "but then again, it sure helped pay the bar tab tonight."

After a long embrace she hops out of the car and skips up to her front door. She stops to blow him a kiss as he pulls away.

An hour later, Kevin Addams is loading plastic crates of milk, half-and-half, yogurt, cottage cheese and sour cream from the warehouse on Ralph Avenue into the back of the delivery truck.

The pounding of hot breath on Murphy's face wakes him. He opens his eyes to find Ralph staring at him, nose to nose. The look in Ralph's face frees Murphy from the sofa. Murphy struggles into his coat and grabs a plastic evidence bag from the kitchen cabinet. He takes Ralph down to the street to do his business and disposes of the evidence.

At three in the morning, Kevin Addams is finished loading. He grabs a carton of chocolate milk on his way out to the truck to begin his route. He rolls out onto Ralph Avenue and heads for his first drop. A beat-up Oldsmobile pulls away from the curb a block behind him and follows.

Addams' third stop is at a convenience store at the corner of Troy Avenue and Avenue J. It is the only retail shop on the street, surrounded by residences. It is dark and deserted at this hour in the morning.

Kevin drains the last of the chocolate milk, climbs out of the passenger door and walks to the back of the truck to remove the order. Rock music blares loudly from the stereo speakers. He leans into the truck to reach a crate of milk quarts. He doesn't hear the man come up behind him. He never knew what hit him.

The man places the crowbar into the back and lifts the boy up into the truck after it. He takes the syringe from his pocket and injects the boy, finding the jugular vein quickly. He closes the back door and climbs into the driver's seat of the truck.

He slowly pulls away from the curb and heads out Avenue J toward Ocean Parkway.

Lorraine DiMarco wakes with her head throbbing. She flirts with the idea of getting out of bed to rummage through her medicine cabinet for something that will make it stop. She remembers that she has already tried everything available and nothing is going to work. She buries her head under a pillow and bears the pain.

He drives up the alley and stops behind the house. He opens the back gate. He pulls the boy from the back of the truck and carries him across the yard to the kitchen door. He opens the door he had unlocked the night before and he drags the boy inside. He closes the door and walks back to the truck. He drives slowly out of the alley and parks the truck on the avenue. He walks back to the house, crosses the yard to the door and grabs the tool satchel from behind the hedge under the kitchen window before going back in.

Vota wakes with a start. It is four in the morning and the upstairs tenant has decided to rearrange furniture. Vota thinks about getting up to complain, but realizes that it could be worse. The guy could be beating on his drum set. Vota covers his head with a pillow and he tries to recapture sleep.

He sits Kevin Addams on a chair and hangs the boy's arm into the kitchen sink. He runs cold water over the boy's hand as he uses the garden tool to sever the boy's finger. He pulls a wood-burning tool out of the satchel and plugs it into a wall socket above the sink. He uses the tool to stop the bleeding. He lays the body on the kitchen floor and reaches into the satchel. This time he comes out with an X-Acto knife, something he once used to cut pictures from magazines for his son. He kneels down and begins to work on the boy's face.

68

He carefully cuts two letters into Kevin Addams' right cheek. He places a handkerchief over the cuts and returns the knife and the wood-burning tool to the satchel. He pulls a pint bottle of Scotch from the satchel and drinks while the cuts dry.

He moves the boy's body into the bedroom and places it on the bed. He finds Kevin Addams' wallet and slips it into his own coat pocket. He takes the orange crayon out of the same pocket and writes the number on the wall above the bed. He stands over the body and examines his work. He says a short prayer for the boy and leaves the room.

He moves back to the kitchen, finds a plastic sandwich bag in a cabinet drawer and places the finger in the bag. He puts the plastic bag and the Scotch into the satchel and leaves the house.

He walks the alley out to the avenue and climbs into the milk truck. He drives back to where he picked up the Addams boy, flinging the boy's wallet from the window of the truck along the way. He parks in front of the grocery store and retrieves the pry bar from the back of the milk truck. He thinks about helping himself to a quart of milk, but he decides that it would be dishonest. He walks to his car and drives home.

Back in his own kitchen, he takes the plastic bag from the tool satchel and places it in the freezer. Alongside the other. He rinses the shears and drops the empty drug vial and the orange crayon into the garbage disposal. He takes the bottle of Scotch into his son's room. The note he had written on the blank side of a coloring book cover lies on the small bed.

He sits on the floor with the bottle.

And that is where he falls asleep.

Surrounded by toys.

SIX

Sunday morning.

Murphy wakes up at dawn. He is pleased to discover that he had found his way to his bed and had not slept the entire night on the sofa, covered in tortilla chips.

Thirty minutes later he is running the track at Fort Hamilton High School with Ralph running to his right as always, a pace or two behind. Murphy alternates his runs between the straight path along the Shore Road Promenade and the school oval.

Murphy completes his final lap and stops to run in place for a slow count to sixty. Ralph uses the opportunity to chase a squirrel across the field. They return to the apartment and Murphy takes a quick shower before cooking eggs for himself and his dog.

George Addams has received two phone calls already and it is before seven in the morning. So much for getting some sleep on one of his few days off. The calls complain about missed dairy deliveries and Addams is thinking about how he is going to wring his son's neck when he gets his hands on the kid. The third phone call has Addams out of the bed and quickly getting into his clothing.

"What is it, George?" his wife asks.

"That was one of our customers. He just arrived to open his shop and found the delivery truck sitting out front," says Addams.

"Kevin?"

"I don't know. This guy says that the truck was abandoned. I'm going down there."

Addams hurries quickly to his car and races out toward Troy Avenue.

. . .

Vota wakes from a bad dream. The dream had something to do with fingers. Fingers not attached to hands. He becomes aware of his own hand. It has swollen over night, the skin tight across his knuckles. He tries to make a fist and finds it difficult and painful. Vota wonders how it will affect his ability to handle his firearm. Then he wonders why he would be thinking about having to use his gun.

George Addams pulls in behind the delivery truck. He gets out of his car, goes to the truck and opens the back door. He knows that this is the third stop on the route; Kevin would have arrived here shortly after three this morning. He can tell that the first two deliveries were taken off the truck. The order for this drop is still onboard.

The convenience store owner is out in front of his shop, his coat collar turned up against the early morning chill. He is untying bundles of Sunday newspapers and arranging them on a metal stand just outside his door. Addams is thinking about taking the store's delivery off the back of the truck. It is a habit. Then he sees the blood on the truck bed. Addams jumps into his car and speeds up Avenue J to the 63rd Police Precinct, four blocks away on Brooklyn Avenue. The store owner watches Addams race off, wondering if he will ever see his milk and cream.

Murphy calls down to the computer lab and checks in with the phone bank. Nothing has come of the search for drug dealers marketing anything like Pavulon. Nothing has come up running the initials J and G against known violent offenders. There are no remotely similar MOs. The phone calls to area hospitals, to inquire about recent missing pharmaceuticals, have not yet begun. Murphy asks again that the request be given a high priority.

. . .

The report of a teen leaving his job in the middle of a shift doesn't sound like a call-to-arms situation to the desk sergeant at the Flatlands Precinct, despite Addams' insistence that his son would not have just walked away.

The appearance of blood in the back of the truck does peak Sergeant Santiago's interest slightly, at least enough to send a squad car over to look at the vehicle.

The cell at Rikers Island is a large, rectangular room, fifty feet long by twenty feet wide. There are two commodes against the back wall, sitting out in the open. On the wall to the right of the toilets are two small porcelain sinks. Along the same wall, running up to the front of the cell, are five tables with bench-type seats, looking like discards from a picnic ground. Mounted high on the wall at the front of the cell, facing into the room and away from the front bars, is a small television. It is always on. The prisoners have no control over the channel selection. It is always tuned to ESPN or the Discovery Channel. In order to watch anything else a written request has to be made, endorsed by at least seven of the twelve cellmates.

Along the opposite wall are the twelve individual cells, each four by seven feet. Each has a sleeping bench, bolted to the floor and wall. These cells remain open to the main room all day, between wake-up and lights-out. The bright lights remain lit during this fifteen-hour period. At ten in the evening the prisoners need to be in these cells, when the barred doors slide into place and the cells go dark.

At seven each morning, the lights flash on and a shrill alarm rings through a speaker mounted on the wall above the TV. The prisoners have fifteen minutes to be ready to leave the cell, or miss breakfast. There are two more trips to the mess hall during the day, for lunch and dinner.

When prisoners aren't out of the cell on work duty or yard privileges, they sit at the wooden tables playing card games or dominos. Some sit reading law books; others write or stare blankly at the television screen.

Bobby Hoyle remains in his small cell.

Hoyle is afraid of the other cellmates. He is frightened by the incessant yelling and arguing, the throwing of objects and the physical altercations.

Bobby has not used the toilet in two days except to urinate. It is partly due to the constant knot in his stomach and mostly due to his modesty. Hoyle passes his hours sitting or lying on his bed, blinded by the harsh white light.

Hoyle has to keep reminding himself that it is Sunday morning, and that his brother Ron has promised to get him out the next day.

As unaccustomed as Bobby is to appealing to a higher power, he prays that he can make it through another day.

George Addams is filling out a short missing persons questionnaire in a small room at the 63rd Precinct. Kevin Peter Addams. Age 19. 170 pounds. 5' 11". Hair brown. Eyes brown. Three clustered scars on left leg from being spiked in a high school baseball game.

Addams thinks about calling his wife, but he doesn't know what he could say. He could try convincing her that everything will be alright, if he could convince himself. He has a bad feeling. He has been waiting for his cell phone to ring, waiting to hear from his wife that Kevin has come home and that she is preparing Sunday breakfast for Kevin and the girls and that he should hurry back before the waffles get cold. He decides not to call and drives back to the delivery truck.

Lorraine DiMarco wakes with a song going through her head. It is something by the Lovin' Spoonful called "Do You Believe in Magic." It was a song on one of the vinyl record albums that her brother left behind when he went off to Vietnam, that her mother saved when Sal didn't come home alive and that Lorraine had spinning on the turntable constantly throughout her adolescence. While other kids her age listened to punk rock, Lorraine listened to the Doors, Jimi Hendrix, Bob Dylan, and the Supremes.

When the song stops playing in her head, Lorraine realizes

to her happy surprise that the headache is gone.

Murphy calls Samson at home to bring him up to speed on the progress of the investigation.

Detective Murphy doesn't like the idea of bothering the lieutenant on Samson's day off, but then again it is supposed to be a day off for Murphy as well.

And what makes it less agreeable is that there is really no progress to report at all.

After Murphy's phone call, Samson feels a pull to go into the Precinct. He wants to be doing more; he wants to believe that something more can be done.

At the same time, he wants to stay home with his family, do something with the girls and have a talk with his son. He wants to know more about what his son is doing and who he is doing it with. He puts thoughts about going into Brooklyn out of his mind. Lou Vota will be there manning the fort, and Lou will call if something comes up.

Samson shifts his attention to preparing breakfast for the kids.

George Addams gets back to the convenience store and finds a squad car parked behind the delivery truck. Two officers sit in the car, engine running to battle the cold.

A young woman stands alone at the back of the truck, slipping on a pair of plastic gloves. She turns to watch Addams as he approaches and offers him a smile.

"Detective Rosen. I'm as close as they could come to an evidence collector this early on a Sunday morning," she says, avoiding the words *crime scene investigator*.

"George Addams. It's my son who is missing."

She turns her attention to the truck and speaks while she takes a sample of the blood from the truck bed.

"Do many people drive this vehicle? I was wondering how many sets of prints we might find."

75

"Quite a few," says Addams.

"We'll need to keep the truck here for awhile, until we can give it a thorough going over. The keys are in the ignition; maybe you could do me a favor and check if it turns over. Try not to touch anything in the cab. In fact," she says, pulling another pair of gloves from her coat and handing him one, "use this to turn the key."

Addams goes to the front of the truck, pulling on the glove as he walks.

The store owner stands in his doorway looking on, as do a few curious people on the street.

The truck starts with no trouble.

A Frank Sinatra tune pours out of the speakers.

"You can shut it down now," Rosen calls from behind.

"Kevin would never have been listening to that radio station," says Addams, coming back to Detective Rosen.

"Oh?" says Rosen, putting a cotton swab into a plastic evidence bag.

"He'd listen to an FM rock station, or a CD."

"Maybe someone else drove the truck," Rosen says, more aloud to herself than to Addams.

"I need to make a few phone calls," says Addams, as he moves away from the vehicle.

Addams calls the dairy and asks that another truck be loaded and sent out to complete the missed deliveries. Then he reluctantly calls home. His wife is trying to sound calm; she is preparing breakfast for their two daughters. Addams tells her that there is nothing to worry about, that everything will be alright. He ends the call knowing that neither of them was convinced and returns to Rosen.

"Is there anything I can do?" he asks the detective.

"I think the best thing you can do is go home to your family."

Seeing the look on the man's face, Rosen knows better than to tell him that there is nothing to worry about.

Ron Hoyle has made a deal to sell the 1965 Mustang. Ten thousand dollars. Much less than it is worth.

Hoyle will need cash for the bail bondsman and the earliest the buyer can come up with that kind of cash will be the following morning. But Ron has kept his promise to his brother; he will have Bobby out of jail on Monday. He prepares for a visit out to Rikers to give Bobby the good news. He tries not to think about giving up the car. As Ron Hoyle dresses, he practices trying to sound *very* happy about the good news when he sees his brother.

Lou Vota polishes off a plate of French toast at the New Times Restaurant. He has been leafing through the pages of the Sunday *Daily News* as he eats. The newspaper is jammed full of advertisements for jewelry stores, with Valentine's Day less than a week away. Vota has been thinking for some time about popping the question, asking Lorraine DiMarco to be his wife. He is thinking that this just might be the right time.

A waitress approaches Vota, looking out of the window as she reaches the table.

"Look at that place," she says. "It stands out like a sore thumb."

Vota follows her gaze across Coney Island Avenue.

"The Happy Horse," Vota says. "Been there as long as I can remember."

"With all of the fancy new buildings and businesses coming into the neighborhood, it's very distracting. No matter how much better the avenue begins to look, that run-down old dump always catches my eye," the waitress says.

"A blot on the landscape."

"Excuse me?" she says, tearing her attention away from the Happy Horse.

"Next time you need a tire repair or a hubcap, I bet it will be the first dump that comes to mind."

"Probably a good bet. Can I get you anything else?"

"No, thank you."

She places the guest check on the table and glides back to the kitchen.

Vota takes a last swallow of coffee, places a ten-dollar bill on the table to cover the meal and a healthy tip, folds the paper under his arm and walks across Coney Island Avenue to the Precinct.

Alone in the detectives' squad room, Vota makes a few phone calls. Nothing found on 7.19.15 as a birth date for any violent offenders or parents of violent offenders in the NYPD database.

The central phone bank is backed up by a request put in earlier by Detective Murphy and it will be a while before they can get around to checking combinations of the two letters cut into the Ventura boy's face and the five digits written on the wall against phone numbers in the 212 and 718 area codes. For something to do, Vota plays around with the task himself. He places a number of phone calls, but all he achieves is infuriating a number of people who are sick and tired of being bothered by phone solicitation. Vota soon abandons the idea and revisits the jewelry ads in the *Sunday News*.

Tony Territo sits on his large leather chair behind his large oak desk in his large oak-paneled office behind the showroom of Titan Imports on 4th Avenue at 89th Street in Bay Ridge. The late morning has turned warmer, the sky is clear and the temperature is expected to reach the mid-forties. A balmy day for Brooklyn in February.

A good day to sell cars.

Less than three miles away, on 41st Street, in the shadow of the Gowanus Parkway near Third Avenue, Tony Territo leases a twenty-thousand-square-foot garage from Dominic Colletti. It is in this building that Territo stores his inventory of high-end stolen vehicles.

Colletti owns most of the buildings in the area, including Mom's Bar on 42nd Street, where Colletti can be found most weekend nights guarded by Sammy Leone.

Along with the lease to the building where Territo keeps his cache, Colletti provides a level of protection against intruders.

Particularly those wearing uniforms.

The cars brought into the garage are all late-model, high-priced vehicles. They are either sold south of the border on the black market, after minor identification alterations, or chopped up for expensive parts.

Territo ran a small, trusted crew. He would never use a fuck-up like Johnny Colletti. More than that, vehicles were never taken from their owners in the way the Colletti kid tried to grab the Mustang. Territo's people were pros. They knew how and when to take a car. Johnny Colletti was a fucking purse-snatcher. Dominic Colletti understood that and this is what angers Tony most—that the old fuck could even suggest that Territo was remotely responsible for the actions of Colletti's idiot nephew and that Colletti would have the audacity to threaten Tony's family.

Territo tries to put Colletti out of his mind. He jumps up from his leather seat and puts on his showroom smile. The sun is shining and Tony has cars to sell.

The temperature has climbed to fifty degrees and the sun is shining. Samson decides that it is mild enough to take the girls over to Alley Pond Park. He asks Jimmy to come along.

Jimmy Samson has places where he would rather be, but a quick look from his mother convinces Jimmy that it would be a good idea to accept his father's invitation.

Kayla and Lucy sit on adjacent swings; Samson and Jimmy stand behind, giving the girls a ride.

"So," says Samson, "tell me about Nicky Diaz."

"Nothing much to tell," says Jimmy. "Just a friend from school. We play basketball together."

"And you had dinner with his family last evening?" asks his father.

"Cheese enchiladas with rice and beans," says Jimmy, not sure where his father is going with the interrogation. "Nicky's mother is an excellent cook."

"And his father?"

"His father runs a pool hall over in Flushing; Nicky helps out there on weekends."

"I don't want you hanging around a pool hall, son."

"I've never been there, Dad. It doesn't really interest me."

"Push me higher, Jimmy, up to the sky," calls Lucy from

her swing.

Murphy pushes his empty plate away.

"That's it, Mom," he says. "I have absolutely had enough."

"I hope you saved room for dessert," says his mother. "I baked a pineapple upside-down cake, I know it's your favorite."

Murphy feels as if he is about to burst.

"Where's Michael?" Murphy asks.

"Michael is hardly ever here. Since he lost his job and had to move back home, all he does is run in to shower and change clothes and grab something from the refrigerator. I worry about him, Thomas. He never talks to me about what he's doing and he always seems so unhappy."

"He brought it on himself, Mom."

"That is not true, Thomas," insists Margaret Murphy. "I don't believe for a minute that Michael took that money. Your father and I did not raise thieves."

"Why would his boss lie?"

"I don't know. I only know that Michael wouldn't do it. And he loved that job. It was the first time in a very long while that he felt good about himself. Why would he jeopardize that?"

"The kid has been trouble ever since Dad died."

"Maybe it would help if his older brother took a little more interest."

"Mom, you know I've tried with him, more times than I care to remember. And every time I get him out of a mess he jumps right back into another. I've had enough. Even Dad would have given up on the kid by now."

"How can you say such a thing, Thomas? Your father would never have given up on one of his boys; he never gave up on you."

Murphy realizes how upset his mother truly is about her youngest child.

"I'm sorry, Mom, I didn't mean that. I'll talk with Mike. Try not to worry so much. How about some of that pineapple cake?"

Lorraine DiMarco is at home, trying to catch up on domestic chores. A few loads of laundry, a quick vacuum, and the impossible task of paying bills and attempting to balance a very unbalanced check book.

Lorraine gets a call from Ron Hoyle. He tells her that he will have the bail money sometime early the next morning. Lorraine assures Hoyle that if he can get it to the bondsman before noon, Bobby will be out of Rikers in time for dinner.

Lorraine asks Ron to call her as soon as he has the cash in hand. She will meet Hoyle at the bondsman's office and they can walk across to the courthouse to take care of the paperwork.

A few minutes after Hoyle's call, Lorraine's phone rings again. This time it is Lou Vota, calling from his desk at the Precinct. There is nothing going on there. He has already gone as far as he could with the Sunday crossword, which wasn't very far. He asks if she is free for dinner, maybe a movie afterwards. Lorraine is feeling pretty well, chores mostly taken care of, things looking a little better for Bobby Hoyle, and miraculously the headache has not returned. Yet.

She tells Lou that she will be ready at six.

George Addams has called the 63rd Precinct every thirty minutes for the past four hours. There is still nothing to report. He is told he can pick up the delivery truck anytime; they have done what they could to gather evidence. The desk sergeant *is* able to tell Addams that they were unable to lift prints from the steering wheel or from the dashboard, which suggests that the inside of the cab may have been wiped clean and which sounds like very bad news.

Tony Territo is with a customer in the showroom. He is hoping to close on a $110,000 Mercedes coupe, when his father walks in.

Territo signals for his best salesman to take over and leads his father back to the office.

"I spoke with Colletti last night," Vincent Territo says, as soon as they are seated. Wasting no time.

"And?"

"His mind is set on you doing this thing for him. He has a distraught sister-in-law on his hands, but I think that it is just as much a test. To see what he can expect of you in terms of tribute. Colletti wants to see you again, and he insists that his inquiry about your daughter was innocent."

"So, what do we do now?"

"I warned you about getting involved with Colletti. You make more than enough selling those cars out there."

"Well, Pop, maybe I'm sorry I didn't take your advice, but that's no help. We have to deal with the situation at hand. And I'm all ears. What do I do?"

"You see Colletti and tell him you'll take care of it. Just try to buy some time. I'll set up a meeting with John Giambi in Long Island. Giambi can get Dominic Colletti off your back if he can be persuaded to do so."

"I hate for you to have to see Giambi, Dad."

"I appreciate the sentiment, but as you say, we have to deal with the situation at hand."

"You don't have to rub it in, Pop."

"Be careful with Colletti. Don't upset him. Just try to put him off long enough for me to work this out."

"Okay. I'll be a sweetheart. And thanks."

"I have to go," says Vincent. "Your mother is waiting in the car. And you had better get back out to the floor before your stand-in blows the sale."

Samson gets a callback from Desk Sergeant Kelly. He had phoned Kelly earlier and asked that Nicky Diaz and his father be run through the computer. According to Kelly, the boy came up clean. No offenses, good student, all-county high school basketball star.

Alicia Samson had guessed right, Jimmy's friend didn't have a rap sheet. But Nicky's father, Felipe Diaz, a.k.a. Phil the Pill, does have a sheet. As long as his arm.

Samson stores the information in his mental filing system and thinks that he may want to stop in for a game of pool the next time he is passing through Flushing.

SEVEN

When Serena Huang looks into the mirror, she sees a rising star. A much talked-about investigative journalist behind a large desk piled high with research in the busy City Room of the *Washington Post* or the *New York Times* and a future spot with a very popular TV news magazine.

Serena is nine months out of New York University with a master's degree in Journalism and the only work she has been able to land is two freelance pieces for the Arts and Leisure section of *New York Newsday* and a tenuous job as a stringer for a local weekly called the *Brooklyn Eagle.*

This week's assignment will have her standing outside of a movie theater on a Sunday evening, stopping patrons as they exit, jotting down inane answers to questions addressing the merits of the most current releases.

If nothing else, the result will necessarily showcase her imagination.

Samson has decided to drive to Brooklyn after all. It has been two weeks since he visited his father. The girls want to go along, but are told that he expects them to be long asleep by the time he gets back. Samson thinks about asking Jimmy to ride with him, feeling it would be good to spend more time with the boy and knowing how much it would please the boy's grandfather. But something that he cannot quite put his finger on has Samson deciding to go alone.

Murphy gets a call from the central phone bank. It has been determined that two vials of pancuronium bromide were taken from a cabinet at the emergency room of Lutheran Medical Center in January. Ralph is groaning, barely able to move, paralyzed from too much of Mom's cooking. The dog won't be much company for a night at home. Murphy decides to run over to the hospital to see what he can learn.

Dr. Bruce Wayne is showing his new assistant around the crime lab. He has waited two months for a replacement, and they send the rookie over on a Sunday. Wayne attempts to look glad to be there. From Robin Harding's perspective, Wayne's attempt is far short of the mark.

A nasty flu that ran through the 68th in Bay Ridge has the police station shorthanded. Officers Stan Landis and Rey Mendez of the 61st are picking up overtime covering the three-to-midnight patrol for the rival precinct. Rey suggests a Mexican joint at 5th and 73rd for their dinner break.

Joe Campo closes the grocery and walks the half block to his son's house on West 10th Street. It is the house he grew up in, the house where he spent the first twenty years of his life.

The house was full of family when Campo grew up.

His father's parents, Italian immigrants, lived in the small basement apartment.

Campo had lived on the main floor with his parents and his two sisters. His mother and father had both come from Sicily as young children, from villages only a few miles apart, and had finally met as young adults in Gravesend.

His father's brother lived on the second story with his wife and had raised three daughters there. Campo was brought up in a house full of female children.

When Campo met and later married Roseanna, they moved into her parents' home on West 9th Street between Highlawn Avenue and Kings Highway, just two blocks from the Campo house. They raised their three children there. When his in-laws retired to Florida, Joe and Roseanna inherited the house where they still lived. Their daughter Millie lived in the apartment above with her husband and two children. A second daughter, Josephine, had moved across to Staten Island after her marriage. She and her husband ran a small pharmacy.

Joe's oldest child, Charles, had moved back into the house on West 10th Street with his wife and children after Joe's father passed away. Charlie had the entire first floor and basement remodeled. The children had bedrooms and a spacious play area downstairs. There was a master bedroom and a guest room on the main floor, a living room, a dining room, a roomy bath, and an enlarged kitchen with sliding glass doors opening out to a rear deck.

Joe's aunt and uncle, both in their nineties, still live in the apartment above.

Roseanna and her daughter-in-law, Angela, are in the kitchen preparing dinner. Charlie Campo is in the living room, reading a story to his son Frankie with the Knicks game playing in the background. The granddaughters are down in the basement, quietly watching a video.

The house is full of family still.

When Joe arrives he greets his son and walks back to the kitchen to his wife. He leans over to kiss her on the cheek. Angela looks on and smiles. Joe walks to the glass doors and gazes out into the yard, where two fig trees had stood when he was a child. He feels a tug on his pant leg and looks down to find Frankie. Joe lifts the boy up into his arms, and tries not to think about the boy on the roof.

Lou Vota and Lorraine DiMarco leave the New Corner Restaurant at 72nd Street and 8th Avenue and drive over to Gravesend to pick up her parents. Lorraine thought it would a nice gesture to invite Sal and Fran to join them for a movie, and Lou didn't argue.

Afterwards, Lorraine reminds Vota, they can drop her parents' home and go over to the 25th Avenue train station to check if the homeless man called Sully had made it back from his weekend getaway in the Bronx.

. . .

Sandra Rosen sits in the front room of her apartment, a second-story floor-through in a brownstone on Garfield Place near 8th Avenue. She soaks her feet in a large basin of warm water and Epsom salts, sips from a snifter of brandy, and browses the latest issue of *Runner's World* magazine.

Rosen has been running five miles, four mornings a week in Prospect Park. She is planning to increase her distance to six miles on Monday morning. She is already preparing for the New York City Marathon, nine months off. Rosen is determined she will be ready this time.

She grabs the phone receiver on the second ring. It is an update from the Precinct on the missing Addams boy. She jots down a few notes and calls the boy's father.

"Kevin's wallet was found," she tells George Addams, "in the street along Ocean Parkway near Church Avenue. Can you think of a reason why he might have been in the area?"

"None," says Addams.

Rosen isn't really surprised; she has a strong idea that someone else drove the delivery truck. What puzzles her is that there was more than three hundred dollars in the wallet when it was found.

Detective Rosen doesn't quite know how to phrase her next question, so she simply asks.

"Is Kevin an intravenous drug user?"

"Absolutely not," says Addams indignantly. "What would ever give you that idea?"

She could say it was the hypodermic needle discovered in the back of the truck, but she decides not to mention it for the time being.

"I'm sorry, it's just routine. We'll have cars out all night, running between the grocery store and the spot where Kevin's wallet was discovered, and we will continue to canvass the neighborhood around the grocery tomorrow. I'll call you as soon as I hear anything."

Addams is afraid to ask what the detective thinks the chances are for Kevin's safe return; Rosen is unwilling to volunteer an educated guess.

Rosen ends the call, drains her glass and realizes that her feet are sitting in a tub of ice-cold water.

. . .

Murphy is sitting at a small table in an office off the Lutheran Medical Center emergency room, looking over the names of all patients and hospital personnel known to be in the vicinity of the ER on the night the Pavulon turned up missing. The list is impressive, and Murphy doesn't really have any clever ideas about how to narrow it down. He is beginning to think that it might have been more fun staying at home and watching Ralph suffer.

Samson sits with his father in the day room of the Jefferson Street Nursing Home, getting beat time and time again at checkers. Samson hates seeing his father in this place, but Isaac Samson insisted. Since Samson's mother passed away nearly a year earlier, Samson begs his father at every visit to come to Douglaston to live with his family. Isaac refuses to leave the neighborhood; he has many friends in the area, including a few in the home itself.

"Besides," Isaac says, slyly watching for his son's reaction as he takes Sam's last checker off the board, "have you had a good look at the nurses in this place?"

Tony Territo finally calls it a day at the dealership. Making the sale on the Mercedes was huge, and badly needed. Territo climbs into the Jeep and is reminded of how much he misses the BMW. He has been waiting more than three weeks for parts to arrive. Tony thinks it very ironic that he could literally build a car from the inventory down in the garage on 41st Street and has been having so much trouble finding what was needed to take care of his own vehicle.

Territo could have easily replaced the car, but he is strongly attached to it. It is a classic 1972 coupe and it has brought good luck to him for over ten years. The Belt Parkway accident didn't do any damage to the chassis; the fix-up was completely cosmetic.

Territo uses cars from the lot or his wife's Grand Cherokee

while he waits for the BMW. The last of the parts is due in the next day and a paint job is scheduled for Tuesday. He has been assured that he will be back in the driver's seat by Wednesday afternoon. He tries to think of it as something to look forward to. He tries not to think about having to see Dominic Colletti again, something he is absolutely not looking forward to.

Territo pulls the Cherokee out onto 4th Avenue and over to 86th Street for the short drive home.

Bruno Graziano has done an expert job laying out the Ventura boy for the wake. The small coffin is open. The cuts on the boy's face are so well camouflaged, even the boy's parents can almost forget they are there. The boy's hands are arranged in such a way as to hide the mutilation.

Paul and Mary Ventura see the last of the mourners out to the street and then return together to the sitting room to be alone with their son for a while longer.

Bobby Hoyle sits in his jail bed after what they call dinner at the Rikers prison cafeteria. He is trying to read something he picked off a rolling book cart earlier that afternoon. Bobby is looking forward to lights out; it will be that much closer to the time he can get out of this ugly place.

When one of the other inmates walks into Bobby's small cell, the look on the man's face convinces Hoyle that his visitor is not there to borrow a cup of sugar. When the man suddenly assaults him, Bobby uses every frantic move he ever picked up on the street to fight off his attacker.

Minutes later, Bobby is at the bars of the main room yelling for a guard. The other man is lying still on the floor of Bobby's cell, blood flowing from his right ear.

Susan Graham and David Levanthal enter the Brooklyn Battery Tunnel, at the end of a six-hour drive from Vermont. Susan realized an hour out of Stowe that she had forgotten her ski boots at the lodge and Levanthal was unwilling to turn back, insisting that the boots would be shipped home to her long before she would be needing them again. They had argued for two hours and not said a word to each other for the last three.

David takes the 39th Street exit off the Gowanus and heads up 4th Avenue to Susan's house on Bay Ridge Avenue.

Lou Vota drops Lorraine and her parents in front of the Marlboro Movie Theater on Bay Parkway. They will pick up tickets while he finds a place to park the car.

Vota can hardly believe his luck when he spots a black Cadillac limousine pulling out of a parking space up ahead as he is turning onto West 9th Street.

Sammy Leone pulls the Cadillac away from the curb and heads up West 9th toward 21st Avenue.

"How did it go with your sons this morning?" he asks.

"They assured me the problem will be settled tonight," says Dominic Colletti from the back of the limousine.

Margaret Murphy sits in one of the two overstuffed armchairs facing the television in her home off Glenwood Road, close to Brooklyn College. She sits in the chair that her husband used when he was still alive. Sitting in Patrick Murphy's chair somehow calms her anxieties. She is half-watching a typical Sunday night made for TV movie, the kind billed as family entertainment. From what Margaret has caught of the story so far, she wonders if the writer ever actually had a family.

Michael Murphy walks into the house and heads straight for the kitchen. He has passed his mother without saying a word. Margaret rises from her seat and follows.

Michael is rummaging through the refrigerator. He pulls out a large platter, leftover London broil from Sunday dinner.

"There are potatoes and vegetables," his mother says. "Let

me warm up a plate for you."

"I'll make a sandwich," he says, grabbing a loaf of bread from the counter and a carving knife from a cabinet drawer.

"Your brother was here for supper. He was sorry that you weren't home."

"I bet he's sorry he missed a chance to ask to see my license and registration. Did he bring beer at least?"

"That's not fair, Michael. You know that your brother cares about you."

"Sure, Mom, I know. Everybody worries about poor little Mikey, everyone's favorite failure."

"Please, son."

"I see how proud you are of Tommy. How proud you were when he made Detective. I couldn't even pass the test for traffic cop."

"Michael, I never wanted either of you boys to join the Police Department. And believe it or not, your father felt the same way. And I never loved the idea of your father being on the force. All we ever wanted was for you and Thomas to be happy."

"Well I appreciate you wanting me to be happy, Mom," says Michael, walking away toward his room with a plate of food and a bottle of Samuel Adams, "and I really hate to disappoint you. But I have other plans."

He sits alone in a rear pew at Our Lady of Angels on 4th Avenue at 73rd Street. The church has emptied after the completion of the Sunday evening service. Father Donovan has disappeared to a small room behind the altar to remove his vestments. The man in the rear pew glances around the church, finding it both marvelous and frightening.

Father Daniel Donovan's sermon had been about love and forgiveness, as the priest's sermons often were. Love thy neighbor, turn the other check, repay evil with goodness.

Donovan always steered clear of the Old Testament. The man in the rear pew, clutching a large manila envelope in his lap, is *immersed* in the Old Testament.

How could he love his neighbor, when he saw himself as a

man without neighbors? How could he turn his other cheek when he had already used both? One on the night his son died. The other on the day his wife left their home with his small daughter. How could he repay evil with goodness when the God of the Old Testament called out to him for retribution, demanded that he bear witness?

He rises and walks to a rack of candles along the east wall of the church. He lifts a wooden stick and lights a candle from the flame of another. He says a short prayer for his firstborn and for the other children God has asked him to reclaim, so that their elders can find repentance.

He steps into a confessional that stands adjacent to the prayer candles. He kneels and places the envelope on the floor of the booth. It is simply addressed in blue crayon to Father Donovan. Inside the envelope is a note in orange crayon on the blank side of a coloring book cover.

And with it the testimony.

He walks out of the large church doors. The evening has turned cold, the temperature dropping quickly after a fairly mild February afternoon. He pulls a knit cap onto his head and tightens his coat. He walks up 73rd Street to 5th Avenue.

As he walks toward 72nd Street, he sees a police car parked in front of a Mexican restaurant. Glancing in as he passes, he spots two uniformed officers at a small table. He thinks about Billy Ventura and Kevin Addams. He fights off the strong urge to go inside and tell these officers about his important work.

Landis is so hungry he could eat tofu. Unfortunately it wasn't on the menu, so he and his partner opted for the chicken burritos. They have been waiting so long for their dinner order that Officer Landis is wondering if he should run back to the kitchen to help the cook catch the bird.

"Why in God's name would this be taking so long?"

"Why do you think they call them waiters?" says Rey Mendez, grabbing the last tortilla chip.

. . .

At 69th Street and Fifth Avenue he turns toward home. Across the street, in front of the Alpine Movie Theater, a young woman is holding a microphone up to another woman's face. He continues down 69th to his house just past Vista Place. He walks up to the porch and lets himself into the front door.

Serena shivers as she holds the microphone. The woman who has come out from the show at the Alpine is thrilled to be chosen for an interview. She claims that it was a great date movie. It might make good copy if Serena had any idea what it meant. On top of that, the woman doesn't appear to have a date. Serena hopes that the recorder is getting it, because she can barely pay attention. She sees a car turn onto 69th Street, a pair of skis strapped to a rack on top.

It has Serena thinking of yet another of the many things she would rather be doing.

He takes the bottle of Scotch into his son's room. He sits on the floor and begins drinking, surrounded by toys.

David Levanthal double-parks in front of the house, gets out of the car, opens the trunk and removes the suitcase without a word. Susan Graham picks up the suitcase and walks to her door, without a word.

As Levanthal's car pulls away, Susan realizes she is glad to be back home.

EIGHT

February. The day has turned much colder. All of the warmth is inside. The time in Vermont passed quickly. The drive home was interminable. Back to work tomorrow. First a shower, a brandy, a cup of coffee. First get into the damned house. Holding the screen door with her left foot, suitcase in left hand, keys in right hand searching for the lock. Unlocked, front door pushed open, stepping inside, screen swinging back, placing the suitcase down, shoving the front door shut, locking door, switching on living room light. Home sweet home. What's wrong?

A feeling. Something you feel walking into a house Sunday evening for the first time since leaving it Friday afternoon. A feeling you have walking into a house that you had left unoccupied for the past fifty-two hours. A feeling that someone has been here while you were away.

And then just as quickly the feeling is gone.

She picks up a few pieces of mail at her feet, tosses them on the small table in the kitchen and starts a pot of coffee. Carrying the snifter of brandy with her to start the water in the shower because it takes a while to get hot. Another sip of brandy, placing the brandy glass on the bathroom sink, stepping into her bedroom as she slips off her jacket, tossing it with her right arm toward the bed, right hand now to the light switch as the left hand pulls off shoes, right hand already working on her blouse buttons, left hand on zipper of skirt—wait a minute.

That feeling again.

Someone has been here?

Now, why would you even want to think something like that?

And then she finally turns toward the bed where her jacket has been casually tossed across the knees of a 170-pound

95

surprise guest.

The call comes in on 911. The caller is trying to remain calm.

"Do you know the person in your bed, Miss?"

"No."

"Where are you calling from?"

"The house next door, my neighbors'," she says, giving the address. The neighbors spy through assorted windows.

"Is the man dead?"

"It's a boy, a big boy. I don't know. I think so."

"Don't go back to the house. A squad car is on the way. Please stay on the line until the officers arrive."

Landis feels the cell phone vibrate. An emergency call to an address six blocks away. Landis and Mendez rush out to their car just as the waitress is finally coming to the table with their chicken burritos.

Mendez hits the siren as Landis makes the turn onto 69th Street, tires squealing.

Serena Huang, shivering from the cold in front of the Alpine Movie Theater, looks up from her tape recorder and watches the patrol car scream toward 6th Avenue.

"I think I hear a siren," Susan Graham says into the receiver.

And the neighbor asks, "Would you like some coffee?"

"Yes, please."

"Say again, please," says the emergency operator.

"I said I hear a siren." And it's right out front, and it goes silent, and the two uniforms are at the door. And they are in the neighbors' house, moving to her. And one of them takes the phone from her hand, and the other wants to talk with her and has to take her shoulders and sit her down on the nearest chair as she finally comes out of the fog she has briefly visited.

. . .

Less than five minutes later, Landis and Mendez are moving to the front door of the adjacent house.

The door is opened, suitcase on the floor to the left of the door. Water running somewhere, the smell of fresh coffee, guns drawn, heading to the bedroom. Coming into the room. Body on bed. Male. Age nineteen. Twenty tops. Lying on bed with legs straight, together. Arms straight, at sides. Woman's jacket across knees. Eyes closed. Mendez looks for a pulse, touching nothing but the boy's neck, transfixed by the cuts on the boy's face.

Landis is staring at the numbers written in crayon on the wall above the bed.

"Dead," says Mendez.

They go through the rest of the house, quickly, thoroughly.

They have spent four minutes in the house and spoken only one word between them when Landis picks up the phone with a rubber-gloved hand to call Homicide.

The call to Homicide is routed to Chief of Detectives Trenton. When he hears of the cuts and the numbers on the wall, Trenton tells the dispatcher to call Samson only.

Samson has just walked out of the nursing home and almost makes it to his car when his cell phone rings. He wonders why he is being called for a homicide in the 68th Precinct. Samson is at the scene in eighteen minutes. He meets Landis at the door. Before Samson can ask, Landis tells him that the evidence guys are on the way.

Samson is taking everything in as he scans the front room of the small, one-story house. Samson cannot touch anything, but he can look. There will be a house full of people soon. More uniforms to secure the scene, evidence technicians, ambulance personnel, the medical examiner. There is already a crowd forming out front. Samson goes through each room very quickly, trying to form a first impression while it is still fairly quiet and uncluttered. He comes finally to the bedroom, finds Mendez posted at the door, and walks in. He confirms that the man, no, the *boy* on the bed is in fact dead. Whether or not this is ruled a homicide will have to be officially determined by the M.E. But hey, this kid didn't die of natural causes.

And after seeing the victim's hand and face, Samson understands exactly why he was brought in.

Leaving Mendez at the bedroom door, Samson returns to the front room with Landis at his heels.

"Who called it in?"

"Lady who lives here," says Landis checking his notes. "Susan Graham, twenty seven years old, ad executive, lives here alone, was gone all weekend."

"Does she know the kid in there?"

"Says no."

"Where is she now?"

"Next door."

Samson opens the front door and steps out. Two more squad cars pull up, spilling four more uniforms out onto the pavement. Here we go.

"Keep these guys out here, and I don't want to see any civilians within fifty yards of this place. You stay here at the door. Only the evidence team, the ambulance guys and the medical examiner get in. Only the M.E. goes into the bedroom," says Samson over his shoulder. "Find Vota, get him down here. Tell him that I went next door."

"Expecting any brass?" asks Landis.

"I hope not, but if we get any ask them very nicely to keep their hands in their pockets," says Samson. "And keep the press far away from here, even if you have to fire a warning shot."

Vota has just come from parking the car. He joins Lorraine and her parents in the Marlboro Theater lobby.

As they are about to go into the auditorium to take their seats, his cell phone rings.

. . .

Serena tries to get closer to the house, careful not to be too obvious. She has hidden the tape recorder in her coat; she is not advertising the fact that she is a newspaper reporter. She feels a strange sense of excitement and works at hiding that also.

Vota drops Lorraine and her parents at the DiMarco house, apologizing all the way for the disrupted movie plans. He speeds off to the address on Bay Ridge Avenue.

Sal DiMarco has volunteered to drive his daughter home. Fran DiMarco insists that they go in for coffee before Lorraine leaves.

Susan Graham is sitting at the neighbors' kitchen table, said neighbors out in the street with the curious. Holding a mug of coffee with both hands, she looks up as he approaches her. Samson is a menacing six-foot-three, two hundred thirty pounds, and as black as the night. But she cannot remember ever seeing anyone so nonthreatening.

She stands.

"Please sit," he says.

"Would you like some coffee?"

"Sure."

She pours a cup, places it on the table, and sits.

He sits. They look at each other, eye to eye across the table. He begins doing what he does best. Calming. Caring.

"Ms. Graham, I'm Lieutenant Samson. I'm afraid that it will be a while before you can return to your home. Do you have somewhere you can go, perhaps spend the night?"

"I can go to my mother's."

"Good, I can arrange a ride."

"Thank you, I called her. She's on her way to pick me up," she says, and then adds, "when you are done with me."

Very bright lady, thinks Samson. Intuition tells him that she really has no idea how the kid next door landed in her bed.

But Samson knows that intuition is only part of the equation.

And that this particular problem will have an ugly solution.

"Ms. Graham, I appreciate your cooperation in talking with Officer Landis. There may be more questions, but it can wait. You can leave with your mother as soon as she arrives. In fact, I wish you would. It's quickly becoming a zoo out there. We'll let you know as soon as it's okay to return home. I truly regret this disruption in your life. We will try our very best not to make it worse."

"Thank you," she says, and then letting the grip she had so admirably held on her emotions slip just a little she adds, "I feel really sorry for the boy in there."

And his big hand quickly and gently covers her rather small, fragile hand. And this instinctive gesture and her silent gratitude succeed in stopping the tears.

Then a uniformed officer is at the door to tell the lieutenant that Vota has arrived.

Samson walks slowly back to the Graham house.

Serena Huang has moved in as close as she can get, a few hundred feet from the ambulance parked in front of a small house. The police have blocked the street at the corner of 6ᵗʰ and Bay Ridge Avenue. The crowd outside is growing; people in nearby houses stand at their doors. A large detective, obviously someone with authority, walks toward the house where all of the activity is centered.

Serena glances back toward 6ᵗʰ Avenue. A uniformed officer stands at the passenger window of a late-model Pontiac, talking with the woman behind the wheel as he shines a flashlight at some papers in his hand. He moves the barricade and the car continues up the street, pulling up in front of the ambulance.

Serena jots down the license plate number.

A minute later, Susan Graham gets into her mother's Pontiac and the car drives away.

. . .

Vota greets Samson at the door. The house is alive with the business of death. Samson can tell that sometime during his absence someone has made the official determination that homicide is where it's at. A two-man evidence team is dusting, scraping and scrounging. Cameras clicking and flashing. Ambulance team waiting.

Landis and Mendez, first to arrive, last to leave, pacing.

"What do you know, Lou?" asks Samson.

"Kid's been dead for a while. No ID. We can safely rule out suicide, accidental death and natural cause. What do you know, Sam?"

"Lady who lives here is in the clear if the time of death was anything more than an hour ago. M.E. get here yet?"

"He's in with the kid now."

"Who'd we pull?"

"Batman."

Dr. Bruce Wayne was often difficult to work with, but he was the best, and Samson was glad to hear that Wayne was on this one. He knew that Wayne would take his time with the examination before releasing the body to the morgue. He also knew that Wayne had exiled Vota from the room and that they would not get back in until Wayne was ready to invite them back.

"Evidence guys come up with anything?"

"Not much," says Vota. "There's a back door connecting the kitchen to a fenced yard. The lock on the back door was forced open and the guard chain broken. The yard borders an alley. They're checking the yard and alley, but may have to wait until daylight to get a decent look. We haven't found anyone yet who heard or saw anything, front or back."

"Anyone call Murphy?"

"Yeah, he's down at the Precinct checking with Missing Persons to see if we can ID the kid in there."

"Sergeant Vota." Lou turns toward the woman's voice. "Dr. Wayne would like to see you and the lieutenant now."

"Thank you, Ms. Harding." She moves back toward the bedroom.

"Batman finally get his new assistant?" asks Samson as they start after her.

"Yup."

"At least her name's not Grayson," says Samson.

"No, it's Harding. Robin Harding," says Vota as straight-faced as possible.

"Murphy's going to have a field day with this one."

"I can hardly wait," says Vota as they enter Susan Graham's bedroom.

"Let's save the Batman and Robin jokes until later because the ambulance guys are getting real antsy and we may as well save it for Murphy who does it better anyway," says Wayne the moment they walk in. "First, the obvious. Male. Caucasian. Nineteen, maybe twenty years old. Dead fifteen to twenty hours. The kid was a perfect physical specimen, could've been an athlete."

Wayne paused. Samson and Vota wait for him to move from the obvious to the gruesome. Here was where Wayne was most effective, and Robin Harding was ready to be educated.

"I'm almost positive that he wasn't killed in this room, and I doubt he died in this house."

"You think he was killed somewhere else and brought here?" asks Vota, even though that is what Wayne just said.

"That's what I think," says Wayne, even though that is what he just said. "I'll know more when I get him down to the lab. But I can tell you this. If you have any doubts that this boy was killed by the same person who killed the Ventura boy, put them out of your mind. And if there is nothing else, I'll let him go."

"Any thoughts, Ms. Harding," asks Lou Vota for some unknown reason.

"None that I would care to verbalize," Harding says, and then surprises all of them, including herself, by adding, "There's a seriously screwed-up person out there."

"I'll send in the stretcher," says Batman.

Wayne and Harding leave the room. Samson and Vota remain looking down at the body.

When the paramedics come in with the stretcher, the two

detectives get out of their way.

"Why did they say *person*?" asks Samson.

"Huh?" says Vota, as they move out to the front porch.

"Wayne and Harding, they both referred to the killer as *person*. I never considered for a minute that this could have been done by a woman."

"Maybe you're a sexist," suggests Vota.

"I'm sure I am to some extent, but what do you think?"

"I try not to," Lou Vota says, wishing he were better at it.

"Let's go back to the Precinct, see if Tommy got anything on who this poor kid might be," says Samson.

Serena manages to get to the front steps of a house two doors from the crime scene by starting up a casual chat with the man standing there. She is within thirty feet of the ambulance. The police officers are occupied, paying more attention to the body being carried out than they are to the people on the street.

As the paramedics transfer the stretcher to the back of the ambulance, the boy's arm slips out from under the sheet and hangs down to the ground.

Serena tries to get closer, to be certain that she is seeing what she thinks she is seeing. A chilling shiver runs through her body that has absolutely nothing to do with the damp, cold wind that has suddenly come up.

Serena is staring at a dark brown, possibly burnt and definitely bloody stump where the boy's right ring finger should have been.

Vota spots the woman as he moves to his car.

"Who are you?" he asks.

"Just a curious neighbor," she says. "What happened in there?"

"An accident," Vota says, "nothing for you to be concerned about. Please move back to your home."

Serena says goodnight and walks off toward 6th Avenue. After Vota leaves, she works her way back to the scene.

NINE

Lorraine and her father get into his car for the ride to Park Slope. She is carrying her sister's old coat. As Sal pulls away from the curb, Lorraine turns to him.

"Could you do me a big favor, Dad?"

"Of course, anything."

"Could you take me over to the 25th Avenue train station before we go over to my apartment?"

For a moment, Sal thinks about asking why. Instead, he turns right onto Avenue U and heads out to Stillwell Avenue without a question.

Back at the Precinct, Murphy has found a possible ID through Missing Persons.

"College student, Kevin Addams, nineteen years old, last seen around three this morning," Murphy reads from his notes. "Description fits."

"Any unusual physical characteristics?" asks Vota.

"The kid has three scars on his left leg," Murphy says. "And according to his girlfriend, all of Kevin's fingers were in good working order as of last night."

"You heard about the finger already," says Samson.

"Bad news travels fast," says Murphy.

"Who's the lucky guy gets to see the parents about a possible ID?" asks Vota.

"I'll do it," says Samson.

"You did the Ventura ID," Murphy reminds him.

"That's why I'll do this one also; I already have the bad taste in my mouth."

"Well, you might want to call the 63rd. If this is the kid, he disappeared within their precinct in the middle of a delivery route. They already have an investigation going and I'm sure they'll want in on this," says Murphy.

"I'll call over there," says Samson. "Lou, I want you to contact Wayne tonight and make arrangements to go over the medical findings with him first thing tomorrow morning. He should be able to begin his exam as soon as I can get a positive ID. Tommy, I want you over at the scene early to overlook the forensic team. Have them fill you in on all they learned or didn't learn inside the house. They'll be out searching the alley and the yard at daylight. Take Landis, Mendez and at least two other uniforms along to do a door-to-door canvass. If this is the Addams boy, I'll send the parents' home tonight and I'll wait until morning to question them, find out what I can about the kid."

Samson stops to take a breath and leave an opening for any questions. Vota and Murphy wait.

"There should be a single underlying consideration in everything we do, everything we see, everyone we speak to. We're looking for any connection between these victims."

"There may not be any connection, Sam," says Vota.

"I'll be surprised if there isn't," says Samson, "but we can hope. Let's meet here at noon and compare notes."

"How about the numbers on the wall?" asks Lou.

"We'll look at that tomorrow afternoon. I want the two of you to get out of here and get some rest," says Samson. "It's going to be hell when the sun comes up."

Lorraine and her father walk up the stairs to the elevated platform at the 25th Avenue train station.

Lorraine carries a coat over her arm; she spots Annie from Bay 38th when they reach the platform. The woman is sitting up on her bench, with a green wool blanket wrapped around her shoulders and a beat-up paperback in her hands.

"What are you reading?" Lorraine asks as they walk up to the bench.

Annie holds up the book, enabling Lorraine to see the tattered cover. *Twelfth Night.*

"Do you like Shakespeare?" Lorraine asks.

"Only the comedies," Annie says. "That's Sully over there,

he just got back."

"I thought you could use this," says Lorraine, holding the coat out to the woman.

"That's very kind," she says, accepting the offering. "A little young for you, isn't she, Pop?"

Sal DiMarco doesn't quite know how to react.

"This is my father, Sal, and I'm Lorraine."

"I'm joking, Sal. The one thing I haven't lost is my sense of humor. Take it easy with Sully, dear. I told him that you were looking for him. I didn't tell him that your friend was a cop. Sully is a little shy when it comes to the police."

"Thank you," says Lorraine.

Sal starts to follow Lorraine as she crosses over to a nearby bench. The man, Sully, sits with a brown paper bag in his hand. In the shape of a wine bottle.

"You go on, Lorraine," says her father. "I'll wait and watch you from here."

Without questioning her father, Lorraine walks over to the man on the bench.

Sandra Rosen glances at her watch when the telephone rings. Rosen is thinking it is George Addams, making his hourly call. She wonders when she might have good news for the man. She is about to find out that she never will.

"Detective Rosen, this is Lieutenant Samson of the 61st. Sorry to call you at home. Sergeant Santiago at the 63rd gave me your number."

"How can I help you, Lieutenant?"

"We have a DOA at 6th and Bay Ridge Avenue; we think it may be the Addams boy who went missing last night."

"I'm sorry to hear that," says Rosen. "Isn't that in the 68th? I thought you said you were with Gravesend."

"I did. It's a long story. I was about to visit the boy's parents, get someone down for a possible ID. I thought you might want to ride along."

"Sure, I've met the father. They're in Mill Basin. Why don't I meet you there?"

"I would rather pick you up and go over together. I can fill you in on the way, and you can tell me what you know.

"Sure," says Rosen. She gives him her address.

"Give me twenty minutes," he says.

"Bobby Hoyle is only twenty-two years old, he's a good kid and he's in big trouble," says Lorraine. "They're charging him with murder, saying it was a drive-by shooting. Sully, if you saw anything that could convince them otherwise, you would be saving an innocent and very frightened kid."

"The police will arrest me for taking the wallet and the gloves," Sully says.

"We can get around that. Bobby is locked up at Rikers Island and I'm really worried about him. Please. Help us."

"And I won't be locked up myself?"

"I promise you won't."

"The boy that was shot, he was about to get into the car. The other boy ran over, they struggled and a gun went off. After the car raced away, I went over to the body. I knew he was dead. I took his wallet."

"I'd like to get a written affidavit. I can prepare it and have you sign. We could arrange to meet tomorrow, I can buy you lunch. Are you willing to do that?"

"Sure. I should have said something to the police that night. I haven't been thinking straight. It's the wine. It's a curse. All I could think about was getting my hands on some money. I'm sorry to hear that I may have caused this boy unnecessary suffering. I'll do what I can to help."

"Thank you. Where can I meet you for lunch?"

"How about the Del Rio Diner on Kings Highway and West 12th?" he says. "I don't have the wardrobe for anything more formal."

"The Del Rio is fine. How about noon?"

"I'll be there," he promises.

"You're talking serial killer," says Rosen.

They are in Samson's car heading out to the Addams home at Mayfair Drive in Mill Basin. Rosen has told Samson about their investigation, the syringe, her strong belief that the killer drove the truck. Samson has told Rosen about the Ventura boy.

"It would be my first," says Samson. "Something I always wished I would be able to leave off my résumé."

"You're certain?"

"Well, from what I've heard, the experts prefer to wait until the tally is three before they make that call. But in this case, they might skip the formalities."

"Wow," she says.

"That's one way of putting it. I was hoping you would talk to the father, since you've talked with him before. I would like him to come down alone for the ID and leave the mother out of it for the moment. We're going to have to convince him that it is very important to keep the details quiet. I don't have to tell you how much easier our jobs will be the longer the media vultures stay away from this."

"Okay."

"Ask him if he knows of anyone who might have had it in for his son, but leave it at that. I'd rather do the bulk of the questioning in the morning, after he has time to be with his wife. You're welcome to join me then, also."

"How about someone having it in for him," asks Rosen, "and hurting him through the son?"

"Go on."

"Let's say these two crimes are connected by a motive, something other than random insanity. I doubt an eight-year-old boy would have that kind of enemy."

"Hold that thought, and let me think about it," says Samson. "Here's the house."

"I was curious about why you stood back at the train station, Dad," says Lorraine. They are on their way to her apartment in Park Slope.

"I know that man. I was afraid that I might embarrass him."

"Oh?"

"His name is Frank Sullivan. Frank and his brother used to

run a luncheonette at 26th Avenue and 86th, just up from that train station. The place was very successful. They had a very big breakfast crowd, commuters stopping before hopping the train to Manhattan. Lots of coffee takeout. They did a busy lunch—shoppers on 86th. And the place was always packed after Sunday Mass at St. Mary's Church down the street. Then they built the McDonald's three years ago—it was nearly next door—and Sully's place lasted less than a year. I heard that his brother moved out to Jersey and started up a new business—his wife had an inheritance. I never knew what happened to Frank. It's terrible."

"It's horrible," says Lorraine, "but what can you do."

Maybe I can do something, Sal DiMarco thinks.

Lou Vota has talked with Batman. Wayne is waiting for Samson to bring in the father for an ID. Then he and Robin Harding will begin the exam. Wayne tells Vota that he is off to a medical examiners' conference in the morning, but assures the detective that they will have the results ready before he leaves and that Dr. Harding will be available to answer any questions and discuss their findings.

Vota phones Lorraine, but her answering machine picks up the call.

Murphy opens the door to his apartment. Ralph is standing on the other side looking like it's just in the nick of time. They run down the stairs to the street.

Not long after the ambulance took Kevin Addams' body from the scene, the crowd of curious onlookers began to quickly disperse. The forensic team had taken all they could from inside the house and would have to wait until daylight for a meaningful search of the back yard and alley. The street barricades were removed. Landis and Mendez were last to leave. Mendez making a comment to his partner about how lucky they had been to avoid reporters.

110

Serena walks up to the house from the opposite side of Bay Ridge Avenue. A woman comes out to the porch of the adjacent house, the house another woman had exited earlier before being carried off in the Pontiac. The woman lights a cigarette and gazes out along the street. Serena crosses over and slowly approaches her.

"What happened here tonight?" Serena asks, casually.

"It was terrible," says the woman, dragging deeply on her cigarette, seeming anxious to talk. "My neighbor, Sue, she came home and found a dead boy in her bedroom."

"A stranger?" asks Serena.

"Yes."

"How did the boy die?"

"I don't know. You're not a news reporter are you?"

"No. I live on the next street. I was out walking and saw the police cars. Why do you ask?"

"They told us not to talk to any reporters.

"Sounds like good advice," says Serena. "I'm a teller at the Citibank on 79th. As a matter of fact, I've met your neighbor, Susan...oh for God's sake, I should remember—I've seen her at the bank, more than once. I just can't seem to recall her last name."

"Graham, it's Susan Graham."

"That's it," says Serena.

"It's turned very cold," the woman says.

"You said it. I'm freezing. You should get inside."

"It's very frightening. You never expect it to come so close to home," the woman says. "Maybe I'll see you at the bank sometime."

"I'm sure you will. Goodnight."

Serena walks briskly to her car, parked in front of the movie theater.

She scribbles notes as she walks.

Brooklyn Chief of Detectives Stanley Trenton receives a call at home from Central Dispatch. The captain of the 68th Bay Ridge has phoned, ranting and raving about being left out of a homicide investigation in his own back yard. He threatened to lodge a complaint to the commissioner's office in the morning if he didn't get a good explanation.

Trenton calls the captain and explains the situation. The captain isn't satisfied; he wants one of his detectives in the loop. Trenton wants to tell the captain to fuck off, but he understands city politics well enough to know that he should try to placate the man.

"Absolutely, Captain," Trenton says. "It was always my intention to bring you in. Who do you recommend from your squad to help us out?"

"I have a young detective, Andy Chen. He knows the area very well, particularly the Chinese gangs from Eighth Avenue."

That should help a lot, thinks Trenton.

"Good, I'll have Lieutenant Samson get in touch with Detective Chen and bring him up to speed. Thank you for offering to lend a hand."

"Glad to," says the captain. "Goodnight."

"Idiot," says Trenton, after hanging up the phone.

Fran DiMarco is at the kitchen table, waiting for her husband. When Sal returns from dropping Lorraine at her apartment, he seems deep in thought.

"Were there any suits, shirts or slacks in the things you packed up for Goodwill that are still decent enough to wear?" he asks.

"Most of it is still good," she says, "and there are shoes. I'm hoping they will be of use to someone. That's the idea of donating them, isn't it? What's this about?"

"We'll talk in the morning. Now, I'm very tired."

"Well, then, I guess we should get ready for bed," she says, taking his hand and leading him out of the kitchen.

George Addams has identified the body discovered at Susan Graham's house as that of his son, Kevin. Detective Rosen talks with him alone after the ID, explaining the importance of keeping certain details from the public.

Addams cannot think of anyone who would have wanted to hurt his son, particularly in such a vicious manner.

Samson is with Batman, telling him that he can begin the medical exam immediately.

Samson and Rosen drop Addams back at his home. Samson tries to imagine what it would be like to have to face your wife with this kind of news. It is beyond his imagination.

As he drives over to Park Slope to drop off Rosen, he thinks about how impressed he was by her work tonight.

"I'd like to talk to your captain about bringing you in on this case, if you're interested," Samson says as they pull up in front of her apartment.

"I would really like that," she says.

"I have a feeling that the chief is going to want a special task force on this one. It will sound good in the press when they finally get wind of this."

"I'm really surprised that it hasn't broken already. I didn't know about the Ventura boy until tonight, and I read the rags pretty thoroughly."

"It's one of the advantages of being in Brooklyn," Samson says, "if you can call it that. Anyway, I'll talk to your captain if Chief Trenton decides to go that way."

"How about tomorrow morning? Do you want me along when you go back to talk to the parents?"

"I thought about it. If you wouldn't mind, you could deal with the mother. It might be easier for a woman to talk to another woman."

"Could be. Depends on the women," Rosen says.

"I'll call you," Samson says as she leaves the car.

He watches until she is safely inside and heads to the BQE for the ride home to Douglaston.

He had sat out on his front porch with the bottle of Scotch to keep him warm until the very last police car had driven off. He had watched the activity in awe, finding it difficult to believe that he could be the cause of all of this commotion.

He had stopped a woman who was hurrying past his house soon after the first squad car arrived.

"Good evening," he called from the porch.

"Hi."

"Aren't you the one I saw talking with a woman outside of the movie theater earlier?" he asked. "I thought I saw a tape recorder."

"Yes, that was me. I was doing an interview," she said, anxious to get to the next block.

"What happened down there?" he had asked, following her gaze toward 6th Avenue.

"I'm not sure; I was on my way to find out."

"I'll let you go, then," he said. "I guess I'll have to wait and read about it."

He watched as she moved off.

When the last police car leaves he goes back into the house. He wonders what he will use, now that the Pavulon is gone. He wonders when Father Donovan will discover the envelope. Then he remembers that he has more pressing concerns to consider. He needs rest. He needs to be back at the unemployment office early in the morning for another humiliating interview. They will ask him what he has done lately to find work.

He could tell them he *has* found work.

God's work.

He walks into his son's room.

He chooses the boy's bed for a change instead of the floor cluttered with abandoned toys.

He falls quickly into a dreamless sleep.

TEN

Monday morning.

Murphy is down to the Graham house after a very early jog with Ralph along Shore Road. He is in the rear yard with the two-man forensic team, watching them do their job. He is taking notes as one of the investigators fills him in on everything they learned from their work inside the night before.

Murphy has Landis, Mendez and three other uniforms out on the street doing a house-to-house. They are there early enough to catch residents as they are heading out to begin the workweek.

The interviews are quick.

Did you see or hear anything in or around the Graham residence during the very early hours of Sunday morning?

No.

Thank you for your help.

Murphy drives up to 5th Avenue to pick up coffee and bagels for the troops.

On his return drive to the house, Murphy stops to let a battered gray Oldsmobile back out of a driveway at 69th Street and Vista Place.

At 8:00 a.m., as Dr. Bruce Wayne is boarding a jet for a conference in Chicago, Robin Harding is rousing herself from a two-hour nap to prepare for her meeting with Lou Vota at nine.

Detective Vota is sitting at the counter of the Red Hook Coffee Shop, working on sausage and eggs.

. . .

Samson drives directly from Douglaston to Mill Basin for the interview with George Addams and his wife. He had called Rosen and asked her to meet him there, so he could go directly to the 61st Precinct afterwards for his meeting with Murphy and Vota at noon.

Lorraine DiMarco wakes with a terrible headache, a rude reminder of the MRI two days away. She is very anxious to get into her office. She expects to hear from Ron Hoyle and she has good news about a witness who may be able to clear Bobby.

Lorraine walks briskly up Washington to catch the bus on Atlantic Avenue that will take her within two blocks of her office on Remsen Street in Brooklyn Heights.

The roar of the bus does nothing to ease the throbbing pain.

Fran DiMarco finds her husband in the garage, making a total mess of the neat work she and Lorraine had done in packing up clothing for Goodwill and the Salvation Army.

"Okay, Sal," she says. "You were tossing and turning all night and I don't think you slept a wink. Now tell me what this is about."

"Do you remember Frank Sullivan, ran the luncheonette near St. Mary's Church with his brother?" Sal DiMarco asks as he rummages.

"I do remember Frank Sullivan. I've wondered what happened to him and his brother after they lost the shop."

"His brother is back in business somewhere in New Jersey from what I've heard. I ran into Frank last night. The man is living in the train station at 25th Avenue."

"My God, how horrible."

"I thought we might be able to help him out with some clothing. It's the least we can do," says Sal, with a very noticeable emphasis on the word *least*.

"I know that look, Salvatore," says Fran. "What are you thinking about?"

He tells his wife about the idea that kept him from sleep most of the night.

Tony Territo is having a very bad day, and it is not yet nine in the morning.

It began when Territo discovered that his son had forgotten to roll the two large plastic trash cans down to the foot of the driveway for the Monday morning garbage pickup. Now, he had two very full containers until the next pickup on Thursday. His rant about the irresponsibility of his worthless thirteen-year-old son almost had Anthony Jr. in tears.

After that, there was a blowout with his sixteen-year-old daughter. Brenda insisted she would not be dragged off to Atlantic City the following weekend. Tony was calling it a "family" outing. Brenda was calling it bullshit.

"It's cold as hell down there, the beaches are closed and there is nothing to do," she said. "Family, my ass. You and Mom will be gambling all weekend and we'll be stuck in a hotel room watching some shitty movie."

"What kind of language is that?" Territo yelled.

"Descriptive," Brenda yelled back.

Brenda had plans whether her parents knew about it or not. Friday was Valentine's Day, but her new boyfriend had to work. He promised to take her to dinner and a movie on Saturday night. The boy had a brand new driver's license, and his father had the coolest red Camaro.

Brenda stormed out of the house to school before the issue was resolved.

And to make matters worse, after the children were gone, Territo's wife took Brenda's side.

"Let her stay, Tony," Barbara says. "She's right, she'll be bored to tears. Anthony can bring the PlayStation. He can keep himself occupied."

"I don't want her staying here alone all weekend."

"She's nearly seventeen, Tony. She's been alone before. What's the big deal?"

Territo is thinking about Dominic Colletti. He hasn't

mentioned anything to Barbara yet about his little problem.

And Territo is thinking about having to see Colletti again that afternoon, and about how a bad day is just going to get worse.

"Tony, wake up, I'm talking to you."

"What?"

"I was asking if you needed a ride to the dealership," says Barbara. "I need my Jeep this morning to get to the health club in Sheepshead Bay."

"Go ahead. I'll have one of the lot boys come to pick me up," he says. "Christ, will I be fucking glad to be back in my BMW on Wednesday."

He woke to find himself in his son's bed. He looked at the clock on the bedside table. He remembered buying the clock, and using it to teach Derek how to tell time. It was a wind-up alarm clock, two metal bells sitting on top and a brightly colored picture of Spiderman on its large face.

When his arms point to the twelve and the eight, son, then you will know it is eight o'clock and time for bed.

Because I'm five?

Yes.

When I'm six can I stay up until nine, Dad?

We'll see, Derek.

He noticed that he had overslept. He had planned to be at the unemployment office when they opened the doors at 8:00 a.m. If he hurried, he might still be early enough to beat the crowd, be in and out in less than an hour.

He quickly shaved and showered and jumped into his car. As he backed out of his driveway, a car coming up 69th Street stopped to let him go ahead. He crossed 6th Avenue where 69th became Bay Ridge Avenue. He glanced briefly at the house as he passed, where all of the activity had been focused the night before. He saw two uniformed police, one on each side of the street, talking with residents at their front doors.

Before turning onto 7th Avenue, he saw the car behind him stop at the house and a man get out of the car carrying a tray full of coffee in paper cups.

He switched on the car radio and found the station that played the only music he could listen to: big bands, Frank Sinatra, Broadway tunes. He drove 7th Avenue until it ended at Dyker Park and then on to the parkway entrance at Bay 8th Street for the drive to the unemployment office.

Victoria Anderson looks up from the stacks of file folders sitting on her desk when Lorraine comes into the office.

"Nice hair," she says. "What did you do, run from the bus stop?"

"I didn't want to miss Ron Hoyle's call. I have good news for him about Bobby."

"He called ten minutes ago, and the way he sounded he could use some good news," says Victoria.

"What did he say?"

"He was pretty incoherent; he said that he had tried calling you at home. I told him that you were probably on your way here."

Lorraine walks back to her private office, sits at her desk and phones Ron Hoyle.

"Ron, Lorraine. What's wrong?"

"I got a call from the prison. Something happened last night. Bobby hit someone."

"Not a guard."

"Another prisoner. The man is in critical condition. They put Bobby in maximum security lockup. They wouldn't say anything else."

"Was Bobby hurt?"

"I don't think so."

"Okay, Ron, try to calm down. I'll find out what happened," says Lorraine, just as Victoria buzzes her on the intercom. "Hold on, Ron, I have another call, don't hang up." She puts him on hold and hits the interoffice line.

"It's Assistant DA Lawrence for you, on line two."

"Marty, Lorraine," she says, taking the call.

"Bobby Hoyle put another inmate into intensive care last night. There's a hearing set for eleven this morning with a motion to revoke bail."

"What happened?"

"I really don't know the details yet; I'm calling so you can arrange time to speak with your client before the hearing. They should have him at the courthouse by half past ten."

"Thanks for calling, Marty." What else could she say? "I'll see you in court at eleven."

She goes back to Ron Hoyle.

"Ron, are you still there?"

"Yes."

"Listen, meet me at the courthouse at ten-thirty. Bobby will be there and we'll find out what's going on."

"What about the bail money? I'm supposed to meet the guy in twenty minutes to close the sale of the Mustang."

Jesus. What a mess.

"Try to reach him, tell him something came up, an emergency. Ask him if you can postpone until tomorrow morning."

"Okay," he says, his voice sounding as if it is coming from the bottom of a fifty-five gallon drum.

"Ron, I have to go now. Maybe I can get information from Rikers, find out their side of the story before I see Bobby. I'll meet you at the courthouse. We'll work this out," she says, not believing a word of it.

Lorraine takes a deep breath and goes to her Rolodex for the number of the warden's office at Rikers Island.

The pain in her head is pounding furiously.

He was in and out of the unemployment office in fifty minutes. He answered all of the questions honestly.

Have you worked since your last claim?

No.

Did you refuse work, quit a job or were you dismissed from a job?

No.

Were you able to work, available for work and looking for work?

Yes.

Have you answered all of these questions honestly?

Yes.

A waste of precious time. Thankfully, he would not be asked to come in person for another six to eight weeks and could make his claims by simply pushing ones and nines on his touchtone phone from home. If it mattered.

On his way to the parkway, he stops at a traffic light at the corner of Sheepshead Bay Road and Voorhies Avenue. A bright red Grand Cherokee parked on the street catches his eye. The license plate reads *TITAN2*. A strong feeling tells him it is no coincidence, God has heard his prayers.

He parks the Oldsmobile in an open space a few cars down from the Jeep, kills the engine, sits and waits.

Lorraine is almost out the door of the office, with ten minutes to get over to Court Street for a consult with Bobby Hoyle, when she remembers Sully and the plans to meet for lunch at the Del Rio Diner.

"Shit."

"What now?" asks Victoria.

"Can you do me a big favor at noon?"

"Sure."

"No, wait. Let me call my father," Lorraine says, heading back to her phone.

"Go right ahead," Victoria says.

"Dad, I need another favor. An emergency came up; I need to be in court. I don't have time to explain."

"No need to explain, what can I do for you?"

Sal DiMarco tells his daughter that he would be glad to meet Frank Sullivan at the diner.

"Are you sure, Dad? I hate asking you. You were reluctant to confront him last night."

"No problem, sweetheart. As a matter of fact, I was planning to see Frank anyhow. I have clothing he might use and an idea that I wanted him to consider."

Lorraine is curious, but has no time. She thanks her father and rushes out to the courthouse.

. . .

"I'll be seeing Frank Sullivan at noon," Sal DiMarco tells his wife. "Are you sure it's alright with you, what we talked about earlier?"

"Yes, it's fine with me. I wonder what it will sound like to him."

"What do you mean?"

"Some people have a difficult time accepting help. Some people have a *very* difficult time understanding an unusual act of kindness."

"Well, all we can do is offer," says Sal, "and thank you, Frances."

Bobby Hoyle is a wreck.

"The guy attacked me, Lorraine. I was scared senseless. I pushed him; he slipped and hit his head against the wall of the cell. It's solid concrete. He went down like a ton of bricks. I ran out to get help."

"Try to calm down, Bobby."

"They're going to revoke bail," Bobby cries.

"We don't know that yet," Lorraine says. But she does know. And all she can think about, other than her headache, is what might happen if the other inmate dies.

Ron Hoyle sits with them, unable to think at all.

Sonny and Richie Colletti find their father in the living room of his large house on Beaumont Street and the Esplanade at Manhattan Beach. The huge bay window looks out on the Atlantic Ocean.

"Bad news, Pop," says Sonny.

"I don't need any bad news," says Dominic Colletti.

"Something went wrong last night. The con we paid to take care of the Hoyle kid wound up with his head cracked open," says Richie.

"*Accidenti a lui!* Is there anyone out there who isn't completely worthless?" Colletti yells, throwing his newspaper across the room. "Will he talk?"

"From what we heard, he can't talk at the moment," says

Sonny. "He may never talk again."

"The way things have been going, I doubt I could be so lucky," says Dominic.

"What should we do about the Hoyle kid?" asks Richie.

"Stay far away from him until this thing settles down. I'm more concerned right now about the other fuck waking up and shooting his mouth off," says Colletti. "Not to mention having to deal with your fucking Aunt Carmella."

"Sorry," says Sonny.

"The perfect fucking word for it," says Colletti.

He has been sitting in his parked car for nearly an hour when he sees the woman climb into the Cherokee. He starts the Oldsmobile and pulls out to follow. She takes the Belt Parkway toward Manhattan, the same route he would be taking to go home. Just before the Bay Parkway exit, he looks across the parkway to the spot where his car went into the chain-link fence on the night Derek died.

At the 4th Avenue exit, he follows the Cherokee off the parkway and onto Shore Road. The house sits like a fortress at the corner of 82nd. The woman pulls up to a wrought iron gate at the foot of a driveway on the street side. She uses a remote in the Jeep to open the gate and drives up to the double garage. The gate slides shut behind her.

He rolls slowly past the driveway as the garage door lifts, but as she pulls into the garage he sees no other vehicle. He continues on 82nd Street and parks at Colonial Boulevard. He takes the Bible from the seat beside him, gets out of the Oldsmobile and walks back. He crosses Shore Road and sits at a bench outside of the park, directly opposite the house.

He is waiting for a BMW; he is waiting for *TITAN1*.

He opens the Bible and begins to read.

He is prepared to wait for as long as it takes.

PART TWO

THE BOROUGH OF CHURCHES

Whoever fights monsters should see to it that in the process he does not become a monster. And when you look into the abyss, the abyss also looks into you.

Friedrich Nietzsche

ELEVEN

Brooklyn Chief of Detectives Stanley Trenton drives through the Battery Tunnel back to his domain. He has met with the commissioner at One Police Plaza in Manhattan. A hell of a way to begin the week. The two homicides have not been connected in the press. In fact, there has been surprisingly little coverage of the two deaths.

The commissioner wants very much for it to stay that way. The commissioner would be very unhappy to hear about a third killing.

Trenton comes out of the tunnel into the daylight. He remembers the large sign that once stood on the right side of the Gowanus.

Welcome to Brooklyn, 4th Largest City in America.

If it had never become part of greater New York City, which most Brooklyn-born might have preferred.

Breuckelen, never forgetting it was chartered before Nieuw Amsterdam. And cost more than Manhattan Island.

Never forgetting that the first East River crossing was called the Brooklyn Bridge.

Brooklyn, fighting tooth and nail at the turn of the twentieth century to avoid being relegated to simply one of the five boroughs. One of the "outer boroughs."

Brooklyn, still resisting the merger after more than a hundred years.

Brooklyn was, in fact, the third-largest city in the country before being absorbed into New York City; when the towns of Flatbush, Flatlands, Gravesend, New Lots and New Utrecht became part of Kings County and the consolidated City of Brooklyn boasted a population of more than two million. Only the cities of Chicago and Los Angeles were more populated at the time.

Brooklyn, where maybe they could keep a lid on this thing

127

for a while longer. Where maybe they could stop it before it happened again and the often overlooked borough made the national news for all the wrong reasons.

Trenton shudders at the thought, but it might not be too soon to call in the FBI.

The hearing is short. There are no witnesses, the other inmate isn't talking, and Bobby Hoyle is curtly informed by the court that his bail is revoked until further investigation. Lorraine DiMarco has no arguments, only a terrific headache. Though hardly a consolation, it seems that Ron Hoyle can hold on to his cherished 1965 Mustang for a while longer.

Sal DiMarco approaches the entrance to the Del Rio Diner on Kings Highway. He carries a large shopping bag. Sully is already waiting in front; the man is surprised when Sal speaks to him.

"Mr. Sullivan, I'm Sal DiMarco. You spoke with my daughter last night. Lorraine is very sorry she couldn't be here—an unexpected emergency in court. I was hoping that you would let me buy you lunch."

"Do I know you?"

"I was a frequent visitor to your restaurant."

"I see," says Sully.

"I brought some clothing, shirts, slacks, shoes," says DiMarco, indicating the bag. "If you could use them."

"That's not necessary, and you don't need to feel obligated to feed me."

"I don't, I would simply like to. And there is something I would like to talk with you about."

DiMarco can read the skepticism in Sully's face. Sal remembers his wife's warning, and he has prepared himself for rejection. After what seems like painful deliberation, Frank Sullivan speaks.

"Okay, sure," he says.

Still holding the bag, Sal leads Sully into the diner.

. . .

At noon, the three detectives huddle around a large pizza. They each draw from a deck of playing cards to determine who will begin. High card first. The king of spades earns Samson the dubious honor.

"Okay. The Addams kid arrives to load up the milk delivery truck at around two in the morning. He's stocked and on his way just before three. I spoke with the last two people who saw him alive. He dropped his girlfriend at her home around one; they'd been out drinking and dancing."

"Was he drunk?" asks Vota.

"She says no."

"Anything happen while they were out? Did she notice anyone watching or following? Did the kid get into any kind of hassle? Piss someone off?" asks Murphy.

"No again. The girl says there was no trouble, they stayed to themselves. She doesn't know of anyone who may have had it in for Kevin."

"Big help."

"The last person to see him was the night man at the dairy. He says the kid grabbed a carton of chocolate milk on his way out, said goodnight and drove off. Guy says he didn't see anyone follow the truck, but he wasn't really looking. I had a couple of uniforms canvass the neighborhood around the grocery store; no one saw a thing. There was blood in the truck, and a spent syringe. I guess we'll hear about that from Lou when he goes over his meeting with Batman."

"Actually it was with Robin, the girl wonder. Wayne had a plane to catch," says Vota.

"Whatever. It looks like the killer drove the truck, used it to transport the body over to the Graham house. He must have known, somehow, that the house would be empty. He ditched the kid's wallet, but didn't take the money."

"I talked to someone who saw the truck over near the scene, parked on 7th Avenue," says Murphy.

"Okay, hold that thought. I'll wait to hear from Lou before I bet the farm, but it seems pretty certain that the two boys were killed by the same person."

"Bet the farm," says Vota.

"If that's the case, then it's very possible that the victims were chosen randomly and that neither one knew the assailant. And that's very bad news," says Samson.

"So much for the usual suspects," says Murphy.

"We've got an eight–year-old with thirty-five cents in his pocket and a nineteen-year-old carrying three hundred bucks, all of which is tossed out onto Ocean Parkway. Not to mention that neither family ever heard of the other," says Samson. "We've got no motive to explain either murder. There's no connection."

"How about this?" says Vota. "The guy has reason to kill one of them and kills both to make it *look* random."

"Do you really buy that?" asks Samson.

"Not at all," says Vota. "We've got no connection."

"Or to put it another way, we're fucked," says Murphy.

"I hope you're wrong," says Vota. "Is that it, Sam?"

"I was counting on one of you two having some happy news about clues."

"Don't hold your breath," says Murphy. "Who's next?"

"Does a jack of diamonds beat a four of hearts?" asks Vota, holding the four.

"Alright," says Murphy, throwing a pizza crust into the Prince of Pizza box and rising to take center stage. "Physical Evidence 101."

"Anyone want that last slice?" asks Samson.

"Eat it," says Vota.

"I don't want to eat it, but it's getting pretty stuffy in here and I thought we might use it to hold the door open."

"How about we get on with this while my delightful chat with Robin Harding is still fresh in my mind," says Vota, grabbing the last slice of pizza.

"The evidence guys were at it all night and all this morning," says Murphy. "No prints. They found traces of blood in the kitchen sink, ground pieces of flesh and bone in the disposal. They say it wasn't the whole finger."

Vota takes a look at the pizza slice in his hand and throws it down onto the desk.

"The back door was busted into, probably a pry bar. It

wasn't a neat job. Door chain broken. Tire tracks in the alley behind the house; they're going to try matching them against the milk truck. No one on the street saw or heard a thing. I did find one guy who came home from bartending at a joint on 5th Avenue at half past three and noticed a milk delivery truck parked across from his house on 7th. Said he'd never seen it before. Said he came out to walk his dog at four or so and the truck was gone."

"Sounds like a whole lot of nothing," says Vota.

"Well put. I went to talk with Susan Graham before I headed back here."

"And?" asks Samson.

"Nice lady," says Murphy. "Still a bit shaken up. Staying with her mother until we're done at her place. Went into work this morning, took a break to talk to me. Says she left her place Friday afternoon around four. Her boyfriend picked her up, and dropped her back at about nine last night. He didn't go in—she says they had a fight on the way back and weren't talking. They spent the weekend at a condo in Vermont, skiing and whatnot. Landis called the boyfriend, David Levanthal, after questioning Graham last night. Same story. No reason to think they weren't where they said they were. We're checking it anyway just to be doing something. Graham says she kept a couple of lights on in the house while she was away. Discourage burglars."

"Good thinking," says Vota.

"She remember seeing anyone near the house when they left?" asks Samson.

"Nope."

"How'd the perp know the house would be empty?"

"Good question."

"Anyone see them get back?"

"Next-door neighbor was out having a cigarette; she confirms the time of arrival at around 9:00 p.m. Says Graham was frantically beating on her front door less than fifteen minutes later. Graham called it in from the neighbor's place, but you already know that."

"Okay, what about the autopsy report, Lou?" asks Sam. "Anything there that we don't already know?"

"It's not pretty. Let's get some air into this room," he says. "I'm gonna grab a pot of coffee from the hall."

"Hey, speaking of coffee," says Murphy, "either of you guys seen my coffee mug?"

"It's over at the lab for tests. They're hoping to discover the origin of life from the residue in the bottom of the cup," says Samson.

Robin Harding seemed to be nothing if not businesslike that morning when Vota came into what she would call her office and what Laurence Olivier would call *upstage left* of Batman's office. Harding stood up when he entered and offered him a seat, absentmindedly tapping the file folder in her hand against the corner of the desk between them. She caught herself doing it, reseated herself, and dropped the report on the cluttered desktop. A deep sigh betrayed her slightly as she began relating the autopsy findings as if she were reading aloud from a grocery list.

"Kevin Addams, age nineteen, apparently in excellent health, no unusual physical characteristics aside from scars on left leg. Dr. Wayne's initial estimate on time of death will have to suffice, approximately fifteen to twenty hours before the body was discovered. We found traces of the same drug that we found with the Ventura boy, pancuronium bromide, administered by injection. It's difficult to be certain, but by the look of the massive blow on the back of his head and the heavy amount of blood loss, I doubt that the drug was necessary."

"So, why use it?"

"You're the detective," she said without malice.

"What about the finger?" asked Vota, unable to move the conversation to a more pleasant subject.

"Same as the Ventura boy," Harding said. "Snipped off with small shears, we're guessing garden variety. And dull. It looks as if it took some work. Then something hot was used to burn the flesh and stop the bleeding."

"A flame?"

"More like an iron, probably smaller. The surface could

not have been much larger than the finger itself. There were no burn marks elsewhere on the hand; a common household iron would lack such exactness. A wood-burning tool maybe, definitely not an open flame."

Vota flinched, took a deep breath, his mind clicking off and on, his brain searching with caution and futility for a way to ask.

"But they were already dead when the killer took their fingers?" he said, hoping for a definitive *yes.*

"Again, it's impossible to be certain. But I would say that they were already deceased."

The answer would have to do.

She was very good. Very professional. Very bright. She had picked up more than knowledge from Dr. Wayne in a very short time. She had adopted his cool, almost cold tone and demeanor in the discussion of very disturbing details. As much as this detachment never ceased to amaze Vota, he couldn't help admiring it. And appreciating it, because it somehow made it a little less impossible to ask the next question.

"And the cuts on the boy's face?"

"Two letters. P and R. Same kind of cuts as before, a small razor knife. We found traces of cotton fiber in the wound. We're guessing that he placed a cloth, maybe a handkerchief over the cuts, to stop the bleeding. And he used something to clean the cuts afterward, alcohol-based. It's being tested now; we should have something on it in an hour. If you need anything else, give me a call."

"And that was it?" says Samson.

"That was it," says Vota, tossing the four of hearts into the pizza box, "except that after she thanks me for my patience and I thank her for her spellbinding presentation, she tells me that even though I may not think so, the whole thing upsets the hell out of her."

"And you say?"

"And I say I'm glad to hear it. And then she's off to do another one."

"Call the Lab, Lou. Try to get a quick answer on the alcohol. Tell them to put Murphy's coffee mug on the back burner if they have to."

"I think the guy was drinking," says Murphy.

"Oh?" says Samson.

"They found a few drops of liquid on the kitchen floor. The evidence guys felt pretty sure that it was booze. He might have used it on the boy's face."

"You're saying that this maniac was standing over a corpse having a cocktail while he waited for his hankie to do its work," says Samson, an involuntary spoken thought.

"Believe me, I hated suggesting it," says Murphy.

"I, for one, am baffled," says Vota. "I think we need a shrink in on this one."

"How about the detective from the 60th, the Russian?"

"Ivanov?"

"Yeah, I met her at the Ventura scene. She mentioned that she has a degree in Forensic Psychology."

"Phone her, Tommy," says Samson. "Find out when she can meet with one or all of us. Shit, that reminds me, I have to make a call. Lou, ring the lab and see if this guy was drinking. Maybe we can get some DNA, not that it would do much good unless we catch the bastard."

Samson phones the 68th Precinct and asks for Detective Andrew Chen.

"Detective, I talked with your captain and we both thought it would be very helpful if you would come in with us on this investigation," Samson says, trying to sound sincere.

"I'd love it," says Chen, sounding very sincere. "Is it true that there was another homicide closely related to the one out here?"

"How about we meet for breakfast tomorrow and I fill you in? How does the Narrows Diner at nine sound?"

"I'll be there."

"Great," says Samson.

"Lieutenant?"

"Yes?"

"Would you mind if I took a peek at the scene on Bay Ridge Avenue?"

"Hold on," Samson says. "Tommy, is there anyone left over at the Graham Place?"

"I left one uniform and a couple of guys cleaning up. Graham would like to get back home tomorrow. I'm guessing that the cleanup is complete. I asked the officer to hang there until he heard from me."

Samson goes back to Chen.

"Okay, take a look. Let the uniform go when you get there and lock up when you leave."

"Great, I'll see you in the morning."

"Yes, you will."

"They think it's Scotch," says Vota when Samson is off the phone.

"Son of a bitch," Samson says.

"Ivanov can be here first thing in the morning," says Murphy.

"Okay, good. Make sure one or both of you are here to meet with her, I'm tied up at nine," says Samson. "It's hard to imagine anyone making sense of this thing, but who knows, maybe she's a psychic."

"Or at least a Gypsy," says Murphy.

Suddenly Landis is standing at the door.

"Save me a slice?"

"When have we ever?"

"Here's that photo you wanted—the numbers on Graham's bedroom wall. The expert says it's a definite match to the writing at Avenue S."

Samson takes the photograph. 242113.

"Six numbers this time," he says. "What the fuck is this guy trying to tell us?"

TWELVE

Tony Territo has a lot on his mind. And none of it is very good.

A shipment of cars from his garage in Brooklyn was stopped and impounded inside of Mexico, a driver arrested. It was costing Territo a ton of money to keep his name out of the discussion, with no guarantees. Not to mention a quarter million dollars' worth of metal on wheels that he wouldn't see a penny of.

Business was slow on the car lot. The time of year, the economy, every fucking thing working against him. And Mondays sucked. The credit report on the high-roller he thought he had sold a Mercedes to on Sunday indicated that the deadbeat couldn't finance a Geo let alone a $110,000 German coupe.

The situation at home wasn't much better. Tony's son was beginning to look like the Goodyear blimp, the doctor warning that if the kid didn't get off his 100 percent greasy fast-food diet and begin exercising he would be a heart attack statistic before he reached sixteen. His daughter was an ungrateful bitch who would only say no if Tony said yes. And she dressed like the girls that Tony, growing up, had always thought of as *good enough to fuck, but not to take home to meet Mom and Dad.* And his wife Barbara, God love her, thought that money grew on fucking rose bushes.

All Tony wanted was to have a nice family weekend in Atlantic City, to take his mind off the daily disasters, and no one in the fucking family wanted to cooperate. If it weren't for that lame De Niro/Billy Crystal film, Tony might have seriously considered seeing a headshrink.

On top of all of that, the very last thing that Tony Territo wanted to do that Monday afternoon was to meet with Dominic Colletti and sweet-talk the old fuck. Tell the old relic that *sure I'll take care of the Hoyle kid; give me a little time.* And why have to drive way out to Sheepshead Bay to listen to Colletti's bullshit, to a fucking restaurant he couldn't even pronounce the name of?

Although Territo was so fucking hungry, he could have eaten vegetables.

What Tony Territo *wants* to do is to tell Colletti to drop dead and call over for a delivery from Pete's Pizza on 94th Street.

But Territo takes his father's warnings seriously.

So instead, he climbs into a Jaguar from off the lot, looks at the address on Knapp Street that Sammy Leone had given him that morning, and heads out to Sheepshead Bay.

"How did it go?" asks Frances DiMarco when her husband returns from his lunch with Frank Sullivan. "I see that you came back without the shopping bag."

"He accepted the clothing," says Sal. "He was a little unsure about the other offer. He said that he would have to think about it. I believe that if Sully felt he could contribute even a small amount, he could be persuaded."

"Maybe Joe Campo could use some help at the store," says Fran.

"That's a good idea, I'll walk over and talk to Joe this afternoon," says Sal DiMarco. "How did you get to be so smart?"

"I learned a lot from my students all those years," she says.

Detective Andy Chen arrives at the Graham house just before two in the afternoon. The cleanup team is gone and the officer on duty is pacing the front room like a caged animal.

"Lieutenant Samson said you could take off when I got here," Chen says. "I'll lock up when I leave."

The uniformed officer is out the front door without hesitation.

Chen walks through the rooms, starting in the kitchen. Not really looking for anything, only trying to get a feel for the place. The place where a young man was tortured and killed. Chen feels a strange sense of excitement.

And he has heard the rumors. Serial killer.

Andrew Chen has waited a long time for something like this. Four years beating the crowded streets of Chinatown in Manhattan. Finally a promotion to Detective, only to be reassigned to Brooklyn's own Chinatown on 8th Avenue. Typecasting. A second-class cop sent to babysit third-class citizens. Pearl Harbor, the Korean and Vietnam Wars, had painted persons of Far Eastern heritage as untrustworthy at best, as the enemy at worst. Inside the Police Department and out in the streets. Even those like Chen, who were born and raised as Americans and had never been anywhere near a rice paddy.

Maybe this was Andy Chen's chance to be accepted as a detective instead of as a Chinese detective. This is what Chen is thinking as he walks through the Graham house, this is what he is thinking when the buzzer summons him to the front door.

And when Chen opens the door what he finds is not a beautiful young woman, but a beautiful young Chinese woman. And he forgets what he was thinking before he saw her.

"Oh," she says, combining a charming look of confusion with an irresistible smile. "Is Susan at home?"

"I'm afraid not," Andy Chen says, "but perhaps I can help you."

Chen steps out to the porch to talk with Serena Huang.

Tony Territo pulls up in front of the Knapp Street address. As he steps out of the Jaguar, Tony spots Sammy Leone pacing at the entrance as if to remind Territo that he is three fucking minutes late. The sign above the door has Tony thinking that his very late lunch will be some kind of swishy French cuisine until he realizes that it says *Meditation*, not *Mediterranean*.

"You're late," says Leone.

Territo bites his tongue, takes a deep breath, and is about

to ask what the fuck they are doing here. Sammy Leone rushes into the building before Territo can form the words. Tony follows.

Territo is led into a small room, off a larger room. The floor is covered with foam mats. In the center of the room, Dominic Colletti is on the floor, arms crossed over his concave chest, legs tied in a knot. Colletti is wearing gym shorts and a sleeveless T-shirt. The wrinkled old fuck looks like a week-old boardwalk pretzel.

Colletti's eyes are closed. He looks to Tony like something a taxidermist fucked up. Territo is about to speak, but Leone silences him with the wave of an arm. They stand and wait. Territo's stomach is growling, and there is not a menu in the place. Finally, the old man opens his eyes and speaks to Territo.

"Tony, thank you for coming," Colletti says. "Have you tried yoga?"

Territo briefly pictures the thick slimy white slop his wife wolfs down with fresh fruit every morning. Then he is fighting off visions of a sausage roll smothered in marinara sauce from Pete's on 4th Avenue.

"Can't say that I have," Territo finally manages.

"I strongly recommend it. Very calming and relaxing," the old man says. "You look as if you could use it. You look all wound up."

"I appreciate your concern, Mr. Colletti," Tony says, trying to control himself. "I'm very busy this afternoon. It was difficult getting away from the dealership. I just wanted to assure you that I will take care of the thing we talked about; in fact, I'm already working on it. I only need a little more time to iron out the details."

"It won't be necessary," says Colletti.

"Really?" says Territo.

Territo doesn't know whether to feel relieved or more worried. Colletti quickly clears it up.

"There is something that you *can* do for me," Colletti says. "My youngest boy, Richard, turns thirty years old this week. I would like to do something special for him. He tells me there is a car he has seen on your lot that he would love to own, a

1972 BMW coupe. Why my son would want a car that is older than he is puzzles me, but he insists it will make him very happy. And the happiness of my children is important to me. Please let him have this vehicle."

Territo is speechless. He can't believe his ears. The old prune wants Tony's cherished BMW, for his fucking deranged son Richie, as a gift. Tony would rather whack Bobby Hoyle than give up the car. Territo thinks of his father, Vincent, and tries to be extremely careful when he finally finds his voice.

"Don Colletti," he says. "I have many other vehicles that are much more desirable, all brand new models, any of which I will be very happy to offer in appreciation for all of the help you have given me."

Territo feels as if all of the oxygen is going out of the room.

"Richard has his heart set on this specific automobile and I am very determined to have it for him."

Suddenly, Tony Territo knows that he is being tested. And he understands immediately that he will fail the test.

"I'm sorry, Mr. Colletti, but I can't help you. In case you were not aware, the 1972 BMW is my own personal vehicle and I am extremely fond of it."

"Please, Anthony, do not make the mistake of denying my request."

"Please, Mr. Colletti," Territo says, throwing all caution to the wind and wanting badly to get the fuck out of that closed, stinking place, "don't make the mistake of threatening me."

And then Sammy Leone is stomping his feet, his neck the color of a hothouse tomato, yelling something about disrespect. And Colletti calmly commands Leone to be quiet, to not disturb the tranquility of the room, and Leone goes silent.

"I beg you to act sensibly, Tony," the old man says. "I will expect to hear something much more positive from you before Saturday. Sammy, please show Mr. Territo to the door. I need to do my deep-breathing exercises. It will help me to clear this unfortunate misunderstanding from my mind."

Colletti closes his eyes as Sammy leads Tony away.

. . .

Samson has been on the phone with Chief Trenton; the phone call he was hoping would not come, as certain as he was that it would. Trenton wants to know what they are doing to solve this case, because the commissioner is on Trenton's back like Quasimodo's hump. Samson manufactures a progress report and slams down the receiver. He looks around the room and realizes that they are doing nothing.

"Tommy, I want you back at Lutheran. I want to find out who lifted those drugs. I don't care how many people you have to talk to, I don't care if it's a floor washer or the head administrator of the hospital. Lou, take Landis and a few uniforms with you over to the first scene. Tommy has the name of a woman who saw a car. Try to get a better description and then canvass the neighborhood again. Send Landis and one of the officers over to the school, maybe someone noticed a car there. This guy had to use a vehicle to take the Ventura kid to the apartment building. Someone had to see something. I'll go back to the grocery store on J. If he drove the milk truck to the Graham house, he must have left a vehicle near there. I'll send Mendez over to the dairy. I want a list of every vehicle that anyone saw that was not familiar: year, make, model, color, condition, plate or partial plate numbers. I don't care how long the list is. We need to find some kind of match."

"Why is he even using the drug at all if he's bashing the victims' brains in?" says Murphy.

"I don't know. Let's concentrate on how he got the stuff and we can fucking ask him when we find him," says Samson.

"Where are the fingers?"

Vota didn't realize he had said it aloud.

"Maybe the guy likes knuckle sandwiches," Murphy says, grabbing his coat and heading toward the door.

"How can you joke about this shit?" asks Vota.

"I can joke about anything. It's therapy. Comic relief if you will."

"Comic relief is a lot more effective if it's funny, Tommy," says Samson.

"He cuts off a finger from each victim," Vota says, more to himself, since no one else seems to be listening. "He doesn't leave it, he doesn't send it to anyone, so he must take it with him. Hold on to it. What the fuck for? What the fuck does he do with them?"

"Let's focus on questions that may have a rational answer, Lou," says Samson. "Let's get out and try to find the fucking car."

"He's going to kill again, and soon," says Vota.

Serena Huang and Andrew Chen sit in a booth drinking coffee at the Ridge Diner on 5th Avenue. They have been at it for more than an hour. Serena is way out on a limb.

She is thankful that she has made it past the fabrications concerning her acquaintance with Susan Graham, an old college buddy she decided she would surprise while she was down from Albany. Serena made Andy Chen for a cop the moment he had opened the door, and she had instantly begun creating a fictitious character.

Serena then moved on to more fiction. Her job with the state health department, which would have her in New York City for a few weeks for planning sessions.

Serena half listens to Chen talk about his rookie year on the police force, while trying to come up with a subtle way to bring the conversation back to the body on Bay Ridge Avenue.

She decides to test the limb a little further.

"What a horrifying experience for Sue. I ran into one of her neighbors before I got to Susan's door. Is it true that the victim's finger was cut off?"

Chen tightens slightly, like a person who thinks he has heard footsteps from behind. Something in the crafty innocence of the question, or maybe in the hypnotic smile accompanying it, puts his guard up.

"I really shouldn't talk about it," says Chen, though he wants to.

"I understand," Serena says, biting the inside of her cheek.

"Off the record?" Chen says.

The use of this particular expression startles Serena initially. Then the irony has her in full theatrical mode.

"Sure, who would I talk to? After the meetings this morning, I can assure you that no one listens to a single word I say."

"There was a homicide, Friday afternoon, an eight-year-old boy. There are similarities that may point to a common perpetrator," he says, and then finally catches himself. "I really can't say more."

"I really don't think I want to hear more," she says convincingly. "The big city spooks me enough as it is."

"Oh, it's not all that bad, especially if there's someone to show you around. Maybe I can give you a tour of Brooklyn while you're down here. It's a world of its own."

"That would be nice."

"How can I reach you?"

"I may have to switch hotels. How about I call you?" says Serena, pedaling fast.

Chen hands her one of his cards.

"You'll call?"

"I will," she says, and then she casually glances at her watch. "Wow. I completely lost track of time, and it's entirely your fault. I have a 4:00 p.m. meeting in Manhattan."

"Can I drop you at the subway station?"

"Sure, that would be great."

Chen watches as she walks down the stairs to the 68th Street Station on 4th. Chen marvels at life's unexpected surprises. He drives off toward the Precinct.

A few moments later, Serena Huang comes back up to the street. She walks back toward the Graham house, back to where she had parked her car. She drives to the office of the *Brooklyn Eagle*. She has a mundane article to complete on new movie releases. And she has to find out everything she can about the recent murder of an eight-year-old boy.

Lorraine DiMarco sits at her desk in the law office. There is work she should be doing, regardless of the fact that there is little she can do for Bobby Hoyle. Except to pray that the inmate Bobby threw against the wall stays alive long enough to talk with the police.

Instead, Lorraine is leafing through a brochure on magnetic resonance imaging. MRI.

How to prepare for the test. What to expect.

Don't eat in the morning, leave the jewelry at home, and the IUD. Use the bathroom before the test begins, tell the technician about any allergies, ask for a sedative if you are unusually nervous, lie still for twenty to forty-five minutes. And be prepared for possible side effects, most commonly a headache.

The thought of the test giving her a headache was almost comical, but not funny enough to ease her fear of Wednesday's appointment. Or stop her agonizing about when and how to tell her father. Or help her make up her mind about whether she could tell Lou Vota about it at all.

Sal DiMarco walks the three short blocks to Campo's grocery.

"Need some more boxes?" Campo asks as DiMarco walks up to Joe and his wife.

"Thank you, we're all set. Good afternoon, Roseanna," says Sal. "Joe, I was hoping you had a minute to talk."

"Sure, let's step outside. I could use a smoke."

Campo leaves Roseanna behind the counter and follows Sal out to the street.

"Do you remember Frank Sullivan?" Sal asks, as Campo lights up a Camel.

"He had the restaurant over on 86th with his brother?"

"Yes. I ran into him. He's not in very good shape. I want to help him out. I want to have him take the small apartment in our basement."

"He is without a home?"

"Yes. He's been living on the streets. I'm afraid he won't accept if he can't afford to contribute at least a token payment for rent. I was hoping that perhaps you could use some help here at the store. Frank is a good man, and he ran his business well."

Joe Campo takes a long drag of his cigarette and puts it out in a bucket of sand sitting at the grocery entrance.

"Your timing may be perfect, my friend," says Campo. "My daughter-in-law Angela is expecting another child very shortly. We had talked about my wife having more time to assist with the older children when the new child comes. Let me speak with Roseanna about this and I will get back to you soon. I believe that we can work something out for Mr. Sullivan, and it could help us out as well."

"Wonderful," says DiMarco. "Thank you, Joe."

"This is a very honorable thing you are trying to do, Salvatore."

"I pray it is the right thing," says DiMarco.

He has been sitting on a bench across from the Territo house for hours. It is getting colder, but he doesn't seem to notice. There has been no sign of *TITAN1*, but he feels certain that he has been guided to the right place.

He has seen two children arrive. First, a teenage boy, perhaps fourteen. Later, a girl. Older. The thought that the oldest child may be female concerns him. He had not considered taking a girl. He will have to be certain, but he will do what he has to do.

He hasn't eaten all day. And he has other business to consider. He needs to find a place to use, an empty place, not far from here.

He decides to leave. Maybe he will come back tonight, to look for the BMW. Or tomorrow. Or the next day.

He has developed the patience of a saint.

He tucks the Bible under his arm, rises from the bench and walks slowly back to his car.

THIRTEEN

The Brooklyn-Queens Resident Agency is a satellite branch of the Federal Bureau of Investigation New York Field Office. The B-Q office is located at Kew Gardens Road near 80th Road in Queens, near the impossible intersection of Queens Boulevard and Union Turnpike and the southern tip of Flushing Meadows-Corona Park, home of both the old and the new Mets' ballparks and anything else left from the 1964 World's Fair. The office is either located in Kew Gardens or Flushing or Jamaica, depending on where you are standing when asked.

Ripley is trying to slip out of his office early on Monday afternoon. Ripley is the SAC, the Special Agent in Command, of the B-Q Field Office. He reports to the ADIC, the Assistant Director in Charge, of the New York FBI Headquarters at Federal Plaza in Manhattan.

For Ripley, the assignment is a promotion, and a return home. He is back in Queens, not far from where he grew up, after nearly ten years in suburban Virginia and an office at Quantico. Ripley has been back in New York City for nearly eight months, and he is finally beginning to feel reacquainted. For Ripley's two young sons, however, born and raised in the woods of Wilderness, Virginia outside of Fredericksburg, it is a new universe.

Ripley missed Quantico. The pulse of the place. The excitement. The challenges. And at the same time, its seclusion, its eerie silence.

Ripley's office in Queens offered a picturesque view of three very large parks: Corona Park, Forest Park and Maple Grove Cemetery. But it was far from tranquil. The incessant noise of automobile, bus and air traffic often made it difficult to think. Queens Boulevard, Union Turnpike, the Grand Central Parkway, Jamaica and Parkway Hospitals, LaGuardia

Airport, Arthur Ashe Tennis Stadium, the ballpark, all coming together in a cacophony of horn blasts and squealed brakes, cheers and jeers, departures and arrivals, life and death.

Ripley is halfway to the door of his office, halfway to escape, when his assistant enters.

"This just came in from One Federal Plaza," says Winona Stone, waving a sheet from the fax machine.

"Come in," says Ripley, returning to his desk.

"Were you on your way out?" she asks.

"What do you have?"

"The Mexican government has the driver of a transport that carried seven very expensive unregistered German-type automobiles across the border and they want to know what to do with him."

"And what does it have to do with us?"

"The driver wants to cut a deal."

"Where's he from?"

"New Haven."

"Send it to Connecticut."

"Connecticut doesn't want it. They're claiming that the vehicles came out of Brooklyn, so they hot-potatoed it to One Federal Plaza and Manhattan threw it to us."

"Doesn't New York have some kind of auto theft task force?"

"Yes, they certainly do. But there's the rub, Chief. The driver is from Connecticut. It's the interstate noncooperation syndrome, no one has the courage to cut a deal without the blessings of the State Department, so they all figure they might as well drop it in our laps."

"Great," says Ripley, "and don't call me Chief."

"The driver dropped a name, Titan Imports in Brooklyn. He claims he can help put the main man away, for a little immunity. What do you want to do?" asks Stone.

"Get out of here, take my kids to a hockey game."

"Okay. What do you want *me* to do?"

"Look into Titan Imports, find out what you can about who operates the place. Let me know what you learn. Don't try talking to anyone."

"Look, but don't touch?"

"Yes. For the time being."

"Okay," says Agent Stone, "you can go now."

"Thank you."

"Enjoy the game, although I must say that I think hockey is a bit violent for young boys."

"Maybe so, but believe it or not it is a lot tamer than TV or video games and they hardly pay attention. They love the crowd. It'll have to do until the baseball season begins. We can only hope that none of the players' dads are there."

Twenty minutes later Ripley pulls into the driveway of his sister's home in nearby Rego Park to pick up his two boys. They play with their cousins in the back yard while he quietly sips the cup of coffee that Connie had quietly placed before him. They sit facing each other across the kitchen table. She knows better than to ask him anything about how he feels or about what he is working on. If he wants to talk he will talk. If he has nothing to say, he is not going to say a thing.

"I'd better get going," he says. "I'm taking the boys to see the Islanders tonight."

"That'll be nice," she says. The best she can do.

"Thanks for the coffee."

"Anytime."

And thanks for being like a mother to my children, he thinks to say but doesn't.

Collecting the boys, collecting their things, heading for the car, and eight-year-old Kyle is already asking the question as he climbs into the front seat.

"Daddy, is Mom mad at me?"

"Dad, Mommy me?" parrots four-year-old Mickey.

"No, son. Your mother loves you."

"Then why did she leave?"

Why did she leave?

She left because she happened to get caught between a lead-footed drunken teenager and his pathetic destiny.

She left because it wasn't enough to be a beautiful, intelligent and loving wife and mother; you had to be able to dodge speeding out-of-control Chevrolets as well.

She left because a God who was so busy creating the sick maniacs that Ripley was paid to track down couldn't possibly find time to worry or care about her. Or about the one man and two young boys who lost the best friend they ever had.

"She left because God missed her and wanted her with him in heaven and she is with him now watching over us and loving us very, very much," Ripley says.

"Oh, yeah," says Kyle, "that's right."

"So, who's going to win the game tonight, kiddo?" says Ripley, trying to change the subject before one of the boys asks if he can visit Mom in heaven.

"The Orioles, silly," says Kyle, to which Ripley shakes his head and smiles.

"I wanna Oreo," says Mickey, squirming in his car seat.

"Would you settle for a hot dog and a beer?" says Ripley, which earns a smile from the older boy.

"I'm a'scared of bears," says Mickey, which has both his father and his big brother laughing out loud.

"Tell you what," says Ripley. "You have the Oreos and milk, Mickey, and Kyle and I can handle the hot dogs and the bears."

"I'm not a'scared of hot dogs, Daddy."

Neither am I, except when they're in out-of-control Chevrolets, thought Ripley.

Serena finds it lost in the Saturday *Daily News.* An eight-year-old boy found dead on the roof of an apartment building at the Gravesend-Bensonhurst border. Cause of death attributed to a fatal head trauma. Very few details otherwise. The boy's name. The name of the owner of a grocery at Avenue S, said to have discovered the body.

The police were investigating.

Serena jots down the name Joseph Campo, and the location of the crime scene. Then she begins phoning the local funeral parlors until she learns that the viewing is scheduled to continue at the Graziano Funeral Home on 86th Street and 24th Avenue from seven until ten that evening.

Serena Huang leaves the *Brooklyn Eagle* office and drives home to her apartment on South Portland Place in Fort Greene. To wash off the dust of the day and find something appropriate to wear to a wake.

Murphy has been flapping his lips at Lutheran Medical Center for hours. His tongue feels like a bar of Bonomo Turkish Taffy about to snap. He finally finds a lead.

Victor Sanders, a night maintenance worker, let go by the hospital three weeks earlier. Sanders was suspected of taking drugs from an emergency room cabinet. The hospital authorities had no solid proof, but could not afford the risk of keeping Sanders on. The decision was made to fire Sanders and wait to see if he would sue the hospital for wrongful termination. Sanders never had.

Personnel gave Murphy an address in Sunset Park.

Eddie Conroy has almost completed his work. At least for this Monday. Eddie is exhausted and anxious to be home with his family.

It has taken all morning to prepare the large basement room for a fresh painting. Father Donovan wanted the room ready for a Valentine's Day event on Friday night, open to unmarried members of the congregation. For hours, Eddie had folded the tables and chairs, stacking them in the center of the floor, and covering all of it with a canvas drop.

The cloth exhibited a splattering of multicolored smears of paint, remnants of previous projects around the church. The underside displayed a mural of the manger at Bethlehem, used in a Christmas play performed by the grade-school children at Our Lady of Angels. Conroy fondly remembers how proud he was of his daughter, who bravely played one of the Three Wise Men.

After moving everything he could move away from the walls and carrying six gallons of white paint from the storage area into the room, Eddie shut down the lights and moved to his work above. He would begin with the ceiling in the morning.

After lunch, Eddie cleaned the stained glass windows, from the inside. The weather prediction for later in the week called for temperatures in the fifties, unusually mild for February. If the meteorologists were correct for a change, Eddie would tackle the outside of the windows on Wednesday or Thursday, once the downstairs painting was done.

Conroy spends the remainder of his day running a broom through the church, up and down the rows of pews and the center and side aisles. With a little time left before his shift ends, Eddie takes a soft cloth and a bottle of wood cleaner to dust and polish the confessionals.

Conroy notices the large manila envelope on the floor of one of the confessionals and lifts it up. He feels its weight. It is simply addressed to Father Donovan. Eddie is mildly curious about the contents of the envelope, and why it was left there and not delivered. But not intrigued enough to interrupt his work.

When he is done with the confessionals, he carries the envelope into Father Donovan's office. Donovan is out of town attending an ecumenical council meeting. Eddie places the envelope on Donovan's desk, alongside the mail that had arrived that morning. The priest could deal with all of it when he returned from Albany on Wednesday evening.

Eddie locks up before leaving, climbs into his car, and rushes home to dinner with his wife and children.

Murphy finds the address on 47th Street in Sunset Park. He had thought of calling for backup. Then he remembered that everyone else was out looking for a nondescript car that might belong to a nondescript multiple murderer, so he decided to rough it alone. Murphy drives past the house, parks up the street near 4th Avenue, and walks back.

The doorbell is answered by a lanky man in his late twenties. He greets Murphy with a smile.

"Victor Sanders?" Murphy asks.

"That would be my brother," the man says. "Are you another bill collector?"

"Not exactly. Is your brother at home?"

"I'm afraid you're out of luck. Vic left town yesterday morning. To look for work. He said something about

Philadelphia."

"Any idea where in Philadelphia?"

"Nope. Though I suppose I'll find out sooner or later—he'll be looking for a handout."

"If you do, would you give me a call," says Murphy, handing the man a card. "It's important I speak with him."

"Detective Murphy? Has Victor done something wrong?"

"It concerns drugs that went missing from Lutheran."

"Vic says he didn't take the drugs."

"Do you believe him?"

"Hey, he's a fuckup, but he's my brother. I have to believe him."

"Do you," says Murphy, not really a question. He is thinking about his own brother, Michael. "Listen, if you hear from your brother tell him that the drugs may have been involved in the murder of two boys. Tell Victor that if he can help us, we can help him."

Murphy caught something in the man's eyes when he mentioned the word *murder*. He is about to ask for some identification when the man shoves the front door into Murphy's body, knocking the stunned detective to the ground.

Sanders races off toward 4th Avenue.

Murphy jumps up and takes off after Victor Sanders.

Brother. Fuck.

At 4th Avenue, Murphy spots Sanders on the opposite side heading toward the subway station. He negotiates the busy avenue, dodging a bus in the process. Murphy can hear the R train rumbling below the street. He watches Sanders take the stairs down to the 45th Street platform.

At the subway entrance, Murphy has to snake his way through the crowd of commuters coming up. When he reaches the platform, he see the doors of the subway cars close and the train jerk to a start and pull out of the station.

Fuck. Fuck. Fuck.

Murphy pulls out his cell phone, a futile thought that he can call ahead to 36th Street. He gets no signal from the phone.

Worthless piece of shit.

Murphy runs back up to the street. His car is two blocks away. The phone will work up here, but the chance of catching Sanders at 35th or even Pacific Street are slim. And there's no way of knowing where the fuck will get off the train. For a moment, Murphy considers hailing a cab. As usual, there is never a taxi when you need one.

Instead, Murphy calls in an APB on Victor Sanders, mumbles *motherfucker* under his breath, and walks back to his car.

Lorraine DiMarco is ready to call it a day. A shitty day. As she gets into her overcoat, her office desk phone rings.

"How did it go, sweetheart."

"I've spent all afternoon trying to visualize how it might have gone worse, Dad," says Lorraine. "No luck. How did it go with Frank Sullivan?"

"What are you doing for dinner?"

"I haven't given it much thought, why?"

"There's something that I want to talk with you about. Your mother is at one of her functions at St. Mary's and I thought you and I could have supper together."

"Sure. Want to go out?"

"There's enough leftover lasagna here to feed the Italian Army, how about that?"

"Okay, as long as you let me eat it cold from the refrigerator," Lorraine says. "I'll be over at seven."

Lorraine walks down to the bus stop for the ride back to her apartment. She wonders what her father has to talk with her about. She wonders if she will have the courage to talk with him about a certain medical test, only thirty-nine hours away.

Lou Vota questions the woman who Murphy had spoken with two days earlier.

"Signora Valenti," Vota says, hoping that the use of Italian might garner more thoughtful cooperation. "You described the vehicle to Detective Murphy as gray or green, please try to remember. *È importante.*"

"*Grigio. Chiaro,*" she says.

"Light gray, *bene,*" says Vota. "*Sportelli?*"

"*Quattro.*"

"Four doors, are you certain?"

"*Credo di si,*" she says. "I think so."

"Good enough. *Per favore,* Signora, tell me everything else you can remember about the car."

The woman tells Vota that she saw the car parked on West 11th Street at the southwest corner at Avenue S on the day the Ventura boy was discovered. She had never seen such a car in the neighborhood before. She remembers the car because of the terrible damage to the rear on the passenger side, and the child seat in back on the same side. She has no clue as to the make or model, only that it was large and looked American. She did not see the license plates.

Not much, but the best anyone has come up with near the Ventura murder scene after nearly five hours of walking and talking through the area.

Vota can't believe that the killer carried the boy from a car on 11th to the apartment building a block away, along Avenue S in broad daylight, without being seen by someone. He is sure that the killer must have driven into the alley alongside the building, carried the boy up the rear fire escape to the empty apartment, unlocked the door from inside, left the building and moved the vehicle.

Then the killer would have walked back to the building and calmly entered the apartment, unnoticed.

Vota is beginning to believe that they are searching for an invisible man.

Vota decides to call it quits, at least for the day, and heads back to the 61st Precinct.

When Vota walks into the Homicide squad room, Lieutenant Samson is on the telephone.

"Okay, enough Tommy," Vota hears Samson say. "Don't beat yourself up. Go home."

Samson places the receiver in its cradle.

"What was that?" Vota asks.

"Tommy made the guy who may have lifted the drugs

155

from Lutheran," says Samson. "The suspect ditched him. We've got an APB out. Any luck?"

Vota tells Samson what little he learned from talking with Signora Valenti.

Samson fills Vota in on what he learned on the Addams case.

"Someone I spoke to saw a car parked on Avenue I that he'd never seen before," says Samson, "not far from where the milk truck was found. A light gray Oldsmobile, four-door sedan. He thinks it was a mid-eighties model. It was sometime after three, Sunday morning. The car had a smashed quarter-panel, passenger side."

"Bingo. Anything on the plates?"

"No. Only that he's pretty sure they were New York, and he noticed a bumper sticker. *Baby on Board.*"

"That's something at least."

"It's really not very much help, Lou. Only another indication that the same perp did both boys. And we didn't need one. We'll put it out to all of the precincts; have them stop and check anything that fits the description, and piss off a lot of citizens."

"What now?" asks Vota.

"I don't know about you, but I'm going to Douglaston to see if my kids remember me."

"Well, get going. I'll call in the all-points on the Oldsmobile."

"I'll see you in the morning, after my meeting with the detective from the 68th. Don't forget to be here for Ivanov," says Samson, grabbing his coat.

Vota calls in the description of the suspect vehicle to Central Dispatch.

"Are you joking, Sergeant? We'll be stopping half the cars in Brooklyn."

Vota assures the dispatcher that he is dead serious.

Vota phones Lorraine. Her machine picks up the call. He scoops up his overcoat and heads home to Red Hook.

He sits at his kitchen table over a bowl of chili. He is

feeling better today. He feels certain he has found the man who killed his boy. He feels so good, in fact, that he has taken the time to heat the chili. As opposed to eating it, as he often did, straight from the can. The bread is a week old.

On his way back home, he noticed a *For Sale* sign on the lawn of a house not far from the Territo residence.

The house sat on a large corner lot, across from the high school. The place looked unoccupied and would be fairly dark and quiet after school hours. He decides he will check it out more closely the next day.

He places the empty bowl into the sink and runs hot water into it.

He takes a bottle of Scotch into the boy's room, and with it his Bible.

He sits on the floor of his son's bedroom.

And reads.

And drinks.

Battling sanity.

FOURTEEN

Serena goes with basic black. She arrives at the Graziano Funeral Home at six-thirty, thirty minutes before the showing is scheduled to begin. She is banking that the boy's parents had spent the afternoon at the wake and were taking a dinner break before the evening hours begin. She is hanging from her thumbs and thinking on her toes.

Serena explains that she is one of Billy Ventura's grade-school teachers, that she has a PTA meeting at seven and wants to see the boy one last time. She claims it may be her only opportunity. A Graziano son reluctantly shows her into the empty viewing room.

Serena moves quickly to the casket and kneels before it. The door closes behind her host, who is off to prepare for the evening visitors. She stares at the boy's small arms, one small hand covering the other. Serena takes a self-conscious glance behind her, confirms that she is alone, and lifts the boy's arm at the wrist; holding on to what she is fairly confident is the sleeve of the boy's first dress suit. His First Holy Communion suit.

The small finger of the boy's right hand is missing. Serena gasps, unsure of how loud a sound she has made.

She carefully replaces the one hand over the other.

Serena takes a long, hard look at her work. As sure as she is that she has succeeded in masking the damaged hand, she cannot help seeing it. She is certain that she will continue to see it for a long time. She hears a sound at the door behind her and collects herself. Serena rises and turns to the door as the Graziano son walks in.

"The parents called, they're on their way," he says. "If you could wait ten minutes, you might catch them."

"I wish I could," she says. "I'll try my best to get back here before ten."

159

Serena walks past the man, leaves the room and the building. She has done something terrible. She has done something remarkable.

She is ashamed and excited at the same time.

Serena Huang believes that she has finally grabbed hold of a ticket to the big show.

Tony Territo sits at the dinner table watching his family eat. Barbara has prepared grilled salmon, fresh broccoli rabe with lemon juice and garlic, and a salad of romaine and tomatoes. She has made every effort to avoid oil and fat and cholesterol.

Anthony Jr. will have none of it, and instead gnaws on a large cheeseburger reheated in the microwave.

Brenda, who believes that teenage girls should look like something from the streets of Bombay, sits staring into space.

Barbara is fishing hunks of garlic from the serving bowl.

Tony Territo has lost his appetite.

"Is the dinner okay?" his wife asks.

"It's fine," he says.

"Is there something wrong?"

"What could be wrong?"

Frank Sullivan has been standing outside the door of Levine's Liquor Store for an hour, debating whether or not to enter.

Finally Sully walks in, grabs a bottle of inexpensive red wine from a shelf, and carries it to the counter.

"Did you hear about Annie?" Levine asks as he rings up the sale and bags the wine.

"What about Annie?" Sully asks.

"She threw herself in front of a train," Levine says.

Sully walks quickly out the door.

"You forgot the wine," Levine calls after him.

Frank Sullivan hears nothing.

. . .

160

Samson helps Alicia with the supper dishes. The girls are preparing for bed, with all of the teeth brushing, hand washing, pajama locating and general procrastination that the nightly ritual entails.

"I'm sure you told me," he says, "but where is Jimmy?"

"Basketball practice. He'll be home any minute."

"Is he free Friday night?"

"For what?"

"To babysit the girls, I thought that we could go out for dinner, maybe a movie."

"Are you asking me out on a date?"

"Yes."

"What's the occasion?" Alicia asks, knowing full well.

"German Unification Day," says Samson, poker-faced.

"Well, then, absolutely. Let's ask the boy as soon as he gets back."

As if on cue, Jimmy Samson bops into the kitchen.

"Listen. I was thinking," says Jimmy. "If you guys wanted to get out on Friday night for Valentine's Day, I could stay home and watch the girls."

"Sure, that would be great," says Samson, catching the conspiratorial glance between mother and son.

And loving it.

Unable to find Lorraine at home or at her office, Vota decides to visit his mother's sister in Bensonhurst. Of course, his aunt insists he join them for dinner.

"How is Lorraine?" asks his Aunt Donna, as she sets the after-supper cake and coffee on the table. Donna has taken to mothering Lou ever since his mother passed away.

"Very well and very busy," Vota says.

"When are you going to make an honest woman of her?" asks his Uncle Alfredo.

"Lorraine is the most honest person I have ever known," says Vota, suppressing a laugh.

His aunt shakes her head over her husband's lack of finesse. Lou and Donna exchange smiles, they both realize that Alfredo means well. He is an old-timer. Born in the old country, he has so little knowledge of American custom.

"What I meant was, when are you two lovebirds going to tie the knot?" Al asks. Clueless.

"Actually," Vota admits, more for the benefit of his aunt, "I've been thinking about asking her soon, you know, with Valentine's Day coming up."

"It doesn't have to be a special holiday," says Vota's aunt, surprising him. "You'll know when the time is right."

"What's Valentine's Day?" asks his uncle.

Detective Murphy sits on a wood stool at Joe's Bar and Grill on Avenue U. Murphy is working on a large plate of steamed mussels from the kitchen, a glass of bourbon and a mug of beer nearby to wash them down.

Augie Sena is behind the bar, hobbling back and forth, his leg in a tall cast. A relentless workaholic, Augie was back behind the bar less than four weeks after a collision with a keg of Budweiser.

"When is it coming off?" asks Murphy, trying to read the array of graffiti scribbled on the cast. "Stand still a minute. What did Mendez write there?"

"I've been assured it will be off before the baseball season ends. I'd like to tear the fucking thing off right now. I've got an itch down there that's driving me insane. Mendez wrote: *Plastered again.* Rey thinks that if he can come up with really bad puns, people will forget that he was born in Puerto Rico. Landis wrote: *Let thee who is without sin, stone the first cast.* So people will forget that he was born in Gravesend."

"Try a wire coat hanger," says Murphy, "for the itch."

"So, do you have a hot date lined up for Friday night, Tommy?" Sena asks, trying to move on.

"What's Friday?" says Murphy.

"So, Joe Campo called me less than an hour after I spoke with him and said that he could give Frank Sullivan work at the store," says Sal DiMarco, finishing the story.

"That's great, Dad," says Lorraine, helping herself to

another healthy slab of cold lasagna.

"Tomorrow I'll try to find Sully and tell him the news. I think he'll go for it."

"Do you need any help getting the basement ready?"

"No. I cleaned up some this afternoon. It's ready. It's a nice little apartment."

"It's a great little apartment," says Lorraine. She had used the rooms herself, while she attended law school at Queens.

"There's salad in the refrigerator," says Sal.

"This is good," says Lorraine. "I have to get going soon."

"Wait for your mother; she should be back any minute. We'll have coffee."

"Sure," says Lorraine, unable to say no.

But the longer she sits there the more difficult it is to keep quiet. And finally she lets go.

"Tell me," says Sal, taking his daughter's hand.

Bobby Hoyle has been moved to another cell.

All ten inmates from Bobby's former cell had signed a petition. They wanted to be able to watch the Islanders game on TV. They didn't want Bobby back in with them.

The inmate who attacked Hoyle remained unconscious.

Bobby sits on his cot, tormented, unable to believe that all of this happened because he went out that night, because he couldn't get through one single night without a cigarette.

Bobby sits on his cot, crying, thinking about how badly he could use a cigarette right that minute.

"Who's winning?" asks Kyle. "I forgot."

"New York," says Ripley.

"Good," says Kyle.

"Good," says Mickey.

Ripley looks down at the younger boy, not sure if he is mimicking Kyle or referring to the hot dog, a healthy chunk of which is hanging out of Mickey's mouth.

A loud buzzer signals the end of the second period.

"Is it over?" asks Kyle.

The older boy is courageously fighting to keep his eyes opened.

Mickey is staring at the gob of mustard in his lap.

"Not yet, but we should get going," says Ripley. "It's late. You have school tomorrow. We can watch the end of the game on television while you guys get ready for bed."

"Will we see us on TV, Dad?" Mickey asks.

"Maybe," says Ripley, smiling.

"When does Mickey start regular school, Dad?" asks Kyle.

"Next year," says Ripley.

"Good," says Kyle, mischievously.

"Are you chewing, partner?" Ripley asks.

"Yes, Dad," Mickey says, after displaying a number of exaggerated mouth movements and managing to swallow.

"Good, let's go," says Ripley.

Ripley carries Mickey in his arms and Kyle hangs on to Ripley's coat as they move toward the Nassau Coliseum exit.

"Can I get some ice skates, Dad?" asks Kyle.

"Do you want to play hockey?"

"No. It looks like it hurts too much. I like the ones in the Olympics," says Kyle.

"Yeah, the limpics," says Mickey.

"Why not," says Ripley. "I'm sure we can find you a pair of figure skates."

"Yeah, figger skates," says Mickey.

After thanking his aunt for dinner, Vota climbs into his car for the ride home. When he reaches Avenue U, Vota decides on another detour.

He turns left and drives the five blocks to Joe's Bar and Grill.

Murphy is still at the bar when Vota walks in.

"Hey, Tommy, drinking your dinner?" he asks.

"Helping it down," says Murphy.

Vota slides onto the stool beside him. He glances up at the television above the bar. Jean-Claude van Damme is rearranging someone's facial features with a six-foot length of two-by-four.

"Is this the one where he plays twins?" asks Vota.

"I don't think he ever made one where he didn't play twins," says Murphy.

"Who won the game?"

"Islanders, 2–1."

"I'll have what Tommy ordered," Vota says to Augie.

"You want them all at once, or a few at a time," Sena says, pouring a bourbon.

"And another round for Detective Murphy," Vota says. "How's the leg, Augie?"

"I'll let you know in a few months when I find out if it's still in there."

"Here's to law enforcement," Murphy says, lifting his glass.

Vota lifts his drink and clinks it against Murphy's.

"Is that marinara sauce on your collar, Tommy?" Vota asks after draining the shot glass.

"It's a mussel shirt," Murphy says, draining his.

"So, what went down in Sunset Park?" Vota asks.

"The guy threw me a curve ball. I swung and missed. He beat me in a footrace to the 4th Avenue Local. There's a two-man stakeout in case he comes back to the house, and they're working on a search warrant for the place. Any luck identifying a vehicle?"

"Narrowed it down slightly. Light gray four-door Olds sedan, crushed quarter-panel passenger side," says Lou.

"Good work."

"Wait, there's more," says Vota. "A child seat in back. And a bumper sticker. *Baby on Board.*"

"Jesus."

"What?"

"I saw a sticker like that," says Murphy, "recently. I can't remember where or when."

"Remember the car?"

"Nope. But then again, memory is not my strong suit, especially after three hours here with Augie pouring."

"Well, no matter," says Vota, "there's probably a million of them out there like it."

"I don't know, most of the bumper stickers around these

parts display messages like *God Bless America* or *Unless You're a Hemorrhoid, Get Off My Ass*," says Murphy. "*Baby on Board* is pretty sophisticated. Hey, Lou, do you know what Friday is?"

"Valentine's Day."

"I told you, Tommy," says Augie Sena. "You've got to be the only person alive who didn't know."

"I told you I was one of a kind, Augie."

"Not quite, Tommy," says Vota. "You'll have to make room for my Uncle Alfredo."

The three sit huddled around the kitchen table in the DiMarco home.

Frances, back from St. Mary's Church, holding her hands over her cup of coffee, palms down, for the little warmth it offers.

Lorraine, finally regaining a hold on her composure, trying it on for size.

Sal, fighting off an image in his mind. A flag-draped casket carried off a military plane at LaGuardia more than thirty years earlier.

"Dad?" Lorraine says.

"I know you are frightened, Lorraine. It will be alright," Sal DiMarco says. "I promise you."

How he can say such a thing, Lorraine is thinking, *and be so convincing?*

"I'm sorry," she says, "for being such a coward."

"Nonsense," says Sal. "You are the bravest person I've ever known. And whether you realize it or not, you're more concerned about worrying us than you are about yourself. So give us a little credit, we're all in this together."

"Thank you, Dad."

"And talk to Lou," says her father. "I'll take you over for the test Wednesday morning. Don't argue."

"Okay."

"I can make another pot of coffee," Fran says.

"That's alright, Mom, I really have to get going."

"Please make one anyway, Frances," says Sal. "I may be

up for a while. I'll walk you out, Lorraine."

"It's turned very cold," says Lorraine when they reach her car.

"It's supposed to warm up by Wednesday," DiMarco says. "Call me tomorrow; we'll make arrangements for getting over to the hospital for the MRI."

"I will."

"And Lorraine."

"Yes, Dad?"

"Call Linda. Your sister is a pretty tough cookie herself. She should hear about this from you."

"I will."

Lorraine gives him a kiss on the cheek, climbs into her car, and pulls away.

Sal can smell the fresh coffee as he comes back into the house.

"I'm sorry that I kept it from you, Salvatore," Fran says as she pours.

"It's alright. Just don't make a habit of it."

A few minutes later the doorbell rings.

"Who could that be at this hour?" says Fran.

"Maybe Lorraine forgot something," Sal says, rising and moving to the door.

When Sal DiMarco opens the front door he finds Frank Sullivan standing there, a shopping bag in one hand and a small suitcase in the other.

"I came to accept your offer," says Sullivan. "If it's still open."

"Come in, Frank," says Sal, "it's freezing out here. What happened?"

"The woman, Annie. You saw her the other night. Your daughter gave her an overcoat," says Sully, following Sal into the front room.

"Yes."

"She's dead. She killed herself. She reached a point that I don't want to reach myself. I need your help."

"Put the bags down, Frank, and let me take your coat," says Sal. "There's fresh coffee."

"Thank you."

"You're welcome," says Sal DiMarco. "Please, make yourself at home."

He wakes to find himself on the floor of the boy's room. The Scotch bottle lies flat on the carpet. The bottle has miraculously held its contents from spilling over the toys surrounding him.

He splashes water on his face from the kitchen sink, gets into a heavy coat over a heavy sweater, and leaves the house. He walks to the phone booth at 5th Avenue, outside the dark movie theater.

He phones Victor Sanders again. There is no answer. He has been trying to reach the man for days. As he walks back to the house, he decides that he will need to come up with an alternative solution.

He first learned about pancuronium bromide from an article he read in a doctor's office waiting room. His son's doctor's office. How the drug was used in capital executions.

After Derek was killed, he recalled more of what he had read. How the drug had a unique effect.

Much like being submerged in water.

Like baptism.

It was then that he decided to seek the drug out, and was finally pointed in the direction of Victor Sanders. The man had supplied two vials, and promised that he could get more.

He was able to begin his work, punish the perpetrators of the crime against him, against his son. And protect the sacrificed innocents by cleansing them from sin.

Baptism.

He would find another way.

He goes back to the boy's room and takes a crayon, blue this time, and writes another note on yet another cover torn from an unused coloring book.

He has another package to deliver.

FIFTEEN

Tuesday morning.

Before leaving Joe's Bar and Grill the previous night, Murphy and Vota had arranged to meet in the third-floor Homicide office at the 61st at eight forty-five. They would both be present for the appointment with Detective Marina Ivanov of the 60th.

At precisely 9:00 a.m., Ivanov walks into the squad room.

The three detectives exchange greetings and take seats around Murphy's desk. No one seems to know how to begin.

"Can I get you something to drink, Detective," asks Murphy. "Coffee or a soda?"

"Thank you, I'm good," she says, lifting the very full coffee cup from the desk in front of her.

"If I recall correctly," says Vota, "there's a blackboard underneath that pile of coats. We could clear it off for you."

"That's okay," says Ivanov. "Listen, before we begin, let me tell you where I stand. I'm not good at lecturing. I'm better at trying my hand at specific queries. And I'm not one of those who gets into the mind of the killer—it's the last place I'd want to go. I've looked over the files. Maybe you could ask questions."

"What's the killer's home address?" asks Murphy.

"Okay, let's try this," Ivanov says. "A few general thoughts based on what I've seen. I don't believe that we are dealing with a textbook case. If there is anything even resembling a useful profile of a serial killer, this guy doesn't fit it. There are important elements missing. There is nothing sexual, for one. More telling, there appears to be no psychopathic rage. Granted, the killer is doing unusual harm to the bodies of the victims, but it is done calmly, methodically, purposefully if you will. He is not interested in the act of mutilation. He is communicating. He is attempting

169

to send a message. The message is the key."

"What's the message?" asks Vota.

"I don't know," says Ivanov, "but it's related to the numbers written on the wall."

"Isn't there rage in clubbing the victim on the head with a blunt weapon?" asks Murphy. "With enough force to kill?"

"I don't think so. It's primitive, but effective," says Ivanov. "It is a method of subduing and killing that would be used by someone who most likely had no experience in either. Knock them on the head, carry them away. Make sure that they don't wake up before the detailed work is done."

"Why bother with the Pavulon?" asks Vota. "The M.E. is almost certain that the blows were enough."

"That's the sixty-four-thousand-dollar question," says Ivanov. "The drug is not really necessary, unless related to its clinical use or its particular effects."

"It's used in capital punishment. Has he instituted his own personal justice system?" asks Vota.

"I think that punishment may be part of this," she says, "but what's the connection between the two victims? And what could an eight-year-old have possibly done to deserve a death sentence?"

"We've got no connection," says Murphy. "So. We are right back where we started."

"Not necessarily, we just have to look closer. Look at it differently," says Ivanov. "I have a strong feeling that there is a tie-in somewhere, connecting the victims, at least indirectly."

"A strong feeling?" says Murphy.

"Okay," says Ivanov, "a hunch."

"So, why is he leaving clues?" asks Vota. "Not that they're any help."

"Remember, I'm only speculating," says Ivanov. "This is pure guesswork based on rudimentary knowledge and very minimal experience."

"So stipulated," says Vota.

"He's leaving messages. They look like clues because they are incomplete, not fully spelled out. I believe he will eventually tell us why he is killing. He wants to."

"What's he waiting for?" asks Murphy.

Ivanov hesitates long enough for Vota to answer the question.

"He needs time to finish."

"I think so," says Detective Ivanov. "I'm afraid he has another victim lined up. Or worse, maybe more than one. But I believe that there will be an end to it. And he'll let us know everything when he's done."

"We need to know before he kills again," says Samson, standing in the doorway.

Back from his meeting with Detective Chen, Samson has listened to part of the conversation.

"This is fucked, Sam," says Murphy. "No fault of our friend here from the 60th, but we're getting nowhere."

"I had a thought on my way in this morning, something the detective from Flatlands said. If this guy is doling out retribution of some kind, why a young kid like Billy Ventura?" says Samson. "And I keep coming back to what the boy's father said, about the guy who got into his cab and threw the Bible at him."

"Someone threw a Bible at the boy's father?" asks Ivanov.

"Not literally—the guy was going on about Abraham and Isaac," says Samson.

"It's the parents," says Marina Ivanov, an involuntary reflex. "That's the connection."

"Yes, that's exactly what I was thinking. This guy is punishing the parents by taking the children," Samson says.

"So, we need to see the parents again, find out what the link is," says Vota.

"I hate saying it, but the parents may not know," says Ivanov.

"I think they do know," says Samson, "whether they know it or not."

"Huh?" says Murphy.

"I think something happened to this guy that set him off," says Samson, "and a parent of each of the victims was responsible somehow, even if unaware. We need to question all of them again, try to discover what it may be."

"It won't be much fun suggesting to a parent that he or she

may be somehow responsible for the death of their own child," says Ivanov.

"Who said anything about fun," says Samson.

"I'd like to help," says Ivanov.

"Sure," says Samson. "We can use all of the help we can get."

"Are you up for one more question?" asks Murphy.

"Go ahead," Ivanov says.

"Can the Knicks make the playoffs?"

"Only mathematically."

"What about the fingers?" Vota asks.

"I'm not sure," Ivanov says.

"Jesus. Forget about being sure. What do you think? What's your hunch? Why does he take them? What does he do with them?"

"Calm down, Lou," says Murphy.

"I don't know," says Ivanov.

Sully has greeted the day in many strange places since he lost his business and ultimately lost his home. He wakes on Tuesday morning in one of the most unusual places he has found himself in for many months.

A bed.

He looks around the room. His bedroom.

It is the smaller of the two main rooms that make up the basement apartment. A single bed, a nightstand with lamp and clock radio, a chest of drawers, a small closet. He unpacks his possessions, fills drawers and hangers.

There is a small bathroom off this room. A sink, a toilet, a shower stall. There are clean towels, soap and shampoo. A new razor and a can of shaving cream. A fresh tube of toothpaste and a packaged toothbrush. A wrapped roll of toilet tissue, an unopened box of facial tissue. He shaves and showers.

He dresses and moves into the larger room.

A kitchen area, a narrow gas stove, a refrigerator, a small dining table, two chairs. A small sofa, a low coffee table, a television.

Two windows letting in light from the side driveway, just above ground level.

On the counter near the kitchen sink, an old toaster, an electric coffee percolator, an unopened can of coffee. In the cabinets, a few dishes, bowls and glasses. In the counter drawer, silverware, a can opener.

He is overwhelmed by the consideration.

Sully hears knocking on the door at the top of the stairs.

"Come in," he calls.

"Good morning," says Sal DiMarco as he walks down. "Please join us for breakfast, Frank; you can shop for groceries later today. Is there anything else you need down here?"

"You were very thorough, Mr. DiMarco. I really don't know what to say. Except to thank you."

"Enough said. Let's eat and then we can walk over to see Joe Campo at the store. And please, call me Sal."

"Thank you, Sal."

Sully takes a quick glance back at his new home as he follows DiMarco up.

Ripley sits at his desk, face buried in a file folder, similar folders spread out in front of him. Agent Winona Stone taps at his door.

"Come in," says Ripley. "Sit."

She takes a seat opposite Ripley.

"I found out some things about Titan," she says.

"Refresh my memory," he says, looking up from the folder. "Titan?"

"Titan Imports. The car shipment stopped in Mexico."

"Got it. What do you know?"

"The owner is Tony Territo. His father, Vincent, was a captain in the Giambi crime family until he retired in the early eighties, when Giambi moved the operation out to Long Island."

"I didn't know they were allowed to retire."

"Vincent was given special permission by John Giambi," says Stone. "Territo lost his oldest son in a private war with another family twenty years ago. The kid was nineteen years old. Vincent Territo told Giambi that he'd had enough."

"Where did you get all of this?"

"Google search. Tony Territo has a clean record; he's had the dealership on 4th Avenue in Bay Ridge for ten years. Sells very expensive foreign cars."

"Interesting, Stone, but there's really nothing there. I've got a desk covered with work that needs to get done. There are court dates coming up fast. We don't have the time or the manpower to watch this guy Territo with the outside chance he might screw up. And that's if he's done anything to begin with."

"The driver in Mexico claims to have the goods."

"They always do," says Ripley, "and from a Mexican jail you would finger your own mother to make a deal. I think we should throw it back to New York or Connecticut. Let the auto theft insurance companies hash it out."

"Okay," says Stone, rising from her seat.

"Okay, keep an eye on Territo. A few days, tops. Don't forget to record your mileage."

Tony Territo arrives at the dealership shortly after eleven on Tuesday morning. As he crosses the showroom, one of his salesmen is showing a Mercedes convertible. Territo fights off the urge to get involved.

Territo sticks his head into the small office behind the cashier's window.

"Good morning, Tony," says Theresa Fazio with a big smile.

"That's a lovely dress, Terry."

"Oh, this old thing," she says, blushing.

"It's very flattering," he says. "Any calls?"

"Charlie from Ciaburri's garage called. He said that the BMW got done yesterday and is going in for the paint job at noon today. He said he can deliver the car here tomorrow afternoon. Charlie said you can call him if you have any questions. I bet you'll be glad to have your car back."

"You'd win that bet. Anyone else call?"

"Your cousin Stevie said he had the information you wanted."

"Great, thanks. How about having lunch with me today?"

"I'd love to."

"Let's make it around one," he says.

Territo walks to his office and sits at his desk. He thinks about Colletti, about Colletti's imbecile son, about the thought of the fuck wanting his car. Territo has the crazy idea of calling the garage, asking that the BMW be painted an entirely different color. The thought passes. Richie Colletti is an imbecile, but he's not *that* stupid.

Instead, Territo calls his cousin Steve.

"The kid you wanted to know about, Bobby Hoyle," says Stevie. "He was supposed to get out on bail yesterday, but it didn't happen."

"What did happen?" asks Territo.

"From what I could find out, one of the goons in his cell attacked the kid, unprovoked. The Hoyle kid tried to defend himself and got in a lucky punch. The other guy is in the hospital."

"Is he going to make it?"

"I heard that it's touch and go," says Stevie, "and he hasn't talked to anyone. The Hoyle kid is going to stay inside, no bail, at least until the thing is cleared up."

"Okay, stay on top of it; I want to know the minute this guy comes around. If he ever does."

"You think Colletti was behind it?"

"I'm sure of it, but I'd like to have some proof," says Territo. "I could use a little leverage right about now."

"You got it, Tony. I'll keep you informed."

"Thanks, Stevie," Territo says and disconnects.

Tony Territo tries to put his mind on more pleasant thoughts. Lunch with Terry Fazio. He calls to find out what's on the room service menu at the Hotel Gregory on 83rd Street.

Frank Sullivan and Sal DiMarco walk the two blocks to Campo's grocery. Sully is quiet, nervous. It has been a while since he talked with someone about a job.

When they arrive, Joe Campo makes it simple.

"I figure you could use a day or so to get settled," he says, "so you can start tomorrow or Thursday, it's up to you. Just let me know, so I can tell my wife that she can take off."

"I can begin tomorrow," says Sully.

"Fine, do you have a driver's license?"

"Yes."

"Good, you can help make deliveries. You'll also be helping receive deliveries, stocking the shelves and covering the counter. You won't be doing anything that I don't also do myself. I can start you at twelve dollars an hour, if that suits you, and I can help you get medical insurance if you need it."

"Thank you," says Sullivan.

"Thank *you*. It will be a great help. There will be weekend work required, is that alright?"

"Yes."

"Good. I'll see you tomorrow morning. Come in around seven. I have a big delivery every Wednesday."

"I'll be here."

"Good. Grab that box on your way out. Consider it a sign-on bonus."

Frank Sullivan looks down at the cardboard box at his feet. Breakfast cereal, milk, eggs, bread, canned tomatoes, pasta, sugar, salt, canned tuna.

"There's some sliced ham and cheese there also," Campo says, "and grab a few cans of soup from the shelf. I wasn't sure what you liked."

"Thank you, Mr. Campo. You won't regret this."

"It's Joe, Frank, and I'm sure I won't. Listen, Frank, I realize that this is quite a step down from running your own business, but my intention is to treat you as an equal. I only wish I could afford to pay you more."

"You are being more than generous, Joe," says Sully. "This is not a step down; it is an incredible step up."

A man with one hand, unaffectionately known on the streets as Stump, is trying to sell two tickets to a sold-out Neil Diamond concert when Mendez appears. The price is seventy-five dollars apiece, the buyers are delighted, the tickets are phony. When the uniformed police officer comes up to them outside the train station at West 7th and Avenue U, the couple takes off toward 6th Street and Stump is left holding the tickets in his left hand. His only hand.

"Jesus, Rey," says Stump, "could your timing possibly be any worse?"

"I need some information, Stump," says Mendez.

"It's going to cost you, Rey. You just blew a hundred-fifty-dollar sale."

"Don't push me; I'm not in the mood. We're trying to find a guy named Victor Sanders from Sunset Park. The guy sells pharmaceuticals he's been lifting from Lutheran. We need to talk with him. Right away."

"Never heard of the guy."

"Ask around, Stump, do what you do best. Call me," says Mendez. "Soon."

"Okay, but let me have something, Rey, I'm totally tapped out."

Mendez pulls a twenty-dollar bill from his wallet and passes it to the informant.

"Jesus, Rey, what the fuck am I supposed to do with this?"

"I told you not to push me, Stump."

"Okay, I heard you twice the first time."

Murphy sits in the squad room, alone.

Everyone else is out on the streets.

Vota is teamed with Ivanov. They decide to talk with Paul Ventura's employers and co-workers. See if the man had any enemies at work, or had a problem with a customer. Maybe something Paul Ventura didn't necessarily know about.

They also planned to visit the bank where Mary Ventura worked as a loan officer. Maybe she turned down the wrong person. The burial of the Venturas' son was scheduled for this morning; the detectives agreed to wait until it was behind them before they confronted the boy's parents again.

Samson would try to talk with George Addams at the funeral home where his son's wake begins today. Try to catch

Addams before the afternoon viewing. Try to discover if the man had any problems with clients, disgruntled ex-employees, anything. Samson calls Sandra Rosen at the 68th and asks if she could join him. Maybe she could talk with the wife again. Detective Rosen says she would meet Samson at the mortuary.

"Murphy," says Officer Landis from the doorway.

"Come in, Stan. What do you have?"

"The report just came in from the search at Victor Sander's place. They said it was like a drugstore. None of the Pavulon, but just about everything else you could think of."

"No surprise there," says Murphy.

"The guy had caller ID. They were able to get numbers for all the incoming calls for the last two days. Mostly solicitors, a call from his mother, and a call from a pay phone. That was it."

"It's hard to picture the guy having a mother. Does she know where he is?"

"She says no."

"I guess she would. Where was the pay phone?"

"Corner of 5th Avenue and 69th Street."

"Are you kidding?" says Murphy.

"Nope. Less than two blocks from where the Addams kid was found."

"I want someone on that booth twenty-four-seven."

"Already arranged," says Landis.

"Jesus," says Murphy. "How do you like that?"

He parks the Oldsmobile next to the dumpster in the Staples parking lot on 5th Avenue at 94th Street. He walks into the store. He needs new blades for the X-Acto knife. And a box of crayons.

At the checkout counter a young girl rings up the sale. He pays in cash.

"Would you like a free bumper sticker?" she asks.

"Excuse me?"

"Here," she says, putting it in the bag. "Take it. It's free."

He walks back to his car and places the bag on the front passenger seat. As an afterthought, he pulls the bumper sticker from the bag.

It reads: *God Bless America.*

He carries it to the rear of the car, peels off the backing, and sticks it to the bumper. Covering the one that is already there.

The one that read: *Baby on Board.*

As he slowly returns to the front, he glances into the rear seat. He opens the back door, unbuckles the seat belt that holds the child seat, and removes the child seat from the car. He carries the child seat around to the dumpster and tosses it in.

He climbs into the passenger seat and drives off.

SIXTEEN

Wednesday morning.

Sal DiMarco picks up his daughter out in front of her apartment for the drive to NYU Medical Center. Lorraine had made the MRI appointment for 10:00 a.m., hoping that the morning rush into Manhattan will have tailed off by 9:30.

As they cross the Manhattan Bridge, Sal asks if she has told Lou Vota about the medical test.

"I never got around to it," she says. "Maybe it's nothing. And Lou has enough to deal with in his job."

Sal thinks about scolding his daughter for not giving Lou the benefit of the doubt, for not trusting that Vota could handle the news. But Sal realizes that there are times when it is best not to compound a loved one's fears and anxieties with more bad news. It is for this reason that Sal has not told Lorraine about the homeless woman, Annie, about her final act of desperation.

"What's the latest with the Bobby Hoyle case?" asks Sal, changing the subject.

"It's not too good. I've been working up a brief. There's a hearing scheduled for Friday morning. The man who attacked Bobby has a long record of violence, which may help in our argument of self-defense. I'm hoping that we can at least clear Bobby of the shooting incident. I'll need Frank Sullivan to sign an affidavit and appear in court on Friday to swear to what he witnessed that night."

"I'm sure Frank will be glad to help. Let him know what time Friday, so that he can make arrangements with Joe Campo. Sully began his new job this morning."

"That's great, Dad. How does he like the apartment?"

"Very much. After he spoke with Joe about starting work, Frank insisted that he and I discuss payment for the rooms. We finally agreed on a monthly rent. I had to fight to get him to lower his offer. And he wants to invite us all down for dinner soon."

"It just goes to show that things can turn out well, even when unexpected," says Lorraine. "It makes me feel less anxious about the test this morning. And it makes me think about Annie from Bay 38th. Maybe something good is headed her way."

Sal is silent, staring through the car window, like someone who cannot make up his mind. Lorraine knows the look on his face.

"Dad?"

"Should we take First Avenue or the East River Drive?" Sal DiMarco asks.

Serena looks over the latest issue of the *Brooklyn Eagle*, hot off the presses this Wednesday morning. She finds her article on page 37. Short, boring opinions from four Sunday evening moviegoers below a photograph of the reporter and a headline with all the imagination of a rainy day weather report.

What's New on the Big Screen.

God.

Serena closes the paper in disgust. Her consolation is the belief that before long her work will appear on page one. And not page one of a fifty-cent weekly.

She will need help. Information on the two killings has been incomplete at best. Serena needs more. She decides that she will need to be patient. She does not want to rush forward with a story that is pure sensationalism. Serena wants to show the world, or at least New York City, that she is a serious, professional journalist. She will take her time. Serena can only hope that someone with a tabloid mentality doesn't beat her to the punch.

Serena knows that she has a very advantageous head start. She knows that the two murders are connected. She knows about the fingers. And she has Detective Andrew Chen's card on the desk in front of her.

. . .

Vota and Ivanov have arranged to meet with the boy's parents at half past noon. Paul Ventura will join them at his wife's home during his lunch break from the auto parts store. Mary Ventura has decided that she would not return to work until the following week.

Before leaving for the appointment, Lou Vota phones Lorraine at her office.

Victoria Anderson takes the call.

"Lorraine is out this morning," she says. "She should be back here by two."

"Is she in court?"

"No, she had a doctor's appointment."

"Is she ill?"

"No. Just a regular checkup," says Victoria, wishing she knew less.

"Please tell her I called," says Vota. "I'll try back this afternoon."

"I sure will."

Murphy walks in as Vota prepares to leave.

"What've you been up to this morning?" asks Vota.

"Walking the streets around the Graham house, looking at bumper stickers. It's really amazing what people will put on their cars. I saw one that read: *Honk if you believe Britney Spears is a Virgin.*"

"Sounds like an anti–noise pollution campaign," says Vota. "Any idea where Samson went off to?"

"He had a meeting with Chief Trenton."

"I bet he was looking forward to that."

"Like a root canal," says Murphy.

As predicted, the day has warmed considerably, the temperature rising into the low fifties. It has been an unusually mild season. It almost seems as if winter has lost its place in the rotation.

Stump finds Dwayne Harris alone on a bench, watching a half-court basketball game in the park opposite Lafayette

High School. Harris is drinking Colt '45 malt liquor from a quart bottle, no brown paper bag, no pretensions.

"Stumpster," says Harris. "Grab a seat. I'd offer you a drink but I forgot the paper cups."

"I just came over from the train station on U," says Stump, sitting. "I was trying to unload a pair of concert tickets and I saw something I thought you'd be interested in."

"There's not much that doesn't interest me on Avenue U," says Harris. "What is it?"

"I saw a guy selling to a couple of school kids on 8th Street."

"Selling?" says Harris, suddenly *very* interested. "Selling drugs?"

"Looked like cocaine."

"You've got to be joking. Who would be crazy enough to sell coke in my neighborhood? The guy must be from fucking Mars."

"Dyker Park, I think."

"This dead man have a name?"

"Jesus, Dwayne, I had it a second ago, it's on the tip of my tongue."

Harris digs out a large roll of cash, peels off a fifty and hands it to Stump.

"Pacheco," says Stump, stuffing the bill into his shirt pocket. "José Pacheco."

"No fucking way, José," Harris mutters.

"Dwayne, you know a guy named Victor Sanders from Sunset Park?"

"The name sounds familiar," says Harris, holding his hand out, palm up. "It's on the tip of my tongue."

"It's not important," says Stump.

"I'm yanking your chain, Stumpy, never heard of the guy. What kind of concert tickets are you hawking?"

"I sold them. Anyway, I don't figure you for a Neil Diamond fan."

"Neil Diamond, are you kidding? The cat is from fucking Brooklyn. Jesus, 'Brother Love's Travelling Salvation Show' is like my all-time favorite tune. Let me know if you get your hands on any more tickets."

"Sure," says Stump, not certain whether Harris is still yanking. Not really caring.

A teenager trots across the avenue from the direction of the high school. She is out of breath when she reaches the bench. She sits near Dwayne Harris. Very near.

Harris looks at the girl and then looks to his other side at Stump, who sits as if waiting for an invitation.

"Don't forget to bring a cup next time," Harris says.

Stump might have been offended if not for the fifty-dollar bill in his shirt pocket, nestled up against the twenty he got from Mendez.

Stump rises, tips his ball cap, and walks off toward Stillwell Avenue.

Headquarters of the Brooklyn Detective Bureau is located at the 67th Police Precinct on Snyder Avenue in Flatbush. Southeast of the Prospect Park exit at Woodruff and Ocean Avenues, south of the State University of New York Health Sciences Center and University Hospital of Brooklyn, and west of Holy Cross Cemetery.

Samson meets with the Brooklyn Chief of Detectives in Trenton's 2nd floor office. Though it has been informally understood since the second body was discovered, Trenton has brought Samson in to make it official. Samson is in charge of this investigation.

"I want you to put together a special task force on this one, Sam," Trenton says. "It will sound good in the press when they get wind of this, and they will."

Samson is a few steps ahead of the chief.

"I think I've got everyone I need on board. Vota, Murphy and I, with Mendez and Landis assigned to us full-time. Marina Ivanov from the 60th; a background in psychology and she speaks Russian. Andrew Chen from the 68th, per your request to placate the captain over there. I don't know how much help he'll be. He's green. But he's eager. And Sandra Rosen of the 63rd; she was first on the Addams case when the kid was still just a missing person and she's sharp as a tack."

"Good," says Trenton. "Try to get them all together after

the weekend so they look something like a team if we have to introduce them as a special unit. Where are we on this?"

Lieutenant Samson fills the chief in on everything they've learned thus far. It doesn't take very long.

"Keep me informed, Sam. I want to hear from you every day. If you need more people, just ask. The commissioner is shaking in his Thom McAns. I've been toying around with the idea of contacting the FBI; what's your feeling on that?"

"I think you know, Chief."

"I don't want to wait too long, they have resources that we don't have. I know the SAC in the Brooklyn-Queens Field Office. He's recently up from Quantico, but he was born and raised in Flushing. Maybe I can have lunch with him, bring it up casually."

"Can you hold off a while?"

"I'll wait until next week, Sam, but I don't want to wait until another body pops up."

"Fair enough. I think I'll save myself a lot of grief and not mention the Feds to Lou and Tommy until you decide you can't wait any longer."

"I'll give you ample warning. I've let all of the labs, phone banks and computer people know that any requests from you have top priority."

"Thanks," says Sam, rising. "I'd better get to work."

"Lieutenant, do me a really big favor," says Trenton as Samson moves to the door. "Catch this fucking guy."

Lorraine walks into the law office shortly before two.

"How did it go?" asks Victoria Anderson.

"The test wasn't bad. The table was very comfortable, and the technician had the most calming voice I've ever heard. It was hypnotic; I fell asleep," says Lorraine. "I have an appointment to talk with a neurologist about the results on Friday afternoon. Any calls?"

"Lou Vota called; he said he'd call back later."

"What did you tell him?"

"I told him that you had a routine checkup."

"Thanks. Is that it?"

Victoria displays all of the characteristics of someone who has something to say, but would rather walk barefoot over broken glass than say it.

"Say it," says Lorraine.

"The inmate who attacked Bobby Hoyle," Victoria says, "he's dead. He never regained consciousness."

"Shit."

"What are we going to do?"

"We are going to convince the judge and prosecutor to drop the charge against Bobby on the shooting, or at least reduce the charge to involuntary manslaughter based on Frank Sullivan's testimony. We are going to request that bail be reinstated. We are going to argue that the inmate who died instigated the confrontation, based on the man's prior history of violent criminality. There's been no charge yet in that incident—we'll see if they want to go ahead with one or not. In the meantime, maybe Bobby can get out of there before something else horrible happens to him."

"You think we can pull it off?" asks Victoria. "That we can actually get Bobby out of Rikers?"

"I have to think so. We'll give it everything we've got. And it should take my mind off the MRI results."

"How did it go with Chief Trenton?" Murphy asks, when Samson returns to the office.

"Better than being dragged to the Little Neck Mall to procure back-to-school shoes for the girls," says Samson.

"How much better?"

"Negligibly."

"Tell me that Trenton didn't suggest reaching out to the FBI," says Murphy.

"Trenton didn't suggest reaching out to the FBI."

"Thanks for lying."

"Don't mention it."

"Don't mention what?" says Vota, walking in.

Tony Territo sits at his desk in his office at Titan Imports.

A sound draws his attention to the open doorway.

Charlie Chiaburri stands there, jingling a ring of keys in his raised right arm. It is music to Territo's ears.

"Your BMW is out on the lot, Tony," says Chiaburri, tossing the keys to Territo. "The way it looks it belongs in the showroom. And it runs like a dream."

"Need a ride back to your garage?" Territo asks.

"My brother is out front in his car. He followed me over," says Chiaburri. "We're gonna grab a bite in the neighborhood. Wanna eat?"

"No thanks, Charlie," says Territo. "I think I'll go for a nice long drive."

The telephone on Lorraine DiMarco's desk rings. She can tell from the newly installed caller ID display that it's Lou Vota calling. After two more rings she picks up.

"Gotham Sex Line," she says, "Mandy speaking. What are you wearing?"

"How did you know it was me?" asks Vota.

"Is that you, Lou?"

"Very cute, DiMarco. How did your checkup go?"

"Fine," she says, like a third-grader asked about school.

"You don't sound too sure."

"I could stand to lose a few pounds," she says.

"Not in my opinion, but then again I was hoping to take you out for a very big dinner tonight."

"I'm sorry, I can't. I have less than two days to get ready for a hearing Friday morning. I probably won't have time to eat at all, which might work out well. I can eat a horse at dinner on Friday night."

"What's Friday night?"

"Very cute, Vota," says Lorraine. "Listen, maybe you can help me. Lombardo, the inmate who Bobby put in the hospital—he didn't make it. I doubt he would have admitted to anything that would have helped Bobby out of this mess, but we'll never know. I refuse to believe that not one single person in that cell saw a thing that night. Lombardo was a real nasty character; maybe someone saw him attack Bobby and was shy about saying so while Lombardo was still breathing."

"I'll look into it. Don't hope for too much."

"Thanks."

"I'll give you a call if I learn something, and I'll see you Friday night."

"What's Friday night?" Lorraine says.

Serena Huang telephones the 68th Precinct and catches Detective Chen just as he is about to leave.

"I thought I'd take you up on your invitation to be introduced to the wonders of Brooklyn," she says. "If the offer still stands."

"Absolutely. How about dinner for a start?"

"Tonight?" she says, crossing her fingers.

"I can't tonight," he says, wishing that he could. "How about tomorrow?"

"Sure, tomorrow would be good."

"Do you like Chinese food?" Chen asks.

"You've got to be kidding," says Huang.

"I am kidding. How about Spanish food? I mean like the kind they might eat in Spain. There's a really good restaurant here in Bay Ridge, Casa Pepe. It's not all that far from where we met. It shouldn't take you more than forty-five minutes from Manhattan."

Serena is totally ad-libbing.

"Actually, I'll be staying in Brooklyn now, at least while I'm down here in the city."

"You took a hotel in Brooklyn?"

Serena pedals faster.

"One of the women from the Manhattan office has a large apartment in Fort Greene. We hit it off real well, and she has an empty bedroom. She offered and I couldn't refuse. It will save me money, and she'll have a place to stay the next time she comes up for meetings in Albany."

"Great. What's the address? I can pick you up."

"How about I meet you at the restaurant?" Serena asks. "How about seven?"

"Sure. It's on Bay Ridge Avenue between Colonial Road and Narrows Avenue. Will you be coming from Fort Greene?"

"Most likely."

"Take the 4th Avenue bus to 69th Street and walk west, toward the shore. I can drive you back afterwards."

"Great," says Serena.

"Are you sure you can find the place?"

"No problem," she says, neglecting to mention that she has been to Casa Pepe more than a few times before.

"Okay, I'll see you tomorrow at seven."

"See you then," she says.

Andy Chen puts down the telephone receiver.

Stay cool, boy, he is thinking, *this is a woman worth trying to impress.*

Serena Huang places the receiver down at her end.

What will it take, Detective Chen, she is thinking, *to get you to talk shop.*

He sits on a bench, just outside of the park, facing the Territo house across Shore Road. He has spent every afternoon on this bench for the past three days.

Today, Wednesday, he arrived shortly before two.

The temperature was a pleasant fifty-five degrees. The sky clear.

He would occasionally shift his attention from the Bible to the large white house.

He saw the woman leave in the Cherokee and return thirty minutes later.

He saw the boy arrive home just after three.

He saw the girl return soon afterwards.

He had seen no other children during his vigils. He concluded that the girl was the oldest child. He would have to get accustomed to the idea.

A delivery truck from the local supermarket pulled up to the gate at four. The gate opened and the truck drove up the driveway. He understood that there must be a camera at the gate, to identify visitors. He would check it out, and keep his eyes opened for other such devices.

At half past four, a Hispanic woman left the house. He could make out the white uniform below her overcoat.

A cleaning woman he guessed.

He saw no BMW.

He realizes that he is hungry. He walks to his car and drives to a 3rd Avenue restaurant for quick dinner.

After eating, he drives to Fort Hamilton High School and finds a parking space along the fence that encloses the running track and the playing field. The house that he has tentatively chosen sits at the opposite corner, a realtor's sign on the lawn in front. He will explore the house when he returns for his car, when there is no longer daylight.

He walks to Shore Road and back to the Territo home. He realizes he has forgotten the Bible in the Oldsmobile. He purchases a copy of the latest *Brooklyn Eagle* from a street vending machine. He returns to his bench and leafs through the pages of the newspaper.

He spots the photograph. The young woman he had seen outside the movie theater Sunday night, had spoken to as she hurried to the commotion on the next street. He tears the small article from the page and places it in his coat pocket.

Soon the sun begins to set behind him. Behind Shore Road Park, the Narrows, Staten Island, New Jersey. It has turned cold. He decides to move on to other business.

As he crosses Shore Road, a car approaches from the direction of the parkway exit at 4th Avenue. An indefinable sensation tells him that his answer has come.

The vehicle turns onto 82nd Street and stops at the gate. A small lightbulb illuminates the license plate. *TITAN1*.

He passes as the BMW moves up the driveway. He stops long enough to watch the driver exit the car. The man turns toward him as if feeling his presence. He recognizes the man, even in silhouette.

He could never forget.

He quickly walks on.

He returns to the house near the high school. He approaches from the back. The house across the alley is shielded by tall trees. The trees shield him as well.

He crosses to a screened-in porch. The door to the porch is unlocked. The porch connects to a large kitchen. The kitchen door will be no problem.

This is where he will take the girl.

He leaves the back porch and moves toward a window to the north. Standing on his toes, he is able to peer inside. It is a spacious bathroom. An old-fashioned wrought iron bathtub sits perched on four metal feet.

This is where he will perform the baptism.

SEVENTEEN

Father Daniel Donovan had returned from his trip to Albany much later than he had planned the previous evening. A three-car accident had closed the Major Deegan Expressway down to a single lane; it had taken him nearly two hours to drive from Yankee Stadium to Our Lady of Angels Church.

He had arrived exhausted. Exhausted by the traffic tie-up, and exhausted by the constant bickering during the three-day conference.

It was small wonder, he found himself thinking, that poverty, malnutrition and poor medical care, evils running rampant even here in the most affluent nation in the world, had failed to be meaningfully addressed. Had been overshadowed, subjugated by concern and paranoia surrounding scandals arising from the sad and senseless behavior of a handful of troubled priests.

It was small wonder, Donovan found himself thinking, all of the death and destruction in the Middle East, in Northern Ireland, around the world, caused by the worship of adversarial deities, conflicting truths. Small wonder when clergy from the *same* Roman Catholic Church, from towns and cities in the *same* state of New York, could not come to agreement on the message of the *same* Gospel.

The golden rule was badly tarnished.

Donovan rises Thursday, glad to be back. Home to his small congregation, the everyday tragedies and triumphs of his community, of people he can greet by name. Home where he can measure the value of his calling, see the tangible results of the help that he can offer, and appreciate the blessing that enables and allows him to serve.

Father Donovan spends the morning working. Going over a checklist of preparations for the upcoming Valentine's Day

193

event. Outlining his sermon for the following Sunday.

Writing an evaluation of the ecumenical council meetings, laboring to express his impressions in a positive way.

After lunch, Father Donovan walks through the church. Eddie Conroy has finished painting the basement room, and has set the tables and chairs in place for the following night. Donovan finds Eddie cleaning the exterior windows, taking advantage of the unusually mild February weather. Conroy climbs down from the tall ladder to welcome the priest home.

"How was the conference, Father?" he asks.

"Difficult. Too much talking and not enough listening," says Donovan. "The basement turned out very well. Thank you for taking care of it."

"I'm only doing my job, Father."

"That is very commendable these days."

"The mail has just arrived," says Conroy, "and there is a mountain of it on your desk."

"I noticed," says the priest. "I've been putting it off. I'm sure that it is mostly bills."

"I hate to bring it up, but it's well past time to begin a donation campaign for a new church furnace."

"Everyone is so burdened by their own personal and financial concerns. How can I ask them to reach into empty pockets?"

"They come here seeking help with those concerns, Father," says Eddie Conroy. "They should at least find shelter from the cold."

Donovan gathers the mail from the box out front and returns to his office. He sits at his desk and places the mail on top of the existing pile, debating whether or not to deal with it. A large manila envelope catches his eye. Donovan pulls it out from the stack. It is addressed to him in red crayon.

He opens the envelope, feeling its weight. He peers inside. He spills the plastic bag onto his desk.

He trembles as he makes the sign of the cross.

Twenty minutes later the phone on Samson's desk rings.

"61st Detectives, Samson speaking."

"Lieutenant, this is Andy Chen. I'm at Our Lady of Angels Church on 4th and 73rd."

"I didn't realize you were Catholic, Detective Chen."

"Lieutenant, I think we have Billy Ventura's finger down here."

"I'm on my way. Don't touch a thing," Samson says and hangs up. "Murphy, get the best forensic team that we have available to 4th and 73rd, the church. Call the lab and make sure that someone is down there and is ready to work. Lou, come with me."

Samson grabs his coat and rushes out the door. Vota hurries after him.

They arrive in fifteen minutes. Two uniforms stand at the door of Donovan's office, Eddie Conroy with them. In the office, Chen sits with the priest. The plastic bag is exactly where it had fallen when Father Donovan dropped it out onto the desk. The envelope lies beside it.

Samson opens the small leather case he has brought in from the trunk of his car. Inside lies an assortment of evidence gathering paraphernalia.

Samson pulls on a pair of latex gloves. He places the plastic bag into another plastic bag. He hands it to Chen. Samson picks up the envelope and reaches inside. He slides out the coloring book cover. He places the cover and the envelope into separate flat, clear plastic bags.

"Is there a copy machine here, Father?" Samson asks.

"In the basement," answers Eddie Conroy from behind him. "I can show you."

"Who are you?" asks Samson.

"Eddie Conroy, our custodian," says Donovan. "He found the envelope on Monday, in one of the confessionals, and placed it here with the other mail. I was away; I just got around to opening it."

"Stay here, Eddie," says Samson, "we'll want to speak with you. Lou, take these down and make copies. And call Tommy. Ask him to find Ivanov and get her over to the 61st as soon as possible. Bring the copies and the originals back up here. We need to get them to the lab right away."

Vota heads out to find the copy machine. Samson asks one

of the uniformed officers to tag along.

"What should I do with this?" asks Chen, holding the bag containing the small finger far from his body, as if afraid it might poke him in the eye.

"Try not dropping it," says Samson. "Okay, let's begin with you, Mr. Conroy. Tell me about finding the envelope."

"Thank you for coming in," says Lieutenant Samson.

"Anything I can do to help," says Father Donovan.

The priest had driven with Samson to the 61st Precinct, where Murphy and Ivanov were waiting in the squad room.

Vota had gone to hand-deliver the three evidence bags to the Central Crime Laboratory. He would join them later.

Samson had asked Detective Andy Chen to remain at the church, where a two-man forensic team would begin searching for evidence throughout the building, particularly the area in and around the confessional where the envelope was first discovered.

Eddie Conroy had been questioned and sent home.

"Does this mean anything to you?" Samson asks.

He hands the photocopy of the note written on the coloring book cover to Father Donovan.

Testimony to the crime of Gibeah.

"Gibeah," says Donovan. "I know it only from the Old Testament. Is there a Bible here? I didn't think to bring one."

"There is a Bible here," says Murphy.

He walks over to the bookshelf and digs out a beat-up Bible, wedged between volumes of New York state statutes and dog-eared detective novels. He carries it to Father Donovan.

"How long has that been there?" asks Vota. "I didn't know we had it."

"About twenty-five years," says Murphy. "My father kept it here when he was on the job; he left it behind when he retired."

"I hope I can find it," says Donovan, turning pages. "I'm fairly certain that it is somewhere in the Historical Books, which follow the first five books that comprise the

Pentateuch. We may have go to the Internet, do a keyword search."

"Take your time, Father," says Samson.

"Should I make a fresh pot of coffee?" asks Murphy.

"Please," says Ivanov.

"I could use it," says Samson.

"Father Donovan?" asks Murphy.

"I wouldn't mind a Diet Coke, if one were available," says Donovan, not looking up. "Here it is. Judges, 19th Chapter. Give me a minute to look this over."

Murphy starts the coffee and then goes out to the hall to fetch a soda from the vending machine. Samson and Ivanov sit silently, watching the priest read.

After a few minutes, Father Donovan closes the book, holding the place with his thumb.

"This is very disturbing," the priest says.

The three detectives wait for him to continue.

"In reaction to the crime of Gibeah, human body parts were sent out to the twelve tribes of Israel."

"My God," says Ivanov, involuntarily.

"What was the crime?" asks Samson.

Donovan reopens the Bible. After a moment he reads.

"*And they went off the road there with the purpose of stopping for the night in Gibeah and he went into the town, seating himself in the street, for no one took him into his house for the night.* Judges, 19:15."

"And?" says Samson.

"The inhospitality of the people of Gibeah resulted in a death," says Donovan, "and the body of the deceased was portioned and delivered throughout the land as testimony to the crime."

"Did you say 1915, Father?" asks Murphy.

"Yes."

"The number on the wall, Sam, at the Ventura crime scene. It was 71915."

"Yes, that would be it," says the priest. "Judges is the seventh book of the Old Testament, although it would normally be indicated by the standard abbreviation, by the letters JG."

197

"Well," says Murphy, "what d'ya know."

"And the letters PR, Father?" asks Samson.

"That would be Proverbs."

"The twenty-fourth book?"

Donovan opens to the front of the Bible and runs his finger down the list of contents.

"Why, yes," he says, surprised, "the twenty-fourth book."

"And 242113. Proverbs 21:13?" asks Samson.

Donovan quickly finds the place.

"He who shuts his ear to the poor man's cry shall himself plead and not be heard."

"I want the parents contacted," says Samson. "I want them all down here, together. First thing in the morning."

Sonny Colletti finds his father at Fontana Sushi of Bay Ridge at 3rd Avenue and 96th Street.

"How can you eat raw fish?" asks Sonny.

"With chopsticks," says his father, demonstrating. "It's brain food. You should try it. What do you want?"

"Lombardo kicked the bucket."

"Sonny, please, show some respect for the dead," says Dominic Colletti. "Did he talk?"

"No. Do you want me to make other arrangements for the Hoyle kid?" asks Sonny.

"We don't need another fiasco like this one. We'll wait until he is out on bail before we make another move."

"It could be a while. Bobby Hoyle's bail was revoked. There's a hearing in the morning, but I doubt they'll let Hoyle out unless they can be convinced Lombardo was responsible for the attack."

"I don't have a while. Your Aunt Carmella is torturing me."

"Then we have to hit him inside," says Sonny.

"I have a better idea. We help get him out," says Colletti. "Find out who is defending Hoyle at the hearing tomorrow. We'll make sure that they have some good news before going into court."

"Okay, Pop, I'll take care of it. Did you get the BMW for

198

Richie?"

"I'm still waiting to hear from Tony Territo."

"How long are you going to wait? Richie's birthday is Saturday."

"I'm well aware of that. I'll wait until tomorrow."

"And if you don't hear from Territo?" asks Sonny.

"Sonny, you are ruining my appetite," says Dominic Colletti. "Get out of here and do what you need to do."

Detective Marina Ivanov drives Father Donovan back to Our Lady of Angels.

"Father," she says, "I'm having trouble understanding this man's actions, from a strictly psychological point of view. I think we would agree about his motivation, based on what we've learned. It seems as if this man suffered a terrible trauma, and holds the Venturas and Addams somehow responsible. It seems as if he may have reached out for help and was turned away. It seems as if he has taken it upon himself to determine and execute punishment."

"I would agree with those assessments," says Donovan. "Our training in these areas is probably quite similar. I hold a master's degree from Columbia University in Clinical Psychology. Our approaches to analyzing the behavior of an extremely troubled human being would not be very different. Where we might differ is in our counseling."

"I understand that, Father. What has me stumped is *why has he targeted the children*? Granted, Kevin Addams was nineteen years old. It is plausible he could have been one of the persons who somehow sinned against this man. But Billy Ventura? He was only eight years old. I have to believe he was innocent. Why the boy? There is nothing I can recall from my textbooks that helps me to explain it. I was hoping that there might be an answer in yours."

"In the Bible?"

"Yes, since this man seems to be using that particular text to express himself."

"I can only speculate."

"I understand."

"I can only speculate," Donovan repeats, "based on the reference to the events of Gibeah as described in Judges, that there was a death involved. I believe that this man has lost someone very dear to him. So dear, that he has been pushed far beyond reason. I believe that he no longer perceives, no longer imagines, any other choice but to seek retribution. And I am afraid that I must come to the sad conclusion that this man lost a child of his own."

"A child for a child?" says Ivanov, horrified by the suggestion.

"The God of the Old Testament," says Father Donovan, "was not one to pull punches."

"Father?"

"Yes."

"If this man truly believes that he is following a mandate from God, that he is complying with a course of action demanded by his faith, then *is* he insane?"

"If you are asking if this man could or should be considered *legally* insane, I don't know the answer."

"What I am asking, Father, is do you think that this man has lost his mind?"

"He has lost much more, Detective," says the priest. "He has lost his soul."

Brenda Territo sits up in her bed reading a novel by D. H. Lawrence. She is interrupted by a knock at her bedroom door.

"What?"

"Brenda, dinner is ready," says her father.

"I'm not hungry."

"Brenda, can I talk with you?" asks Tony Territo.

"I'm doing my homework," she answers, putting the novel under her pillow and reaching for a trigonometry workbook.

Territo opens the door and steps into the room.

"I wanted to make sure you were ready for tomorrow. We are leaving around three. I want to beat the traffic and be down there in time for dinner."

"I told you that I'm not going."

Territo has tried every other argument, and every time it

has ended in anger and shouting. Tony decides to try a new tactic.

"Please, Brenda, it will make your mother happy."

"If you want to make Mom happy, stop fucking the office help."

Territo moves quickly across the room and slaps his daughter's face.

"Fucking tough guy," she says, hiding the pain. "You are pathetic."

"I'm sorry, Brenda. I lost my temper. Please be reasonable."

"Do you think no one notices the way she looks at you. She may as well have it written across her forehead. The only idiot who doesn't seem to know that you're fucking the whore is Mom."

"You don't know what you're talking about."

"Get out," Brenda says, giving her father a look that scares Territo more than ten Dominic Collettis ever could.

"Brenda," he says, backing away.

"If you are not out of this room in two seconds I will march downstairs and tell my mother about you and your slut secretary."

"Is Brenda coming down?" Barbara Territo asks when Tony takes his seat at the dinner table.

"She's not hungry," says Tony. "We had a little talk. I agree with you, there's really nothing for her to do down in Atlantic City. She may as well stay home."

"Can I stay home, too?" asks Anthony Jr.

"Shut the fuck up and eat," answers his father.

Serena spots Chen standing out in front of Casa Pepe. She turns her coat collar up against the stiff, chilly wind that has come up from the Narrows and the Atlantic.

"It's cold out here," she says as she approaches, "you could have waited inside."

"I wanted to reach you," he says. "I needed to cancel dinner tonight. I didn't know how to get in touch with you. I'm sorry that you had to come all the way out here."

"That's okay, it didn't take me long. It's my fault for not letting you know how to reach me. I'll give you the phone number where I'm staying. We'll do it another time, if you would still like to."

As she reaches into her purse for a pen, Serena can see the anguish in Chen's face. Illuminated by the light from the restaurant window.

"I *would* like to," Chen says. "I just can't be with anyone tonight. I wouldn't be very good company."

She waits for him to say more, but he doesn't speak.

"Did something happen?"

"I really can't talk about it," he says, fighting to hold his tongue. "I can't think about it."

He knows that he can't let himself look at her. He knows that he needs to get away from there.

"Andy, what's wrong?"

He lets his eyes meet hers.

"It was so horrible, you can't imagine," he says, losing the battle. "I held it in my hand, in a clear plastic sandwich bag, as if it were some sort of gruesome leftover. I can't get it out of my head."

Serena Huang wants to hear every detail. She is smart enough to know not to push him.

"It's alright," she says, reaching out to take his hand. "Let's just walk, quietly. Whatever it is that's upset you, please try thinking about something else. You don't need to talk about it."

But Andy Chen does need to talk about it.

And as they walk, he does.

Frank Sullivan cleans the dinner dishes.

Sully had prepared a humble meal for himself. Baked chicken breast with garlic and basil, steamed broccoli, a cucumber and tomato salad. Nothing very special. Except for the fact that it was served on a ceramic plate, with real silverware, and a cloth napkin.

At a table, seated on a chair.

It has been a very long time since he has enjoyed a meal so

much.

He has left the ranks of the homeless.

Sully throws the switch on the electric percolator and finishes the cleaning while the coffee brews.

It had been a long day.

Arriving at Campo's grocery at seven in the morning. Lifting cartons of canned and dry goods from the foot of the metal ramp that ran from the street down into the store basement, breaking out the individual units and setting the inventory neatly on shelves. Campo taking over the heavy work from time to time as promised.

Standing in for Joe at the front counter when Campo was down below. Meeting many of the regular customers, the neighbors. Helping set out the various salads, the rice balls, the sausage and peppers and other cooked foods that Roseanna Campo had prepared at home that morning and had delivered before the lunch hour. Preparing sandwiches for takeout, on fresh Italian bread from the local bakery.

In the afternoon, taking the van to make deliveries.

It had been a tiring day, but an important day.

It has been a very long time since he has felt so useful.

He has left the ranks of the jobless.

Sullivan pours coffee into a ceramic cup and carries it to the bedroom. It has been a long time since coffee has tasted this good.

He goes through the small closet, selecting the clothing he will wear the following morning.

Tomorrow will be another important day.

He will stand witness in a court of law, his testimony will be recorded, his voice will be heard.

He will leave the ranks of the disenfranchised.

He chooses a pair of slacks, a shirt, a necktie. He hangs them on the outside of the closet door.

He walks into the bathroom, looks into the mirror above the sink.

His face is clean-shaven, his hair is neatly cut, his eyes are clear.

It has been a very long time.

You have rejoined the world of the living, he whispers to

his reflection.

The face in the mirror speaks back, but the words fall on deaf ears. Deafened by newly regained innocence.

The world of the living is a perilous one.

Beware.

204

EIGHTEEN

Lorraine DiMarco arrives at her office very early on Friday morning. She had been up half the night, dividing her attention between writing and rewriting a statement for the Hoyle hearing and fighting a merciless headache.

She sits at her desk, putting finishing touches on her motion to reinstate bail. She feels confident that with the testimony of Frank Sullivan she will ultimately be able to bargain a plea of self-defense in the Colletti shooting, involuntary manslaughter at worst. That she will be able to win an argument for probation with no jail time.

The assault at Rikers is much more problematic.

Lorraine had not heard from Lou Vota. No one has come forward with any help. Lorraine will have to argue reason. Lombardo was a violent, repeat criminal. Bobby Hoyle is an unfortunate victim, having no prior trouble with the law. Very convincing on paper. But Lorraine understands that reason is the weakest possible argument in a courtroom.

The telephone on Lorraine's desk rings at nine. The phone conversation is short. A few minutes later she is standing at Victoria Anderson's desk. The expression on Lorraine's face is one of unmistakable disbelief.

"Pinch me, so I know I'm not dreaming," she says.

"My God, Lorraine, sit down before you fall down," says Victoria. "What's happened?"

"Bobby Hoyle's defense in the Rikers incident was just handed to us on a silver platter."

Lorraine takes a seat before continuing.

"One of the inmates who shared the cell with Bobby and Lombardo came forward. He's ready to testify that Lombardo had been talking all that day about what a pretty boy Bobby was, about how tasty Hoyle was going to be."

"Tasty?"

"I'm only relating what I was told. The witness will also testify that he saw Lombardo go into Bobby's cell, and that he clearly heard Bobby protesting before Lombardo hit the wall."

"It sounds too good to be true."

"Absolutely," agrees Lorraine, "but I'm not inclined to look this gift horse in the mouth."

"Okay then," says Victoria. "How about we accept it as incredible good fortune?"

"I don't see how we can do otherwise," says Lorraine, suddenly reminded of the doctor's appointment scheduled for later that afternoon. "I can only hope it doesn't use up my daily quota of luck."

They somehow manage to get all four parents to the 61st Precinct by nine-thirty on Friday morning. With Samson is Sandra Rosen of the 63rd, called in to be a familiar face for Mrs. Addams. Also present is Lou Vota, who is meeting Detective Rosen for the first time.

Lieutenant Samson had prepared a speech, had gone as far as practicing aloud on his drive in from Douglaston.

"What I have to say is not easy for me to say," Samson begins, wondering why it had sounded so much better in the car, "and will be difficult for you to hear. I only ask that you keep an open mind, that you believe I have no wish to offend anyone, and that you make very certain not a word of it leaves this room."

He pauses, expecting questions.

Vota resists the strong urge to raise his hand, ask if Lieutenant Samson would be kind enough to restate his demands.

Murphy would not have missed the opportunity.

Samson continues.

"We have come to the conclusion that both your sons were killed by the same man," he says, hearing one or both of the mothers gasp at the suggestion, "and we have come to the conclusion that these boys were targeted for a reason, that they were not random victims."

"My God, what reason?" cries Mary Ventura. "Our Billy was eight years old."

"That is what we are trying to find out," says Samson. "That is why we need your help."

"How could any of us possibly help you?" asks George Addams. "What could any of us possibly know about a sick maniac who kills innocent children?"

"We believe something happened to this man that hurt him profoundly. That somehow he holds you accountable."

"That's crazy," says Paul Ventura. "What in God's name are you talking about?"

"Something that you or your wife did, or didn't do, Mr. Ventura. And you or your wife, Mr. Addams, or perhaps Kevin himself. Something that you did, or failed to do, which may have caused the loss of someone very important to this man."

"This is scandalous," George Addams yells. "Are you trying to blame us for our son's death, trying to blame Kevin? Trying to justify the actions of a murderer?"

"We are not trying to blame or excuse anyone. We are pleading for help. We are asking that you think about it. That you try recalling something, anything you might have done, without malice, which nevertheless may have been seen as turning away from someone in dire need of assistance."

Twenty minutes later, the three detectives are alone in the squad room.

"That went well," says Samson.

"Don't beat yourself up, Sam, you played your heart out," says Vota. "I haven't heard a better speech since Governor Cuomo at the '88 Convention. And you remember how much that one did to get Dukakis elected."

"Oh, you're a big help," says Rosen.

"Lou has a point," says Samson, "and he was being relatively kind. If Murphy was here, I'm sure he would have brought up Al Gore's concession speech."

"That thing about helping to prevent another innocent child from being senselessly killed was a nice touch," says Vota. "Face it, you were playing a tough crowd, Sam."

"An impossible crowd," says Samson. "These people are in

total denial."

"Don't give up hope quite yet," says Rosen. "I was watching George Addams very closely."

"And?" says Samson.

"He was thinking about it."

"What will it take for him to start talking?"

"What everything takes," says Rosen. "Time."

"We don't have time," says Samson.

Officer Landis sits with Detective Murphy in Murphy's Chevy on East 3rd Street near Avenue V.

"What convinced you we'd find him here?" asks Murphy.

"Our informant gave it to us with a money-back guarantee," says Landis.

"That's good enough for me."

"Stump says the guy's mother lives here," says Landis. "Word has it she's down in Philadelphia visiting her *other* son," he adds, trying unsuccessfully to repress a laugh.

"Not that funny. You know what to do, Stan. We need to get him outside."

"I know exactly what to do, and I feel ridiculous in this thing. How do I look?"

"Please don't ask me how you look, and don't forget that it was your idea."

"I just thought it was wasteful. The Department paid a lot for it," says Landis, "and it hardly gets used."

"Well, there you are," says Murphy. "Let's go. And please fix your nose, it's crooked."

They leave the car and walk over to the house.

Landis awkwardly climbs the stairs to the front porch. He places a hundred-dollar bill at his feet.

Murphy moves out of sight to a spot at the side of the stairs, near the entrance to a basement apartment.

Landis rings the doorbell. A minute later the door opens slightly and Landis puts on his goofiest smile.

"Who the fuck are you supposed to be?" asks the man standing behind the partially opened door.

Landis grins and bears it.

"I'm collecting donations for the Ronald McDonald House."

"I gave at the office, Ronald; try me again in a few months. Nice shoes by the way," the man says, and notices the money on the ground.

"Thank you, sir," says Landis. "Have a nice day."

Landis turns his back to the man and moves toward the stairs, stopping momentarily to gaze up the street. He can hear the man step out of the doorway and onto the landing. When Landis turns back, the man is standing with his foot covering the hundred-dollar bill. Landis quickly moves to block the front door.

"Hey, what the hell is this?"

Landis pulls his badge from the pocket of his baggy yellow pants and pulls the bushy orange wig off his head.

"Victor Sanders," Landis says, "you are under arrest for the sale of stolen pharmaceuticals."

Sanders scoops up the cash and charges down the front stairs. Murphy steps out to meet him at the bottom.

A well-placed kick in the shin has Sanders face down on the pavement. Murphy has Sanders cuffed before Landis can maneuver the huge floppy shoes down to join him.

"Good seeing you again, Vic. Glad we caught you," says Murphy. "Let's take a ride."

Landis helps Murphy lift Sanders to his feet.

"I can't believe I got taken down by a fucking clown," Sanders mumbles as they lead him away.

"Sorry, Victor, luck of the draw," says Murphy. "The Bearded Lady was out on another bust."

Lorraine DiMarco walks out of the Brooklyn Courthouse. With Lorraine is Frank Sullivan, Bobby Hoyle, and Bobby's brother Ron.

"I don't know how you did it," says Bobby.

"I'm not quite sure myself," Lorraine says. "We still have a trial to deal with, but it's looking very good for probation."

The judge had not reinstated bail. Instead, with the testimony of Frank Sullivan and the witness from Rikers, bail had been waived and Bobby Hoyle released on his own recognizance.

"Thank you, Lorraine," Bobby says, "and thank you, Mr. Sullivan. You saved my skin in there."

"I should have come forward sooner. I caused you a lot of unnecessary trouble," says Sully.

"Better late than never, Mr. Sullivan," says Ron Hoyle. "We realize that it wasn't easy for you."

"Call me Frank. After all, we're neighbors now."

"Neighbors?" says Bobby.

"I rented the apartment in Sal DiMarco's basement," says Sully.

"That's great, Frank," says Ron, "and convenient. We can give you a ride home."

"Did you come in the Mustang, Ron?" Bobby asks.

"Yes, I guess I'll get to keep it after all. Need a lift anywhere, Lorraine?"

"No thanks, I'm just walking back to the office," she says, and starts toward Remsen Street.

The three men move off in the opposite direction.

In spite of the nasty headache and her anxiety over the impending doctor's appointment, Lorraine can't help but shake her head and laugh when she hears Bobby's pleading voice behind her.

"Can I drive?" Bobby Hoyle asks his brother.

"Pancuronium bromide, Vic, Pavulon," says Murphy. "We need to know who you sold it to."

"I don't know who the guy was. I try hard not to know. And I don't know how he found me," says Sanders. "He called on the telephone; he told me what he wanted and how much he was willing to pay."

They sit at a table in the Precinct interview room.

"Did he ask for Pavulon, specifically?"

"Yes, or anything else like it," says Sanders. "He wanted something that would approximate the sensation of being held under water. I thought it was some kind of kinky sex thing. Figured him for one of those freaks who puts his head in a noose when he beats off, or whose wife likes being choked while he's banging her."

"There are people who do that?" says Landis, finding it hard to believe.

"Are you kidding?" says Sanders. "You've been away with the circus too long, pal."

"Alright, Vic," says Murphy, "let's stayed focused. So, he called you?"

"And I told him to give me a few days and call back. And he did, and we met to do the deal."

"Where?"

"Nowhere. Anywhere. What's the difference? Who the fuck remembers? The train station at 59th Street and 4th, maybe."

"Calm down, Vic. What did he look like?"

"He looked like every other fucking clown out there. No offense, officer," he says, scowling at Landis. "I could ID the guy if I saw him again, but I can't tell you what he looked like. The thing is, I think I'd seen him before."

"Oh?" says Murphy.

"At the unemployment office, over in Sheepshead Bay. I'm pretty sure it was the same guy. I doubt he remembered me. The only reason I remember him is he had a little kid with him, a boy. I nearly tripped over the kid. He was sitting in the middle of the floor, drawing in a coloring book, crayons spread out all over the fucking place. Had the whole room jammed up."

"Don't you think it was quite a coincidence, seeing the guy before?" asks Murphy.

"Sure it was a coincidence. The world is chock full of coincidence, Detective," says Sanders. "I ran into you twice, didn't I? And I've been very cooperative; I hope you won't forget that."

"You haven't given us shit," says Murphy, "and I've forgotten you already. Stan, go lock this asshole up and call over to the 68th for someone to come get him out of here."

"Let's go, Sanders," says Landis. "The show is over."

"And please lose the costume, Stan, before you get too attached to it," says Murphy. "We'll take a nice, leisurely drive over to Sheepshead Bay; try to find out if anyone at the New York State Department of Labor office can remember stepping on a Crayola."

Vota tries reaching Lorraine at her office. Victoria tells him that Lorraine is in court. He tells Victoria he will call back.

"What are you up to, Lou?" asks Samson.

"Nothing really."

"Let's do something."

Samson stops at Kelly's post on the way out.

"If anyone cares, we're out looking for a beat-up Oldsmobile," Samson says.

"Try Garcia's Bargain Lot on New Utrecht," suggests Sergeant Kelly.

The trip out to the unemployment office turns out to be a colossal waste of time.

The place is nearly empty. A few people, looking very bored, filling out endless forms. Only one office employee, looking much more bored.

"Where is everyone?" Murphy asks.

"It's Friday afternoon, it's Valentine's Day, and it's the start of a three-day weekend. What do you want?" says the clerk.

Murphy struggles to be polite. He asks about kids.

"They bring their brats in here all the time," says the clerk. "What do they think this is, a day-care center?"

"Okay, look, we can see that you're very busy," says Murphy, unconsciously clenching his fists. "We'll be out of your hair in a minute. Try to recall a specific child. A boy, a coloring book, crayons."

"You should talk to Mrs. Livingston. She's the one who usually deals with the little animals. Millie's the grandmotherly type. She'll be in Tuesday."

"Is that what the unemployed have to go through just to get the measly few hundred bucks they've earned?" asks Landis as they walk out. "Makes you feel lucky to have a job."

"As long as it's not his fucking job," says Murphy. "How about a hot dog while we're in the neighborhood?"

They sit at the counter at Nathan's on Surf Avenue in Coney Island. Murphy has three hot dogs on a paper plate in front of him. Smothered in mustard and sauerkraut. Landis works on a solitary potato knish.

"How can you eat those things?" Landis asks.

"Are you kidding? I adore these things. Remind me to grab a couple for Ralph before we leave."

"Where to after this?" asks Landis.

"I don't know, guess I should check back in at the Precinct," says Murphy. "Why, you have something to do?"

"I was hoping that I could get off early today."

"Oh, right, Valentine's Day. Have a hot date?"

"We'll see," says Landis.

"Who's the lucky guy?"

"He's new; I met him last weekend at church."

"Another cop?"

"God forbid," says Landis. "How about you?"

"How about me what?"

"A date tonight?"

"I haven't had a date in so long I've forgotten the feeling of anxiety and terror."

Lorraine DiMarco was about to meet Dr. Rowdy Barnwell for the first time.

Dr. Barnwell had been referred by Dr. Laura Vitiello, Lorraine's primary care physician. Lorraine knew that Dr. Vitiello, a board-certified gynecologist and a very radical feminist, would never have recommended a male neurosurgeon unless Barnwell was the best in his field.

"Rowdy?" Lorraine had said. "It sounds like a nickname for a cattle hand."

"It's actually his real name," Dr. Vitiello had said. "His nickname is Headhunter."

Dr. Barnwell's office is located in the NYU Medical Center at 33rd Street and First Avenue in Manhattan, where Lorraine had come for the MRI.

Lorraine takes the subway from Boro Hall in Brooklyn. She arrives exactly on time at 3:00 p.m., and is sitting with Barnwell at exactly 3:02.

"This is a first," she says. "No waiting, no stack of forms to fill out."

"I don't believe in waiting rooms, and I have all the paper I need from the medical file that Dr. Vitiello faxed over," says Barnwell. "So, how would you like it, straight from the hip or beating around the bush?"

"Shoot," she says.

"The MRI showed a tumor. About the size of a grape. It is most consistent with, which is to say most likely, a meningioma. A meningioma is *usually* benign and *seldom* fatal. As you can tell by the adjectives, there are exceptions. The tumor is pressing against the optic nerve, causing the headaches. It is operable. The success rate is above average. Any questions before I go on?"

"What kind of grape, Thompson or red globe?"

"More the size of a flame seedless," says Barnwell. "Here's the clinical jargon if you're interested, and I have pictures."

Lorraine reaches over for the written consultation.

After a quick look, she hands it back.

"Why don't you read it to me, Doctor. I'm sure you could do it more justice."

Barnwell reads in a deep melodic voice: "*Axial T1, T2, FLAIR and sagittal T1-weighted images of the brain were obtained before and after the administration of intravenous contrast. Study demonstrates a well-circumscribed extra-axial homogeneously-enhanced mass located near the left anterior clinoid process measuring approximately 1.5 centimeters at its greatest dimension. This is most consistent with a meningioma. The optic nerve canal is poorly visualized and the optic nerve at this level is felt to be compressed. There are no additional areas of abnormal contrast enhancement. The ventricles and sulci are normal. There is no evidence of a brain mass lesion, midline shift, mass effect, or extra-axial collections. There is no parenchymal signal abnormality.*"

"It rolls right off the tongue, doesn't it," says Lorraine.

"It's my favorite language. I find it very musical, but I've found that most patients prefer the English translation first."

"I appreciate that. So, what now?"

"We go in and get the little devil out of there. That should take care of the headaches. Then we can take a closer look at how nasty the tumor really was."

"When?"

"As soon as possible. I would recommend scheduling no later than a week from Monday."

"Okay, a week from Monday it is," says Lorraine.

Murphy cuts Landis loose and heads back to the 61st. When he finds the squad room empty, he buzzes Desk Sergeant Kelly.

"Where is everyone?"

"Samson and Vota are out killing time, Mendez is off duty, and according to my notes Landis should be with you," says Kelly. "If you get too bored, Murphy, come down for a beating at gin rummy."

"I'd rather read the sports section in the *Post*," says Murphy.

"That's a cruel thing to say," says Kelly.

He had come directly from the other house. The house near the car accident, where the woman had turned him away while his son bled in a car on the highway.

He had watched the house for two mornings now, taking his turn there before moving on to his bench on Shore Road. Two mornings, six hours during each of the past two days, and not a soul had come or gone. Not a child to school. Not a father to work. Not a visitor. Not the woman.

He would have to be more aggressive, he would need to take active steps to discover who in this house would be chosen to atone for the crime of ignoring his plea for help on the night his firstborn was taken from him. He knew that his time was running short. He understood that after he took the girl behind the iron gate, he would have to move along quickly. He knew that he would be discovered soon. It was inevitable. He needed to complete his work, complete God's work, before his time ran out.

He would take more active steps.

Tomorrow.

But this afternoon, he has been sitting at the bench on Shore Road, across from the Territo home, for two hours. To his surprise, he has seen all four arrive back at the house by three.

He now watches as the man and the boy load suitcases into the Jeep Cherokee.

The mother and the girl come down from the front of the house and wait on the sidewalk for the Jeep to come around. His heart sinks at the thought that they are leaving, most likely for the weekend, and he will have to delay his task.

The Cherokee turns onto Shore Road and pulls up to where the women are standing.

Suddenly, the girl and her mother embrace. The woman climbs into the front seat of the vehicle and the Cherokee drives off. The girl waves and walks back up to the house, safely behind its iron gate. She is alone, perhaps for a few nights. She is safe for the moment, he cannot reach her inside.

But he is sure that this is God's blessing.

She is a teenager, free of her parents.

She will be coming out.

He waits.

NINETEEN

The phone on the desk rings loudly, causing Murphy to jump. He realizes that he had dozed off.

"We got a homicide, Tommy," says Kelly, "a young girl. Two uniforms are there at the scene."

"Tell them I'm on the way."

Murphy grabs his coat and runs down. Kelly is holding out a slip of paper with the address.

"I'll try to find Samson and Vota," Kelly says.

"That's okay," says Murphy, heading out the door. "If I need them, I can find them myself."

Samson and Vota have been driving around Brooklyn for hours, mostly around the area of the Graham house. Nothing.

Vota has finally reached Lorraine and confirmed their dinner date for later that evening. Vota thinks he hears something odd in her voice, but he lets it go.

Samson is looking forward to a night out with Alicia.

"I need to take a break, Lou. My car is at the Precinct. You can drop me back there and then you can call it a day," says Samson. "I'll run in and check on Murphy, then I'm headed home myself."

Twenty minutes later, Samson watches Vota drive away from the Precinct. His cell rings before he gets inside.

"Where are you, Sam?" says Murphy on the other end.

"Standing in front of the 61st, where are you?"

"I'm on my way to pick you up. I'll be five minutes."

"Jesus, Tommy, it's Valentine's Day."

"That's why we guys without a date have to do all the dirty work," says Murphy.

"I *have* a date."

"C'mon, Sam, get over it. It's only your wife. I'll be there in three minutes."

Samson calls Alicia to apologize.

"It's okay, Sam."

Alicia's unfailing understanding only makes Samson feel more guilty.

"I'll get there as soon as I can."

"You'll get here when you get here," she says. "I'm not going anywhere. Just be careful."

Samson promises that he will and snaps the cell phone shut as Murphy pulls up.

"Jeepers," says Murphy. "If I didn't know better, I'd swear you're not glad to see me."

"What's this?" Samson asks, picking the paper bag off the dashboard as he climbs into the passenger seat.

"A couple of Nathan's hot dogs for Ralph. If you'd like one go ahead, he won't mind."

"No, I don't want one," says Samson, tossing the bag into the back seat. And what do you mean Ralph won't mind. How would he even know about it?"

"Oh, he'll know."

"Where are we going?" Samson finally asks.

"You won't believe this."

"Try me," says Samson, unimaginatively.

"A twenty-two-year-old girl gets a box of candy from her boyfriend, takes a bite out of an almond cluster and drops dead."

"Do we have the boyfriend?"

"Coney Island Hospital has him, under heavy sedation. The guy's a mess. Called it in himself. He was just about to bite into one of the candies, which, by the way, was laced with hydrogen cyanide, when he watches the girl go into convulsions. She was DOA."

"By any chance did he mention how the candy came to be poisoned before they doped him up?" Samson asks.

"You have to understand this kid was blubbering a lot—incoherent would only approximate his condition. He works for a messenger service and the candies were something he was sent out to deliver. The company he works for confirms that he was dispatched this afternoon with a box of candy addressed to a Mrs. Evelyn Campbell on West 5th Street, with a card reading: *Happy Valentine's Day from Your Loving Husband.*"

"What'd Evelyn have to say?"

"Evelyn told him that she wouldn't accept the candies. She said she didn't want anything from her scumbag husband. That's a direct quote," says Murphy. "So Miller, our boy in the hospital, decides that instead of sending them back he'll keep them and give them to his girlfriend who likes them so much that she's on the third one before the cyanide kicks in and KOs her."

"Unbelievable."

"I hate to say I told you so," says Murphy. "Just for your further edification, a representative of the messenger service said that it was against policy for an employee to keep an undeliverable item."

"Good policy. And the loving husband?"

"Estranged husband. I'm taking you to see him as we speak."

"Anyone ahead of us?"

"We're the first. Just plain lucky I guess," says Murphy as he swings the car into the driveway of a small brick house on Quentin Road, "and here we are."

There is no answer to their doorbell ringing, knocking or calling. The door is unlocked so they go in, announcing themselves as police officers as they do. Their guns drawn, they split up the search through the six rooms.

Samson finds Mr. Campbell in his bed.

Samson shouts at the man, yelling at Campbell that he has killed the wrong person.

He shouts at Campbell, yelling that the man has fucked up a special evening planned with Alicia.

He shouts at the man, telling Campbell that he'd like to wring his fucking neck.

Samson asks Campbell, as Murphy comes into the bedroom to find out what all of the shouting is about, how the man could resort to using something as sinister and malicious as candy laced with poison on Saint Valentine's Day.

But the bullet hole that Campbell has put into his own right temple has left the man unresponsive.

"What'ya gonna do now," asks Murphy, "read him his rights?"

"You know," says Samson, "it wouldn't be very hard to get tired of this shit."

"Yeah, but isn't it nice to get an open and shut case occasionally," says Murphy.

Serena Huang walks the corridors of the NYU School of Journalism. It feels like years since she's been here; it seems like yesterday.

Off the halls, in small rooms and offices, students sit alone or in twos or threes, silent, noisy, surrounded by books, staring at monitors. They look so young; Serena is feeling old at twenty-five. Every one of these young people has one goal in mind. To get the big story. They are all anxious to get out and take Serena's job, the job she hasn't landed yet.

Serena reaches the door of Dr. Jenkins' office. The door is open. She knocks lightly. Jenkins waves her in, indicates a seat, and holds up a single finger all in a fluid movement of her one free hand, while the other holds a phone receiver to her ear. *Come in, have a seat, I'll just be a minute.*

Sharon Jenkins is the youngest full professor in the long history of the department, and a contributor to the *New York Observer*. Jenkins was Serena's teacher, advisor, mentor and remains Serena's idol. Serena sits and waits.

"Okay," says Jenkins, completing her phone business, "you made it sound urgent and I'm running late. I'll just say that you are looking well and we can skip the rest of the small talk. What kind of help do you need?"

"I need advice."

"Okay."

"I stumbled on a story," says Serena. "Two murders in Brooklyn, similar if not identical ritual elements. No one else has it yet."

"You're certain they're connected?"

"I saw evidence with my own eyes that was extremely

convincing, and I have a very reliable source for confirmation, someone inside the NYPD."

"Leading the investigation?"

"No."

"And you want to know how to proceed?"

"Yes," says Serena.

"Okay," says Jenkins, "here's the bottom line. More important than breaking the story is being there at the end. You need to convince the lead investigator that you have enough to bury them in reporters, but are willing to hold if you are promised the exclusive inside track. It's not as easy as it sounds, because a smart detective may call your bluff, will try to convince you that you may be endangering lives. Which may be true."

"How do I deal with that?"

"Seven words: *The Public has a right to know.*"

"And if it doesn't fly?"

"Then you have to decide what's more important, your career or the consequences. I can't help you with that one. I can only remind you that if you swim in the Devil's lake, you may bump into the Devil."

"Should I try to presell the story?"

"That's tricky also. If you went to the *Times* or the *Voice* you would be walking a thin line. You would have to tell them enough to create interest, but not so much that they consider it too big for someone with no track record and decide to go after it without you. At the same time, it helps when you talk with the Police Department if you have someone with clout standing behind you, some kind of credentials," says Jenkins. "I'll tell you what I can do. Find the lead investigator, ask for a face-to-face, tell him or her what you know, and ask for an official comment. Say that you're freelance for the *Observer* and use my name. I'll back you up. And then play it by ear."

"Thank you, Dr. Jenkins."

"Let me know how it goes, if I don't read about it first. Now go, I have to meet my husband for dinner. It's our anniversary."

"You were married on Valentine's Day?" says Serena.

"It happens," says Sharon Jenkins.

He is parked at the corner of 82nd Street and Shore Road. From where he sits, he has a clear view of both the front and side entrances. If he can take her near either of the gates, it will be less than a hundred feet back to the car.

Inside the house, Brenda Territo takes a final look into the mirror. She puts a finishing touch to her eye makeup and smiles.

Not bad, she thinks.

She glances at her watch and hurries to collect her coat and purse. Brenda turns off the upstairs lights and skips down the stairs.

He sees the lights go out on the second floor. The light above the front door comes on.

He sees the girl step out onto the front porch.

She stops to lock the door.

He switches off the dome lamp in the Oldsmobile before stepping out onto the street. The girl moves down the front stairs of the house. He crosses to the corner of the property. He stands in the darkness, no more than fifty feet from the girl, and waits for her to come through the wrought iron gate.

And waits.

Until she finally comes out to the sidewalk as a car pulls up in front of the house.

And she is quickly in the car and the car is quickly gone.

"What time do you have to be home?" asks Brenda.

"One," says Diane as she drives. "I'll have to drop you back by twelve-thirty."

"What if I stayed at your house tonight? My house is a little spooky when no one else is home, and it'll give us an extra half hour."

"Great idea," says Diane, pulling out her cell phone. "I'll call my mom and tell her that you're going to spend the night."

"So, what's this great party?" Brenda asks when Diane is off the phone.

"My sister's friend rents a Victorian with some other girls

222

in Midwood. There'll be a lot of guys from Brooklyn College."

"Well, then, step on it."

"What about the new boyfriend?" asks Diane. "Jason?"

"Jason is tomorrow night. Tonight is tonight."

"What I'd really like to know is how you got out of going to Atlantic City?"

"Leverage," says Brenda. "Serious leverage."

Father Donovan moves through the crowd in the basement at Our Lady of Angels. He is pleased with the turnout.

Men and women. Young, unmarried. Some not so young, never married, widowed. Some talking, getting acquainted. Some standing quietly, watching, waiting.

All glad for an alternative to spending the evening alone. On this annual evening in mid-February when being alone is made to seem almost shameful.

Donovan spots the young woman. She seems to be carefully studying the crowd. He works his way over to her.

"I'm happy to see you here," he says, "thank you for coming. Are you looking for someone special?"

"To be honest, I am looking for someone in particular. Thank you for inviting me, Father," says Marina Ivanov.

It is nearly 10:00 p.m. when Samson finally makes it home to Douglaston. Before he is out of the car, Alicia is at the side door waiting to greet him.

She stops him before he can speak.

"Don't waste any energy apologizing again," she says. "I would prefer you put whatever strength you have left to better use."

"Oh?" he says, removing his coat as he follows her into the house.

"Here, let me get that for you," Alicia says, taking the coat as she hands him a glass of wine.

She places the coat on a chair and picks up the other glass from the kitchen table.

"Happy Valentine's Day," she says, touching her glass to his.

They each take a drink.

"What smells so good, and why is it so dark in there?" he asks, moving toward the doorway connecting the kitchen to the dining room.

"It's called a late dinner."

The dining room table is set for two, decorated with fresh flowers and illuminated by two tall candles.

Alicia steps up beside him in the doorway. Samson puts his arm around her shoulder.

"There's something missing," he says.

"What's that?"

"Why am I not tripping over the children?"

"The children are at my mother's, for the night. I thought that if we had to stay at home, it would be much more fun if we were alone."

"Why don't we make that late dinner a little later?" he says, leading her up the stairs to the bedroom above.

Murphy sits on his usual barstool.

There are a good number of patrons at Joe's Bar and Grill, some in pairs, some not. Some shooting pool, some watching the Knicks game, others holding hands while the jukebox shouts out silly love songs.

Murphy calls to Augie for another drink.

"What's the matter, Tommy?" Augie Sena says, placing the shot and the beer chaser in front of Murphy. "You look lost in thought."

"I was thinking about Ralph. Home all alone on Valentine's Day."

"Imagine how my wife feels, although the ruby earrings seemed to ease her disappointment quite a bit," says Augie. "I hope you got Ralph a present at least."

"Of course I did," says Murphy, draining the glass of bourbon and trying hard not to picture the condition of the Nathan's hot dogs sitting on the back seat of his car.

. . .

Rosen closes the novel; she's having trouble staying awake. She had fixed a dinner of stir-fried vegetables and nearly polished off a bottle of Merlot. The night spent alone at home would not have been half-bad if her mother hadn't called three times to ask Sandra how she was doing.

Serena Huang picks up the call on the third ring.

"Sorry to phone you so late," says Andy Chen.

"No problem, is everything okay?"

"It was kind of a rough night, I guess," Chen admits. "I was going to call you earlier, but I figured you would be out."

"The woman I'm staying with had a hot date," Serena says. "I watched videos."

"I was hoping we could get together, maybe tomorrow?"

"Sure. I'm wide open."

"Great, I'll call you during the day to work out the details. And Serena."

"Yes?"

"About last night, I was upset. I said a lot of things that I shouldn't have said. About my work."

"Andy, I told you there's no need to worry about it. I wouldn't mention anything that you said. I'm sorry that it has been so emotional for you, but I'm glad if talking about it helped in any small way. Trust me, I won't say a word," she says. "I'll see you tomorrow."

Serena places the receiver down, unnerved, wondering how she could bring herself to be so deceitful.

But only for a moment.

They lay quietly in Lorraine's bed. She curls into his arms. It was by any standards a memorable evening.

Dinner at Peter Luger's, Lorraine wondering how Lou could have possibly managed a reservation. The waiting period was at least two weeks for a weeknight, no telling how long for a Friday night. And for Valentine's night? Either Lou had made arrangements back in the fall of '98, or being an NYPD detective had perks that even an attorney could not imagine. Lorraine was able to fully enjoy the remarkable dinner because she knew that Detective Vota was not one to abuse his power.

Afterwards, an all-Mozart concert at the Brooklyn Academy of Music and dessert at Junior's on Flatbush.

Lou and Lorraine lay there, side by side, tired and satisfied, each occupied with private thoughts, each with something to say and each having no idea how to say it.

Vota has been trying all night to somehow work the word *marriage* into the conversation. He runs his fingers along Lorraine's back, trying to decide if it is not too late to squeeze it in.

Junior's cheesecake is without argument the best on the continent, will you marry me?

"Were you about to say something?" Lorraine asks.

"I had a terrific time tonight," he says.

"So did I, you thought of everything."

And, by the way, I have an appointment, a week from Monday, to remove a brain tumor.

"Thank you, Lou."

"Don't mention it."

"Goodnight," says Lorraine, kissing him on the cheek.

They are both asleep in minutes.

He looks at his wristwatch. It is nearly midnight. He somehow knows that the girl is not coming back tonight.

He is somehow positive.

He is also certain that tomorrow night will be the night.

He decides to leave the car there. He does not want to give up so perfect a parking spot. He takes the manila envelope off the seat and climbs out of the Oldsmobile.

He walks to the house near the high school. He comes in through the back yard and onto the screened porch. The door into the house itself is as simple to enter as he knew it would be. He places the envelope at the threshold and steps in.

He goes to the bathroom; he sets the plug in place and runs

water into the tub. While it fills, he writes on the wall in blue crayon.

He turns off the tap, examines his work, and moves back to the kitchen. He picks up the envelope and leaves the house. He feels prepared.

He begins walking, down to and then along 4th Avenue. He stops for a moment to drop the envelope into a corner mailbox.

As he reaches Our Lady of Angels, groups of people are leaving the church. He notices the priest, talking with a young woman on the sidewalk in front of the rectory.

"Good evening," he says as he walks past.

"Good evening," says Father Donovan.

"Have a safe night," says Marina Ivanov.

He crosses the avenue and continues home.

He comes into his house. There is a stack of new mail on the floor, beneath the slot in the front door. He kicks it aside. It becomes part of the larger pile of personal mail and junk flyers laying underneath the small table to the left of the doorway. He places his keys on the table. A greeting card in a bright red envelope catches his eye. He reaches to pick it up and carries it into the kitchen.

He pours a tall glass of Scotch.

He carries the glass to the boy's bedroom, leaving the Valentine's card from his wife on the kitchen counter.

Unopened.

TWENTY

Saturday morning.

There is a knock on the study door.

"Come in."

"You wanted to see me, Mr. Colletti?"

"Yes. Sammy, sit," says Dominic Colletti, holding a large tumbler filled with what looks to Leone like bright orange mud. "Would you like a glass of fresh carrot juice?"

"No, thank you."

"I haven't heard from Territo about the vehicle," says Colletti. "His time is up."

"What would you like me to do?" asks Leone.

"Remind him of the importance of respect."

"When are the children coming home?" asks Samson, refilling their coffee cups.

"That's up to you," says Alicia. "Are you going in today?"

"I wasn't planning to, I'm hoping to be home all day."

"Then the children will be coming home later," says his wife.

Lou Vota opens his eyes to find Lorraine beside him, sitting up in bed reading. She is wearing a terry cloth robe and her hair is still damp.

"What time is it?" Vota asks.

"Almost nine, Van Winkle. Are you working today?"

"Yes, and I'm late, but I'm all yours tomorrow."

"Well, you'd better get into the shower," she says. "I saved you some hot water. I'll start the coffee."

He leans over and kisses her forehead.

"That's a beautiful mop of hair you've got there,

Counselor," he says, heading for the bathroom.

Not for long she thinks.

Murphy arrives at the 61st Precinct at nine.

"Anyone in?" he asks Kelly at the desk.

"Samson is off. Vota called, he's on his way."

"When was the last time you had a day off?"

"What century is this?" Kelly answers. "Actually, I have tomorrow off, and the holiday on Monday."

"Holiday?"

"Presidents' Day."

"Which president?" asks Murphy.

"Who cares?" says Kelly.

Gabriel Caine walks slowly up the front steps of the corner house at Cropsey Avenue and 26th Avenue. He looks up at the street address above the door. Gabriel rings the doorbell and takes a step back. A moment later, a man stands in the open doorway.

"Can I help you?" he asks.

"Mr. Randall?"

"No, I'm afraid there is no Mr. Randall here."

Gabriel pulls a slip of paper from his briefcase and gives it a quick look.

"I'm very sorry to have bothered you," says Gabriel. "They apparently gave me the wrong address at the office. I have an appointment to see a Mr. Henry Randall about a college tuition fund for his children."

"Would you like to use the telephone?"

"Excuse me?"

"To call your office, see if they can find the right address."

"That would be very kind," Gabriel says.

"No problem, I know how it is. I'm a salesman myself, Jim Bowers," the man says, holding out his hand.

"Gabe Caine," says Gabriel, accepting the handshake.

"Come in," Bowers says. "Do you only work local?"

"Yes," says Gabriel, following Bowers into the house.

"You're very fortunate, I have to travel quite a lot. You can use the phone on the table."

Bowers walks off into another room, leaving Gabriel alone to make the call. A few minutes later he returns.

"Any luck?"

"Yes, I've got it. It's over on 24ᵗʰ Avenue. Thank you very much."

"Who's here, James?" calls a voice from the kitchen.

"A young man selling investment savings plans, for college tuition."

"Did you inform him that we have no children," says the woman, walking into the room, "or did you neglect to inform me that you're planning to go back to college?"

The woman is smiling brightly. Gabriel looks into her eyes. They are remarkably blue, unusually beautiful.

And they are the eyes of a blind woman.

"This is my wife, Hannah. Hannah, this is Mr. Caine. He was sent here by mistake."

"I don't believe in mistakes, everything happens for a reason," says Hannah Bowers. "Can we at least offer you coffee, Mr. Caine?"

"No, thank you, Mr. Randall will be waiting. It's very generous of you to offer. It's very unusual."

"I certainly hope that it hasn't become unusual to show hospitality to a fellow stranger," says Mrs. Bowers. "It is a blessing to be able to help others. Sadly, I seldom get the opportunity. I'm glad that James was at home. It's very difficult when I'm here alone."

"It's my fault. I'm overprotective and I'm a bully," says Bowers. "I insist that Hannah be very careful when I'm away. The world can be a scary place, particularly in the dark."

"I'm glad I had the chance to meet you," says Gabriel.

"Good luck," says Bowers, following Gabriel out to the front porch. "If you're ever back in the neighborhood, stop by and say hello. Hannah would like that."

"God bless you both. You are truly good people," says Gabriel, as he walks down the stone steps to the street.

· · ·

Ripley pours from the office coffeemaker and turns to find Agent Stone standing close enough to touch him.

"Jesus, Win," he says, nearly dropping the cup, "you scared the hell out of me. What are you doing here? This is Saturday."

"I might ask you the same thing."

"You might?"

"I'm sorry I startled you."

"I'll get over it," says Ripley, moving to his desk. "I'm trying to clear up a little work today so I can avoid being back here until Tuesday. Don't forget that Monday is Presidents' Day and coming to work on a government holiday is a federal offense."

"I won't forget."

"So, to get back to the original question, what are you doing here?"

"I've been following up on Anthony Territo."

"Sit down, Stone," Ripley says, taking a seat behind his desk. "Let's get this out of the way."

"I followed Tony Territo to a garage near Sunset Park in Brooklyn yesterday afternoon, and I stuck around after he left. Just after dark, a brand spanking new Mercedes convertible arrived and was taken in."

"You told me the guy owns a dealership; maybe the car needed repairs."

"I spoke with an NYPD dispatcher this morning, talked him into showing me a list of reported car thefts."

"How did you manage that?" asks Ripley.

"I think he liked my suit."

"And the Mercedes was on the list."

"Yes, sir. Taken from a driveway on East 11th and Avenue X around seven."

Ripley walks over to the Brooklyn-Queens wall map.

"That's the 61st Precinct, call it in if you haven't already," says Ripley.

"I would have, but I wanted to speak with you first. About the garage."

"What about the garage?"

"The building is owned by Dominic Colletti."

"This Dominic Colletti," says Ripley, lifting a thick file folder from his desk.

"The very one," says Stone.

"Do me a favor; find out who's in charge at the 61st."

"Yes, sir," says Stone, jumping out of her seat with the enthusiasm of a kid heading for the tree on Christmas morning.

"Didn't I ask you to stop calling me sir?"

"Actually, sir, you asked me to stop calling you Chief."

"Can you call me Ripley?"

"Yes, I can do that."

"Great. And Stone," he says as she reaches the door.

"Yes, Ripley."

"Good work."

George Addams rises from the kitchen table after lunch at home with his wife. They had buried their son three days earlier.

"I need to make a phone call," he says.

"Why not make it right here?" asks his wife.

"I'll use the phone in my study," he says, leaving the room.

The call is answered by the on-duty desk sergeant.

"63rd Flatlands, Santiago speaking."

"Detective Rosen, please," says George Addams.

"Detective Rosen is off duty today. Can I help you?"

"When will she be back?" asks Addams.

Santiago quickly checks the Precinct schedule sheet.

"Monday morning. Would you like to speak with another detective?"

"No, thank you, I'll try back on Monday."

"She may check in, can I tell her who called?"

"I'll phone Monday," says Addams.

He returns to the kitchen where his wife is pouring the coffee.

"What is it?" she asks. "What's on your mind?"

"Nothing."

Their two girls run in before she can challenge him.

. . .

Gabriel comes into his house, leaves the briefcase at the door, and walks back to the bedroom. After getting out of the suit and into a pair of blue chinos and a Brooklyn College sweatshirt, he moves to the kitchen.

Gabriel hunts through the refrigerator for something to eat and settles on a piece of cold fried chicken. He sits at the counter. He is thinking about the woman, Hannah Bowers. The kindness behind those sightless eyes.

He notices the red envelope. He tears it open. A card from his wife. From Florida. A large heart on front. Three words printed inside. *Happy Valentine's Day.*

Five one-hundred-dollar bills wrapped inside a short note in her timid handwriting. *We are doing fine. I've tried reaching you. Please call. I've seen to the mortgage payment. I miss you very much. Your daughter misses you.*

Gabriel places the card and note on the counter.

I was meant to protect and provide for them, he thinks.

He violently throws the cash to the floor.

God has spared Hannah Bowers, now only two remain.

First, the girl.

Gabriel goes into his son's room and lies down on the floor, among the toys. He will rest. Until dark.

And then he will go to take her.

Later that afternoon, a woman watering the plants on her sixth-floor fire escape on West Street near Gravesend Neck Road saw her upstairs neighbor float past her on his way to a fatal rendezvous with the sidewalk below. Then she heard a voice from above say: *If your girlfriend calls again, I'll tell her you stepped out for a minute.* The woman below dropped her watering can, which landed on top of the body on the ground, and ran in to call 911.

The first officers at the scene went to check out the corpse and found the watering can lying on the victim's back and a dent in the man's skull into which the tapered end of a steam iron would have fit perfectly. Then a woman's voice from above screamed: *You stay away from my husband*, and a moment later a heavy object fitting the description of the likely murder weapon hit the pavement, missing the younger of the two patrolmen by a few inches. Considering the possibility that something like a blender or sewing machine could be next, the two policemen quickly took cover in the vestibule of the building and opted for waiting right there until the Homicide detectives arrived.

When Vota and Murphy pull up and get out of the car, the younger officer yells for them to move quickly out of the line of fire.

"She's armed with household appliances," he says.

Just as they come into the vestibule, a four-slice toaster lands at their feet.

"Should we call the bomb's away squad?" asks Murphy.

"C'mon, let's go," says Vota, not too amused, and leads the way to the elevator.

When the door of the lift opens on the eighth floor a cast-iron skillet bounces into the elevator and skids to the back of the cage.

"Fucking great," says Vota, not knowing whether to pull his gun or grab the frying pan to level the playing field.

"Maybe we'd better call the SWAT Team and tell them to bring the anti–wedding shower gift gear," suggests Murphy.

"Can't you quit even for a minute?" asks Vota.

"Are you going to shoot her?"

"No."

"Do you want to get nailed by a flying tea kettle while you try to subdue her?"

"No."

"Do we have any helmets or armor in the car?"

"No."

"Then what's your plan?" asks Murphy

"Let's go down and call for the SWAT Team," says Vota.

Frank Sullivan mans the front counter while Joe Campo is off on a delivery to West 7th Street. Sully uses a large stainless steel spoon to freshen the salads in the refrigerated display case. Suddenly, a small pair of eyes peers at him through the glass.

"Good afternoon," Sully says, standing, "and what's your name?"

"Frankie," the boy answers. "Where's Grandpa?"

"Well, how about that? Frank is my name, too. Your grandfather will be back very soon," says Sully.

Sullivan can see something of Joe Campo in the boy's handsome features.

"How about an olive, Frankie?"

"Too sour," the boy says.

"I see you've finally met the Terror of Tenth Street," says Joe Campo, walking up to them.

"You're silly, Grandpa."

"What brings you up here, Frankie?"

"Grandma needs some tomato glue," the boy says, trying to stifle a laugh.

"You know where the tomato paste is, grab a can off the shelf," says Joe. "I'll walk you home. I'll be back in ten minutes, Sully."

"No problem, take your time."

"Listen, Frank, Roseanna is over at my son's house down the street, cooking up a storm. Eggplant parmigiana, if I'm not mistaken," says Campo. "We would be pleased to have you join us for dinner. If you don't have any other plans."

"I would like that," says Frank Sullivan.

"Good, you can quit for the day as soon as I return. We'll plan to eat at seven."

"I'll bring wine," says Sully.

"Very good," says Joe Campo.

Samson checks in with Murphy at five-thirty.

"Did I miss anything?" he asks.

"A woman on West Street knocked her husband out of a sixth-floor window with a Proctor Wrinkle Master. We had to call in the SWAT Team."

"The husband die?"

"Oh, yeah. At least once."

"Anyone else hurt?"

"One of the SWAT guys took it on chin. An electric wok. He'll be okay. Lou split. I'm out of here at six."

"I'll be in tomorrow," says Samson.

"I won't be. So have a nice day, bro," says Murphy.

"God bless you, Sully, you look wonderful," says old man Levine.

"Thanks. I feel wonderful."

"What can I do for you?"

"I need a very good bottle of Chianti, Sol," says Sully. "If I can pay you next week."

Levine walks out from behind the counter and takes a bottle from the shelf. He slips it into a long paper bag.

"The wine is on me," says Levine, handing it to Sully. "A gift."

"Why?"

"Just look at yourself, Sully," the old man says. "It's the least I can do. You've made my day."

Murphy finds a parking spot in front of his building. There are plenty of empty spaces on a Saturday at dinner time. Other people go out.

He stops in for takeout food before going up.

"I went with spare ribs, shrimp with lobster sauce and cold sesame noodles," Murphy announces as he walks into the apartment. "If you don't like the menu you can eat Alpo."

The length of Ralph's tongue says that spare ribs will be fine.

Gabriel sits in the Oldsmobile. It is parked on the corner, across from the Territo house, where he had left it parked the night before.

A flashy, bright red Camaro pulls up in front of the house. The car horn blasts three times.

Brenda Territo blots her lipstick and grabs her coat. She is almost out the door of her room when she remembers her ring. A gift from her father for her sixteenth birthday. She runs back to her dresser and slips the sapphire onto her finger. She turns off the lights and heads down.

Gabriel sees the lights go off, and a minute later the girl is out on the front porch. As she locks the door, an idea comes to him.

Brenda skips down the steps and out of the gate. She hops into the Camaro. The car speeds away.

Gabriel waits a few minutes before climbing out of the Oldsmobile. He moves slowly to the front gate, glancing up and down Shore Road as he walks. At the gate, he pulls out a ring of keys. He finds a key that he had used at his job, when he had a job. He can't think of why he had saved it.

Gabriel manages to partially work the key into the lock. He snaps it off and returns to his car.

And he waits.

The last of the guests are gone soon after eleven. Dominic Colletti had invited a small group of friends and family to celebrate his son's birthday at the house in Manhattan Beach. Only Sammy Leone and Colletti's two boys remain, and Dominic's sister-in-law collecting empty plates and glasses.

"Carmella, stop already. I pay a cleaning girl good money for that. Richard, please, drive your Aunt Carmella home," says Colletti.

Dominic is afraid that if she asks one more time about Bobby Hoyle he will tear her tongue out.

Richie Colletti looks at the 24-carat gold Rolex, the birthday gift from his father. He was expecting a BMW.

"Why can't Sonny drive her home?" Richie asks, knowing that the old hag would say something about the car if he had to take her home in his three-year-old Chrysler.

"I need Sonny for something else," says Colletti. "Now go. Find your aunt's coat. Carmella, I beg you, put those plates down."

When Richie finally gets the woman into her coat and out the door, Dominic turns his attention to Sonny.

"I need you to give Sammy a ride over to Bay Ridge," he tells his son.

"Sure, Pop, what's up?"

"It is time to settle with Tony Territo. It broke my heart seeing how disappointed Richie was tonight."

"What are we going to do?"

"Sammy is doing, you are driving, go," says Colletti. "Sammy is waiting out front."

Sonny goes out to his Porsche and finds Leone standing at the passenger door. Sammy is holding a large shotgun.

"Jesus, Sammy, what the hell is that for?"

"We're going to do a little bodywork on a certain BMW coupe," says Leone.

They climb into the Camaro after leaving the Fortway Theater.

"Damn it, Jason. I couldn't even watch the movie, fighting to get your hands off me the whole time," says Brenda. "Please take me home."

The boy pulls the Camaro away from the curb and heads toward Shore Road, confused. Everything he had heard about Brenda Territo had convinced him that she was a sure thing.

Ten minutes later, in front of Brenda's house, Jason gives it one more try.

"I told you that you can't come in, Jason," Brenda says. "You don't know my father; he'll have the house checked for fingerprints when he gets back."

Jason ignores her and puts his hand on her bare knee.

Brenda slaps his hand and jumps out of the car.

"C'mon, Brenda, get back in the car. Let's just sit for a while," he says. "I promise I'll behave."

"Go home and take a cold shower, Jason. Call me when you cool down."

"Brenda."

"Goodnight," she says, slamming the car door.

"Bitch," he says under his breath as he punches the gas pedal.

Gabriel hears the Camaro peel away and sees the girl stand

239

watching as the car tears off. He had crossed to the corner of the house when they had arrived, and stood there with the crowbar in his hand. Gabriel starts toward the girl as she moves to the gate.

Two blocks down on Shore Road, Jason pounds on the brake pedal.

"Fucking girls, shit," he mutters, making a reckless U-turn back toward the Territo house.

Brenda is struggling with her key. She checks to make sure it's the right one.

"Fuck," she says, loudly.

Her voice startles Gabriel and he misses his mark. The pry bar strikes her in the neck and shoulder.

Brenda falls heavily to the ground. Gabriel gets down beside her; he can't tell if she is alive.

The Camaro jumps the curb and screeches to a stop, inches from Gabriel and the girl.

"What the fuck!" Jason yells, as he jumps out of the car.

When the boy reaches the front of the vehicle, Gabriel lands a violent blow with the iron bar to Jason's knee. The boy goes down, holding the leg, screaming in pain.

In the light of the Camaro's headlamps, Gabriel sees the sparkle in the girl's sapphire ring. A glowing star. The boy is crying out for help. Gabriel pulls the ring from the girl's finger and runs for the Oldsmobile.

"Turn onto 82nd Street and stop at the side entrance. They're out of town, but Territo was nice enough to leave the Beemer out in the driveway," says Sammy Leone. "When I'm done, it's going to look like Swiss cheese."

As they approach the corner of 82nd Street, a large car suddenly backs out onto Shore Road. Sonny Colletti brakes just in time. The Oldsmobile speeds away.

"Fucking maniac," yells Sammy Leone.

"What's going on here?" says Sonny, driving up to the Camaro.

They can now hear the boy screaming.

Sonny gets out of the Porsche and moves toward the two

bodies on the ground.

"Sonny, get the fuck back here," yells Leone.

"These kids are hurt."

"And if the cops find us here with this shotgun, we're fucked. Let's go."

Sonny stands glued to the spot.

"Sonny," Leone yells again, at the top of his voice.

A light comes on, in front of the neighboring house. Sonny Colletti rushes back to his car and jumps behind the wheel. He throws the Porsche into gear and races off.

Jason is still screaming when the first patrol car rolls up to the scene.

The bell in the tower at St. Anselm's strikes twelve times, ringing in a new day in the Borough of Churches.

PART THREE

A BLOT ON THE LANDSCAPE

From the middle of the building an ugly flat-topped octagonal tower ascended against the east horizon, and viewed from this spot, on its shady side and against the light, it seemed to be the one blot on the city's beauty. Yet it was with this blot, and not with the beauty, that the gazers were concerned.

Thomas Hardy

TWENTY ONE

Sunday morning. Murphy has the day off.

He starts his day as usual, the three-mile run with Ralph. They begin their run at eight on Sunday mornings, two hours later than their weekday jogs.

The last quarter mile back to Murphy's apartment is taken at a brisk walk, allowing both man and man's best friend to wind down and resume normal breathing by the time they reach home.

The routine rarely changes, and ends with the three-flight climb to the apartment and four eggs shared equally between them. Murphy's scrambled, well. Ralph's sunny-side up. The difference this morning is that someone is in the apartment when they return, and they both feel it as they reach the door designated 4B.

There are many ways to react, and Murphy knows them all, has used them all. Go down and call for backup. Go in fast and low. Stand ready and wait in the hallway for someone to come out. Murphy and Ralph look at each other as if helping each other decide.

Then Murphy knocks on the door.

"It's open, come in," calls a voice from inside.

"You should stay home this morning, Sam," says Alicia, "until you feel a little better."

Samson had been up all night with stomach cramps and nausea.

"Do you think it was something I ate?"

"I think it has to do with what that poor girl ate, poisoned Valentine candy," says Alicia, "and this case you're working on, the two murdered boys. It would make anyone sick to his stomach."

"I'll call Lou, see if he can cover for me. At least for a few hours."

"Want a couple of eggs?" asks Murphy, as he and Ralph walk into the kitchen.

"How about French toast?" asks the younger man at the card table, which served as the dining table when it wasn't surrounded by very serious poker players.

"This isn't the fucking House of Pancakes, get your feet off the table and what the fuck are you doing here anyway?" says Murphy.

Ralph adds something unintelligible.

"I've got a problem."

"You've always got a problem, and you could have at least started the coffee."

"This is serious, Tommy."

"Listen, Michael, the only thing serious about you is that you are a serious fuck-up. I told you to keep your nose clean or stay the fuck away from me. I'm not bailing you out of trouble again. And if you get far enough out of line, I swear I'll take you in."

"Cop talk."

"That's what I am Mike, a cop. What the fuck are you?"

"Your brother."

"Don't rub it in. And it's not enough reason to put up with your bullshit."

"Mom thinks it's enough. Dad would think so."

"Keep them out of this because you're just going to piss me off. All you do for Mom is worry her. And if Dad would have lived to witness half the shit you've pulled, he would have kicked your ass out a long time ago."

"Before he died, he asked me to take care of Mom."

"I take care of Mom; you can't take care of anything," says Murphy, and then he takes a deep breath and tries his best to calm himself. "Look Mike, I'm getting very angry and I don't have time for this crap. If you want to join Ralph and me for breakfast, you're welcome. Afterwards or otherwise, get the hell out of here and don't bother coming back unless you've got good news."

"I think I might have killed a guy."

"What the fuck is that supposed to mean?"

"It means I think I killed a guy. I don't know. I cut him a few times, but I didn't stick around to take his pulse or nothing."

"What the fuck happened?"

"I stopped this guy for his wallet and the guy jumps all over me. I stuck him a couple of times to get him off me and I ran."

"And you didn't call it in?"

"I'm telling you."

"And you leave him to die, you fuck. What time was it?"

"About two this morning. I didn't know what to do. I've been walking around all night. The fucking guy was about sixty fucking years old. He shocked the shit out of me. What happened to just giving it up?"

"Did he see your face?"

"I don't know. Probably."

"And you didn't get his wallet."

"No."

"Cocksucker. You better pray that this guy is still breathing somewhere. I'm not scheduled to go in to the Precinct today. How the fuck am I going to find out if this guy turned up? I'll have to wait until tomorrow morning to check the blotter. God fucking damn it, Mike, I should take you in right now."

"You can't do that."

"Don't tell me what I can or cannot do, Mike. I could fucking break your neck. I want you to get out of here and go home. Don't talk to anyone. Don't talk to Mom about this. I'll tell her you were here, but otherwise you never saw me this morning. And if you don't stay at the house until I'm ready to decide what to do with you, I'll find you and drag you by the fucking hair down to lock-up."

"Tommy."

"Don't fucking Tommy me, just get out."

"I'm scared."

"Yeah, well I'm fucking terrified. How's that?"

After cooking two eggs for Ralph and none for himself, Murphy calls his mother.

"Hi, Mom."

"Thomas, Michael didn't come home last night."

First words out of her mouth. Tell me about it.

"Yeah, Mom, I know. He stayed with me. He showed up around midnight, I didn't want to call you so late. Sorry to worry you. He's on his way home now. Please ask him to call me as soon as he gets in, okay?"

"Is anything wrong, son?"

"No, Mom. Nothing's wrong."

"Are you coming for dinner this afternoon?"

"Does a bear poop in the woods?"

"Thomas."

"Wouldn't miss it. Be there around four."

"Bring Ralph, I'm making corned beef and cabbage."

Oh, Christ.

"His favorite," says Murphy. "We'll see you at four."

Vincent Territo sat in the corridor with his daughter-in-law and his grandson, outside of the intensive care unit at Victory Memorial Hospital. Vincent had been notified of the attack on his granddaughter and had made the call to Tony in Atlantic City. Vincent had waited outside of the emergency room as the doctors worked to keep Brenda alive, and then at the ICU waiting for his son.

Tony, Barbara and the boy finally arrived after four in the morning.

Brenda Territo had lost a lot of blood. She remained unconscious. The doctors were doing all they could to keep her stable with blood transfusions and antibiotics.

The question about permanent damage due to the severe blow on the neck would have to wait.

Tony Territo and his wife had been interviewed by the investigating detective after being given some time to talk with doctors and nurses.

"Do you have any idea who may have wanted to harm your daughter?" asked Andy Chen.

"What do you mean?" asked Tony, surprised and alerted by the question. "I thought she was mugged?"

"We discovered that the lock on the front gate had been tampered with. She couldn't get in," said Detective Chen. "We believe that someone may have been waiting for her, may have marked her. If it weren't for the boy, well, it could have been much worse."

"What boy?" asked Barbara.

"Your daughter had just returned from a date with a young man. He had dropped her off in front of the house after some kind of argument and then he decided to come back to apologize. He may have saved her life."

"What happened to the boy?" asked Tony.

"He's here, in the hospital," said Chen. "His kneecap was shattered by the assailant. Does the word sunny mean anything to you? Maybe a name?"

It took every muscle in Territo's face to manufacture an ignorant look.

"No. Why?"

"The boy heard the word spoken," said Chen. "Are you sure there's no one you can think of who would have reason to hurt your daughter?"

"I'm sure," said Territo. "Can we go back to Brenda now?"

"Sure," said Chen. "I may need to speak with you again."

"We'll be here," said Tony.

"I hope your daughter comes through okay," said Chen, wondering what it was that Territo wasn't telling.

A few hours later, Territo has found Jason's room and waits until the boy's parents leave for breakfast before going in. The boy repeats what he had told police. Jason had heard the word or name sunny called out, and then he saw a silver Porsche speed away.

Territo returns to his father, wife and son outside the ICU.

"Any word?" he asks.

"Not yet," says Barbara. "My God, who would want to hurt our little girl?"

Tony and Vincent exchange a private glance.

"I don't know," says Tony. "I'll be right back; I need to make a phone call."

Mike had called to say he'd made it home, Murphy reminded him to stay put. Michael said that he would.

Twenty minutes later, Vota calls to ask if Murphy would give up part of his day off and come down to the Precinct for a few hours.

"Samson is going to be in late, if at all," says Vota, "and it was a busy Saturday night for the bad guys. I need a little help following some of it up."

Although lucky was not how Murphy felt, it was a lucky break. He had spent the past hour wondering how the hell he was going to survive until the next morning not knowing whether his brother had actually killed someone.

Now, he could check the overnight crime reports without having to demonstrate conspicuous interest.

Stevie arrives at Victory Memorial and finds them all outside the ICU.

"Jesus, Tony," says Stevie, taking his cousin's hand in his own. "Is she going to be alright?"

"I don't know," Tony says.

Stevie moves to give Barbara a hug and then embraces his Uncle Vincent.

"I need a favor, Steve," says Tony.

"Anything."

"Let's take a walk," says Tony.

"Let me join you," says Vincent.

"Please, Pop," says Tony, with all of the insistence he can respectfully direct at his father. "Please stay here with Barbara and Anthony."

"What can I do?" asks Stevie, when they are out on the street in front of the hospital.

"What kind of car does Sonny Colletti drive?" asks Tony.

"A silver Porsche."

"I need you to find Sonny and stay on him constantly," says Territo. "I want to know where he is at all times."

Murphy stops at the front desk as soon as he comes into the Precinct. Sergeant Kelly is on duty.

"I thought you were off today," says Murphy.

"I am off, just like you," says Kelly.

"Let me see the overnights, Borough-wide."

Murphy finds it quickly. On the very long list, which included five shootings, more than a dozen B-and-Es, nine armed robberies, fourteen muggings, two attempted rapes, three wife beatings, two hit-and-run accidents and eight stabbings was the one stabbing that Murphy guesses he is looking for.

Kenneth Wolfe, 58, found stabbed twice in an alley between U and V off Ocean Avenue, not very far from the Precinct. The victim was discovered by a taxi driver at 2:17 a.m. and rushed to Coney Island Hospital. Lots of blood lost, the victim was moved from the ER to intensive care at 5:03 a.m. The investigating officer, Jackman, had not yet been able to question Wolfe as of the time of the report. The time of report was listed at 6:45 a.m.

Murphy resists the strong urge to call the hospital to inquire about Wolfe's status. It was now 11:00 a.m. Jackman would amend his report as soon as he could talk with the victim.

Murphy would have to wait.

"Are any of these people dead?" Murphy asks Kelly, referring to the list as he hands it back.

"Two."

"Which ones?"

"One of the shootings. Twenty-year-old punk shot by a nineteen-year-old punk. We've already got the shooter in custody," says Kelly. "One of the stabbings, Vota's got it on his desk."

Murphy walks anxiously up to the squad room.

"Hey, Lou. I heard we got a stabbing homicide last night."

"Latin kid named Pacheco, drug thing; I've got Mendez out on it. He'll call if he needs us. Meanwhile, we have a shitload of other overnights to follow up," says Vota, handing Murphy half the stack. "Grab a seat."

"Is Sam coming in?" asks Murphy.

"Don't know yet. Something wrong Tommy? You look worried."

Jesus, is it that fucking obvious.

"My mother is planning to feed cabbage to Ralph today. Last time she did, he almost blew out my car windows on the way home."

Lieutenant Samson is feeling well enough, and guilty enough, to finally drag himself to Brooklyn, arriving at the Precinct before three.

"Which one of you guys would like to get out of here first?" asks Samson, coming into the squad room.

"Let Tommy loose, he needs to pick up Ralph and get to his mother's," says Vota. "Mrs. Murphy is preparing Ralph's favorite dish."

Murphy manages to choke out a thank you and heads out.

At 3:20, Officer Rey Mendez calls in with a lead in the lethal stabbing of José Pacheco.

Mendez had a tip from his informant, Stump.

The suspect in the Pacheco stabbing is Dwayne Harris, who was known to Mendez as a twice-convicted drug dealer and lives at the Marlboro Projects on 86th Street.

Vota leaves to meet Mendez at the apartment complex.

Samson remains to man the squad room.

At 3:30, Samson gets a call from Kelly.

"There's a woman here to see you, Lieutenant," Kelly says. "She claims she's a newspaper reporter and that it has to do with the Ventura and Addams cases."

"Send her up," says Samson.

Fuck.

At 3:40, Mendez is rapping at a door of an apartment at the Marlboro Projects with Vota beside him. After more knocking and no answer Mendez tries: *Police, open up.*

The gun blast is quickly followed by a bullet that tears through the door and catches Mendez in his right side. Vota watches Mendez go down hard and thinks about kicking in the door. Instead he pulls out his cell phone and calls for backup and an ambulance.

At ten-to-four, Murphy and Ralph are greeted by his mother with news that Samson needs him to call right away.

"Tommy, sorry to blow your day entirely, but I'm in a jam. I have a situation here at the Precinct that I have to deal with. Lou is out with Mendez and I need you over at Coney Island Hospital. Ask for Officer Jackman."

"Jackman?" says Murphy.

He is trying to sound as if he never heard the name.

"We've got a street stabbing that was just upgraded to a homicide."

"I'm on my way," says Murphy.

Fuck.

"Where's Michael, Mom?"

"I don't know, he left about an hour ago. He said he would be back by the time you got here."

"Listen, Mom, I have to go. I'm sorry. Is it okay if I leave Ralph?"

"Sure. Somebody's got to help me eat all of this food."

"I'm sorry, Mom, really."

"It's okay son, be careful."

"And Mom, when Mike gets back, keep him here if you have to sit on him to do it."

"Can you tell me how you obtained your information, Ms.

253

Huang?" asks Samson.

"I can only tell you that I have most of it firsthand," Serena says. "I've seen both bodies."

"And what exactly do you want from me?"

Here goes, thinks Serena.

And then she spells it out.

At 3:58 p.m., three squad cars are screaming up 86ᵗʰ Street. An ambulance siren is blaring a few blocks behind.

Vota is holding Mendez in his arms, after kicking in the door and finding the apartment empty.

Vota uses his jacket to slow the bleeding.

At five, as testimony to the veracity of the adage *life goes on*, Ralph is gorging himself on corned beef and cabbage.

Lorraine DiMarco is swallowing another three aspirin.

Susan Graham is playing indoor tennis with Daniel Levanthal.

The Ventura family is visiting the cemetery.

George Addams is staring at his telephone.

Officer Landis is purchasing a movie ticket.

Frank Sullivan is preparing lentil soup.

Bobby Hoyle is shopping for new shoes.

Stevie Territo is looking for Sonny Colletti.

Murphy is searching for his brother.

And five-year-old Lucy Samson is sneaking her hand into the cookie jar.

Brenda Territo died shortly after five.

A brief story was reported on New York One, just after the 6:01 p.m. weather report.

Agent Winona Stone crosses from her television to the telephone and calls the 68ᵗʰ Precinct looking for details.

Lou Vota walks into the squad room, after riding to the

hospital in the ambulance with Mendez.

"Rey will be okay," he says, before Samson can ask.

"Thank God, how about Harris?"

"Went out the window," says Vota. "What happened to you? You look like you've seen a ghost."

"Worse than that," says Samson. "I've seen a reporter. Somehow she put the Ventura and Addams cases together."

"Fuck."

"Tell me about it."

"What did you tell her?"

"I asked her to hold off for a few days. I had to throw her a few bones."

"Did she agree to wait?"

"She said that she'll give us until Wednesday."

"Fuck," says Vota.

"Tell me about it."

Ripley watches his youngest boy attempting to open his mouth much wider than anatomy will allow. It calls to mind the age-old advice, *never eat anything larger than your head.*

"How about I cut those into smaller pieces for you, Mickey?" he asks.

"Okay."

"Dad?"

"Yes, Kyle?"

"How do they get the cheese inside the raviolis?" asks his oldest.

What happened to the easy questions, like why is the sky blue, thinks Ripley, just as the telephone rings.

"I'll be right back, son, and we'll figure it out," he says.

"Ripley, it's Stone. I'm sorry to bother you at home on a Sunday."

"I imagine you would be."

"Tony Territo's teenage daughter was assaulted in front of her house last night. The rest of the family was out of town. She died this afternoon."

"That's a terrible story, Stone, and I grieve for her family. Why exactly are you telling me this?"

"I spoke with the investigating detective, Andrew Chen from the 68th Precinct in Brooklyn. You can understand why the incident piqued my curiosity."

"Sort of."

"When Chen took the call, I introduced myself as FBI. Before I could say another word he says: *If this is about the two boys who were killed last week, you'll need to speak with Lieutenant Samson at the 61st.*"

"What two boys who were killed?"

"I didn't ask; I wanted to talk to you first," says Stone. "I told him that we were already working with the lieutenant, and I stressed that it was very important to keep our involvement quiet."

"Jesus, Stone, what made you say that?"

"I don't know, instinct. Something in Detective Chen's voice, something that told me he wasn't surprised to be getting a call from the Bureau. I quickly changed the subject and asked about the Territo girl."

"And just how did you explain the FBI interest in that particular incident?" asks Ripley.

"I asked if she had been sexually assaulted. I said that we were working on a case that might involve a serial rapist. And again, I swore him to silence."

"You never cease to amaze me, Stone."

"So, I got what details I could about the Territo girl. They have reason to believe that her attacker was waiting for her to arrive home. The front gate lock was tampered with, so she couldn't get in."

"*Was* she sexually assaulted?"

"No, but someone came along during the attack, so whatever her assailant had in mind was interrupted."

"Any suspects?"

"None. Only a word or a name, sunny or Sonny. And a witness who saw a silver Porsche."

"So, what are you thinking, Stone?"

"I'm thinking it's intriguing that we're looking into this guy Territo and then suddenly his daughter is attacked and killed."

"Intriguing?"

"Coincidental, whatever. And I'm thinking there's something else going on in Brooklyn that we may need to know more about."

"Let's pay a friendly visit to Lieutenant Samson on Tuesday morning and ask him about the two boys who were killed," suggests Ripley. "Then we can decide whether or not it should concern us. We can talk about the Territo girl afterwards."

"Why not tomorrow?"

"Because tomorrow is Presidents' Day and you recall what I told you about working on a federal holiday. And I'd like to spend the day with my boys, who will be home from school tomorrow. And if the lieutenant has children of his own, he'll likely want to do the same. I could probably come up with a few more reasons if pressed."

"Those will suffice."

"I'll call the 61st on Tuesday morning, make sure that Samson is in," says Ripley. "Then I will call you."

"Roger that," says Stone. "Over and out."

"How are you guys doing?" asks Ripley, returning to the supper table.

Mickey is trying to figure out how to keep his straw from flopping around in his glass of milk.

"I got it," says Kyle, proudly.

"Got what, son?"

"They make two pieces of ravioli and put the cheese in between and then stick the pieces together."

"That's exactly what they do," says Ripley.

"Where's the Scotch tape, Daddy?" asks Mickey, still trying to solve the straw problem.

"They don't use Scotch tape on raviolis, silly," says Kyle, "they use Elmer's."

Gabriel Caine writes the note in green crayon, on the blank side of a sheet of yellow construction paper that he finds on the floor of his son's room.

On the other side of the sheet of paper is a crude drawing, something that a five-year-old scribbled. Something that an adult could never understand.

He places the sheet into a manila envelope.

He takes the plastic bag, which holds the girl's star sapphire ring, and drops it into the envelope also.

The ring would have to do.

TWENTY TWO

Monday morning. Presidents' Day.

Lorraine DiMarco wakes up with a terrible headache. Her operation is eight days away. She has to talk with Lou Vota.

Soon.

Murphy can't locate his brother, and he isn't too sure what he would do if and when he did. Kenneth Wolfe is deceased, and Michael is Murphy's prime suspect.

Mendez is alive, but would be off his feet for at least a week. He is recovering after the removal of a .38 caliber slug from his right abdomen, which missed his stomach by less than an inch.

Vota is on the streets trying to hunt down Dwayne Harris, wanted for questioning in the lethal stabbing of José Pacheco and the shooting of Officer Mendez.

Landis along.

Samson has decided to go into Brooklyn on the holiday after all. Drop in to see his father at the nursing home, and then check in with Kelly at the Precinct.

Samson also plans to visit Officer Mendez at the hospital, and he wants to be close at hand if there is any word on the suspect, Dwayne Harris.

Samson is being massacred in a game of checkers when his cell phone rings.

"Addams is ready to talk, Lieutenant," says Rosen.

"About what?"

"About not stopping to help someone in trouble."

"Do me a favor, Rosen. Get hold of Detective Chen at the 68th and have him accompany you out to see Addams," says Samson. "I have a few things to take care of. If I don't hear from you first, I'll call you at the Addams place."

. . .

259

Vota and Landis are headed up to another apartment very similar to the one outside of which Mendez had been shot. They had been told that Dwayne Harris might be there, taking sanctuary with his girlfriend.

Samson leaves his father and heads to his car. He calls in to the Precinct as he walks. Kelly tells Samson where he can find Vota and Landis—Landis had called in their location before they entered the apartment building. They hadn't asked for backup, but Samson is tempted to check it out. Samson decides that he will wait until he reaches his car to choose whether to visit Mendez at the hospital or see about Vota and Landis.

When Vota and Landis come off the stairwell onto the fifth floor, a young woman is leaving the apartment where Harris is said to be hiding. Vota quickly approaches her. Before she knows what's happening, Vota is behind her with his left arm across her chest and his right hand covering her mouth. The fear momentarily leaves her eyes when she finally notices Landis in his uniform, and instantaneously returns when she understands the new set of circumstances. Vota eases her out of the hallway and back into the stairwell; Landis remains against the wall to the right of the apartment door.

"Is Harris in the apartment?" Vota asks the woman. "Shake your head, yes or no."

Nod. Yes.

"Where?" asks Vota. "Be specific and speak softly."

"In back, in the bedroom."

"Alone?"

Nod. Yes.

"Okay, I'm going to take your keys. We are going back to the door and I am going to let myself in. You will not have to go in, but if Harris responds to the door opening you will call to him that you forgot something. If you do anything to alert him, I cannot guarantee your safety and you will be guilty of aiding an alleged murderer."

The woman's eyes are the size of grapefruits.

"Do you understand?" Vota asks.

Nod, yes.

"Okay, I'm going to let you go now. Don't be foolish."

Vota releases her. He waits for her to hand him the keys, asking her to identify the one he needs. He asks her to try remaining calm as he ushers her back out into the hall and toward Landis at the apartment door, holding her elbow with his left hand and the key in his right. At the door, he transfers her elbow into Landis' hand, transfers the key to his left hand and draws his service revolver with his right. Landis moves with the girl to the left of the door and Vota carefully pushes the key into the door lock. They all hear the TV come to life on the other side of the door before he turns the key.

"Fuck," mouths Vota, moving away from the door.

He motions for Landis to follow with the girl toward the stairs.

The three duck into the stairwell.

"Get her out of the building and call for backup. Get to the rear of the building and see if there is another way out. Fire escape, whatever. I'll wait and watch the door from here," says Vota.

Landis heads down with the girl and Vota turns his attention back to the apartment door, keeping out of the hallway.

The keys still dangle from the door lock.

The television blares from inside.

Fuck.

When Landis and the girl get down to the ground-floor lobby, Samson is walking in.

"Put her in the car and stay with her until backup arrives," Samson says, whoever she was and for whatever reason Landis had her by the arm. "Tell them to be quiet coming in."

"Lou asked me to check the rear," says Landis, as Samson moves past them toward the stairs.

"I just did, unless this asshole can fly there's only one way out of there," Samson says and starts up.

. . .

So, of course, when Murphy walks into the Precinct, he is on his way up to an empty squad room.

Desk Sergeant Kelly, sitting at his throne, looks up and asks, "Where the hell have you been?"

Murphy could say he's been trying to find his brother who, by the way, knifed someone to death recently.

"You writing a book?" he says instead, and heads up to the third floor.

Two minutes later, he is buzzing the desk.

"Kelly, where the fuck is everybody?"

"Samson went to the hospital, maybe, Vota and Landis are busy hunting the slime who shot Mendez, Chen and Rosen are out on a call."

"Chenanrosen?"

Kelly says, "You can read all about it in the fucking book I'm writing," and hangs up.

"What the fuck is a chenanrosen?" Murphy says as he places the receiver down and the phone rings.

Vota wheels around, gun ready, reacting to the sound behind him.

"A little jumpy, Lou?" says Samson.

"Fuck yes, I'm a little fucking jumpy, this guy shoots through doors. How the fuck did you get here so fast?"

"Took the Belt Parkway. Used my siren."

"What do you want to do?"

"I don't know, Marty, what do you want to do?"

"I want to get this scumbag."

"Okay, Lou, let's go get him."

"Homicide, Detective Murphy speaking."

"Lieutenant Samson, please."

"He's not here. Perhaps I can be of assistance," says Murphy to the woman caller.

"I'm calling about Addams."

"Addams who, Miss?"

"It's Detective, Detective Rosen, Detective."

"Addams is detective detective rosen?"

"I'm Detective Rosen, not *Miss*. And George Addams is the father of the boy found murdered in Bay Ridge. Where have you been?"

What the fuck is this? Do I need this?

"Talking with my desk sergeant about a book that he's writing," says Murphy. "Listen Rosen, excuse me, I mean Detective Rosen, I think that we got started on the wrong foot. Maybe if you could quickly fill me in I could be of some help in Lieutenant Samson's absence."

I seriously doubt it.

"I guess it's worth a try. Chen and I are with George Addams."

"Hold it, I've got another call."

"How do you want to play this?" asks Vota as they approach the apartment door.

"I don't know that play is quite the right word, but putting semantics aside for the moment I say we knock on the door and if he shoots through the door we shoot back through the door," says Samson.

"Just like that?"

"You got a better idea?"

"Nope."

"Okay then, let's do it."

"By the way, Sam."

"Yes?"

"*Play it* was only a figure of speech."

Samson takes the left of the door, Vota takes the right.

Samson knocks. No answer. Vota is thinking it seems so foolishly familiar, they may as well leave originality to the screenwriters.

"Police, open up," is what he says.

And then three bullets rip through the door from the inside and both detectives step out and face the door and each discharge six rounds through the door from the outside and then they retreat to their positions on each side of the door and reload.

And then they wait.

"It's your dime," says Murphy answering the second phone line, Rosen put on hold.

"My dime, your ass," says Kelly. "Just thought you might be interested to know that Samson is up with Vota on the Harris bust. Landis just called in."

"Shit. How come I miss all the fun? They need me up there?"

"I hope not. They got the troops from the 68th heading over. Just letting you know is all, so you don't get too worried everyone went to Hawaii and left you behind."

"You're all heart, Kelly. Truth is that those guys couldn't find the bathroom without me, let alone Hawaii."

"I'll give you that. No one in this place has trouble finding the bathroom with you around," are Sergeant Kelly's last words before disconnecting. Murphy suppresses a laugh as he goes back to line one.

"Okay, Rosen, where were we?" he says into a dead phone. Shit.

Murphy puts down the receiver and the phone instantly rings.

"This is Rosen; you didn't hang up on me purposely. Am I right?"

"Sorry, yes. I mean yes, you're right. I didn't hang up on you; I must have pushed the wrong button."

"You're pushing all the wrong buttons, Detective. Now, would you like to hear about what Addams had to say?"

"I'm all ears, go ahead. Whoa, I got another call."

"Well, what now?" asks Vota.

"Kick in the door?" says Samson.

"Your turn, I did one yesterday."

"How convenient."

"We could shoot more holes in the door and squeeze right

through."

"I have an idea," says Samson, "why don't we just use those keys dangling there."

"Homicide, Murphy speaking."

"Tommy."

"Mike, I've been looking all over for you, you little fuck. Where the hell are you?"

"I'm scared, Tommy."

"Just tell me where you are and wait for me there. I swear to God, Mike, you better not fuck around with me now."

"They find the guy I stabbed?"

"Yeah, where are you?"

"Is he dead?"

Yes, he's fucking dead.

"No, Mike, he's okay. He's at Coney Island Hospital. Now, please tell me where you are."

"Why the fuck would they take him to Coney Island with Beth Israel only a block away?"

"What?"

"You could spit at the emergency entrance to Beth Israel from the spot where I stabbed that guy. Why the fuck would they take him all the way out to Coney Island? You're bullshitting me Tommy, the guy is dead. Oh Christ, I killed the guy."

And then the line goes dead.

Four uniformed officers with riot guns rush up behind Samson and Vota as they step through the door and look down at a very dead Dwayne Harris.

"Wow, I can't believe this fucking worked," says Samson.

"That's an understatement. I'll bet we hit him with ten out of twelve," says Vota.

"Oh, I don't know. Seven, maybe eight tops."

"Fifty bucks says it's ten."

"You're on," says Samson.

. . .

"Fucking fuck," shouts Murphy. Then, remembering the other call, Murphy hits the button for the other line. "Rosen, are you there?"

Nothing.

Great.

"I can't believe this guy," Rosen says to Andy Chen. "He hung up on me again."

"Bet you can't wait to meet him."

"Detective Rosen?"

"Yes, Mr. Addams," she says.

"Lieutenant Samson is on the phone for you."

Murphy is almost out the door of the Homicide squad room, heading down to get the crime reports from Kelly to find out who Mike had actually stabbed if it wasn't poor Kenneth Wolfe who died at Coney Island Hospital, when the phone rings again.

"Jesus, Rosen, I'm sorry."

"Tommy? This is Lorraine. Is Lou there?"

"No, Lorraine. He's out on a call with Sam."

"Anything dangerous?"

"Oh, no. Not at all. Should be back soon. Can I give him a message for you?"

Sure, tell him I have a brain tumor.

"No, that's alright. Just called to say hello."

"How are you?"

"Great, thanks." *Just peachy.* "And you?"

"Yeah, fine, great." *Fucked.*

"Great."

"Okay, I gotta run."

"Okay, then, so long, Tommy."

"Okay, right, later, Lorraine."

. . .

After the shoot-out that left Dwayne Harris a dead alleged murderer, Samson leaves for Mill Basin to meet Chen and Rosen while Vota heads back over to the Precinct to do the paperwork on Harris.

The evidence team at the scene would hopefully find proof that Harris was actually the man who stabbed José Pacheco to death and shot Rey Mendez. It had already been established, in any event, that Harris had been hit with eight bullets, making Samson fifty dollars richer.

Rosen had asked Samson to meet them at a diner near the Addams house.

"Why here?" asks Samson, finding Chen and Rosen at the counter.

"Addams pleaded that we leave before his wife got home and found us there. Apparently he's not ready to tell his wife what he told us," says Chen.

"Which was?"

"That he drove past a car that had gone off the Belt Parkway and then drove past a man walking on the parkway," says Rosen. "And that the man was carrying something, which may have been a child."

"Jesus," says Samson. "What was his excuse for that?"

"He had none, beyond running very late on his delivery route that morning. He claims that he never thought about it being a child until your speech the other day," Rosen says. "Addams says that he did call it in, and felt sure that help was on the way."

"When was this?"

"We found that a call came in on the 16th of January. A car off the road near the Bay Parkway entrance, which is where Addams saw the vehicle," says Chen. "A squad car and a tow truck were both dispatched. When the police officers arrived, there was no one there. They wrote up a traffic citation, put it on the windshield and left."

"Brilliant," says Samson.

"They're running down the citation," says Rosen. "I'm expecting a callback with a car make and license number."

"How about the tow truck?" asks Samson.

"We're trying to track down a driver."

"Good work, how will you hear back?"

"Everyone has my cell phone number," says Rosen, "and your number at the Precinct."

"Let's all go back to the 61st and wait," says Samson.

Murphy goes through the crime reports once again and this time finds the right one. A man with two superficial knife wounds had walked himself into the emergency room at Beth Israel at 2:30 a.m. the previous morning. He reported being mugged, resisting his assailant, receiving the wounds and lying still on the ground until his attacker left the scene. He wasn't badly hurt, but played possum for fear of further harm. An ER nurse treated his wounds and he was interviewed by a uniformed officer. He said he was pretty sure that he could identify the perpetrator and was sent home with an invitation to come into the Precinct at his earliest convenience to work with a sketch artist on a composite drawing. He was expected to come in early Tuesday afternoon. The good news was that Murphy's brother was not a murderer, only an armed robber. The bad news was Michael didn't know that and Murphy had no way of telling him.

Vota gets back to the squad room as Murphy is walking out.

"Lorraine called," says Murphy, "to say hello. What went down with Harris?"

"He went down," says Vota. "It was like Dodge City."

"Where's Lieutenant Earp?"

"He went to meet Chen and Rosen."

"Who the hell are Chen and Rosen?"

"Andrew Chen from the 68th and Sandra Rosen from the 63rd. They're coming in with us and Ivanov on a special unit. There's a meeting tomorrow afternoon. Don't you read your memos?"

"Only when they're about free basketball tickets. What

time tomorrow?"

"Two. Where are you headed?"

"Family business," is all Murphy says before leaving the squad room.

Later that afternoon they sit in the squad room at the 61st, waiting for someone's phone to ring.

Samson, Vota, Rosen and Chen.

"I almost forgot, Lieutenant Samson," says Chen. "I meant to ask you earlier. When did the FBI come in on the case?"

"What are you talking about?" says Samson.

"I got a call from an Agent Stone. She said that they were already working with you, Lieutenant."

"Now, why would she say that, when I've never heard of the woman?" asks Samson.

"The FBI called specifically asking about this case?" asks Vota.

Not exactly, thinks Chen.

And then he realizes that he has fucked up, royally.

"As I recall," Chen says.

And he decides not to mention Agent Stone's interest in the death of Brenda Territo.

"Damn. Trenton said that he would warn me before he contacted the Feds," says Samson.

"When were you planning to warn me?" asks Vota.

Before Samson can respond, Rosen's cell phone rings.

"A 1986 Oldsmobile Ninety-Eight," Rosen says after taking the call.

"Jesus, that's the one," says Vota.

"The tow truck driver is off until Thursday afternoon. No answer at his home," says Rosen. "They'll keep trying."

"This is our man," shouts Samson, slamming his hand down on the desk. "I can feel it. Did you get a license plate number on the Oldsmobile?"

"Yes," says Rosen.

"Give it to Vota. Lou, call in to the DMV and get a name and address," says Samson.

"They're closed, Sam."

"It's not even three-thirty."

"It's a holiday."

"A holiday is the last fucking thing this is," says Samson. "Find someone who can give us a fucking name, Lou. Chen, find out where that tow truck driver lives and sit on the place until he shows up. Rosen, find out if there were any other emergency calls that night, in the vicinity of Bay Parkway and the Belt. And locate Paul Ventura, find out if he was anywhere near the area in his taxicab at the time. I'm going to phone Trenton and ruin his holiday if he doesn't have a damn good answer as to why the FBI is asking questions. This is the first solid lead that we've got since this nightmare began; I want it to fucking lead somewhere. Where the hell is Tommy?"

"He took off," says Vota. "He said that he had family business."

"Find him."

Chen, Rosen and Vota all quickly grab telephones as Samson storms out of the squad room to try cooling off.

Murphy has called his mother three or four times looking for his brother, Michael. No luck.

He is working on his second bourbon with beer chaser at Joe's Bar and Grill when his cell phone rings.

"Mike, where the fuck are you?"

"It's Lou, Tommy," says Vota. "I'm at the Precinct and Sam is looking for you. And he's on a rampage."

"Great," says Murphy. "Tell him I'm on the way."

"Something going on with Michael?"

"Tell Sam I'm on the way," is all Murphy says before ending the connection.

Samson finds a phone at an empty desk on the second floor.

He tries to keep the anger from his voice.

"I'm telling you, Sam. I never contacted the FBI," insists Chief of Detectives Trenton, dragged away from a dinner party by Samson's call.

"Then how the fuck did they catch on?"

"I don't know. Do you want me to find out?"

"No, leave it alone."

"What's going on, Sam?"

Samson fills Trenton in.

"Keep me informed," says Trenton.

"When are you going to get a captain assigned here," says Samson. "I'm not getting paid enough to be running this fucking place."

"Sam, you know that I'm trying to get *you* that job. And if you break this case before someone else is killed, there is nothing stopping you from being Captain of the 61st."

"Thanks for the warning, Chief," says Samson before hanging up.

When Samson returns to the squad room, Chen is gone. Rosen and Vota are waiting.

"Okay, whoever wants to start," says Samson.

"There *was* a second call that night," says Rosen. "A woman, Hannah Bowers, 26th and Cropsey. Not far from the parkway, close to where Addams saw the man walking. Bowers called reporting a car accident. I'm waiting to hear from the officers who responded."

"Forget waiting, I want you to go talk with the woman as soon as we're done," says Samson. "What about Ventura?"

"His last fare that night was to 25th and Bath, around 3:00 a.m. Then he headed to the Belt Parkway service road to Ocean Parkway and home," says Rosen.

"He'd go right past the Bowers place," says Samson.

"Ventura remembers a man trying to flag him down, he said he was really tired and forgot to light his off-duty sign at the last drop," says Rosen. "When he spotted the guy waving, he turned the sign on and drove by."

"Dear God," says Samson.

"The Olds is registered to a Gabriel Caine," says Vota. "I've got an address and a Social Security number."

"Where's Murphy?"

"On his way."

Samson picks up a phone and rings the front desk.

"What?"

"Kelly, when Tommy gets in, hold him there and buzz me."

"He's just walking through the door."

"Hold him there, I'm coming down," says Samson.

"Roger."

"Lou, I want you and Rosen to go see Hannah Bowers. Call me as soon as you speak with her," says Samson, "and give me that address for Caine."

"What's up, Sam?" Murphy asks when Samson gets down.

"Follow me, Tommy, we're taking a ride. Kelly, if Chen calls, give him my cell number."

Samson races out the door, Murphy close behind him.

In the car with Vota on the way to 26th Avenue, Rosen's cell phone rings. Officer Puglia from the 62nd Precinct.

"I heard you were asking about the January 16th call to the Bower's residence," he says.

"What can you tell me?"

"My partner and I arrived at 3:22," says Puglia, looking at his notes. "The Bowers woman would only speak to us through the door; she wouldn't let us into the house."

"Didn't you identify yourselves?"

"We really couldn't, except verbally. The woman said that she was blind, and alone, and afraid to open the door. She told us that a man had been there, shouting about a car accident and an injured child. She left him at the door and called it in."

"Did you find anything?"

"Nothing. We cruised the area, looking for the cars or someone needing help."

"Cars?"

"Bowers thought she heard the man say that another car hit him. If there were two cars involved, we couldn't find either. I did check the log afterwards; there was never an accident report that night for that vicinity."

"And you didn't check the parkway?"

"We were told there was another patrol car covering the parkway," says Puglia.

"Okay. Thanks for your help," says Rosen.

"Here we are," says Vota. "Well?"

"There was never an accident report filed that night, and there may have been another car involved," says Rosen. "Give me a minute. We may need to try getting a neighbor before we go up to the Bower's house."

"How's the family, Tommy," asks Samson as they get out of the car.

"Fine, and yours?"

"Is there some family business you need to be dealing with instead of being here?"

"No."

"Good. In that case, be here."

"I'm here, Sam."

"Good. Let's look around for the Oldsmobile before we go to the house."

Rosen has enlisted the help of a woman from the house next door. Vota and Rosen wait at Hannah Bower's door as the neighbor knocks.

"Yes?"

"Hannah, it's Sadie. There are two police detectives here who need to talk with you."

They hear the door being unlocked from the inside.

Murphy and Samson stand at the door. They couldn't find an Oldsmobile on the street fitting the description. Samson rings the doorbell.

A moment later, a man opens the door and steps out onto the front porch.

"Can I help you?" he says.

"Gabriel Caine?" asks Samson.

"There's no Gabriel Caine here."

"Would you mind showing us ID?" asks Murphy, showing the man his shield.

"Not at all," says the man, reaching for his wallet.

"Thank you, Mr. Lowry," says Murphy, after checking the ID and handing it back. "Sorry for the inconvenience. We had this address from an automobile registration and needed to check it out."

"Maybe he's a former tenant, I've been here almost a year and I still haven't gotten around to changing the address on some of the credit cards I never use," says Lowry. "I can give you the phone number of the property managers; maybe they know where Caine moved to."

"That would be great," says Samson. "Thank you."

"Very cooperative," says Murphy as they walk away.

"It happens occasionally," says Samson.

"Did the man say something, mention a name, anything that might help identify him?" asks Vota.

"I can't remember," says Hannah Bowers. "I don't think so."

"Anything that sounded like Gabriel or Caine?"

"Gabriel Caine. We met a Gabriel Caine," says Bowers. "Saturday. He told us that he was a salesman, sent to the wrong address. My husband was here, Robert let him in to use the telephone."

"When will your husband be home again?" asks Vota.

"Tomorrow evening."

"Please have your husband call us as soon as he can. Here's my number," says Vota, placing a card into her hand and passing another one to the neighbor. "If you hear from Caine again, is there a way you could contact us?"

"I'll program your phone number into Hannah's speed dial, Sergeant Vota," says the neighbor, "and my number is programmed in also."

"Is Gabriel Caine dangerous?" asks Hannah Bowers. "He seemed like such a nice young man."

"I really don't believe that he is a danger to you," says

Rosen, "but we'll put a police car outside the house until we have a chance to talk with him."

Murphy phones the property management office as they drive back to the Precinct. The answering machine tells him that someone will be back at the office at nine in the morning.

Chen calls Samson's cell phone. A neighbor of the tow truck driver has told Chen that the family is out of town until Wednesday evening. Samson asks Chen to leave a business card with a note under the door and call it a day.

Samson and Murphy arrive back at the Precinct shortly after Rosen and Vota arrive.

The four sit in the squad room comparing notes and working out strategy for the next day.

"I'll have Chen making phone calls from his own desk at the 68th," says Samson. "I want him to keep trying the tow truck driver until he gets an answer. Chen will also be trying to get a change of address from the post office."

"Why isn't Detective Chen here now?" asks Vota. "We could have called it our Tuesday afternoon meeting and got it over with."

"The meeting tomorrow is still on. We need Ivanov to be with us, and she's unavailable today," says Samson. "Not to mention that Chief Trenton will probably join in."

"Sorry you mentioned it," says Murphy.

"Rosen, you'll go to the property management office to find out if they have a forwarding address on Caine. Thank God this damn holiday will be over; maybe we can find someone in this city at work," Samson continues. "Of course, he may have lived in more than one place since."

"Speaking of work," says Rosen, "we have a Social Security number. We should at least be able to find out where Caine is employed."

"Good idea," says Samson. "Remember one very

important thing. Finding Gabriel Caine is not enough. We need real evidence. We need to get into his place of residence and into his car. We will need search warrants, and they are not easy to get. All we really have now is circumstantial. We have nothing to prove that he killed anyone."

"You're not going to find an employer for this guy. And I think we can kill two birds with one stone," says Murphy.

"Which two birds are those?" asks Samson.

"I think we can find the address and get enough for a search warrant. Landis and I were planning to check back at the unemployment office in the morning, to follow up on what Victor Sanders said about seeing the guy there. If we can ID Caine as the man who bought the drugs from Sanders, I think we'll have what we need for a search. We'll have to find that asshole Sanders again—he's out on bail."

"I want you down there when they open the doors of that office in the morning, Tommy. Take Landis with you. We'll put out another APB on Sanders."

"Do we have a picture of this guy?" asks Murphy.

"A copy of his driver's license just came in," says Vota. "I have it on my desk."

"Everyone will do what they're supposed to do, in case the unemployment office doesn't pan out," says Samson. "But if Caine is getting checks sent, finding a current address is looking good."

"What are you and I doing in the morning, while all of this is going on?" asks Vota.

"I'll be right here, coordinating," says Samson. "Everyone will call in, regularly. As soon as we get an address, we'll cover the place and cover Caine's every movement until we can get a warrant."

"And me?" asks Vota.

"We don't know why Caine went off the road, but we can surmise, based on what Bowers thinks she heard and the rear damage to the Olds. Suppose he was hit by another vehicle, even though he didn't report it, for whatever reason," says Samson. "The Oldsmobile had a child carrier and a *Baby on Board* bumper sticker. The man who stopped at the Bower's home said that there was an injured child. Addams thinks he saw the man on the highway carrying what may have been a child. And remember what Father Donovan said. If there was a child seriously hurt, or killed, someone has to know about it. Find that someone. Check all the hospitals, Lou, starting with those closest to the accident. Find out who brought a child in on the 16th of January."

"The 16th? That was the night of my birthday."

"Well that's good to know, Tommy. Happy birthday," says Samson. "You should have told us sooner. We could have had some cake or something."

Murphy understands Samson's frustration and lets the comment pass.

"Let me see that driver's license photo, Lou."

Vota finds the photocopy and hands it to Murphy.

"Jesus, I was there. I saw this guy. In the ER at Coney Island Hospital. I was there with Augie Sena, the night he broke his leg."

Murphy looks at the photo of Gabriel Caine.

He can remember the man's vacant eyes.

"The guy was a total wreck. I stopped a doctor who I knew, asked what happened," says Murphy. "The child died."

The silence in the room lasts a good thirty seconds, and then it was shattered by the ringing phone.

Samson picks up.

"That was the 62nd Precinct, Lou. They finally traced the gun that killed Johnny Colletti. It belonged to him. I think that's good news for Lorraine's client. You might want to give her a call. Murphy, can you get over to the hospital, see what you can find out about the child. They may have the address we need on the father."

"Sure, Sam."

"Mind if I ride along?" asks Rosen.

"Not at all. Let's go," says Murphy.

"Call me as soon as you have something," says Samson as they head out. "I'll be right here."

Vota gives Lorraine a call.

Samson takes the opportunity to call home.

"I'm going to be late," Samson says to Alicia. "Don't hold

dinner."

"How late?"

"I don't know, I'll call you before I leave."

"Okay, be careful."

"Did the kids enjoy the day off from school?"

"For the most part. I'd better feed them. Call me."

After hearing from Vota, Lorraine calls Bobby Hoyle.

"I'll talk with the prosecutor in the morning," she says. "Maybe they'll drop the charges entirely."

"That's great news, Lorraine. Can I buy you a drink to celebrate?"

"Not tonight, Bobby, I have a lot of work." *And a whopper of a headache.* "Have one for me."

"Mind if I take off, Sam?" asks Vota. "You can call if you need me again tonight."

"Going to see Lorraine?"

"No, she's busy. And I'm wasted."

"Sure, go ahead, get some rest. Tomorrow is going to be a killer."

"Call if you need me," Vota says again before leaving.

Gabriel Caine collects the five one-hundred-dollar bills from the kitchen floor. He takes a small suitcase from in front of the side door before walking out to his car.

Samson is going stir crazy in the squad room.

The telephone rings.

"Sam, we got an address. 69th Street and Vista Place. It's less than a block from the Graham house," says Murphy. "We're on our way over there."

"Okay. Call as soon as you get there. Look for the Oldsmobile, but don't go near the house yet. I'll send a few unmarked cars over to meet you."

. . .

"Are you sure you can't have a drink with me, Ronnie? This bad dream may actually be over."

"I'd love to, Bobby, but I'm working the swing shift tonight," Ron Hoyle reminds his brother. "I'll take a rain check. Have one for me."

Gabriel Caine parks the Oldsmobile in the long term lot at LaGuardia Airport. He walks into the terminal and finds the ticketing counter.

He purchases a round-trip ticket for Tampa, Florida. He pays cash.

He has a few hours to wait for departure.

Clutching the ticket and the Bible in his free hand, he walks toward the concourse.

"No Olds. And the house looks empty," says Murphy.

"Did the other officers arrive?" asks Samson.

"Yes, two cars. I put one on 6th Avenue, at the near end of the back alley, and the other across and down from the house on 69th."

"Okay, make sure they understand that they're not to approach Caine. All they are to do is call us if they spot Caine coming in, follow and call if they spot him leaving."

"Caine has a wife and another kid," says Murphy. "What if they're inside—how will we know if they're alright?"

"Damn it. If we go in without a warrant, we could blow it entirely," says Samson. "Check with the neighbors, see if anyone knows about the wife and kid."

Ten minutes later Murphy calls back.

"Caine's wife and daughter left town a few weeks ago," says Murphy. "A neighbor says she went down to Florida to take a job with her father, a commercial realtor in Tampa."

"Thank God, that's a relief."

"Do you think Caine went down there?"

"It's a thought."

"The neighbor didn't have the father's name. I called the information in to One Police Plaza and they're going to try tracking her down. I gave them your home and cell phone numbers and both of mine. The two surveillance cars have the numbers also. I guess we wait."

"Thanks, Tommy," says Samson. "I'm going to head home while I have the chance. Why don't you do the same."

"Any luck finding Victor Sanders?"

"Not yet. Kelly is still here if anything breaks."

"Maybe I'll grab something to eat nearby, and check back with these guys before I head home," says Murphy.

"Whatever, just make sure you get some rest. There may not be many more opportunities," says Samson.

Bobby Hoyle comes out of his house starts to walk up West 12th Street, heading for the High Times Tavern over on Avenue U.

"Bobby," calls a voice from behind him.

Hoyle turns to find Frank Sullivan sitting on the front steps of the DiMarco house, two doors down.

"Hey, Sully," says Hoyle. "Care to join me for a drink up on Avenue U? I'm buying."

"No thanks, I've given it up," says Frank, rising to his feet. "But I wouldn't mind stretching my legs. I'll walk up with you, just to the bar door."

In the car parked across the street, the man behind the wheel watches Bobby and Sully walk away.

He decides that it would be best to wait until Hoyle returns.

"Are you hungry?" asks Murphy.

"Starving," says Rosen.

"How about I buy you dinner?"

"I'll have dinner with you. I'm not sure about you buying."

"There's a joint up on 5th. The food isn't half-bad."

"Sure, let's go," says Rosen. "We can order from the good half."

Stevie Territo stands in the shadows near the corner at Avenue T.

He calls Tony Territo's cell phone and finds his cousin at the funeral home, making final arrangements for Brenda's wake.

"He's still here, just sitting in his car, Tony," says Stevie.

"Stay on him, Steve," says Tony Territo. "I'm nearly done here."

"I wanted to apologize for all the telephone mishaps earlier today," says Murphy.

They are having coffee after dinner at the Ridge Diner on 5th Avenue.

"You would do better not reminding me," says Rosen.

"Reminding you about what?"

"So, are you the kind of guy who has birthdays that nobody remembers?" asks Rosen.

"Not really. I work with the kind of guys who have more important things on their minds. Not to suggest that my mother doesn't, but *she* remembered my birthday."

"That's good to hear."

"I need to check on the stakeout up the street," says Murphy, pulling out his cellular phone.

"Well?" says Rosen, after Murphy makes the call.

"Nothing doing. They're not going anywhere until the suspect or their relief shows up. They'll call if they need us. I guess we can hit the sack for a while. Where do you live?"

"Aren't you rushing things just a little, Detective?"

"I meant that we can take off, I can give you a ride home," Murphy stammers.

He's blushing, she thinks.

"My car is back at your Precinct," she says.

"Okay, then, I can give you a ride to your car," he says,

rising quickly and grabbing the guest check from the table. "Mind if I take care of this?"

"Go ahead. I get it next time."

Tony Territo parks his BMW behind Stevie's Jaguar on Avenue T.

He spots Stevie standing near the corner.

"Where is he?" Tony asks, walking up to his cousin.

"About halfway down the block, on this side. He's just sitting there in his car."

"Okay, thanks Steve. I owe you one. Get going, I'll take it from here."

"Be careful, Tony."

"Don't worry about me. I'm a survivor."

"So," says Murphy, letting Rosen out at her car.

"So," says Rosen.

"Drive safely."

"You do the same."

"I'll see you tomorrow."

"See you then," Rosen says, as she climbs in behind the wheel.

Murphy watches her pull away.

And he's feeling pretty good for a minute or two.

And then he remembers his brother.

Bobby Hoyle rises shakily from the bar stool at the High Times.

"I've had enough, Pete," he says to the bartender. "Have a good night."

"Are you going to be alright getting home?"

"I'm walking."

"I know that," says Pete, laughing kindly. "That's why I asked."

Bobby Hoyle staggers out to the street and stumbles the half block to 12th. As he walks toward his house, he sees a man walking toward him.

Bobby squints, but he can't focus, he can't seem to recognize the man's face. He waves and calls hello, in case it's someone he knows. As the man gets closer, he raises his arm and points it in Bobby's direction.

There is something in the man's hand that Bobby can't make out.

Bobby continues to walk toward the man, wearing a stupid smile.

Suddenly a voice from behind the man stops him.

"Sonny," the voice says.

Sonny Colletti begins to turn as the bullet rips into his shoulder, spinning him around to face the shooter.

Two more shots silently tear into Sonny's chest and Colletti's gun drops loudly to the ground.

Sonny's body collapses to the pavement beside it.

Tony Territo steps up to the body and puts another one into Colletti's head for good measure.

Territo turns and moves quickly back to his car.

Bobby finally finds his tongue and begins yelling for help.

Porch lights come on up and down the street.

Territo's car races away up Avenue T.

Bobby Hoyle stands frozen in his shoes as the first of the neighbors begin circling the body.

And the first police siren shouts out its approach.

And Detective Murphy has something to take his mind off his brother Michael again.

For a while.

The telephone rudely wakes Sammy Leone at one in the morning.

"Sammy, Sonny is dead," says Richie Colletti.

"What the fuck are you talking about?" asks Leone, shaking off sleep.

"He was shot, in Gravesend. It looks like he was there to take out the Hoyle kid."

"The Hoyle kid shot Sonny?"

"We don't know, the cops aren't saying much yet."

"What the fuck was Sonny thinking?"

"He was probably thinking about making points with the old man," says Richie. "My father is going nuts. He wants you over here at the house. Now."

"Try to calm him down, Richie, I'll be there in twenty minutes."

Leone quickly throws on clothing, rushes down to his car and climbs behind the wheel. Before he can start the engine, the silencer is pressed against his head.

"Put your hands on the dashboard and rest your head against the steering wheel, Sammy. Don't fuck around."

"Territo?"

"Do it, Sammy."

Leone complies.

"You're a dead man, Tony."

"Not yet, Sammy. Shut up and listen. I'm guessing you heard about Sonny. I know that you were with him when he murdered my daughter," says Territo, playing his hunch. "I want to know whose decision it was. Tell me if Dominic ordered it."

"You're out of your mind, we were only there to fuck up your car, the girl was already down. The old man doesn't even know about your daughter yet."

"It's a sin to tell a lie, Sammy. You might want to think about confession before it's too late."

"I'm telling you that you're wrong, Tony, and you're finished. When Colletti finds out that you killed his son you won't last ten minutes."

"How would he find out, Sammy?"

"I'm going to tell him, you fucking maniac, and I'm going to love breaking the news to him."

"Wrong answer, Sammy."

And then Territo puts a bullet into the back of Sammy Leone's head and climbs out of the back seat of the car.

Gabriel Caine takes a taxi from the airport.

The cab drops him in front of the large ranch house in suburban Tampa.

The house is dark.

He walks up to the door, a suitcase in one hand, the black cloth-covered book in the other.

He looks like a door-to-door Bible salesman, out way past bedtime.

He rings the doorbell.

A man answers the door.

"Gabriel?" says his father-in-law.

"I want to see my wife and daughter," Gabriel says, in a voice without inflection.

"Karen didn't tell us that you were coming. It's very late."

"I want to see my wife and daughter," Caine repeats.

"Come in," is all the man says.

Gabriel follows him into the dark house.

TWENTY THREE

All the well-thought-out strategy of the previous afternoon was unnecessary by Tuesday morning.

All they could really do now was to wait. Wait for Gabriel Caine to turn up. Wait for Victor Sanders to turn up. Wait for a search warrant.

There were surveillance teams stationed at Caine's address around the clock. Front and back. In six-hour shifts. Officers in plain clothes and unmarked cars from four neighboring precincts.

There were also cars at Victor Sanders apartment in Sunset Park and outside of his mother's house on East 3rd Street in Gravesend. And word on the street, using Stump and other police informants and assorted shady characters, that Sanders could expect a sweet deal in his impending drug trial if he showed his face.

All they could do was wait.

Samson walks into the Precinct at eight.

"Good morning, Washington," says Samson, coming up to the front desk. "Kelly finally get a day off?"

"Yes, and just in time the lucky bastard. The shit hit the fan."

"What happened?"

"You'll get it quicker if Murphy fills you in. He's up in the squad room," says the desk sergeant. "He's been here all night."

Samson takes the stairs three at a time.

"Damn," says Samson, "that's all we need right now is a fucking mob war."

"It's fucking pandemonium, Sam. It looks like Sonny Colletti was about to put one into Bobby Hoyle and someone came along and saved the kid's skin," says Murphy. "A few hours later they find Sammy Leone in his car, his brains all over the dashboard. Ballistics says it was the same gun that killed Sonny."

"Speaking of ballistic, Dominic Colletti is going to go insane," says Samson. "I want someone on Colletti and his other son twenty-four-seven."

"It's taken care of," says Murphy, "and Landis is on his way to speak with Bobby Hoyle. The kid was a basket case last night, not to mention falling-down drunk. Maybe he'll make a little more sense this morning. Landis has a couple of uniforms along to talk with neighbors."

"Damn. Fucking Italians."

"C'mon, Sam, they're not all bad."

"Go home and get some sleep."

"I thought you'd never ask," says Murphy, struggling out of his chair.

"And Tommy."

"Yes, Sam."

"You could have called me."

"Yes, Sam, I could have."

"Thanks."

"You're welcome."

"Gabriel, you look terrible," says his wife.

"I'm fine."

"You are far from fine. Listen. My father can cover for me at the office for a few hours, and Mom can watch the baby. Let's go out and have breakfast somewhere. We need to talk."

"There's nothing to talk about. I just wanted to see you and the girl again. To see you and Beth. I can't stay long. I have something I need to do."

"Is it a job?" she asks.

"Yes. Work."

"That's great. Let's go for breakfast, you can tell me about it."

"We'll take Beth. I want to be with her while I can."

. . .

Shortly after Murphy leaves, Samson's phone rings.

Sergeant Washington from down at the front desk.

"I hope this is good news," says Samson.

"Does word that there are two FBI Agents down here looking for you qualify?"

"Not exactly."

"Should I send them up?"

"As opposed to what, shooting them?"

"I'll send them up," says Washington.

Murphy lets himself in to his mother's house. Ralph almost knocks him to the floor in the doorway.

"Careful, pal, you might wake me up," says Murphy. "I can see you've been eating well."

"Is that you, Michael?" his mother calls from the back of the house.

"It's Tommy, Mom. Thanks for babysitting Ralph."

Where the fuck are you, Mike.

"Anytime, son, I enjoy the company," she says when Murphy walks into the kitchen. "Are you hungry?"

"No, Mom, but I could really use a few hours' sleep."

"Use the bed in your old room. The sheets are clean."

"Wake me at noon, Mom. Or if you hear from Mike."

Samson has filled the FBI Agents in on the details of the two murders, particularly their obvious similarities.

He has also run down the evidence, particularly the biblical references, and summarized what he and his team believe it reveals about the killer's motivation.

"We're almost positive that we have the perpetrator identified," Samson says. "Gabriel Caine, lives close to where we found the second victim. We're waiting for Caine to surface, and working on a warrant to search his place."

"He loses a child, and he takes children in return," says Ripley. "Do you have children, Lieutenant?"

"A teenage son and two daughters, eight and five."

"I have two boys, just about the same ages as your girls. And the Caine and Ventura boys?"

"Caine's son was five years old and Billy Ventura was eight," says Samson, considering the fact for the hundredth time.

"How horrible," says Winona Stone.

"Do you mind if I ask how you heard about the Ventura and Addams boys?" asks Samson.

"Does it really matter?" asks Ripley.

"I guess not," says Samson.

"Have you determined who Caine's next target might be?" asks Agent Stone.

"We believe the Bowers woman who turned him away that night is safe. Caine's visit to her home may have convinced him that she had pardonable reason, and she has no children. We're keeping an eye on the house."

"You said that Gabriel Caine never reported a two-car accident," says Stone, "that he never reported being hit by another driver."

"Right. But as I also said, we have reason to believe that there was another vehicle involved."

"If there was a second vehicle, then the other driver obviously didn't stick around to help Caine and the boy," says Agent Stone, "and never reported the accident either. Why not?"

"There are lots of reasons why people fail to report accidents, especially if they're responsible," says Samson, "and unfortunately there are people who walk away."

"I'd say that would make the other driver guilty of a hit-and-run, and would put him or her right at the very top of Caine's get-even list."

"That would suggest that he could identify the other driver. And that's what has been bothering me most," says Samson. "Why didn't Gabriel Caine report a second vehicle if there was one, particularly if we are assuming he could have identified the other driver to the police?"

"I think that Gabriel Caine decided very early on that what happened out there that night was not a matter for the police," says Ripley. "That he chose early on to place the matter into other hands."

"That may be true. And if it is, it's a very scary thought. But it doesn't help us much," says Samson. "I don't imagine someone is going to come forward this late and admit to leaving the scene of an accident."

"You've done a very good job of keeping the connection between these deaths out of the news," says Ripley, "and I certainly understand why you would choose to. But there are times when we can use the media to our advantage, and times when it's necessary. If there was another vehicle, and if you can get the driver to come forward..."

"We may be protecting a child's life," says Samson, completing the thought.

Just as his phone rings.

"Detective Chen is on the line for you, Lieutenant," says Washington. "He needs you over at St. Anselm's Church in Bay Ridge, right away. Something about another manila envelope."

"Tell Chen that I'm on the way. Ask him to try getting Father Donovan over there, with his Bible."

Samson grabs his coat and looks at the two agents.

"Do you have some time to kill?" he asks.

"Sure," says Ripley.

"Let's go," says Samson.

Samson stops at the front desk on the way out.

"If Landis calls, or anything comes in on the Colletti shootings, get in touch with Murphy," Samson tells the desk sergeant.

Ripley and Stone hurry out to the street after Samson.

"We'll take our car, Lieutenant," says Ripley. "We'll be right behind you."

"Did I hear him say Colletti shootings?" asks Stone as they follow.

"Yes you did," says Ripley, "but I think it might be best to wait a while before we bring it up."

Dominic Colletti is pacing the room like a wounded tiger.

He has not stood still since identifying his son's body hours earlier. Richie Colletti has just taken a phone call and approaches his father cautiously.

"Was that Sammy? Where the fuck is he?"

"Sammy is dead, Pop. He was shot in his car outside his place. Executed."

The old tiger is speechless.

"Who's doing this, Pop?"

The old man can hear the fear in his son's voice.

"I don't know. Puerto Ricans, the fucking Russians," says Dominic. "Sammy pushed a lot of people around."

"But why Sonny? And why did you send Sonny after the Hoyle kid?"

"I never sent Sonny there," yells Dominic. "Sammy was going to take care of Bobby Hoyle himself. Sonny went on his own, God knows why."

To fucking impress you, Richie thinks but won't say.

"What if it was Tony Territo?" asks Richie.

"What are you talking about?"

"What if someone saw Sonny and Sammy that night, when you sent them to trash Tony's car?" asks Richie. "What if Territo thinks we had something to do with what happened to his daughter?"

"Sonny was a made man. Even if Territo is insane enough to believe we'd hurt the girl, he knows if he hit Sonny he would have to deal with us *and* with John Giambi."

"If Tony Territo thinks that we had something to do with his daughter's death, he's not going to give a fuck about dealing with Giambi," says Richie. "And nothing is going to stop him from coming after us."

"Find his father. Now. Find Vincent Territo."

Samson, Ripley and Stone find them all in the rectory office. Chen, Father Donovan, and Father Santini, pastor of St. Anselm's.

Samson carries his black evidence case.

The manila envelope lies face down on the desk.

The plastic bag holding the finger lies on the floor near the desk.

Chen and the two priests stand looking down at the bag as if it had teeth.

"I didn't touch anything," says Chen.

"I can see that," says Samson.

The lieutenant pulls out a pair of latex gloves and an evidence bag and hands them to Agent Stone.

"Would you mind?" he asks.

"No. Not at all," says Stone, moving to retrieve the finger.

Samson slips on a pair of latex gloves and crosses to the desk. He turns the envelope face up. It is addressed to Father Santini, in blue crayon, canceled postage in the upper right corner. Before he gets to the contents, Samson notices the writing in the upper left-hand corner.

"Well I'll be damned," Samson says, forgetting for a moment that there are two priests in the room, "there's a return address."

"It's very close to here," says Father Santini over Samson's shoulder.

"Chen, get over there. Call as soon as you arrive," says Samson. "I need to bag this evidence."

"I can handle it, Lieutenant," says Stone. "I'll meet you and Agent Ripley there. Father Santini can show me the way."

"Thanks," says Samson, pulling off the gloves. "Chen, take Father Donovan with you, Agent Ripley can ride with me."

The four men rush out of the rectory.

Stone gets to work bagging the evidence.

Father Santini prays.

The large house sits on a corner lot, opposite Fort Hamilton High School's track and playing field. Samson immediately spots the realtor's sign on the lawn.

"Chen, call that phone number. Get permission from someone with authority to go into the house."

Ripley and Samson walk around the outside of the house in opposite directions while Chen makes the phone call.

Samson approaches the front entrance.

Ripley peers through the back porch and can see the damage to the kitchen door.

"Do we need someone from the realty office down here?" Chen calls out.

"No," yells Samson, "just get a verbal okay."

"Okay," shouts Chen a moment later.

"Back here, Lieutenant," calls Ripley.

"Chen, cover the front door," says Samson as he heads for the rear. "Father Donovan, please stay where you are."

Agent Stone and Father Santini arrive at the scene.

Samson takes out his weapon as he reaches Ripley.

Ripley does the same as they step into the house.

Ten minutes later they are all crowded into the bathroom.

The number 291421 is written on the wall above the bathtub in blue crayon.

"He was planning to bring another victim here," says Samson.

"He still may be," says Ripley.

"This is from Isaiah, Chapter 14, Verse 21," Father Donovan says, consulting his Bible, "*The offspring of the wicked will leave no name behind them. Start slaughtering the sons for the guilt of their fathers. Never again must they rise to conquer the earth and spread across the face of the world.*"

"Why the water in the bathtub, Father?"

"I don't know."

"Chen, call in a forensic team," says Samson, "and we need a few cars watching this house until Caine is found."

"How about this, Lieutenant?" says Stone, holding the large plastic evidence bag that holds the manila envelope.

"Let's have a look," says Samson, reaching for the bag.

Samson removes the note and places it into a separate clear bag. It is written on the inside of a torn coloring book jacket. In crayon.

Samson hands the note to Donovan.

"Would this explain the filled bathtub, Father?"

"Yes, Lieutenant, it would." says Donovan. "It could also explain the use of the drug you mentioned, which I was told had an effect similar to being submerged in water."

"You've lost me, Lieutenant," says Stone.

Father Donovan hands Agent Stone the note.

"It's from the Gospel of Saint Mark," the priest says.

Stone reads the note aloud, "*Go out in the whole world and proclaim the Good News to all creation. He who believes and is baptized will be saved; he who does not believe will be condemned.*"

Gabriel had said very little to his wife at breakfast. She had tried talking, and asking him about the work he had mentioned. All he would say was that he had a job to do. And that it was good work.

Gabriel stares silently at his infant daughter. Pure and without sin. When would she take her first steps, and who would see to it that her innocence was not lost.

After breakfast they leave the restaurant on Bayshore Boulevard, leave her car parked in front, and walk to the end of Baypointe Circle, Gabriel pushing the child's stroller. They sit at a bench, looking out over Tampa Bay.

In silence.

Karen tells her husband that she has to be getting to work. They walk the short distance to her office.

"Here are the car keys," she says to Gabriel. "Can you find your way back to the house?"

"I can," he says.

Karen walks into her office.

Gabriel Caine walks back toward the Bay, to the water, pushing Beth in the stroller ahead of him.

Samson asks Chen to stay at the house, to wait for and remain with the evidence technicians.

Two unmarked cars arrive, carrying officers in street clothing sent to cover the first surveillance shift.

Father Donovan walks back to Our Lady of Angels.

Stone drives Father Santini back to St. Anselm's.

Ripley and Samson talk on the corner of the street, waiting

for Stone to return for Ripley.

"Using pancuronium bromide to baptize his victims, that's way out there," says Samson.

"Caine is far past being rational," says Ripley. "I find it much more fascinating that the man has chosen to administer the sacrament, by whatever means. In his mind, he is protecting the souls of innocents."

"Would you and Agent Stone care to join us for our meeting at two?" Samson asks. "Everyone working on the case will be there. I could treat you both to lunch before we go back to the Precinct."

"I appreciate the offer, Lieutenant, but I have a mountain of work on my desk and you have things well in hand. And here's Agent Stone now. Please, don't hesitate to call us if you feel we can help in any way."

"Good meeting you," says Samson, surprised to be saying it.

"Same here," says Ripley, thankful not to be in the other man's shoes.

Stone pulls the car up to the curb where Lieutenant Samson and Ripley are standing. She watches the two men shake hands.

Samson crosses to his car as Ripley climbs into the passenger seat beside Stone.

"Did you happen ask him about the so-called Colletti shootings?" asks Stone.

"I like the guy, and he has enough on his mind," says Ripley. "I'd rather try finding out through other channels before we bother Samson."

"Understood. Do you have a second hand on your wristwatch?"

"As a matter of fact I do."

"Time me," says Stone. "Ready?"

"Go."

Stone crosses Narrows Avenue, turns right at the next intersection, Shore Road, continues to the next street and stops.

"We're here," she says. "Time?"

"Forty-two seconds," says Ripley. "Where is *here*?"

"Tony Territo's home."

"Are you serious?"

"Oh, yes," says Stone.

"I talked to Vincent Territo, Pop," says Richie. "He can see you at one-thirty. He can come out here and meet you on Emmons Avenue at Randazzo's Clam Bar. He needs to be back to his granddaughter's wake by two."

"Will it be safe?"

"Jesus, Pop, it's Randazzo's not Umberto's. In the middle of a Tuesday afternoon. Of course it's safe."

"Okay, I'll meet him at one-thirty," says Colletti. "And if he cannot convince me that his son had nothing to do with Sonny, I will hang Tony Territo from the flagpole of his car lot with John Giambi's blessing."

Murphy is having a dream. He is twelve years old. He watches as his father applies Mercurochrome to a nasty gash above Michael's eye, a result of a fall from the back-yard swing set. Two-year-old Michael is screaming wildly.

"How did you let this happen, Thomas?" asks his father as he works on the ugly cut. "Didn't I ask you to take care of your brother?"

Murphy feels as if he is being shaken.

"Michael?" he says aloud as he comes out of sleep.

"Thomas, wake up," says his mother. "It's noon. I've fixed lunch for you."

Stone and Ripley sit in a small Greek restaurant on Queens Boulevard, close to the Field Office. Stone had made a few calls as soon as she was back at her desk and came into Ripley's office looking like the winner of an Easter egg hunt. Ripley suggested they talk over lunch.

Agent Stone is trying to sell her theory to Ripley as if it

were the true deed to the Brooklyn Bridge. Stone is so involved; she has hardly touched the grilled octopus.

"Remember I told you that someone heard what sounded like the word sunny or the name Sonny at the scene where Brenda Territo was attacked."

"Vaguely," says Ripley, digging into the lemongrass.

"Dominic Colletti's oldest son was shot to death in Brooklyn last night, shot three times, and then one more to the head after he was down. Less than an hour later, Dominic Colletti's bodyguard, Sammy Leone, was shot in his car. Execution-style."

"Let me guess," says Ripley, "Dominic Colletti named his oldest boy Sonny."

"He sure did."

"And you reckon that if Tony Territo decided it was Colletti's son who assaulted his daughter, it makes Territo the front-runner in the Best Suspect category for the two executions."

"Wouldn't you agree?"

"Absolutely. But don't you think the Brooklyn detectives have already figured that out?"

"I'm sure they have."

"So then, what is this all about? Why are you letting your food get cold over this?"

"What if Sonny Colletti really had nothing to do with the assault," says Stone. "What if he was just at the wrong place at the wrong time?"

Ripley pushes his plate away and gives Agent Stone a hard look.

She is wearing a Cheshire cat smile.

"You think that Tony Territo's daughter was a victim of Gabriel Caine."

"You saw how close the assault was to the house across from the high school playing field."

"Why Territo?"

"What if Tony was the driver of the second vehicle?"

"Jesus, Stone. Is it that small a world?"

"It's Brooklyn."

"Let's try finding out if Territo had bodywork done on any

of his vehicles lately," says Ripley.

"I've already started making calls," says Stone. "Do you think they would warm up the octopus if I ask nicely?"

Officers DeRosa and Andrews sit in an unmarked car on Oriental Boulevard across from Dominic Colletti's home in Manhattan Beach.

"We finally get to wear plain clothes," says DeRosa. "And here we are, freezing our asses off babysitting this old dinosaur and his demented son."

"The view isn't bad," says Andrews, looking out over the beach to the Atlantic.

"I'm sure the view is a lot better from the window of the old fuck's living room," says DeRosa, looking up at the house. "Makes you wonder about crime not paying."

"How are you feeling, *amigo?*" says Landis, sticking his head through the doorway of the hospital room.

"Stop it, Landis," says Rey Mendez, holding his side as he sits up in the bed. "It hurts when I laugh."

"What's so damn funny?" asks Landis, walking in.

"It's the way you say *amigo*, Stan, you make it sound like a letter in the Greek alphabet. Did you stop at Alfredo's on your way over here?"

Landis reaches into his coat and pulls out the roast pork sandwich, wrapped in aluminum foil and still warm from Alfredo's San Juan Deli.

He tosses it over to his partner.

"Thank God," says Mendez, tearing at the tinfoil with both hands. "All they ever feed me in this place is boiled-to-death chicken and blue Jell-O. What the fuck flavor is blue supposed to be? Can you stick around for a while?"

"A short while, there's that big powwow at two. I'll come back later. Try not to swallow that thing whole."

Murphy finds Samson alone in the squad room.

"Are we still on for two?" asks Murphy.

"Yes. And Trenton will be here. I spent the morning with two Feds."

"That must have been a ball."

"It wasn't too bad. The SAC of the Brooklyn-Queens Field Office, Ripley, and his assistant. They were both very sharp. Ripley is no glory hound. In fact, I invited him to join us and he passed."

"Well, that's refreshing," says Murphy. "An FBI Agent who doesn't live and breathe to show us poor city cops how incompetent we are. What are you studying; did someone give you the answers to the Captain's exam?"

"Very funny. I'm studying Gabriel Caine's file from the unemployment office. He was laid off his job six months ago, his benefits are about to run out. He went to work for the company straight out of high school. Downsizing. Twelve years and so long, it's been good to know you. His wife was expecting any day, they lost their health insurance and they had just bought the house before he got the ax."

"Jesus," says Murphy. "Anything on the wife and the other kid?"

"An address for the wife's parents just came in. The Tampa PD is sending a car over there now."

Stretch Sacco parks the large car on the beach side of Oriental Boulevard, halfway between the Colletti house and Kingsborough Community College.

It is a late-model Mercedes sedan that looks as if it came off the assembly line a few days too soon. It is missing the grill, front bumper, both headlight assemblies, trunk lid, side view mirrors, passenger seat, door panels, back seat and nearly the entire dashboard.

Stretch reaches down for the plastic gasoline can.

He gives the inside of the car a thorough dousing.

A moment later, Stevie Territo pulls his Jaguar up beside the Mercedes.

Stretch gets out of the Mercedes and climbs in beside Stevie.

"Yo, Stevie," says Sacco.

"Hey, Stretch," says Territo.

Stretch Sacco strikes a wooden match against his front tooth and tosses it through the open window of the Mercedes as Stevie floors the accelerator.

"Jesus Christ," says Officer Andrews, nearly dropping his coffee thermos. "What the fuck is that?"

"I would say it's a car in flames," says LaRosa.

Officer LaRosa starts the engine and quickly pulls away from the Colletti house toward the burning vehicle.

Gabriel Caine phones his wife at her office. She answers on the third ring.

"Franklin Leasing, this is Karen."

Gabriel stands at a pay phone, holding the Bible.

He speaks the one word loudly, competing with the noise of the busy airport.

"Goodbye," he says.

"Gabriel? Where are you? I can barely hear you."

"Goodbye."

"Gabriel?" she says again before the line goes dead.

Karen Caine quickly calls home, the line is busy.

She hits the redial button, frantically, again and again, begging the telephone to ring. Finally it does ring, and her mother picks up.

"My God. I thought you'd never answer."

"Karen? What is it dear? You sound frightened."

"Mom, where's Beth?"

"Beth is right here, Karen," says her mother. "Pushing around the crayons that Gabriel bought for her after they left you this morning. Gabriel went out again, about an hour ago; he said he needed to walk. Is there something wrong, dear?"

"No, Mom, it's alright. Give Beth a kiss for me."

"Richie, go start the car," says Dominic Colletti. "I don't

want to be late to Randazzo's."

Richie Colletti steps out through the back door of the house as his father moves to a hall closet for an overcoat.

Dominic hears two quiet pops followed by what sounds like a heavy object falling to the ground.

"Richie," he calls.

"Going somewhere?" says Tony Territo, finding Colletti getting into his coat. "I think you need a new driver."

Territo is pointing the weapon directly at Colletti's forehead.

"Territo, are you insane?"

"Are you kidding, I'm just coming to my senses. My father sends his regards. He asked me to tell you that he's sorry he had to miss your appointment."

"You're a dead man, Territo," says Colletti. "John Giambi will have your head for this."

"I hadn't thought about that. I'd better take some time to meditate. Okay, done."

Territo puts a bullet into Dominic Colletti's chest and another into his head after the old man collapses to the floor. He walks out the back door, steps over Richie Colletti's body, and walks out the driveway to the street where Stevie's Jaguar waits to pick him up.

Landis walks into the detectives' squad room a few minutes after two. He is the last to arrive.

"Sorry I'm late, Lieu, I lost track of time sitting with Mendez in his hospital room," says Landis. "You know how engaging Rey can be."

"Don't we all. How is he doing?"

"I think he's planning a breakout. So. Who's who?"

"This is Detective Rosen from the 63rd and Detective Chen from the 68th, and you know Detective Ivanov," says Samson. "Have you met Chief of Detectives Trenton?"

"More than once," says Trenton, walking up to greet Landis. "Officer Landis is very active and vocal on issues involving discrimination in the Department. We've had a number of discussions, Stan to Stan."

"I never realized that Trenton had a sense of humor," whispers Murphy to Vota.

"It's limited," says Lou.

"Okay," says Samson. "Let's get started."

Samson quickly reviews the status of the Gabriel Caine case for the benefit of those in the room who may only have bits and pieces of the whole picture.

He pauses briefly for questions and moves on.

"We're running short on available units for stakeout and surveillance, Chief," Samson says. "We have two cars at the Caine house, one at Victor Sanders' place, one at his mother's, one at the house opposite the high school, and one at the Bowers' house. Not to mention the car watching Dominic Colletti. We'll hold that topic for later, when we get around to new business. If we find Victor Sanders, and if he identifies Caine as the man who purchased the drugs, we should be able to get a warrant to search Caine's house. And if we're real lucky, we'll find enough evidence there to bring Caine in before he does any more harm."

"Is it possible that Caine is done?" asks Trenton.

"I'll let Detective Ivanov address that question."

"I would love to believe that he's done. Let's assume that no one else turned Caine away that night. He's dealt with what he considers the crimes of Ventura and Addams," Ivanov says, "and we believe Caine decided to spare Bowers after learning of the woman's circumstance. If there was another car involved, then someone left the scene without offering help. In Caine's mind, another sinner. Another criminal of Gibeah. And if Caine has identified the driver of that vehicle, there is at least one more family to be concerned about before we can hope that Caine is done."

"What are *our* chances of identifying a second driver, short of waiting to ask Caine himself?" asks Vota.

"I think we need to put word out on TV and radio this evening," says Samson. "I was hoping you could get with the Public Relations people and make it happen, Chief."

"What did you have in mind?" asks Trenton.

"Something short, no specifics. Just that we're looking for anyone who may have been witness to an accident at that place and time, that it is extremely important and that we will guaranty immunity from criminal prosecution to anyone who has knowledge. The NYPD Press Corps should be able to word it much better than I could, but that's the general idea."

"It could alert Caine," says Trenton, "and bring no other results."

"I think we need to take that risk," says Samson.

"Alright," says Trenton. "I'll see to it that a short announcement runs on all of the local news reports at six and eleven today."

"There's a question that has been bugging me," Rosen says. "Where was Caine going with a five-year-old child at three in the morning?"

"The Tampa PD should have his wife located anytime now," says Murphy. "Maybe she can tell us."

"That's all I have," says Samson. "Now, we wait."

"So, are we open to new business?" asks Trenton.

"I suppose we are," says Samson, warily.

"I received word just before I arrived," says Trenton. "Dominic Colletti and his son Richard were assassinated at Colletti's home in Manhattan Beach an hour ago."

"Well that's just *dandy*," says Vota.

"Look at it this way," says Murphy, "it frees up a surveillance unit."

Samson is about to say something when his phone rings.

The others lament over the Colletti situation while he takes the call.

"This is Sergeant Ludlow of the Tampa PD, Lieutenant. We're over at the Franklin home. Mrs. Franklin says that her son-in-law showed up here late last night. She says that Caine went out for a walk a few hours ago and hasn't returned. His wife is at an office downtown; we're about to head over now."

"Okay, Sergeant, we appreciate the call," says Samson. "Would you mind calling back when you're with Mrs. Caine, I have a few questions I'd like to ask her."

"No problem, Lieutenant," says Ludlow. "I'll speak to you then."

. . .

Sharon Jenkins finds Serena at home.

"Serena, I spoke with a good friend of mine. Walter Gately. Walt is an associate editor working Brooklyn and Queens for the *Tribune*," says Professor Jenkins. "He's very interested in your story. I only gave him enough to get his attention. Walt is disposed to giving you a shot; it's a tremendous opportunity, Serena."

"That's fantastic," Serena says, trying to untie her tongue.

"Walt is willing to give you some time to develop the story, but there's a catch. Gately wants something from you today by five, in time for tomorrow's edition. It doesn't have to be very much, just enough to hint at what's to come and to establish the Trib as first to break the story. Which in turn will establish you as the reporter who broke it."

"I told the detective in charge that I would hold off until I spoke with him again, tomorrow."

"You have to speak with him today. Make a deal. Ask him to give you something you can use now, for your solemn word that you'll sit on the major details until later on. This is a chance of a lifetime, Serena," says Jenkins. "I would go for it. I told Walt you'd call him by four."

"Give me his number," says Serena.

Trenton leaves to work on a statement for the evening news. The others move to the subject of Colletti and sons.

"I would bet the farm on Tony Territo," says Murphy. "Territo must have heard somehow that the name Sonny was mentioned at the scene of his daughter's attack, so Tony figures it for Sonny Colletti and goes wild. I don't know how we'll prove it without witnesses. No one saw a thing at Manhattan Beach, at Leone's car, or on West 12th Street. Bobby Hoyle was too drunk to recognize his own brother. The way I look at it, if these fucking Soprano wannabes want to knock each other off, let them have at it. I'm only sorry the poor girl had to get in the middle of it."

"But that's the thing, Tommy," says Vota. "If we let the

lunatics turn Brooklyn into the O. K. Corral, innocent bystanders are bound to get hurt."

"We'll keep an eye on Territo, maybe we catch a break. These guys are egomaniacs; maybe Territo brags about it to the wrong person," says Samson as his phone rings again.

"Don't you just love it when the joint is jumpin'," Murphy says.

"That was Tampa; Caine's wife says her husband was on the way to the hospital *before* the accident," says Samson.

"Oh?" says Rosen.

"His wife says that the boy was ill, they were going to meet the boy's physician at the ER. She thinks Caine has left Tampa," Samson manages to squeeze in before the phone rings again. "Christ, what the fuck is it now?"

"Just when you think it can't get worse," says Samson coming back to the group, "now I've got a fucking reporter on my back. I have to talk with the woman. Chen, you can sit in. I told her to meet us at the New Times, across the Avenue. Lou, why don't you and Detective Ivanov check in with the units at Caine's place and make sure everyone is awake. Landis, see if you can do something to find Victor Sanders. Talk to your contacts on the street again. Throw some more money around if you have to, dig into petty cash. Murphy, you and Rosen try to locate Tony Territo."

"And do what, ask him how good it felt to put one into Colletti's skull?" asks Murphy.

"Why not? He might enjoy telling you."

"I'm sure he's at his daughter's wake," says Rosen.

"So go there, pay your respects, whatever. Just take a good look at him and let him know you're looking," says Samson. "C'mon, Chen, let's get out of here."

"We're not wearing black," says Rosen as they climb into her car.

"I think we can get away with that," says Murphy, "but you probably will need a hat."

"I've got my Mets cap in the trunk," she says.

"I'm sure the funeral home has a stash of modest headwear and neckties for just this kind of emergency. Hang a left on to Coney Island Avenue and another left at Avenue U."

"Reach over and grab the folder on the rear seat. I brought something to show you."

"What might that be?" asks Murphy, reaching back.

"There was a stabbing in my Precinct the other night, near Beth Israel. The victim came in today to work with an artist on a sketch. When I saw the drawing, I had to make a copy for you. I thought you'd get a kick out of it."

Murphy pulls the photocopy out of the folder and takes a look.

"Don't you think it resembles you quite a bit?" Rosen asks.

No, but it looks a hell of a lot like my brother.

"Oh, I don't know. Looks more like Jerry Seinfeld. That's Avenue U coming up."

Samson and Chen sit at a booth in the rear of the New Times. Samson spots Serena walking to the table and rises to greet her.

"Have a seat Ms. Huang," he says. "This is Detective Andy Chen."

"Serena?" says Chen.

Samson looks from one shocked face to the other.

"Excuse us, Ms. Huang," Samson says. "Order whatever you like, it's on the NYPD. We'll just be a minute."

Samson moves to the front of the restaurant and Chen rises silently to follow.

Serena wants to offer Chen some kind of explanation, but realizes she has none.

Samson walks out to the street and Chen joins him.

"So?" says Samson.

"I had no idea she was a reporter, Lieutenant."

"What difference does that make, Andy? I don't care if

she's your fucking manicurist. Why would you *ever* talk about a case to any civilian? Which reminds me, was it you who handled the interview with Territo and his wife at the hospital?"

"Yes."

"Did you mention the boyfriend? The kid who was at the scene when Territo's daughter was attacked?"

"I'm afraid I did."

"Jesus Christ. I don't know if we can continue to work together, Detective. I'm going to need some time to consider."

"I believe I can help you decide," says Chen.

"I don't have the time or the patience for excuses right this minute."

"I think I may have put the FBI on to the Caine case."

"What?"

"When Agent Stone called me and identified herself as FBI, I just assumed that she was calling about the Ventura and Addams boys, so I told her she would need to speak with you."

"Unfuckingbelievable."

"I don't know what to say, Lieutenant. There's really nothing to say," Chen says, turning to leave.

"Chen?"

"Yes."

"If Stone wasn't calling about the boys, what *was* she calling about?"

"She called to ask about Territo, about what happened to his daughter."

Samson is totally lost.

"Why the interest in Tony Territo? That phone call came long before Territo had it in mind to increase the mortality rate of Brooklyn's Italian-American population."

"I don't know. Stone claimed it might be related to another case they were working on, but I have no idea anymore if anything that anyone tells me is the truth."

"You have a lot to learn, Andy. Chalk it up to experience and don't tear yourself apart over it. You fuck up; you try not to do it again. And none of it is going to end the world; it's just a royal pain in the ass that I could easily live without.

Look, I have to get back in there and do some damage control and then I'm going to find out what the FBI isn't fucking telling us. Why don't you take the rest of the day off. I'll call you."

Before Chen can say another word, Samson quickly turns and heads into the restaurant to deal with the reporter.

Rosen and Murphy walk into the room at Torregrossa and Son's Funeral Home where Brenda Territo's body is laid out. Rosen is wearing a black pillbox hat she borrowed from the office, with a net hanging over her eyes. She gives Murphy a look that warns him against commenting.

Territo's wife is over to them the moment they enter, wanting to know who they might be.

"Sandra Murphy," says Rosen. "I was Brenda's English teacher. This is my husband, Thomas."

"Thank you for coming," says Barbara Territo, losing interest immediately and walking off.

"How could you be sure she wouldn't know the girl's teachers?" whispers Murphy.

"By looking at her," says Rosen. "I'm going up to the casket, do you want to join me?"

"I'll pass."

Rosen moves up to the front of the room. Murphy spots Tony Territo exchanging a few words with his wife.

"My God, what a beautiful girl," says Rosen sadly when she returns to Murphy's side.

"Who are they, Tony?" asks Stevie.

"Barbara says the woman is one of Brenda's high school teachers," says Territo.

"They still look like cops to me."

"I need a drink," says Tony.

"There's a bar across the street," says Stevie. "Let's go, I'll buy you one."

Rosen and Murphy follow them out.

Serena Huang is sitting opposite Walter Gately at a table in an espresso bar on Prince Street in Soho. He is reading the short piece Serena had written after agreeing on the ground rules set by Lieutenant Samson.

"It's good, but it's not enough," says Gately. "What else can you give me?"

"Both victims were missing fingers, but I promised I wouldn't include that information yet."

"Include it and we can do business," says Gately. "You can use my office. It's up to you, Serena. Don't take too long deciding; we need the copy in an hour."

"Alright, yes," says Serena, giving up the half-hearted battle with her conscience. "Let's go to your office."

"Bedford Avenue Body Shop, Fred Caravella speaking."

"Mr. Caravella, this is Agent Stone, FBI."

"Oh?"

"We're calling to find out if you did any bodywork on a vehicle for Anthony Territo in the past four weeks."

"Try Ciaburri's on 65th Street. They do all the work for Territo," suggests Caravella.

Murphy and Rosen watch Tony Territo and his cousin Stevie enter the bar across Avenue U.

"Would you like a cocktail?" asks Murphy.

"Sure," says Rosen, "as long as you let me buy."

Michael Murphy watches as his mother leaves her house and walks to another, two doors up the street. His mother has dinner every Tuesday evening with a neighbor. A widow also. The two women take turns hosting the meal.

When Margaret enters the other house, Michael crosses the street. He lets himself in to his mother's house and begins searching, checking all the places where his mother may have cash hidden. When he is done, Michael has a total of sixteen dollars and twenty cents in cash, and a credit card.

Michael decides that there is something else in the house

that he might make use of, and he knows exactly where to find it. Michael goes into the closet in his mother's bedroom and pulls it down off a high shelf above the bar holding the hanging clothing. He stuffs it into his coat pocket and quickly leaves the house.

Theresa Fazio sees the short news announcement on the small television in her office at Titan Imports. Theresa immediately calls Tony Territo's cell phone number.

Territo watches the same announcement on the television above the bar, where he and Stevie work on straight Scotch. Territo is trying not to glance at the schoolteacher and her husband who sit at a nearby table looking more and more like police. His cellular phone rings.

"Did you see the news?" says Theresa, clearly upset. "They're looking for information about the accident."

"Yes, I saw it. Just ignore it."

"They said that it was important, an emergency."

"Theresa, forget it. I was supposed to be out of town that night. How am I supposed to explain to my wife what I was doing riding around Brooklyn with you at three in the fucking morning? Especially now?" Barbara is going through hell as it is. Just forget it, Theresa."

"I want to come over for the wake later this evening."

"Oh, Christ, Theresa."

"Tony, it will look strange if I don't come. All of the salesmen will be going. Barbara will be expecting me."

"Alright," says Territo. "But not tonight, make it tomorrow. And put that accident out of your mind, Theresa. Permanently. Understand?"

"I understand," Theresa Fazio says, thinking it sounds a little too much like a threat.

Rosen is looking at a menu when their drinks arrive.

"How's the food?" she asks the waiter.

"You might want to dine elsewhere this evening," he says. "The cook came in so drunk he'd probably fuck up a baked potato. Pardon my language."

"No problem, it's very colorful," says Rosen. "Thanks for the tip. Can we get pretzels or something?"

"I can bring you a bowl of chips."

"Plain?"

"Barbeque or sour cream and chive," says the waiter.

"Thanks anyway," says Rosen.

"That phone call got our boy Tony a little agitated," says Murphy when the waiter leaves.

"I can empathize," says Rosen. "I'd feel the same if I'd gunned down four people in the past twenty-four hours and someone rudely interrupted *my* quiet time."

"61ˢᵗ Detectives, Samson speaking."

"Lieutenant, we have Victor Sanders in custody."

"Get him down here to look at Caine's photo, Landis. I'll call to get a head start on a search warrant. Good work, Stan," says Samson. "I'll bet you're real glad you didn't have to wear the clown outfit again."

Gabriel drives out of Queens after leaving LaGuardia Airport. He listens to the announcement on his car radio. Interest in the accident that took his son's life tells him he has been identified. Caine knows that he cannot return to the house; he will never sit in his son's room again.

Gabriel fights off thoughts about home, about Derek, about the other children. They are gone.

All but one.

He needs to keep his mind clear, to finish his work so he can finally rest.

Caine comes off the BQE and on to the Gowanus.

Gabriel takes the 65ᵗʰ Street exit off the Belt Parkway and parks on 2ⁿᵈ Avenue. He places the iron pry bar and the Bible into the small suitcase he had carried to Tampa.

He steps out of the Oldsmobile, takes the cloth tool satchel from the trunk, and leaves the car as it is. The keys dangling from the trunk lock. He needs a safe place to stay, for a short time, until he can take the child.

The last child.

Gabriel knows where he will wait. He picks up the two bags and begins walking up 65th Street toward 5th Avenue.

"They're leaving," says Rosen. "Should we follow?"

"I'm not all that hot about hanging at a mortuary," says Murphy. "Why don't we get dinner and come back?"

"Italian?"

"Of course. Joe's Bar and Grill is just the other side of McDonald Avenue, we can walk from here."

"How about the food?" asks Rosen. "Have you eaten there?"

"Once or twice, a week."

"That good?"

"Not bad if you like garlic and olive oil, and not having to wash the dishes."

"Where are you, Lou?" asks Samson.

"In the car with Detective Ivanov, in front of Caine's house. We let these guys take a dinner break," says Vota. "As soon as they return, we'll give the unit at the alley in back a break. What's up?"

"Victor Sanders identified Caine from the driver's license photo. I'm waiting to hear on a search warrant. If we can get one tonight, we go in."

"Let me know, Sam," says Vota. "We'll hang until I hear from you."

Gabriel walks to the back-alley door of Mitch's Coffee Shop. When he is sure no one is nearby, Caine uses the pry bar to break in.

Caine digs a flashlight from the satchel and uses it to guide his way through the back rooms. A small walk-in cooler, a separate closet with sink and toilet, a stove, a table and chairs, a radio, a small TV, a telephone. Everything he will need to survive.

Caine kills the flashlight and walks through the door that connects to the restaurant counter, dining tables and street entrance. The sign on the front door indicates that the shop will be closed until the end of the month. Mitch is taking his San Juan holiday. It will give Gabriel some time to locate and take the last child.

He returns to the back rooms.

After determining that light from the rear will not be seen from the front, Gabriel switches on the ceiling fluorescent.

This will be Gabriel Caine's home for the next week.

My final home, he thinks.

My final days.

Gabriel turns on the small TV and then walks into the cooler to check the food supply.

"Lieutenant, this is Agent Stone. Glad I caught you."

"So am I," says Samson. "As a matter of fact, I was planning to give *you* a call."

"Oh? What about?"

"Agent Stone, you called me. Please, after you."

"We think we know who drove the car that hit Gabriel Caine on the night his son died. We think it was Tony Territo."

"Could you give me a clue as to how you reached that conclusion?" asks Samson. "Tell me about the dots?"

"It all began with stolen cars shipped from here to Mexico; Territo's name came up. We'd never heard of Tony Territo. Agent Ripley wasn't interested until we learned that Territo leased a garage from Dominic Colletti, who the FBI had heard *a lot* about. I followed Territo for a day or so, to his car dealership, his home, the garage he leased from Colletti. He's using the garage to store the stolen vehicles. We were planning to pass the information on to the NYPD, let your auto theft people take it from there and forget Territo. It's not really our business. And then we heard that Territo's daughter had been killed and the coincidence stimulated our interest in him again."

"Are we almost to the dots that connect Territo to Gabriel Caine?" asks Samson impatiently.

"Territo's house is less than a minute from where we found the bathtub full of water this morning. And Territo had front-end bodywork done on his BMW, he took the car into the shop on January 16th."

"It's a daring leap, but it's not enough. Maybe we could bring Territo in for questioning, but he'd just tell us that he smashed into his garage door," says Samson.

"You're probably right. But what's Territo going to say when he hears that Colletti may not have been responsible for his daughter's attack, now that he's wiped out the entire Colletti family?"

"I can't imagine, but I'd like a picture of his face."

"What are you going to do?"

"We'll wait. I'm hoping to have a search warrant for Caine's house anytime now. I want to see what we find. I want Caine a lot more than Territo at the moment. But we'll get around to Tony boy. If we can't pin the Colletti hits on him, we'll teach him something about proper highway etiquette. If Territo did hit Caine's car and left the boy to die, I'll see to it he never drives a car again if he ever gets out of prison."

"Good luck with the search warrant, Lieutenant."

"I'll let you know how it goes."

"So, why did you become a police officer?" asks Rosen.

They are at a table in Joe's Bar and Grill over plates of linguini with red clam sauce.

"My father was a cop; I wanted to be like him."

"Are you?"

"Am I what?"

"Like your father?"

"I don't know. My father was a complicated man."

"And you?" says Rosen. "Are you a *simple* man?"

"How are you two doing? Do you need anything, more bread?" Augie Sena calls from the bar.

"We're fine, Augie, relax," says Murphy. "He's trying to

make a good impression on you. Augie likes to see new customers come back."

"New customers or new women friends of yours?"

"I don't make a habit of bringing women friends here."

"I'm sorry, I ask too many questions. Something about being a detective," says Rosen.

"Why did you become a police officer?" asks Murphy. "Was *your* father a cop?"

"Not exactly. Hey, Augie, maybe we *could* use some more bread."

"We won't have a search warrant until morning, Lou. I have a promise it will be in our hands no later than seven. They're all backed up with requests because of the fucking holiday yesterday," says Samson.

"That sucks."

"It does. If everyone is back from break, why don't you and Ivanov call it quits? I'm going to do the same and head home for a while. Let's plan to be back here by six. I called Murphy and Rosen and cut them loose also."

"Okay, Sam, I'll be ready at six."

Gabriel Caine prepares an omelet.

Cheddar cheese and eggs from the walk-in cooler and mushrooms from a can.

There is plenty to drink. Juice, soft drinks, coffee and tea.

And he has an unopened bottle of Scotch that he picked up outside of LaGuardia earlier.

Gabriel will make note of everything that he eats and drinks at Mitch's, and will make sure that he leaves enough money to cover it all.

Before beginning the humble meal, Gabriel Caine says a silent prayer of thanks for the food and shelter he has been given.

And he solemnly swears that he will remain worthy.

TWENTY FOUR

Vota, Samson and Ivanov stand at Gabriel Caine's door at six forty-five on Wednesday morning, search warrant in hand. The Crime Scene Investigators wait on the street.

Samson rings the doorbell and after a few moments he pounds on the door itself.

Samson steps back to consult with Vota.

"Well?" he asks.

"It's still your turn to kick one in," says Vota.

"It's unlocked," says Ivanov, pushing the door open.

There is a pile of mail at the threshold, a larger pile under a table to the left of the doorway. The living room in front is littered with assorted plates and drinking glasses, clothing scattered everywhere.

"Looks like the maid hasn't been in for a while," says Vota.

The television is turned on, tuned to an all-cartoon network with the sound muted.

A hallway leads from the front to the other rooms in the house. On the left, a small dining room connecting to the kitchen. On the right, two bedrooms. At the end of the hall, the bathroom.

"Bring in the crime scene guys, Lou," says Samson.

The detectives walk into the bathroom. There is a second door connecting to the master bedroom. The medicine cabinet mirror above the sink is smashed. The cracks in the shattered glass move out from a dent in the center of the cabinet door, the size of a fist.

A child's toothbrush lies in the sink basin.

The bathtub is full of water, rubber toys float on its calm surface.

"Start in here," Samson tells the evidence team as he leads Vota and Ivanov into the bedroom.

There is a crib against the wall opposite the large bed. The bed is neatly made, and looks as if it has not been slept in for some time. Framed photographs sit on a chest of drawers. A young boy on a bicycle with training wheels, a proud father at his side. A wedding photo, an attractive young couple, eyes full of excitement and hope.

A photograph taken in front of the house. Gabriel Caine holding the boy in his arms, his wife visibly pregnant, a realtor's sign on the front lawn. *Sold.*

"They were a lovely family," says Ivanov as they move to the other bedroom.

The floor in the boy's room is strewn with toys. An area at the foot of the bed is clear, the size of a man's body. A half empty bottle of Scotch sits at its center.

"He's been sleeping there, on the floor," says Ivanov.

"Look here," says Vota, holding a coloring book in his gloved hand, both covers cleanly torn off.

Samson looks away from the wall above the bed. It is all he has focused on since entering the room. The entire wall is covered with writing, in crayon.

"Quotes from the Bible, most if not all from the Book of Job," says one of the CSI team coming into the room.

"I want photographs of every word," says Samson.

The three detectives move on to the kitchen.

The floor is covered in trash. Newspapers, discarded mail, a greeting card displaying a large red heart.

The sink is full of dishes, glasses and silverware. The stove top crowded with unwashed pans. A package of X-Acto knife blades on the counter, one or two removed.

An unopened box of crayons. A stocking cap.

And a large manila envelope.

Samson reads the address, written across the front of the envelope in crayon. As unbelievable as it seems, he is not surprised.

Samson pulls on a pair of latex gloves, lifts the envelope and reluctantly spills out the contents.

A plastic bag falls onto the counter. It holds a star sapphire ring.

Samson pulls out a piece of yellow construction paper. The

note is neatly written in large block letters, in green crayon.

And all the first born of the land shall die. And throughout the land there shall be such a wailing as never was heard before.

"This explains why Gabriel Caine's third victim was a daughter and not a son," says Samson. "He was going after the eldest children."

"What third victim?" asks Ivanov.

"Whose daughter?" asks Vota.

Samson lifts the envelope and holds it up to Vota and Ivanov. It reads *Titan1*, above a Shore Road street number. An address Samson had very recently become familiar with.

The address of the house where Brenda Territo paid for the sins of her father.

"I don't understand," says Ivanov.

"There really isn't much for us to do here," Samson says. "Let's give the CSI team a little space do their job. Meet me back at the Precinct and I'll try to explain it to you, as much as it defies explanation."

Samson places the envelope down on the counter. Vota and Ivanov silently follow him out of the house. The three detectives leave for the Precinct, in separate cars.

Samson calls ahead to Desk Sergeant Kelly. Kelly has fresh coffee and bagels waiting for them in the squad room when they arrive. Vota and Ivanov dig into the food while Samson fills them in on his talk with Agent Stone.

"How horrible for the parents of these children," says Ivanov. "Especially the innocent mothers."

"So, what's the game plan, Sam?" asks Vota.

"I've done all the talking and you've done all the eating. You're at least as good as I am at game plans, Lou. You tell me."

"First, we put out an all-points. Pick up Gabriel Caine on sight."

"I agree," says Samson.

"I'll do it now," says Vota.

"You ate all the good bagels," says Samson to Ivanov as Vota makes the phone calls. "What are those two sorry looking things you left for me?"

"I'm guessing banana nut and oat bran," says Ivanov.

"Not that it really matters, but which is which?"

"The one sprinkled with what looks like fingernail clippings is the oat bran."

"Pass the banana nut," says Samson, thinking he'd give his left ventricle for a bacon, cheese and egg sandwich.

Murphy is dreaming. A woman is lying close to him in his bed, waking him with a kiss. The woman looks very much like a certain detective from the 63rd.

Murphy opens his eyes as Ralph licks his cheek again.

"The APB is going out now, citywide," says Vota, once he is sure that Samson has given up entirely on the bagel.

"It's possible that Caine may never come back," says Samson. "As far as we know, Territo's daughter could have been last on his list. There's no telling where he went from Tampa. We'll call the airlines, but if he hopped a bus it could take a very long time to track him down."

"I still believe that when Caine is done he will let us know somehow," says Ivanov.

"What do we do about Tony Territo?" asks Vota.

"Find out when the viewing begins at the funeral home and we'll plan to be at Torregrossa's when Territo and his wife arrive. I think that one or both of them will be able to identify the sapphire ring. We'll try getting warrants to search the house, his car, his office at Titan Imports and the garage he leased from Colletti. We'll claim we're looking for evidence to prove that he was involved in the accident with Caine," says Samson. "We'll be looking for the weapon that killed Colletti and for hot German cars."

"We can bring Territo in for questioning while the searches go forward," says Vota.

"We'll do that. If all goes well, we should be able to charge him with grand theft auto, leaving the scene of an accident, maybe even vehicular homicide," Samson says.

"And if it goes *very* well," says Vota, "we can charge

Territo with four counts of first-degree murder."

"Tony Territo is going to have a very bad day," says Ivanov.

Victoria Anderson buzzes Lorraine at her desk.

"There's a Rowdy Barnwell on the line," she says. "I didn't realize the Rodeo was in town."

"Put him through," says Lorraine.

"Ms. DiMarco, an emergency has come up," Dr. Barnwell says. "A very important public official, whose name I can't mention, is scheduled for brain surgery at Bethesda Naval Hospital on Monday afternoon. I've been asked to fly into Maryland that morning for a consultation with the surgeons."

"I'm impressed. So, I guess you're calling to postpone my operation."

"Actually, I was hoping we could move it up to this Friday."

"As in the day after tomorrow?"

"Ms. DiMarco. Is it alright if I call you Lorraine?"

"Go for it."

"Lorraine, let's do it on Friday. Trust me, you'll be glad to get it over with. And besides, if I screw up in Maryland, I may never be heard from again."

"That was a joke, right?"

"Yes it was."

"I'd advise you not to give up the operating room for the comedy club," says Lorraine. "What time on Friday?"

Murphy walks into the squad room at nine. Samson asks Ivanov to bring Murphy up to speed because Samson is tired of the sound of his own voice.

By ten, they have warrants to search Territo's home, his office, the garage on 41st Street and to search and impound any personal vehicles. The wake is scheduled to begin at one that afternoon, Vota and Ivanov plan to be there in time to greet the parents when they arrive.

Samson will remain at the Precinct to coordinate the hunt

for Gabriel Caine and take reports from the warrant teams. He also plans to be there when Territo is brought in, and to be present for Territo's interrogation.

Rosen will work out of her own Precinct, and will be available if needed.

Samson has not yet resolved the question of Detective Andy Chen.

This leaves only Detective Murphy and Officer Landis free to respond to a felony homicide at a liquor store on Avenue X.

A solo gunman had been interrupted during an attempted robbery by a customer who walked in at precisely the wrong time and was shot and killed before the gunman fled.

Murphy and Landis arrive and are filled in by one of the two uniformed officers who were first at the scene.

"Guy over there," says the officer. "Duffy. Owns the place. Comes in this morning, takes about fifteen minutes to set up, opens the door for business. The perp walks in, pulls a gun, and asks for the money. Now, there isn't much cash on hand first thing in the morning. In fact, Duffy makes the point, thinks it's funny or something, that if the guy waits until closing time we're talking three, maybe four grand. As it is, Duffy's got about one-hundred-fifty in the drawer. Duffy's getting the dough out, no argument, and the poor bastard lying on his back over there walks in. The perp gets spooked, turns and pops the guy once in the chest and hits the high road. And that's all she wrote."

"Duffy's the only witness?" asks Murphy.

"I guess someone could have seen the shooter run out."

"Why don't you and your partner hit the street and ask around?" asks Murphy.

When the uniforms leave, Murphy and Landis move to the witness. Duffy is working with a sketch artist, and Murphy watches the artist put on the finishing touches.

Murphy's reaction is just short of audible as he looks down at the drawing.

It looks like his brother, Michael.

Murphy calms down and silently reprimands himself.

Fucking paranoid bastard, every police sketch you see

looks like Michael to you. And you know a police sketch rarely comes close to being a useful ID. Get the fucking needle out of your arm.

"Kind of looks like you," says Landis, standing beside Murphy, thinking it pretty amusing.

"I've drawn this guy, just yesterday," says the sketch artist. "A street mugging. The victim was stabbed. Close to Beth Israel Hospital. I'll check it out when I get back to my desk."

"You okay, Murphy?" Landis asks.

"Depends on what you mean by okay."

"Forget I asked."

"Asked what?"

"61ˢᵗ Detectives, Vota speaking."

"Are you free for dinner tonight, Detective?"

"Yes I am, Counselor."

"How about seven at my apartment? I'll cook."

"I'll bring the wine."

"See you at seven," says Lorraine.

"Everything alright?" asks Vota.

"See you at seven. Ask me then."

"FBI, Stone."

"This is Samson; we got into Caine's house. We found enough to bring him in, but we don't know where he is. We have the entire NYPD out looking, but I it wouldn't hurt to have the FBI out also. Two heads are better than one."

"Sure," says Stone. "I'll bring it to Ripley."

"You were right about Territo, by the way. We found what we're pretty sure is his daughter's ring on Caine's kitchen counter. We're planning to bring Territo in later today."

"Caine didn't have time to take a finger, so he took her ring. It's spooky," says Stone.

"That's one way of putting it."

"Are you sure that Caine is coming back?" The Territo girl could have settled the score."

"According to Delta Airlines, Gabriel Caine took a return flight to LaGuardia yesterday afternoon. And we found his car abandoned on 2nd Avenue and 63rd Street in Brooklyn this morning."

"Lieutenant, would you mind if I took a peek around Caine's place? Maybe there's something that could help us find him."

"Something that we may have missed?"

"That's not what I was implying, Lieutenant," Stone says. "Remember what you said about two heads."

"I'm sorry, Agent Stone. I've heard a lot about how the FBI likes to take over."

"That's just in the movies, and definitely not in Ripley's nature. He's told me more than once to stay out of your hair. Seeing Caine's place is more about my curiosity than anything else, and about my education."

"Feel free to look around all you like, Agent Stone, and if you do find something we may have overlooked, feel free to beat me over the head with it. Please."

"Thank you. And Lieutenant, my name is Winona. If you felt so inclined you could call me Win."

"We'll see how it goes," says Samson.

Murphy returns to the 61st Precinct after he and Landis had accompanied the sketch artist to his work desk.

The artist found the drawing he remembered doing with the mugging victim the day before. Murphy had seen that drawing already, in a folder from the back seat of Rosen's car. Landis and the artist compared the two drawings, and the resemblance was close enough for Officer Landis to note in his crime report that the suspect in the felony homicide at the liquor store was possibly also a suspect in a recent stabbing in the 63rd.

Murphy thought that the liquor store drawing, of the suspect who he was sure couldn't be his brother, looked a lot more like Mike than the earlier drawing of the suspect who Murphy knew *was* his brother. Not a pleasant thought.

A connection between the two crimes made Mike's

situation more dangerous, whether Michael was at the liquor store or not. Murphy thought not, but there was information that he wasn't sharing with his colleagues so he said nothing.

If Murphy didn't find his brother soon, they were both fucked.

When Murphy walks into the squad room, Samson is there alone. Vota and Ivanov had just left for the funeral home.

Murphy calls his mother the moment he reaches his desk. No word from Michael.

"What's up?" asks Samson from across the room.

"Could you be a little less specific?"

"I can give it a shot. That's about the tenth time in the past two days I've heard you call looking for your brother. Is he missing or something?"

"He had a fight with my mother is all. He stormed out of the house, hasn't called her. Probably shacking up with a girlfriend. My mom is upset is all. Why so interested?" asks Murphy, trying not to sound defensive.

"Missing people are the rage these days, is all," says Samson, trying not to sound offensive. "Need any help?"

"No, but thanks for asking."

Rosen walks in and breaks an awkward silence.

"Miss us already?" asks Samson.

"I thought you might want to see this, though I'm sure you don't want to see it," says Rosen, walking to Samson's desk and handing him a copy of the *Tribune.*

"Son of a bitch," says Samson, after quickly reading the short piece by Serena Huang. "Is there absolutely no one who can be trusted. This is all we fucking needed."

"I'll give ten-to-one odds we get a confession today," says Murphy, "and it won't be Gabriel Caine."

"I'm much more worried about a copycat," says Samson.

Everyone is pacing the squad room waiting for the phone call from Vota.

As soon as Territo arrives at the funeral home they will move. Murphy to Titan Imports on 4th Avenue, with a two-man backup along. Landis to the garage on 41st, with three other uniforms along. Rosen to meet Ivanov at the house on Shore Road, with a tow truck on call if needed.

"Reminds me of the Tet Offensive," says Samson.

A stretch limousine pulls up in front of Torregrossa and Sons just before one. Vota telephones Samson as he and Ivanov watch Tony Territo's parents, his wife and son, and finally Territo himself climb out of the limo.

"Got him, Sam," says Vota. "I'll be there shortly."

"Showtime," says Samson to the others.

Vota approaches Territo with his shield in hand.

"Mr. Territo, I'm Detective Sergeant Vota, NYPD. We need you over at the 61st Precinct to answer a few questions."

"Am I under arrest?" says Territo.

"Only if you want it that way," says Vota.

"Barbara, take Anthony and my parents inside," says Territo to his wife.

Barbara Territo quickly complies. Ivanov follows them into the building.

"What's this about?" asks Territo.

"We'd prefer talking at the Precinct," says Vota.

"Do you realize that you are taking me away from my wife and son at a very bad time?"

"I do. We'll try not to keep you long," says Vota.

"And if I won't come?"

"You mean if you won't come voluntarily?" asks Vota, raising his arm to signal the two officers sitting in the patrol car across the Avenue. "We have warrants to search your house and your vehicles, Mr. Territo. You may want to let us have keys. It would save unnecessary damage."

Territo angrily hands Vota a key ring as the two uniformed officers reach them.

"By the way," says Vota, taking a plastic bag from his pocket. "Do you recognize this?"

"That's my daughter's ring. Where did you get that?"

"One of our investigators found it outside your house,

we'll make certain that it's safely returned to you when our investigation is complete," says Vota. "Are you ready to come along to the Precinct?"

"Let me tell my wife I'm leaving."

"My partner is inside letting Mrs. Territo know now," says Vota. "Please escort Mr. Territo to the 61st Precinct, Officers. I'll be following right behind you. I need to get these keys to Detective Ivanov."

"Mrs. Territo, I'm Detective Ivanov, 60th Precinct. I am very sorry to trouble you at such a difficult time, but it's unavoidable," says Marina.

"What is this about?"

"Your husband has gone off with Detective Vota for questioning, in regard to a car accident on the sixteenth of last month. Do you know anything about the incident?"

"My husband was in Boston on business," says Barbara Territo. "His car was damaged in the parking garage at the hotel. What kind of people are you? To take my husband away from his family at a time like this?"

She really doesn't know, thinks Ivanov.

"Enforcers of the law, Mrs. Territo, that's all. Just doing our job. I'm sure we will have your husband back to you soon. I'm sorry to have bothered you. I'm very sorry about your daughter."

Before Barbara Territo can say another word, Detective Ivanov is quickly moving to the exit.

Landis pounds on the large metal door until a man with a wrench in his hand opens the garage entrance.

"Yes?" he says.

"We have a warrant to search the premises."

"Are you crazy or just stupid? This building belongs to Dominic Colletti. It's *way* out of your jurisdiction."

"Dominic Colletti sleeps with the fishes."

I've always wanted to say that, Landis thinks, as three more officers come up behind him.

"Get names, addresses, Social Security and telephone numbers on everyone," says Landis. "Then tell each suspect about the deep shit he's in if he doesn't have sense enough to start talking. Begin with Mr. Jurisdiction here."

Murphy walks into the showroom at Titan Imports and finds the office manager.

"Murphy, NYPD," he says. "We have a warrant to search the premises."

"What is this about?" asks Theresa Fazio. "Is it about the car accident?"

Bingo.

"As a matter of fact it is," says Murphy. "Why don't you tell me about it?"

Samson has kept Territo sitting in an interview room for almost an hour, while the lieutenant waits for reports on the searches.

Territo's lawyer is already with his client.

Landis reported that they found stolen vehicles and automobile parts, and have taken statements from the choir at the garage to back it up. They are in the process of recording vehicle serial numbers.

Murphy in on his way back with Theresa Fazio. She is prepared to testify that she was with Territo on the night of January 16th, when Territo sideswiped another car while speeding onto the Belt Parkway at Bay Parkway. They were on their way to a hotel in Sheepshead Bay after closing a bar in Brooklyn Heights.

Ivanov and Rosen had searched the Territo house, the Jeep Cherokee and the BMW.

When Samson and Vota are finally ready to enter the interrogation room they have enough evidence to charge Territo with leaving the scene of an accident and with grand theft auto.

The bad news is that none of the search parties found a weapon to connect Territo to the Colletti murders.

"I still find it hard to believe that Territo ditched the gun," says Samson.

"We just couldn't find it," suggests Vota. "Territo is a megalomaniac, too proud of his heroic accomplishments to ditch the gun. He probably plans to give it to his son for the kid's eighteenth birthday."

"Jesus, that's it," says Samson, picking up his phone. "We need one more search warrant."

Wednesday evening at half past six, the 61st is quiet.

Tony Territo is charged, arraigned and out on bail.

Lou Vota is on his way to pick up a bottle of wine for dinner at Lorraine's.

Murphy and Rosen have decided to dine together for the third straight evening, trying to remember whose turn it is to buy.

Landis is on his way to the hospital to visit Mendez, stopping at Alfredo's San Juan Deli for chicken, rice and black beans.

"What would you say," asks Barbara Territo, "if I told you that I know about you and your slut secretary?"

Tony Territo says nothing.

Samson and Ivanov are at the funeral home, a search warrant in hand. Evening visiting hours have not begun.

"This is highly unusual, and offensive I might add," says one of Torregrossa's sons.

"We appreciate the editorial," says Samson, "and I'd like to take the time to discuss the merits, but we should do this before the family returns from dinner."

A few minutes later, two funeral employees are lifting Brenda Territo's body from the casket and onto a gurney.

The nine-millimeter handgun, silencer attached, sits on the satin bed.

"You have to appreciate the gesture," says Samson.

"Let's go pick Territo up," says Ivanov.

"It's nearly seven. Territo's probably on his way back here," says Samson. "Let's wait."

"What would you say," asks Murphy, "if I told you my brother is a murder suspect-at-large and that I can't find him anywhere?"

"I would say try harder," answers Rosen.

In the limousine on the way back to the funeral home, Tony Territo's cell phone rings.

A call from a Torregrossa son.

Barbara has not said a word to Tony since confronting him about being with Theresa on the night of the accident.

Tony tells the driver to stop, to let him out, and to take his wife and son ahead.

Barbara doesn't care to ask why.

"What would you say," asks Lorraine, "if I told you that I have a brain tumor, which might be malignant, and that I'm scheduled for surgery to remove and diagnose the little son of a bitch on Friday morning?"

"I would say that you waited long enough to tell me," answers Vota.

"Fuck," says Samson, when the limo arrives without Tony Territo aboard.

"Let's go to his house," says Ivanov, "and put out an APB on the way over."

"He won't be at the house. Let's bring the gun over to the ballistics people, then you can drop me back at the Precinct and you can take off. I'll take care of Territo."

"I don't mind handling it, Lieutenant," says Ivanov. "Maybe you can still get home in time for dinner."

"Thanks. I wouldn't mind that at all."

"They're burying Territo's daughter in the morning."
"He's going to miss it," says Samson.

"What would you say," asks Landis, "if I told you that I saw a rat running across the floor of Alberto's kitchen?"
"I would say pass the blue Jell-O," answers Mendez.

"Stevie, can you pick me up?"
"Sure, Tony, where are you?"
"In serious trouble," says Tony Territo.

"What would you say," asks Samson, "if I told you that I'd really like to retire in a few years, maybe go back to school, do something less insane for a living?"
"I would say why wait," answers Alicia.

TWENTY FIVE

Thursday. The 61st Precinct has remained quiet all morning.

Fortunately for Samson, the flurry of television, radio and newspaper inquiries inspired by Serena Huang's piece in the *Tribune* have all been directed to the NYPD Press Corps.

The Department is stonewalling.

Rosen is at the cemetery for Brenda Territo's burial, on the outside chance that her father will show his face.

Landis has a few days off.

Samson is staring at his telephone.

Murphy is out looking for his brother.

Vota answers the call from Kelly at the front desk.

"Yes?"

"Lou, I got a guy down here says he killed the two boys. The guy said, and I quote, *that will teach the little bastards not to point fingers at me*, end quote."

"Great, did he bring his power garden shears?"

"How'd you know?" asks Kelly.

"Lucky guess. Cordless?"

"Lou."

"Be right down."

Serena Huang has been trying to reach Samson since Wednesday.

She tries a few more times on Thursday morning and is told a few more times that the lieutenant is unavailable.

Meanwhile, Walter Gately has been pressing Serena for more of the story.

"I'm shut out," says Serena. "Samson won't talk to me, and I can't say I blame him. I knew we should have waited. No one is talking to anyone, if that's any consolation."

"What about the detective friend of yours, who gave you the first leads?" asks Gately.

"Thanks to me, that detective is off the case," says Serena. "And he's no longer a friend. I'll be lucky if I have any friends left when this is over."

"I would be much more worried about the state of your career than the status of your friendships," says Gately.

"How much time can you give me?"

"To be truthful, I don't know," says Gately. "If you can't get me something very quickly, something exclusive, I'll have to put one of my veteran reporters on the story. I have people here who know how to squeeze the NYPD press people for information, and so do our competitors."

So long, Sixty Minutes, thinks Serena when he hangs up.

"The guy said he ate them?" says Samson, after Vota gives him a synopsis of the confession.

"Finger food," says Vota. "Just goes to show you that no matter how dark Tommy's humor can be, it can't even come close to the human comedy."

Gabriel Caine takes the Bay Ridge Parkway bus toward Coney Island. He gets off at Stillwell and Highlawn.

He crosses Stillwell. At the corner sits the Avenue Hobby Shop. This is where he picked up the first child.

Caine walks to the street where the last boy lives.

The last sacrifice.

He passes the blue house and casually looks it over.

He continues to the next corner and leans against a car, opens a newspaper, watches and waits.

People on the street seem to pay him no mind. Others lean on automobiles, alone or in pairs, talking. A group of teenagers throw a football around. Women pass, pushing wheeled carts filled with groceries. Cars pass, blasting loud music out onto the avenue. Passersby smile, he smiles in return. A handsome, nonthreatening smile.

Finally, the maroon Ford station wagon pulls up to the

opposite corner and parks. A man and the child step out of the vehicle.

The man stoops to give the eight-year-old a kiss, and watches as the boy walks down the street. The man lights a cigarette and smokes, and watches until the boy reaches the blue house and is safely inside. Then the man puts out his cigarette and walks into the corner grocery store.

Gabriel closes his newspaper and begins walking back toward Stillwell. He waits for the bus that will take him back to Bay Ridge, back to his temporary home.

Gabriel will take this trip again the next afternoon, one more dry run.

And Monday he will be ready.

"Lorraine goes into the hospital today," says Vota.

"How is she handling all of this?" asks Samson.

"I think she's doing better than I am with it."

Samson is trying to come up with an appropriate response when his phone rings.

"Lieu, it's that reporter again, Huang," says Kelly. "Should I tell her you're not here?"

"Put her through, Kelly. I'll tell her myself."

Kelly transfers the call.

"Don't call me, I'll call you," Samson says.

And he disconnects.

Murphy needs to talk to someone about his brother, and is surprised when he finds himself reaching out to Rosen.

She goes directly to his place when he calls at three that afternoon; she hears the urgency in his voice.

They walk with Ralph along the Shore Road Promenade.

Rosen listens without interrupting.

"My mistake was trying to be a father to my brother after Dad died. Michael had just turned sixteen, and he worshipped my father. But what Michael needed was a big brother, not someone trying to be a father who had no idea how to be one.

"Mike started having trouble in school soon after Dad

passed away, and I was very hard on him. Mike had always been a bright kid, and now his grades were falling and he was running around in the wrong circles. I was very busy then, I had recently graduated from the Police Academy. I never thought that I would wind up being a cop, and here I was at twenty-five in uniform. Mike on the other hand had been talking about being a policeman like his dad since he was five years old. But by the time he turned eighteen, he had already flunked out of high school and had been in some trouble with the law around a shoplifting incident. I was able to get him off with just a fine, but there was no way he was going to be accepted into the Department after that.

"Michael kept having brushes with trouble and I kept covering them up when I could and I kept being hard on him. I tried to do what I thought a father should do if his son was fucking up. The thing is, my father would have behaved very differently. And I must have known so because I knew the kind of man my father had been. I knew how he related to us growing up. He was always positive, he always taught through example. My father never lectured, never lost his temper, would never have given up on either one of us. The father who I tried to be for Michael was a negative, pontificating, impatient, loudmouthed tyrant. I have no idea who I was taking after, but it surely wasn't Patrick Murphy.

"Two years ago, I helped Michael find a job at a small coffeehouse in Brooklyn Heights. One of the guys at the station had an older brother who was just opening the place and needed some help. We arranged an interview and Mike was taken on. Michael did very well, learned quickly, was liked by the manager he worked for, and he was turning his life around. He loved working in the Heights, and he met a very sweet girl who worked in a boutique next door to the shop. In less than a year, Mike was promoted to Assistant Manager and given a second pay raise. He talked to Mom and me about getting his own apartment and began looking around Carroll Gardens for a place.

"Then the manager left for a position elsewhere. The owner thought that Mike was still too young to manage, so he brought in a new manager. Mike continued as assistant.

Michael had problems with the new manager from the start.

"Mike complained that the new guy was making his life hell. The new man was never satisfied with his work, was always putting him down in front of customers. He insisted he wasn't doing anything wrong, that for some reason this guy simply didn't like Michael. I told Mike to talk to the owner. Mike told me that he had spoken with the owner and the owner had told him to just do his job. I had a lot on my mind at the time. I was working toward qualifying for my detective's shield.

"I told Mike to just do his job.

"A month later, Mike came to me more upset than I had ever seen him. He had lost the job. The manager had told the owner that he caught Michael stealing money and Michael was fired on the spot. Mike insisted he was innocent, that the manager lied just to get rid of him. I found it very hard to believe that someone would do something like that, and apparently so did the Department of Labor. They denied Michael unemployment insurance benefits after two appeals.

"So, I became a detective and Mike became unemployed with a one-job résumé and no references.

"It all went downhill from there and now my brother is twenty-four and he's out there all alone thinking that he's killed someone and he's afraid to come to me because I've been such a self-righteous bastard."

"And you didn't believe Michael?" asks Rosen. "When he told you that he didn't steal the money from work?"

"I didn't believe him. And today I went to the place and found the owner there. He told me that the manager had taken nearly a thousand dollars from the safe two months earlier and disappeared. He asked how my brother was doing and I walked out. I passed the boutique next door and I caught a glimpse of the girl Michael had dated before his trouble. She wouldn't him see again after he was fired."

"Mike will call, Tommy," says Rosen. "In his heart he knows he can trust his own brother. And what will you do?"

"I'll do everything that I can do to help him."

"Talk to your mother about this, so she can assure him if he contacts her. And talk with Samson and Vota, they can help. I have to get going."

"You won't say anything about this."

"I'm glad if it helped to talk, and flattered that you chose me, but it does put me in a tough spot. I'll keep it to myself and I'll pray that no one asks."

At 4:07, Andre Harris is handing a hundred-dollar bill to a man with one hand, payment for the names and addresses of a couple of homicide cops named Samson and Vota who had put eight bullets into his little brother Dwayne three days earlier.

As a bonus, Stump mentions that Samson has a son who sometimes ran with one of Phil Diaz's boys.

At 4:33, Stump calls Officer Rey Mendez at the 61st Precinct to inform Rey about his chat with Andre Harris. With hopes of scoring another fifty bucks by doing so. Stump is told that Mendez is still on sick leave.

He asks for Mendez's partner, but Landis is off until Saturday afternoon.

At 5:30, Agent Stone introduces herself to the two teams of officers staking out Gabriel Caine's residence before she enters the house.

Stone goes through the rooms. Looking. Taking notes. In the boy's bedroom, she reads the writing on the wall.

I speak of what I know: those who plow iniquity and sow the seeds of grief reap a harvest of the same kind.

It is all one, and this I dare to say: innocent and guilty, he destroys all alike.

There is anger stirred to flame by evil deeds; you will learn that there is indeed a judgment.

The Book of Job.

Stone shudders and leaves the room. She has decided how she will proceed. She starts by gathering every piece of the mail scattered throughout the front rooms and piles it all onto the kitchen counter.

Stone begins examining each item, one by one.

At 6:25 p.m., Salvatore DiMarco drives his daughter to University Hospital of Brooklyn to check in. Frances has come along. The operation is set for ten the following morning.

Lorraine's parents sit with her for a while once she is settled into her overnight accommodation.

"Why don't you get out of here, Lou?" says Samson. "Didn't you tell me that Lorraine was checking into the hospital this evening?"

"Yes," says Vota.

"So, get over there."

"You'll call if you need me?"

"I will."

At 8:20, Murphy is sitting at the bar waiting for Augie Sena to pour another bourbon.

"Don't you think you should eat something, Tommy?" Augie asks when he delivers the drink.

"What are you, my mother?"

"If I was your mother, you'd be calling me up on the phone every ten minutes asking about your brother," says Augie.

At 9:00, Samson calls his wife to tell her that he would be a little later. Again.

Alicia tells him it's okay, and to be careful.

Again.

The phone rings as soon as he places the receiver down.

It is Sergeant Hackett, who works the front desk after Kelly leaves at four.

"Lieutenant, I'm calling out for food from across the street," says Hackett. "Can I order something for you?"

"How about a bacon, cheese and egg on hard roll?" says Samson.

"I'll do it, but only if you promise not to tell your wife that I was an accessory before the fact."

At 9:55, Vota and Lorraine are both exhausted.

It would have been difficult to tell, listening to the reassurances voiced over the past two hours in Lorraine's hospital room, which one of them was scheduled to go under the knife at ten the next morning.

"They'll have to shave my head," says Lorraine.

"I'd imagine they would," says Vota.

"Will you still love me when I'm bald?"

"There is nothing they could possibly do with your hair that would change the way I feel about you, Lorraine," Vota says, taking her hand. "Well, maybe a Mohawk."

At 10:35, Michael Murphy is checking into the Midwood Suites on East 15th Street off Avenue K. Michael thinks seriously about calling his brother as soon as he gets up to his room. He can't bring himself to make the call.

Michael is lucky enough to have a mother who will not report a stolen credit card, so he calls room service for dinner instead.

Michael was unlucky enough to be spotted going into the hotel by a police officer on the street, who thought he recognized Michael's face from a police sketch and headed for his Precinct to check cases.

At 11:15, Samson is still hanging on to the hope that Tony Territo or Gabriel Caine will turn up. He calls his wife again.

"Are the kids all asleep?" he asks.

"Jimmy's still awake."

"When did Jimmy get home?"

"At the stroke of eleven," says Alicia.

"Where was he?"

"With a friend."

"Where and with what friend?"

"With Nicky Diaz at his father's billiard parlor."

Not good, Samson thinks.

At 11:37, Murphy calls his mother again, apologizing for the lateness of the hour.

No word from Michael.

Murphy finishes the last of his drink, wishes Augie a good night, and heads home.

Ralph will be very glad to see him.

At 11:55, Officer Perry returns to the Midwood Suites with two other uniforms along. Perry had found what he was looking for in the warrants file, and was certain that the man he spotted walking into the hotel lobby was the same man wanted for a recent liquor store homicide.

Officer Perry had tried reaching Murphy or Landis, the investigators of record, but the desk sergeant at the 61st Precinct told him that neither was available. Perry took one of the officers in through the lobby with him and sent the other around to watch the alley in back.

At 11:56, Michael Murphy finishes his meal and writes a short note on hotel stationery. *Tommy, I never took the money from my job. I love you. Tell Mom I'm sorry.*

Michael places the note on bed and goes to his coat. He takes the gun and carries it back to the bed.

He sits on the bed with the gun in his hand.

. . .

At 11:56, Samson gets word from Desk Sergeant Hackett about a call that had come in for Murphy and Landis. Samson decides he should go over to the Midwood Suites to check out what was going down.

. . .

At 11:57, Gabriel Caine returns from a short walk.

Earlier in the day, he had repaired the hasp on the alley door and had replaced the lock with a new one from the Ace Hardware on 5th Avenue.

Gabriel reaches for a discarded, day-old copy of the *Tribune* that sits on the ground near the alley door before going back into Mitch's Coffee Shop.

At 11:59, there is a knocking at the door of Michael Murphy's hotel room. Followed by a voice.

"Officer Perry, 68th Precinct, please open the door."

Michael instinctively goes for the window and climbs out onto the fire escape, the gun still in his hand.

TWENTY SIX

When Murphy walks up the hall toward his apartment door he hears the phone ringing inside. It is just past midnight, late for a phone call, so he thinks immediately of his brother Michael.

Murphy runs to the door and in his haste to reach the phone forgets to say *it's me, Ralph* when he pushes the door open. He is instantly knocked down to the floor, and his head hits the concrete hallway floor with enough force to leave him unconscious.

Andre Harris finds Phil Diaz in the pool hall on Queens Boulevard in Flushing.

Diaz owns the place.

Diaz is a small-time hood, dealing in marijuana and pills, uppers and downers. Like most small-timers he is self-important leaning toward overly suspicious.

"Hi, Phil," says Harris, approaching boldly.

"Am I supposed to know you?" is the wary reply.

"Not important, I'm here to do you a big favor."

"Do I need a favor?"

"Uh-huh."

"I'm listening. But not for long."

"It's about your boy."

"Which one?" asks Diaz, scanning the room for familiar and unfamiliar faces.

"Nicky."

"What about Nicky? He was here two hours ago and he was good so what the fuck do you have to say?"

"Doesn't he run with a kid named Jimmy Samson?"

"Yeah, Jimmy was with him. Get to the point, man, you're putting me to sleep."

343

"The kid's old man is a cop."

"So?"

"So, this pig threw his kid in with your boy to get dirt on you."

"That's bullshit."

"No."

"You trying to tell me this cop puts a seventeen-year-old kid, his kid, on the line for him? I don't think so."

"Your kid ever score for you?"

"That's none of your fucking business," says Diaz. But Harris thinks that Diaz got the point.

"Better watch your ass," says Harris.

"Okay, you had something to say and you said it. You say you came here to do me a big favor, so how come I don't feel grateful?"

"Because telling you about the problem isn't the favor. The favor is helping you solve the problem."

"Do I need help?"

"Uh-huh."

"I'm listening."

If dogs could talk, this one would probably have said *Oh, shit* when he KO'd Murphy at the threshold of 4B. Now Ralph is licking Murphy's face as Murphy comes to back to consciousness a few minutes later.

"It's me, asshole," says Murphy, pushing the dog off him. Murphy is halfway to his feet when he realizes that the phone is still ringing.

"What is it?" snaps Samson, listening to unanswered rings from the phone receiver against his ear and turning to Officer Perry coming up behind him.

"A call from Dispatch, looking for you specifically. Sounds like another one of those finger murders."

"Fuck," says Samson, cradling the phone receiver forcefully. "Where?"

And after Perry tells him where, Samson picks up the

receiver again. This time to call Vota.

"Fuck," says Murphy when he picks up the phone and all he hears is the loud sound of a click on the other end.

"Fuck," says Vota when his phone rings, waking him after he finally managed to put pictures of brain tumors out of his mind and somehow fall asleep.

"Lou," he hears before he can even say a word. "We've got another one. Missing a finger."

"Shit, where?"

Samson tells him where and then adds, "Lou, I'm down here at the Midwood Suites and Tommy's brother Michael just got wasted by a cop."

"What the fuck are you talking about?"

"Michael got made by a beat cop down here, Perry. Ties him to a liquor store homicide that went down yesterday and goes in with two other uniforms to make the bust. Two at the door, third down in the alley out back. Michael goes out the window and gets nailed on the fire escape."

"Was Michael armed?"

"Doesn't look like it. Internal Affairs is down here and they're all over the shooter. Name's Davis, twenty-four-year-old rookie. Fired four rounds, almost popped Perry leaning out the window."

"Tommy?"

"Can't get hold of him, and we need to get our asses down to this other thing now."

"I can't fucking believe this shit. Listen, Sam, one of us has to wait for Tommy. I'm closer. Scare up Ivanov or Rosen and I'll meet you after. I don't want some nobody asshole breaking this to Murphy."

"You're right. See you later."

"Nicky."

"Yeah, Pop?"

"That kid you were with tonight, you play ball with, what's his name?"

"Jimmy?"

"Yeah, that's the one. You seeing him tomorrow?"

"Hadn't planned it, why?"

"I need help moving a couple of tables, thought maybe you and he could give me a hand. He looks like a strong kid. Give you each a twenty."

"I can ask him."

"Ask him good," says Phil Diaz. "It's important."

Vota hadn't wanted to leave Lorraine all alone at the hospital earlier, but was surprised by the relief he felt when he did. He wasn't handling her problem very well.

Vota knew that another missing finger and Murphy's brother getting blown away was just about what it would take to get him to forget just how terrified Lorraine's impending operation had made him. And the thing of it was, he was as frightened for himself as for her.

Rey Mendez is sick of being in bed. Mendez can't sleep, again, and decides to call the Precinct.

Maybe a little shoptalk would help.

After Hackett fills him in on all the action he is missing, Mendez only feels worse.

"I need to get the fuck out of here," he complains.

"What's stopping you?"

"These fucking doctors. Test this. Test that."

"They got you tied down?"

"What?"

"Can you walk?"

"Yes, I can fucking walk."

"Then walk the fuck out of there," says Hackett with perfect nonchalance. "By the way, you got a call earlier. Character calling himself Stump."

"What'd he want?"

"Didn't say. Asked for you, then for Landis. Told him you

were both out and asked him if I could help."

"And he said?"

"No."

"Wish I knew what he wanted."

"Really? How much?"

"Enough, thanks," says Mendez and he starts to pull himself out of the hospital bed as he hangs up the phone.

Murphy tries to phone Sandra Rosen—her line is busy. Her line is busy because Samson is calling for her to meet him at the scene of a homicide involving a missing finger. Murphy replaces the receiver just as the knocking on his apartment door begins.

After waking Rosen, Samson goes back to Perry.

"I've got to go, Perry. Unless you hear otherwise from me personally you will not breathe a word to anyone about this kid being the brother of a police detective."

"Nobody?"

"Nobody. Tell me that you understand me perfectly. Nobody. Leave it to me."

"What about my CO?"

"Damn it, Perry, get the shit out of your ears. No-fucking-body."

"Yes sir."

"Don't fuck up."

And then Samson has to go, like so many times before, to where he did not wish to go.

The telephone rings and the bartender picks it up.

"White Owl, Red speaking."

"Is Stump there?"

"Been in and out. You a cop?"

"No, his cousin. If he shows up ask him to call Rey. He knows the number."

"What, 911?"

"I'm not a fucking cop, asshole. Just give him the message," says Mendez.

"Okay already, I'll give him the message," says Red. "Officer."

Murphy is rushing to the door and yelling at Ralph to stop barking.

"Mike, you little cocksucker, I'm going to beat the living shit out of you. Don't you fucking move an inch." And he gets the door opened and it's Vota standing there.

"Lou? What's up?"

"Can I come in Tommy?"

"Yeah, come in."

"Can you get this dog off my leg?"

"Before or after you come in?" asks Murphy smiling. Vota is not looking very well standing there, Murphy calls Ralph off and steps aside to let his partner enter.

"What's going on, Lou?" he asks.

Asking as if he already knows the answer.

Michael Davis is twenty-four years old. Just a kid. And he has just killed another kid his own age. Another kid named Michael.

Harry Jacobs is twice his age, twice his size. Jacobs is from IAB. Internal Affairs Bureau.

Cops learn pretty quickly not to be intimidated by IAB investigators. But Michael Davis hasn't had time enough to learn.

It is routine for IAB to investigate all incidents involving the shooting of a civilian by a police officer. Jacobs had to talk to Vota and Samson about the Harris shooting just days ago. Jacobs has a nickname among the population of cops of which he was once a member. His nickname is fuckface.

Investigators from IAB usually work in pairs. Tonight is no exception. Along with Jacobs to interview Davis is Marty Richards. He is younger than Jacobs, and newer to the Bureau. As such, he may remember more about what it was like to be a regular cop and what regular cops think of cops like him who go after them. Maybe not. His nickname among his former peers is also fuckface.

Michael Murphy was struck by two bullets fired by Officer Davis. Michael fell four stories to the alley below and his neck was broken. Whether Michael was dead before he hit the ground may or may not be determined by the medical examiner.

Davis has told Jacobs and Richards that the suspect was pointing what he thought was a gun and so he fired up at the man.

"I saw something in his hand pointed down at me. It was metal—I could see light reflecting off of it," says Davis.

Davis is very frightened by these two men.

"You hear that line in a movie?" asks Jacobs.

"Fuck you," says Davis, trying something he did hear in a movie.

"No. Fuck you," says Jacobs.

And Davis knows that he didn't pull it off and wishes he would have believed himself when he told himself that he couldn't pull it off before he tried.

"I don't think we need to remind you that no shots were fired other than those you fired and no weapon has been found on or about the body of the alleged felon," says Jacobs, reminding him.

"I think I would like to speak to a lawyer," says Davis, using the last in his limited repertoire of movie clichés.

Jacobs and Richards return to their car.

Richards opens his mouth and lets out the words he has been afraid to let escape because he knows that once they are uttered they can never again be left unsaid.

"It's very hard to believe that this Murphy kid was a suspect in both a stabbing and a homicide and his detective brother didn't know anything about it," says Richards.

"Oh, he knew about it," says Jacobs.

. . .

Vota quits beating around the bush.

"Tommy, it's your brother. He's been killed resisting arrest."

"Motherfucker," is what Murphy says and throws a lamp against the wall sending Ralph scrambling for cover under the kitchen table. "I'd better call my mother."

"It's one in the morning, Tommy. Let her sleep."

"Where is he?"

"At the morgue by now."

"Do I have to go down to identify?"

"No. Sam did the ID at the scene."

"Sam was there? How the fuck...?"

"He arrived after the shooting," Vota interrupts. "It happened too fast."

"Why the fuck did Michael get shot at? He couldn't have been armed."

"He went out a hotel window. An officer down in the alley got nervous and started shooting."

"Who was it, Lou?"

"A cop. Jesus, Tommy, come on. Michael was running. They had him pegged for a felony homicide. Everyone was edgy. It was too fast. No one could slow it down."

"Michael didn't do that liquor store."

"Did he tell you that?"

"He never had the chance, but he was my brother for Christ's sake. I know what he could do and what he couldn't do. It's my fault—I had him and I let him go. I need a fucking drink."

Vota grabs the bourbon. He pours two tall glasses.

"Don't blame yourself," Vota says, hearing how benign it sounds even as he says it and handing Murphy the drink.

Murphy quickly drains the glass and hands it back to Vota for a refill. Murphy is boiling inside. Very close to the surface. He is very angry. At himself, for letting Mike off the hook so many times that this could happen. At the trigger-happy cop who killed his brother. At Vota for being here. At Samson for not being here.

Murphy is raging at his helplessness, his inability to change what has happened.

The finality of it.

And just before his rage and his anger are about to explode out of him, he is overwhelmed by a sincere sadness. The hand that takes the glass from Vota begins to tremble where a moment earlier it would have sent the glass the way of the lamp. He sinks into a chair, brings the trembling hand up to his face and drinks. And he knows that the most difficult thing he has ever had to do in his life will be explaining to his mother why he couldn't protect his little brother.

Her youngest child.

"I'm really sorry," says Vota.

"So am I," says Murphy and then, "Thanks for being here."

"Sam would be here too, you know; if he could."

"Yeah, I know. Of course I know that."

"And I'll go with you to see your mom. If you want," says Vota. "I mean we both will, Sam and me."

And Murphy rises, but not as if he's headed anywhere. And Vota fights the urge to go to Murphy, but loses the battle and is soon holding Tommy in a standing embrace. And Murphy is hugging back. And then the moment passes.

And they are quickly apart and Murphy is heading for the bourbon bottle and Vota is thinking he needs to call in real quick, check in with Samson.

"Shit, I left my cell phone and pager on my desk at the 61st," Vota says.

"Use the landline in the bedroom," Murphy manages to suggest.

"What a fucking mess," says Samson, looking over Batman's shoulder at the corpse on the floor.

"Makes you appreciate how neat and clean Gabriel Caine works," says Wayne, not looking back.

The body is that of a female Caucasian, mid-twenties, attractive, unclothed. Her right hand is missing a thumb. There is blood everywhere.

There are signs that this woman was bound and gagged.

There is a large bruise on her left cheek. She has been sexually abused. She is obviously in her own apartment.

This is a crime of passion. The sight of it is making Samson sick.

And Sandra Rosen, who has come up behind him, looks down and has to quickly look away.

Someone has tried to imitate an MO he read about in a newspaper. The result is nothing even vaguely resembling the previous murders.

The result is much more like a plane crash or a train wreck.

"At least this guy will be easy to find," says Samson to no one in particular, as if there were anything about a mess like this to be thankful for.

"Lieutenant," speaks a voice behind him.

"What is it?"

"Sergeant Vota is on the phone, sir. Wants to know if you need him down here."

"Tell him I don't."

"He said if you didn't need him down here he could use you up there."

"Tell him I'll be there as soon as I can."

"He said to come alone and to bring ice."

"They're bringing in the witnesses to identify your brother," says Vota.

"The guy that got stabbed will say yes; Duffy from the liquor store will say no."

"And what will you say?"

"To fuckface? Nothing. I don't know anything."

"What about a knife, maybe the cop in the alley saw a knife."

"So, he starts shooting? Fuck he think? Michael was going to throw it at him?"

"Maybe he saw *something*, thought it was a gun."

"Did they find a knife or anything that resembled a gun?"

"I don't know."

"Then what are you talking about?" asks Murphy,

reaching for the bourbon bottle.

"I don't know."

"You feeling sorry for the shooter, Lou?"

"I'm feeling sorry for everyone. You. Your mom. The mothers of Billy Ventura, Kevin Addams and Brenda Territo. Myself. Lorraine."

"What's with Lorraine?"

"Pass the bourbon," says Vota, and then, "Tommy, I'm scared shitless about Lorraine."

Samson takes about fifteen minutes with Rosen to make sure she understands everything that needs to be done in the next few hours on the case at hand. He says that he has to leave on important business. He tells her that she is in charge, and where he can be reached if anything broke or she needed advice. Samson tells her that he has Hackett working on getting Landis down to assist her if he could be located.. He tells her that odds are the murderer knew the victim, most likely a past or present boyfriend or husband. He tells her that no suspect was to be approached without first notifying him.

Samson starts to leave.

"Lieutenant."

"Yes."

"Murphy told me something that I think I have to tell you about."

"And that would be?"

"That his brother was the perp in a recent stabbing incident."

"Listen, Rosen," says Samson as calmly as he possibly can. "Very carefully. I know about Tommy's brother, and the situation has changed drastically. I don't want to go into it now; I really need to get out of here. I want you to forget that Detective Murphy mentioned anything to you about his brother. Anything at all. Do you understand?"

"I'm not sure that I do, Lieutenant."

"It's simple. Forget it. Trust me on this, Sandra."

"I need to hear more."

"Can you wait at least?"

"I can wait," says Rosen, "but don't let me wait too long. If I'm putting myself on the line for you or Tommy, I want to know the score."

"Okay, deal. Be careful."

"You too."

"So, how's Lorraine taking it?"

"She's strong, but she's pretty shook up."

"So, what the fuck are you doing here?" asks Murphy. "You should be getting rest so you can be at the hospital first thing in the morning to help her through this."

"I'm here because you just lost your brother."

"Thank you and bullshit."

"I didn't take the news very well, Tommy. And I think that Lorraine sensed it. Shit, Tommy, I feel as if I let her down."

"Is that what you feel?" says Murphy. "Don't fold on her, Lou. Lorraine needs to hear that it's going to be alright. And you'd best start believing it yourself. Don't leave Lorraine out in the cold, the way I left Michael out there all alone."

"C'mon, Tommy, it's not the same."

"It's exactly the fucking same. Something falls hard on the person next to you and you're checking yourself for damage. Someone who you're supposed to love and care about gets kicked in the ass and your first reaction is to cover your own. Mike had no one else to turn to. Lorraine isn't going to wait for you to come around; she needs to know she can count on you. Can she?"

"Yes."

"Let her know. What time is it?"

"Time to stop hoarding that bourbon," says Samson, walking in with a bag of ice cubes under his arm.

"I'm really sorry about your brother, Tommy," says Samson, taking a glass of bourbon from Vota.

"I want to know about the cop who shot him, Sam."

"Tommy."

"It's alright, Lou," says Samson, and then to Murphy,

"Kid's a rookie. Name's Davis. IAB is on it. So, how are you doing?"

"My kid brother just got blown away by Hopalong Rookie. Take a guess."

"The kid thought he saw a gun."

"He thought? Did they find a gun?"

"They're looking."

"They're looking. And what are they gonna *thought* when they don't find one?"

"Look, Tom, I didn't come here to argue with you," says Samson.

"Right. You came to bring ice."

"I came to bring you my condolences."

"IAB is going to chew Davis up and spit him out, and I'm going to be there passing the ketchup. The kid's finished, and the streets will be safer without him out there packing a thirty-eight."

"Don't take it so personally, Tommy," says Vota.

"Just how would you like me to take it, Lou?"

"I'd be more worried about what Internal Affairs has in mind for dessert after they've devoured the Davis kid," says Samson.

"What do you mean?"

"I mean fuckface and fuckface are idiots, but they're not stupid. A kid holds up in a hotel, goes out the window when the heat shows up—his brother the detective must know something about something. I want to know what you think your brother did and what you knew, Tommy. All our asses are on the line, not to mention your little heart-to-heart with Detective Rosen. IAB is going to be all over you and we'd better get this all straight."

"Oh, that's what you mean."

So, Murphy tells the story again, and Vota, who already heard it, decides that he'll call the hospital to check on Lorraine.

"Speak," says Andre Harris, bringing the cell phone to his ear.

"I've been standing here for four fucking hours and this fucking cop hasn't showed."

"What do you want? Need me down there to hold your hand?"

"Fuck you."

"No. Fuck you, Jefferson," says Harris. "You want the bread, fucking wait."

"Officer Landis?"

"What time is it?"

"After two. This is Detective Rosen. I need your help."

"I'm off until Saturday afternoon."

"Everyone else is occupied. Can I fill you in?"

"Not now, I'm still asleep. Give me fifteen minutes; I'll meet you in front of my place. You can fill me in on the way to wherever it is that I'm so indispensable on one of my few nights off."

"I'm sorry."

"Not your fault. See you in fifteen."

Sergeant Hackett looks up as Rey Mendez walks into the station at two-thirty.

"Hi, Rey. You look like shit."

"Thanks, I resemble that remark. Did Stump call back?"

"No."

"I think I know where to find him. If he calls again, tell him I'm headed to the White Owl."

Vota comes back into the living room after calling the hospital. He was told by a nurse that Lorraine was asleep.

"Well?" asks Murphy.

"Sleeping."

"Alright," says Samson, wanting to make sure that they all have things straight. "You tell fuckface that you knew nothing about Michael's trouble."

"Right, I didn't know anything and everyone backs me up,

including Rosen."

"Okay," says Samson. "We'll work it out."

"Sure we'll work it out," says Murphy. "Meanwhile my brother is in the morgue and his mother doesn't know about it yet, Lorraine has some kind of brain tumor and Lou would rather be here listening to us yell at each other, Territo is on the lam, some whacko is out there with a chip on his shoulder and a pair of garden shears, and you're standing there holding that bourbon bottle like you're waiting for fucking Christmas Eve. How do we work that out?"

"Well," says Lou. "In the morning we'll all go and see your mom, then I'll go see Lorraine before they wheel her into the OR, we'll bury Mike, and then we can go catch the bad guys. Meanwhile, break open that bag of ice and pass the bourbon."

"White Owl, Red speaking."

"Stump there?"

"Nobody here. We're closed."

"If you see him tell him Andre Harris called."

"What am I, his fucking answering service? If *you* see him first, you can tell him his cousin Rey called."

"Rey?"

"Yeah, Rey the cop."

"So," says Murphy, "what are you doing here? I thought we had another missing finger."

"What we had was a very sloppy copy. Rosen's on it."

"Anybody got any good news tonight?"

And then the phone rings.

"Maybe this is it," says Samson, moving to answer it. "It's probably for me."

Just as Andre Harris was getting into his car to head over to the White Owl on the chance that he might run into Stump and find out who the fuck Cousin Rey was supposed to be,

Stump was rapping loudly on the front door of that very establishment.

"We're closed."

"Red, it's me, Stump. Let me in."

"We're closed."

"I need your phone."

"Get lost."

"I'll give you twenty bucks."

"Hold your horses, I'm coming."

"That was Rosen," says Samson, taking up the bottle of bourbon. "Seems that tonight's victim dumped her boyfriend recently. Rosen spoke with the dead woman's roommate who says the boyfriend has been stalking the victim since the breakup. Suspect isn't at his residence. Rosen is staking it out with Landis. I told her to call me if he shows."

"Any calls for me?" asks Stump as Red lets him through the door.

"I'm tired of this shit. Why don't you get a fucking phone?"

"There's no hookup in my refrigerator box. Who called?"

"Cousin Rey and a guy named Harris."

"Uh-oh," says Stump as he dials the Precinct.

"Twelfth, Hackett."

"Officer Mendez."

"Not here."

"Did he get my message?"

"You Stump?"

"None other."

"Where are you?"

"White Owl."

"Stay put, he's on his way over there."

"Red," says Stump, replacing the receiver, "let me have a beer."

"Stump," says Red, "let me have my twenty."

. . .

They should probably all be somewhere else. Or at least getting some sleep.

Instead, they pass a bottle of bourbon.

They have decided, for some reason they have already forgotten or perhaps never quite knew, to exchange stories. Like kids sitting around a campfire, they are going to tell scary stories. Because scary things are happening and scarier things can happen yet.

And here is a chance to speak about fear. Aloud and in company.

And they all seem to know without saying that this is a rare opportunity and more important right now than sleep.

And the stories they tell are true stories. And they tell of the fears of boyhood and the fears of manhood. And they tell of the fears of innocence and the fears of guilt. And they speak in turn. First Vota, and then Samson, then Murphy, then Vota again. One scary story after the other, but none told with the intent of outdoing the previous one. The intention is not to compete. The intention is not to frighten but to remember fear.

And in doing so, to remember overcoming the fear.

And by the time Samson is recalling the time he lost Lucy in a department store for twenty minutes, just after Vota relived a hostage situation he was in the middle of in his rookie year, Murphy is snoring loudly on the couch.

And then the phone rings.

"We're closed, goddamnit!" yells Red to the rapping on the door.

"It's Rey," says Stump. "Let him in."

"What the fuck is this, your fucking office?"

"C'mon Red, lighten up. Be a good citizen."

"I got your good citizen swinging. I want both of you out of here in five fucking minutes," says Red, going to the door.

. . .

"That was Rosen, the suspect just arrived home. I'm going to head down there. You stay with Tommy. Let him sleep. Try to get some rest yourself. I'll give you a yell if I need you; otherwise I'll try to be back here at eight-thirty," says Samson. "We'll take Tommy over to see his mother."

"Okay, but you didn't finish the story about losing Lucy in the Kmart."

"And then I found her," says Samson, heading out the door.

"So, who's this guy asking all the questions about Vota and Samson?" asks Mendez.

"Harris, Andre," says Stump.

"Should I know that name?"

"His brother was the cat who plugged you, and then your boys made Swiss cheese out of him."

"Shit, what's he planning?"

"No idea. He just wanted the dope on them. He didn't say why or what for. I don't want to know."

"Didn't you think you might be putting them in danger?"

"Look, Mendez, the dude hands me a C-note and I answer a few questions. It ain't against the law and it's not my job to worry about it. That's why I called you. It's your job to worry about it. So, maybe you could show a little appreciation," says Stump, holding out his only hand.

"Can I use your phone," says Mendez to Red.

"What am I gonna say, no?"

Mendez dials Vota's home number. No answer.

Mendez calls the Precinct.

"Twelfth, Hackett."

"Hackett, it's Mendez. Where are Vota and Samson?"

"Samson's out on a call," says Hackett. "I'm not sure about Vota. Probably at home at this hour."

"Vota's not answering his home phone," says Mendez, "can you beep him?"

"I could, but it wouldn't do much good. He called me earlier tonight to tell me he forgot both his pager and cell phone upstairs."

"Okay, thanks, I'm going to head over to Vota's place in Red Hook and check it out. If you speak to Samson tell him that Harris' brother might be gunning for him and Lou."

"You want some backup?"

"No, I'll call in if I need any."

"How you feeling, Rey. I mean you just climbed out of a hospital bed."

"I'm feeling like I just climbed out of a hospital bed, but I'm doing alright, thanks," says Mendez, putting down the receiver and then turning to Red, "Thanks."

"You're very welcome," says Red. "Now, get the fuck out, both of you."

Junior Jefferson has been waiting outside of Vota's house for more than five hours. He is freezing his ass off. He is calling Harris from the phone both across the street. There is no answer.

"Fuck me," he says.

Andre Harris cruises by the White Owl just in time to see Mendez and Stump walking out together. He continues up the street, makes a U-turn and comes back. The guy who had come out with Stump is gone. Harris pulls up alongside the one-armed informer.

"Stump, get in."

Stump takes off.

Harris doesn't even get off a shot.

"Landis, get to the rear of the house. Rosen, come with me. Heads up."

Samson and Rosen slowly approach the front door, which is well lit by an overhanging lamp. Samson is just about to knock when Rosen gasps.

"Is that what I think it is?"

"It depends on whether or not you think it's a human thumb," says Samson looking down at the ground. The two detectives draw their weapons.

"Are we allowed to break the door down now?" asks Rosen.

"I'm not sure, is a thumb on the lawn more probable cause than a bloody glove?"

"Cute."

"Let's knock; I'm really not feeling up to kicking down this door."

"How about I ring the doorbell?"

"Okay, Rosen, ring the doorbell."

Rosen rings the doorbell.

The call from inside sounds a lot like *Whozzit?*

"It's three-thirty in the morning and this maniac is asking who is it," says Samson, and then raising his voice he says, "Police, open up."

"What do you want?"

"Who is this fucking guy?"

"Name is Roland."

"Roland what?"

"Rodney Roland."

"You call that a name? Mr. Roland, open the door."

"Do you have a warrant?'

"We don't need a warrant; we just want to ask you a few questions. Rosen please put that thumb in an evidence bag before I step on the goddamn thing. Mr. Roland, I'm getting impatient."

"I don't have an evidence bag."

"Have one of mine," says Samson, pulling one out of his inside jacket pocket. "Mr. Roland."

"I want to speak with a lawyer."

"Do you believe this guy? Just open the door, Rodney, then you can call whoever you want. Or is that whomever?"

"I didn't kill her."

"Okay Rosen, on three. One. Two. Three."

The door burst in under the force of two right legs. The two detectives enter with weapons extended.

They find Rodney Roland behind the door.

Knocked out cold.

"Now, I'll have to fill out a goddamn three page report

explaining why we had to trash a door to enter a suspected murderer's residence without a warrant," says Samson, just as Landis comes crashing through the back door.

"Make that two reports," says Rosen, as Roland starts to moan back to consciousness.

"Cuff this guy, Landis. Read him his rights and take him to the Precinct. Make sure that a doctor looks at him. Rosen, call in a team to go over this place and wait for them. I'm going home to get some sleep."

"How is Detective Murphy, Lieutenant?" asks Rosen, walking him out to his car.

"He's fine, Detective. I'll fill you in later. Meanwhile, please don't forget what I said earlier."

"Okay, but don't forget what *I* said earlier."

"Haven't we been through this one before?"

"Yes."

"Okay," says Samson, opening his car door, "and Sandra."

"Yes, Sam."

"Don't forget the thumb in your pocket."

If Lou Vota had arrived home, unsuspecting, Junior Jefferson could probably have gotten the drop on him and followed Andre Harris' order for a hit. Instead, Mendez shows up and spots Jefferson and slowly approaches the phone booth where Junior is trying to reach Harris to complain that the mark was not going to fucking show up tonight.

"Got a match?"

Jefferson's hand goes reflexively to the .45 tucked into the front of his pants when Mendez tackles him to the ground. Mendez has him cuffed in less than fifteen seconds.

"Got a permit for this piece, Andre?" says Mendez, taking the gun.

"Name's not Andre. As far as a permit is concerned, permit me to tell you to go fuck yourself before I exercise my right to remain silent."

. . .

At four-thirty in the morning, Stump is hiding in an abandoned building in Gravesend. He is praying that Andre Harris has given up his pursuit.

Mendez has deposited Junior Jefferson in a holding cell, where Junior waits for his lawyer. Mendez puts out an APB on Andre Harris, wanted for questioning, possibly armed and dangerous. Five minutes later, Mendez is fast asleep on a cot in the squad room.

Rosen and Landis are in an interrogation room trying in vain to get a coherent statement out of Rodney Roland. Batman and Robin are working on the body of Sheryl Lansing, the object of Rodney Roland's warped affection. They had quickly determined that the thumb found on the suspect's doorstep was a perfect match.

Thomas Murphy is snoring loudly on his sofa.

Vota is asleep in Murphy's bed; the warm body lying beside him belongs to Ralph.

When Samson comes into his house everyone is long asleep. As he gets out of his clothing, he thinks about what he has to look forward to in the next few days.

Helping to break the news to Murphy's mother that her other son was not coming home, ever. Watching a friend go into major surgery. Sitting by while fuckface and fuckface dragged Murphy over the coals. Hunting down Tony Territo. Trying to get hold of Gabriel Caine before there were more confessions and more imitators and more than enough news stories to have the entire city in a panic.

It is five minutes to five, Friday morning. Samson sets his alarm clock for 7:00 a.m. and lays down next to Alicia who sleepily turns into his arms.

TWENTY SEVEN

At 8:00 a.m., Murphy shakes Vota awake.

"Lou, I'm heading over to see my mother."

"Wait, I'll go with you."

"No, it's okay. I should do this by myself. You need to get to the hospital."

"Are you sure? Lorraine doesn't go into surgery for another two hours."

"Positive. And Lou."

"Yes?"

"Say something nice to Ralph before you leave. He always feels insecure and vulnerable the morning after."

At University Hospital of Brooklyn, Vota sits in a chair beside Lorraine's bed. They would be taking her down to the OR soon. Her father and mother had been there since eight, and had just left the room to allow Lou and Lorraine a few moments alone.

"Well, how do you like the new look?" asks Lorraine, moving her hand across the top of her head.

"You look pretty tough."

"Like Sigourney Weaver in *Alien 3* or Demi Moore in *G.I. Jane*, right?"

"I was thinking more along the lines of Yul Brynner in *Westworld*."

"Real cute, Vota. Don't you have bad guys to catch?"

"I'm just kidding, Kojak," he says.

Lorraine couldn't help laughing.

"What time is it?" yells Samson, bolting upright in bed.

"Ten a.m.," calls his wife from the kitchen.

365

"Damn. I was supposed to go with Tommy to see his mom."

"I think it is best that they deal with this together," says his wife, coming up to the bedroom door. "Alone."

"What happened? I set the alarm for seven."

"So sue me," says Alicia.

"Please hand me the telephone," Samson says. "I need to call my lawyer."

There is no answer at Murphy's, so Samson calls the Precinct.

"Twelfth, Kelly."

"It's Samson, fill me in."

"Mendez is asleep down here, looks like he just got out of a hospital bed. Jefferson is out on bail."

"Jefferson?"

"Junior Jefferson. It seems he was waiting outside of Vota's place with a contract from Andre Harris to hit Lou."

"Andre Harris?"

"Brother of the cat you and Lou sent to Boot Hill last week. Seems Harris is out for revenge. We put out an APB. We have an unmarked outside Vota's house."

"How about outside mine?"

"Look out the window."

"What else?"

"Rodney Roland is being held for arraignment later today. Rosen and Landis took off. She said she'd like to hear from you; he said he'd rather not. Fuckface called. Said that he and fuckface would love to see you and Murphy this afternoon at four, sharp. I have a corn on the little toe of my left foot that's killing me."

"Did Duffy from the liquor store show up to take a look at Michael Murphy?" asks Samson.

"Oh, yeah, that too. Duffy said the Murphy kid wasn't the shooter."

"Have you tried Dr. Scholl's?"

"You mean the celery soda?"

"Never mind. I'll be here at home for a while if anyone cares."

"Copy that. Over and out, Lieu."

"Are you going in?" asks Alicia.

"Not right away, I'm starving."

"Well then, how about I fix a big breakfast?"

"Sounds perfect. Can I help?"

"Help yourself to some coffee, and throw some bread in the toaster. And go out back to ask your daughters if they will grace us with their presence."

"How about Jimmy?"

"Not here."

"Oh?"

"Went to help a friend move some furniture."

"The Diaz kid?"

"Uh-huh."

"Got a phone number?"

"No."

"Too bad."

Andre Harris is laying low.

Harris knows that Stump fingered him. He also heard that Jefferson had been picked up. Harris doesn't know if Junior had fingered him as well.

Stump is lying very low.

Stump knows that Harris knows that Stump fingered him.

Junior Jefferson is out on bail, lying a little low.

Jefferson knows that he hadn't fingered Harris, but doesn't know if Harris knows that he hadn't fingered him.

The phone rings.

"Hello."

"Hi, Dad."

"Hi, Jimmy. Where are you?"

"I'm with my friend Nicky. His father wants to talk to you."

"Okay, put him on."

"Lieutenant Samson, this is Phil Diaz."

"How can I help you, Mr. Diaz?"

"You may or not know that I've had a little trouble with

the law in the past. I just want you to know that my Nicky is a good kid and that your son is safe with us."

"I hope so."

"That said, there's a guy named Andre Harris who might be looking to do you or your family harm. I can't tell you much more than that, but I assure you that he will get no help from me and he will get a lot of grief from me if he tries."

"I appreciate your candor, Mr. Diaz. I think that until this thing is settled, it would be safer for Jimmy and Nicky if they kept away from each other. If you see or hear from Harris again, please let me know immediately. Thanks for tipping me."

"Sure. I'll explain to Nicky that it's temporary. They're pretty close buddies."

"Absolutely. I'm sure that Jimmy will be disappointed also. Let me speak to him."

"Tommy, it is not your fault. Your brother was very mixed up. No one could have done more than you did to help him. My biggest regret is that your father wasn't around longer to give him guidance. My only relief is that your father is not here to see what happened to Michael."

"Mom, I'll make sure the kid who shot Michael pays for this."

"And do what? Destroy another young man like Michael? Bring suffering to another mother? I'm certain the officer was as terrified as your brother was. He didn't go out to kill someone. He felt that he was protecting himself."

"From what? Mike didn't even have a weapon."

"Are you sure?" asks his mother.

"What do you mean am I sure?"

"Tommy. Your father's service revolver. It's not in the closet."

The phone rings.

"Samson residence."

"Lieu, this is Kelly. I've got some bad news and some very

bad news. Which do you want first?"

"The bad news."

"I just got word that IAB has a gun found in the alley where Murphy's brother was shot last night. It was never fired. In fact, it wasn't loaded."

"Jesus, no bullets. What's the very bad news?"

"The gun belonged to Murphy's old man."

"Murphy's Law."

"Sorry, Lieu."

"Sit on this, would you?"

"My lips are sealed."

Jimmy Samson gets home in time to grab the last two pancakes as Alicia begins clearing the breakfast dishes.

"Want my last piece of bacon?" asks Lucy.

"Sure, thanks."

"Okay. Twenty-five cents."

"Real cute, Luce," says her father, trying to suppress a smile. "Kayla, please help your mom clean up. Jimmy, I'd like to talk with you before I go in to work if you have a few minutes."

"Sure, Dad, anytime," says Jimmy. "Would you take a dime, Lucy?"

"Fifteen cents."

"Deal."

The phone rings.

"Hello."

"Sam, it's Lou."

"Where are you?"

"At the hospital, Lorraine is just now coming out of the OR."

"Where's Murphy?"

"With his mother," says Vota.

"IAB wants Tommy in for questioning," says Samson. "This afternoon at four."

"Jesus, Sam. He just lost his brother. Is IAB that fucking

anxious?"

"I'd like to think they're unaware of the timing, but I wouldn't bet on it."

"I haven't been home," says Vota. "I need to shower and change. Unless you need me now."

"No, go ahead. I'll call if I need you."

"If I'm not home, I'll be back at the hospital. I want to be here when Lorraine is out of recovery."

"No problem. Give her my love. And Lou, watch your back. Looks like we have someone gunning for us."

"What's that about?"

Samson fills him in on Andre Harris.

"Tommy."

"Sam."

"How's your mom doing?"

"Not great, but she's a tough old Irishwoman."

"Listen, Tommy. IAB wants to see us this afternoon. They found your father's gun."

"Good, my mother will want it back," Murphy says. "Michael left the bullets here."

"I can call Chief Trenton, see if I can get him to call off the dogs until after your brother's funeral," says Samson.

"What time this afternoon?"

"Four. They'll come to the Precinct."

"Let's do it, Sam. Get it the fuck over with," says Murphy, "so I can get on with my so-called life."

Junior Jefferson is doing what he always does on a Friday morning, throwing hoops with his homeboys at the local schoolyard.

Jefferson has just sunk a three-pointer when he hears a familiar voice behind him.

"J.J."

"Andre, my man," says Junior. "What it is?"

"Got a minute?"

"For you, bro? Absolutely. Hey Slick, hold my spot. Be

back in a shake."

As they cross the yard, Junior can see the anger in Harris' every motion.

"Heard the man picked you up last night."

"Yeah. You believe that shit. Some gimp spic cop sandbagged me and dragged me to the 61st."

"What did you have to say?"

"Nada. They got nothing on me and less from me. All they've got is a brother with a gun. Big deal. My lawyer says no sweat. Doesn't think there was PC."

"Mention my name?"

"Fuck no. What do you have to do with the price of pinto beans? Don't sweat, bro. You don't figure in this shit."

"Glad to hear it, J.J. Seen Stump?"

"Not in a week, brother."

"I think he fingered me. You see him, you sit on him until you can get me over to chat with him. And if you have to sit on him real hard, don't worry about having to tell me he won't be talking to me. Or anyone. Get it?"

"Got it. What about the cop?"

"Guess I'll have to take care of that myself. You just find Stump. Soon."

Sal and Frances DiMarco sit waiting for news from the doctor. Shortly before noon, Dr. Barnwell approaches them. His expression is neutral. His news could be summed up as so far, so good.

The operation had been successful, the tumor removed, no complications observed. Lorraine was in recovery. She would be tested when she came through anesthesia for any abnormality in brain functions. Again, no reason to expect any problems. A biopsy would be done to establish whether the tumor was malignant or benign.

"So, if the biopsy comes back negative and Lorraine wakes up able to recite the preamble to the Constitution?" asks Sal DiMarco.

"Then she will be pretty much out of the woods and just as she was before this whole business started," says Barnwell.

"The headaches should be gone."

"She has one less headache already," says Lorraine's father.

"How's that?"

"She won't have to worry for a while about what to do with her hair."

"I'm going to love chatting with Murphy and Samson at the 61st," says Jacobs.

"Be easy on the guy, he lost a brother last night," Richards reminds him.

"His brother was a punk, and a criminal."

"You're just upset that the gun takes the Davis kid off the hook," says Richards, trying to lighten things up and wondering why Jacobs seemed to like his job so much.

"The gun puts Murphy right on the hook."

"Ease up," says Richards, hoping he isn't going too far with the senior investigator. "The gun wasn't loaded. And the Murphy kid didn't kill anyone; he was cleared on the liquor store shooting."

"He stabbed a man and left him bleeding in the street, and who knows what else."

"And you're so sure that Detective Murphy knew about it?"

"Positive."

"And how are we going to prove it? He's not going to give it to us on a silver platter."

"Maybe he'll slip up."

"He may have already slipped up, and it cost him a brother," says Richards. "Maybe it's just not worth the hassle. Maybe he's been punished enough."

"I hope you're not going to have trouble executing your duties, Sergeant," says Jacobs.

"Absolutely not, Lieutenant."

"Good, so we go and we get this guy."

. . .

372

Samson finally dragged himself to the Precinct at noon and has been sitting alone in the squad room for nearly three hours. No word on Harris or Caine or Territo.

Ballistics on the bullets from the gun found in Brenda Territo's coffin had been positively matched to the bullets that killed Sammy Leone, Dominic Colletti and Colletti's two sons.

Fuckface and fuckface are due in an hour. Samson decides on fresh air and a stale hot dog. On his way out he bumps into Rosen coming in.

"Howdy, Lieu."

"Well, Sandra, what brings you around?"

"Paperwork on that Roland psycho. Aren't you glad to see me?"

"Always. Can I bring you back a dirty-water frank?"

"How do you eat those things?"

"Chew slowly and use a lot of mustard."

"I'll pass, but you can bring me back a Diet Pepsi," says Rosen. "How's Murphy doing?"

"Rosen, you got a thing for our Tommy?"

"I'd have to be nuts."

"Granted," says Samson. "But that doesn't answer the question."

"I don't know. I doubt it. So, how is he?"

"He's holding his own. A little too much angst if you ask me, but nobody does."

"I'm a little worried about IAB, if they call me in."

"They have no reason to involve you. No offense, but they probably don't know you exist. But I do want us clear on this Michael Murphy thing. Let's see how clear we are when I get back with your soda."

"Just in case fuckface knows I do exist?"

Murphy walks into the squad room at three-thirty. Detective Rosen is already gone.

"Glad you came early, Tommy," says Samson. "We'll meet with Jacobs and Richards in the interview room. Let's have coffee and prepare for our little ordeal."

. . .

"Yo, Slick," calls Andre Harris, interrupting the Friday afternoon half-court basketball game. "Where's J.J.?"

"Didn't know it was my turn to watch him."

"Take a guess."

"Well," says Slick. "If a bus leaves for Baltimore at 1:45 p.m. traveling at fifty miles an hour..."

"What the fuck?" asks Harris.

"Probably somewhere near Philadelphia," says Slick, looking at his watch and then going for the rebound.

"Detective Murphy, a week ago your brother was the perpetrator in an attempted robbery. The mugging victim received multiple stab wounds during the incident."

"Alleged perpetrator," says Samson.

"The victim later identified Michael Murphy from a photograph," says Jacobs.

"That is not a conviction, Lieutenant Jacobs."

"Take it easy, Sam," says Richards. "We're not here to crucify anyone."

"I wish I could be that certain," says Samson, glaring at Jacobs.

"Okay, Lieutenant. Alleged perpetrator. Now, do you think that Detective Murphy can speak for himself?"

"Yeah, I can speak for myself, Jacobs. What the fuck do you want to know?" says Murphy.

"Detective, you are speaking to a superior officer."

"That's a laugh."

"Tommy, shut up," says Samson. "Ask your question Lieutenant Jacobs."

"Were you aware, Detective, that your brother *may* have been involved in the incident?"

"No, I was not."

"Did you have occasion to see your brother after the incident occurred?"

"No, I did not."

"Was it usual that you not see your brother for almost a

week?"

"It was not unusual."

"Even though he lived with your mother?"

"He was out a lot."

"Your mother said that you spoke with him on the phone this past Sunday."

"You bothered my mother?"

"It's routine."

"Routine. She just lost her son you callous fuck."

"Tommy, calm down. Jacobs get to the point."

"Did you speak with your brother on the phone?"

"Are you calling my mother a liar?"

"Lieutenant Jacobs," says Samson, jumping in again. "You asked the detective if he had seen his brother. He told you he had not. Now, you are asking something entirely different, and you introduced the question in an unusually adversarial manner. We are well aware of the fact that you outrank Detective Murphy, but there is no proof that he is undeserving of your respect. Please try to be objective. Ask your questions and let us get back to work."

If looks could kill, Richards would have been the only survivor.

"Detective Murphy, did you speak with your brother on the phone last Sunday?"

"Yes I did."

"And he said nothing about being involved in the incident in question?"

"He did not."

"And were you aware that he was in possession of your father's service revolver?"

"No I was not."

Jacobs pauses. Looks at Richards, back at Murphy, and then to Samson. The room is silent for nearly a minute.

"Is that it?" says Samson.

Jacobs remains silent.

"Good," says Samson. "Nice talking with you fellows. Let's go Tommy."

Samson and Murphy get up to leave.

"We'll be in touch," says Jacobs, finally freeing his tongue.

"Can't wait," says Samson, ushering Murphy out of the room.

"Well?" says Jacobs after they are gone.

"Well, what," says Richards. "We got nothing. Forget it, let it go."

"He's lying through his teeth," says Jacobs.

"So what."

"Ms. DiMarco, I want to talk with you about what was done and what you can expect, before we invite your parents in," says Dr. Barnwell, settling into a chair beside her.

"Okay, and please call me Lorraine."

"Lorraine, please let me lay it all out before you ask any questions."

"I was under the impression that appropriate bedside manner allowed for the patient to jump in at any time."

"It's not my style."

"I'll try. But I am an attorney, Doctor. And I have a habit of interrupting."

"Try your best," says Barnwell, respectfully. "The tumor we removed this morning was a primary brain tumor. Meaning the original source of the tumor was the brain, as opposed to a metastatic brain tumor caused by cancer somewhere else in the body. It was accessible, not deep in the brain and fairly easy to remove."

"Sounds good so far."

"A meningioma tumor is something like a capsule with a sac around it," says Barnwell. "Once the tumor is removed, there are usually no residual tumor cells. But we do keep in mind the fact that even the removal of 99 percent of a tumor can leave a residual of one billion tumor cells."

"As in one billion?"

"Yes."

"Nice number."

"It's not as bad as it sounds. Please let me finish."

"Sure."

"The existence of residual tumor cells could lead to a reappearance of the tumor and a recurrence of the symptoms.

If that is the case, then there are means at our disposal to attack these residual cells. You are probably familiar with procedures such as radiotherapy and chemotherapy, and we are achieving increased success with immunotherapy."

"Don't know that one."

"The employment of a biological response modifier to help the body's natural defense mechanisms to inhibit tumor growth."

"Getting your own immune system to do the job?"

"Exactly. All of these methods have pros and cons and ultimately the decision would be yours as to which, if any of them, to initiate if the need arose. Of course, the most important factor in all of this is what we will find in the biopsy. If the tumor is found *not* to have been malignant, and with the success of the operation in removing virtually all of what was determined to be a low-grade primary brain growth, the prognosis is extremely good."

"So we wait."

"So we wait. We should have the pathology report by Monday afternoon."

"Well, thanks for the facts, Doc. Will there be a midterm exam?" she says, trying on a smile for size.

"You're welcome, there may be a pop quiz," Barnwell says. "If you have any questions let me know."

"That's not the point."

"That's exactly the fucking point, Rey."

"I don't see it."

"What's the last thing he says before he dies?"

"Rosebud."

"There it is. How can you not see it?" says Landis.

"Mendez, Landis, do you read me, over."

"Mendez speaking. If anyone can hear me through this static."

"I read you Rey. Static is a way of life with me. Your boy Stump just called—says Andre Harris is gunning for him and he wants you to bring him in."

"Bring him in?"

"Yeah, he said, and I quote, *I want to come in from the cold*. Leave it to you to have a snitch who thinks he's Richard Burton."

"Kelly, maybe you could settle an argument for us."

"Oswald acted alone."

"What was the moral of *Citizen Kane*?"

"Citizen who?"

"Orson Welles."

"No wine before it's time?"

"Jesus, Kelly, you're unbelievable."

"You want to know where this guy Stump is or not?"

"Sure."

"You going to bring him in from the cold or let him dangle?"

"You thinking he might be bait to snag Harris?"

"It crossed my mind."

"Let us know where he is. We'll play it by ear."

"Don't mess with guys in big houses."

"What?"

"The moral. Never fuck with a guy who owns a mansion in California. San Simeon, Xanadu, Rockingham, whatever."

"Kelly, you're unbelievable."

"I've heard. Stump is holed up at O'Brien's on Kings Highway. Over and out."

After meeting with IAB, Murphy goes back to his place to walk Ralph.

Vota calls to tell Murphy that he is going out to see how Lorraine's operation went and then he would head over to Joe's Bar and Grill to join Tommy for a few drinks.

Landis and Mendez thought that they would let Stump sweat a little. They had decided that they couldn't in good conscience let him swing in the wind; that they would have to do something to protect him. But maybe if Stump had to wait a while, he would be that much more talkative when they got to him.

They walk into O'Brien's just after six and find the bartender.

"We came for Stump," says Mendez.

"Well, you got me stumped. Don't know what you're talking about."

"Look, pal, he called us, asked us to come rescue him. If you don't believe me, go out back or wherever you've got him stashed and ask him. Tell him Rey is here."

"Fuck it. What the fuck do I care? Go back there and tell him yourself. Through the door on the left."

"Thanks," says Mendez. "Say, anyone ever tell you look a lot like a guy works over at the White Owl. Name's Red I think."

"Yeah, our mother tells us all the time. You need an escort?"

"That's alright," says Landis as the two officers head for the back of the bar.

When they enter the back room, Stump nearly hits the ceiling.

"Jesus Christ, Rey, where you been? I called hours ago. This Harris is a lunatic; you gotta get me off the streets."

"Okay, Stump. Calm down, the cavalry has arrived. Where's Harris now?"

"How the fuck should I know? He could be outside this place. When you opened the door, I thought it was curtains."

"Stump. Or is it Mr. Stump?" says Landis. "Ease off a little on the melodrama. This isn't a Jimmy Cagney movie. What do you suggest we do with you?"

"I don't know. Do what you do. Protective custody. Whatever. Just keep me out of this guy's reach until you nail him."

"How about Jefferson?"

"Junior went down to Baltimore to chill. Did you know it's snowing down there? He doesn't have to be back until his court date on that little wrestling match you had with him in a phone booth and I don't expect you'll see him until then. Just hide me somewhere."

"Okay, you're under arrest, come with us."

"What, you're not going to Mirandarize me?"

"Don't get cute or I'll tear off your good arm and beat you over the head with it," says Landis. "Don't forget that you got yourself into this mess and put our detectives in danger while you were at it. I'm not going to forget it and I'm going to keep reminding you if you have a memory lapse. Asshole."

"Show some respect, I lost the hand in Kuwait fighting to keep your gas tank full. Is he always this warm, Rey?"

"Shut the fuck up, Stump, you're pushing it," Mendez says. "You couldn't even spell Kuwait. If you had two hands, I'd cuff you. Now, let's get the fuck out of here."

"Gee, I'm glad I called you guys. I feel really safe now."

"Would you like us to leave without you?"

"Absolutely not. Lead the way."

"Four-score and seven years ago," recites Lorraine, "our forefathers brought forth upon this continent a new nation, conceived in liberty and dedicated to the proposition that all men, and all women I would like to add, are created equal, shall I go on?"

"Very funny, Lorraine," says her father.

"Did I pass the memory test?"

"You should have asked her to recite Shakespeare's twenty-third sonnet," says Vota.

"Piece of cake," says Lorraine. "The Lord is my shepherd, I shall not want. He—"

"Cut it out, Lorraine," says Sal DiMarco, "you have made your point. You are just as smart as you were before the operation, and just as smart-mouthed."

"Dad, I feel fantastic. Except for the drool on my chin. This is the first time in I can't remember how long that I woke up without a headache. By the way, how's my head look?"

"Like a smiley face without the eyes," says Vota.

"I'm in stitches," she says, and then she turns to her mother. "Mom, cheer up. I made it. I can remember my cup size."

"Oh, Lorraine," says her mother, reddening.

"You're worried about the biopsy findings?" Lorraine says, and when her mother doesn't answer, "Try not to think about it. I'm not going to think about it. I'm going to enjoy the next few days thinking about how lucky I am and watching my hair grow."

"I'll do my best, Lorraine," says her mother.

"How's Tommy doing, Lou?" asks Lorraine, trying to move on to new business.

"I think he's still in the *I blame myself* phase."

"Catholic guilt," says Lorraine and then, "I'm sorry. I shouldn't joke. He'll get over it. He has good friends to keep reminding him that he's innocent."

"No one is innocent," says Vota.

"Alright, St. Augustine, let's move on to happier subjects. Where's my ice cream?"

"The nurse said you only get ice cream if you have your tonsils removed."

"Then do me a favor, Lou."

"What's that?"

"Tear my tonsils out of my throat and then go get me some cherry French vanilla," says Lorraine.

"What do you think of the new weatherman on Channel Two?"

Landis is trying to make friendly conversation with Kelly while Mendez is finding accommodations for Stump.

"I don't know. It's too early to call. I'm just glad it's not a woman. I'm so tired of weatherwomen. And now all the women sportscasters. I don't get it. Why would they even want to do it?"

"For the money?"

"I don't even like men sportscasters if they never played the game."

"I thought this new guy was okay. He said it may snow tomorrow—what do you think?"

"Well, it's snowing in Baltimore."

Andre Harris realizes that Junior Jefferson is too far away to be of any help in tracking down Stump. And he's already decided that he is going to take care of the cops who killed his brother without Jefferson's help.

Harris also knows that the cops are looking for him; he will have to stay scarce.

Hunt for Stump, hunt for the pigs, and keep out of sight.

Tricky. But Andre Harris loves a challenge.

Agent Stone catches Samson at the 61st.

"Lieutenant, I've been going through Caine's mail," says Stone. "There was tons of it. I put in time at his place today and yesterday. I have separated out everything that may give us a clue, mostly personal mail. I was hoping it would be okay to take it back to my office. Agent Ripley should be able to get permission to examine the contents."

"I have no problem with that," says Samson.

Landis and Mendez are about to call it a night. Andre Harris hasn't surfaced, and tomorrow is another day.

They pull into the Precinct parking lot to drop off their cruiser. Landis heads to his own car; Mendez drops the keys to the patrol car off with the desk sergeant and stops at the cellblock to check on Stump.

"This ain't working out," says Stump, pacing the cell. "I'm claustrophobic."

"What did you expect, a suite at the Plaza?"

"No sight of Harris?"

"Not a glimpse."

"He's going to make a move soon," says Stump.

"What's that, a hunch?"

"No, it's a fact," answers the one-armed informer.

"What makes you so sure?"

"Conventional wisdom."

Murphy and Vota sit at Joe's Bar and Grill, drinks in hand.

"Here's to Lorraine making it through the operation with flying colors," says Murphy.

"Here's to you surviving IAB," says Vota.

The bar phone rings as they toast. Augie is delivering drinks to a far table.

"Would you grab that, Tommy?" Augie Sena calls.

"Joe's," says Murphy into the receiver.

"I need to place a food order for delivery."

"Go ahead," says Murphy, reaching for pad and pencil.

"A large order of fried calamari, with hot sauce on the side. An order of baked ziti with sausage. An order of shrimp scampi over linguini. And lots of garlic bread."

"What's the address?" asks Murphy.

"Is Augie working?"

"Yes."

"Tell him it's for Stevie T—he'll know."

"Who called?" asks Augie, returning to the bar.

"Food order, for Stevie T. Says you'll know him."

"Stevie Territo, lives right up here on West 5th Street between U and V. Watch the bar for a minute," says Augie. "I'll bring this order back to the cook."

"You thinking what I'm thinking?" asks Vota.

"That's an awful lot of grub for one guy. Maybe his cousin dropped over for dinner," says Murphy.

"How do you deliver, Augie?" asks Vota.

"My dishwasher, Max."

"Could you bring him out with you?"

"Sure," says Augie, heading for the kitchen.

Augie returns, Max follows as far as the kitchen door.

Max is sporting a cotton chef's tunic under a full apron, one or both of which may have been white at one time. Max stands there as if he's afraid to come any closer to the two detectives.

"Jesus, Augie, what have you got him wearing?" says Murphy. "That outfit should be dry-cleaned and burned."

"It's been a busy night, and unlike some I could name, there are those who work hard for a living."

"We need the shirt and apron," says Vota. "We're your new delivery men."

Augie takes Max back into the kitchen and comes out with the clothing.

"Lou will be wearing it," says Murphy.

"Are you insane," says Vota. "That stuff looks like it was pulled out of someone's throat. I'm afraid I'm going to have to pull rank, Tommy."

"Lou, this kid Stevie has seen me before," Murphy says. "It's going to have to be you at the front door."

"Fucking wonderful," says Vota. "Hand me those nasty-looking things, Augie."

Twenty minutes later, Vota is ringing the front doorbell. Murphy has gone around back.

"Let's see, that's the eggplant parmigiana and the fettuccini Alfredo," says Vota when Stevie Territo opens the door. "Seventeen dollars and eighty-five cents."

"What the fuck are you talking about? That's not what I ordered."

"That's what it says right here on the ticket, sir," says Vota. "Shit, I hope I didn't grab the wrong bag."

"You fucking imbecile," Stevie yells. "I'll have you fired."

"What's all the noise about?" says Tony Territo coming to the door.

Territo recognizes Vota immediately and runs for the back. Murphy grabs Territo as Tony bolts out of the rear door. Murphy has him handcuffed by the time Vota appears, pushing Stevie along in front of him.

"You're under arrest for the murders of Sammy Leone, Sonny Colletti, Richard Colletti, and Dominic Colletti," says Murphy. "Did I get them all in, Lou?"

"I think so. You'll be taking a ride with us also," says Vota, cuffing Stevie, "Harboring a fugitive."

"Those fucking Collettis killed my daughter," yells Tony Territo, struggling against his cuffs.

"Actually, they didn't," says Vota. "But we can get to all of that later. Right now, I want you to exercise your right to remain silent. Both of you. Very silent."

"Can we take the food along with us at least?" Stevie Territo asks. "I'm fucking hungry enough to eat eggplant."

. . .

Caine sits at a table in the back of Mitch's, turning the pages of a two-day-old copy of the *Tribune* he picked up off the back alley. He comes across a piece on the murders of two Brooklyn boys. The article states that the boys were killed by the same man, and both were brutally disfigured. The short piece goes on to suggest that the killer is most likely someone who had been abused as a child and may have tortured and mutilated animals in the past. The police are urging parents to be diligent as to the whereabouts of all their children.

Gabriel decides that this reporter needs much better information. He searches the back rooms for a telephone book. He is somehow confident that Serena Huang will have a listed number.

Gabriel finds a Brooklyn phone directory on a cabinet shelf. And sitting beside the book, a handgun.

He carries the book and the weapon back to the table.

TWENTY EIGHT

Saturday morning. Murphy and Ralph run the track at Fort Hamilton High School. Murphy spots the unmarked car sitting directly across from the house where Gabriel Caine had prepared a bathtub for a baptism.

Samson has given Murphy time off. He has told Murphy not to come in until after the church service for his brother. Until after the burial.

Trouble is, Murphy has nothing at all to do. He has no idea what he is going to do with himself all morning.

"Looks like snow," says Murphy. "What do you think?"

Ralph barks in agreement.

Lorraine DiMarco wakes up in her hospital bed. Without hair, sure. But without a headache.

She looks around the cold, gloomy hospital room and then up at the television mounted on the opposite wall. She uses the remote control to turn on the TV.

Lorraine finds an old Barbara Stanwyck film on the classic movie channel.

"Nice hair, Barb," she says.

"This looks like a fine pancake batter," says Ripley to the boys, who decided to make breakfast for Dad. "You weren't going to cook them before I came down, I hope."

"No, we were just getting it ready. We can't use the stove without you to help us," says Kyle.

"Whose idea was it to add the cocktail olives?" asks Ripley, stirring the contents of the large bowl and taking in the thick layer of pancake mix covering the counter and the floor below it.

"Me, Dad," says Mickey, beaming. "There was no blue berries and you love those little olives."

"That I do, son," says Ripley. "Do you have a name for this inventive gourmet concoction?"

"What's a gummy cockshun, Dad?" asks Mickey.

"We call them martini flapjacks, of course," says Kyle with as straight a face as he can manage.

"I bet that the Pancake House would love to have this recipe. How about we clean up some and go down there to tell them about it?"

"And maybe while we're there, we can see if they have any blueberries," says Kyle.

"Good idea," says Ripley, when the phone rings.

"Sorry to bother you on a Saturday," says Agent Stone.

"And so nice and early, too. What's up?"

"I have some mail from Caine's house," says Stone. "I was hoping you could get the okay to open it."

"Not before Monday, so enjoy the weekend."

"You do the same."

"Oh, Win. I almost forgot," says Ripley. "Kyle's third-grade class is doing a field trip to the New York Aquarium at Coney Island on Monday and it's my turn to be one of the tag-a-long parents. I won't be in until Tuesday morning. I'll try to get permission for you to open the mail before then."

"Wow. The Aquarium. That sounds like fun."

"Have you ever been on an excursion with twenty-five eight-year-olds?" asks Ripley.

"No."

"Not fun. Have you had breakfast?"

"No."

"I'm taking the boys to the Pancake House on Queens Boulevard and 73rd Avenue, if you would care to join us."

"Does that sound like fun?" asks Stone.

"Let's just say that it has more potential than two dozen kids crowded around a shark tank," says Ripley. "Be there in thirty minutes if you feel like braving it."

"Why not," says Stone. "Columbus took a chance."

. . .

388

Samson arrives at the Precinct at eight. He finds Murphy already there.

"I said that you could take the day off, Tommy," says Samson. "Shouldn't you be with your mother?"

"My mother is being well taken care of by my father's brothers and her sisters. I needed a sane distraction, so I came to finish the paperwork on the Territo arrest."

"How's Tony doing?"

"Not too well. That lunatic Stump is in the adjoining cell, chewing Territo's ear off."

"Have you had breakfast?" asks Samson.

"I can't remember, but I can always do breakfast."

Kelly stops them on their way out to the New Times.

"Lieu, we got a situation on Fulton Street downtown. A Union rally at one of the department stores has turned ugly. I just got a call that they could use a few more cars down there. I was wondering if we could pull the car sitting over at Vota's place."

"Let me call Lou, see what he thinks."

"I'm on my way to the hospital to see Lorraine," says Vota when Samson calls. "I'll send those guys in front over to Fulton Street on my way out. I'll be in later."

"Done, Kelly," says Samson. "Let's eat, Tommy."

The film was *The Strange Love of Martha Ivers* and, although Lorraine preferred Bette Davis, she found herself getting wrapped up in it. She thought that her father and Lou would probably like this one. Her father was a big Kirk Douglas fan, and this was Douglas' first film. And the crime element might appeal to Lou. She thought about calling them, but decided that her father had probably seen it a hundred times and Lou probably didn't need another murder mystery on his hands. Just when Van Heflin arrived back in Iverstown, there was a knocking on the door of her hospital room.

"I'm guessing it's open," she calls.

"How are you feeling, Lorraine?"

"Not bad, Doctor. I don't know what they have in this IV, but I haven't felt like worrying for a few hours."

"Good. I can give you our preliminary findings. It is looking very good," says Barnwell. "Based on the shape of the tumor, and the sac that surrounded it, we're almost certain that the cancer was not malignant. I'll have the pathology report, based on microscopy in the laboratory, by Monday afternoon. I'll go over the report with you when I return from Bethesda. I believe that we can avoid drug or radiation treatment entirely, unless symptoms recur."

"Great."

"We are giving you Dilantin, which is an antiseizure medication, with the recommendation that you remain on the drug for a few weeks. Surgery will often cause swelling of the brain, which can cause seizures," says Barnwell. "We'll also administer a drug to decrease any apparent swelling if necessary."

"When can I get out of here?"

"I think I can let you go in a week, if everything continues to look good. I recommend that you rest for a few weeks, stay away from your office."

"I can do that."

"I'll stop in to see you again a few times before I leave for Maryland," says Barnwell. "And when I get back, we should know all we need to know. I'm very optimistic."

"Thank you, Doctor. Can I call you Rowdy?"

"No," says Barnwell. "By the way."

"Yes."

"I don't usually like Barbara Stanwyck movies, but that's a very good one," Barnwell says before leaving the room.

Everyone's a movie critic, she thought, running her hand across her head.

He was much better in Shane, Lorraine thinks when Van Heflin returns on screen.

"The lieutenant is out to breakfast," says Kelly. "He should be back soon. I'll tell him you called, but I doubt he'll be interested."

"Tell him that it is very important, that things have changed," says Serena Huang. "Tell him that I received a phone call from a man who isn't done with his crayons yet. The lieutenant will understand."

"Give me your phone number," says Kelly.

"That's great news, Lorraine," says Vota when she fills him in on the preliminary results.

"Yeah, not bad huh."

"Close shave."

"Are you making fun of my head again, Lou?" Lorraine asks.

"I love your head."

"I'll let that one pass. Is it swelling?"

"Is what swelling?"

"My head."

"Not as much as it did when you won your last big court case."

"Get out of here and go to work," says Lorraine. "My breakfast should be arriving soon and I am not sharing my stewed plums."

"I'll lay off your plums. But I want to stay to see how the movie ends."

"Heflin finds out that Martha Ivers killed her aunt," says Lorraine. "Now go make the streets safe."

"See you later," says Vota.

"That reporter called, Lieu—something about crayons," says Kelly when they walk in. "Here's the phone number."

Samson grabs the number and races up to his desk, with Murphy at his heels.

"I don't know where he is, Lieutenant. He phoned."

"Do you have caller ID?"

"He said that he was calling from a phone booth," says Serena, "I do have the number."

"Run this number right away, Tommy," Samson says, and repeats it as Serena reads it to him. "What exactly did Caine say, Ms. Huang?"

"He said he wants to help me get the story straight," says Serena. "He doesn't believe everything that he reads in the newspapers."

"I'm not surprised," says Samson. "Where on earth did you get all of that nonsense about an abused childhood and dead animals?"

"Straight out of a textbook, Lieutenant, but have you seen some of other news stories lately? They're saying he may be homosexual, because his victims were boys. That he may be eating the body parts. One writer had a wild idea that Caine was carving up his victim's faces. The less you tell the media, the more they feel that they have to dream something up. I don't think getting the real facts out is such a bad idea," says Serena.

"What does he want?" asks Samson.

"Caine wants people to understand that he is saving these children, sending them to heaven, protecting them from being damned by the sins of their fathers. He said he's a soldier of God. He said that if I could help make his intentions clear, he would turn himself in."

"And you scoop the big story," says Samson.

"That's the last thing on my mind, Lieutenant."

"I'll bet."

"Lieutenant, Gabriel Caine said that he would turn himself in *after* he had saved the last child. I'll do whatever you believe is best."

Jesus.

"Lieutenant?"

"I'm still here. I'll have to talk to Chief Trenton. I'll get back to you."

Samson puts down the receiver.

"It's the booth at 5th and 69th, Sam," says Murphy. "It's just up the street from his house."

Samson calls the 67th Precinct, trying to locate Chief Trenton.

. . .

"It may not be a bad idea, Sam," says Trenton. "We have a panic growing that will only get worse the longer these news stories continue to become more irresponsible. We already have a flood of missing persons reports, a number of confessions, and one of the radio stations has offered a huge reward for information. It won't be long before people start turning each other in. If the public hears that the victims were chosen for a reason, no matter how insane the reason, people may at least understand that not every child in the city is in danger."

"So, we let her go with the story?"

"I think we have to, Sam. Make sure we see it before she turns it in and that we stay with her day and night in case Caine contacts her again," says Trenton. "He told her that he was planning to kill another child?"

"Yes."

"We can't let that happen, Sam."

"I am sending a Detective Marina Ivanov over to you," says Samson. "She will read your story before you bring it to the *Tribune*, she will escort you to drop it off, and she will stay with you until Gabriel Caine is apprehended. Is that perfectly clear?"

"Yes, it is," says Serena.

"I've got a car at the phone booth, Sam. Where the fuck do you think Caine is?"

"Close," says Samson.

"Lou called; he's on his way here from the hospital."

"When Lou gets in I want you out of here, Tommy," says Samson. "You have funeral arrangements to attend to and a mother you should be with. I have all the help I need. And Tommy."

"Yes."

"This was found in Michael's room at the hotel," says Samson, handing Murphy the note, feeling that he had been holding it from Murphy for far too long.

"Did you read this?" asks Murphy, after reading it himself.

"Yes."

"Do you think that Mike went there to kill himself?"

"I don't know, Tommy," Samson answers. "I don't know."

Murphy runs home to see to Ralph's needs. Feeding, walking and reassuring the animal. Murphy has some time before he needs to pick up his mother for the drive to the funeral home to make arrangements for the wake, so he decides to make a quick visit to the hospital to see Lorraine.

"I'm really sorry about your brother, Tommy. I don't know what else to say."

"What can you say? I'm glad the operation went well."

"So."

"So."

"So, I heard you had to meet with Internal Affairs," says Lorraine. "Were they surprised when you strolled in without counsel?"

"I told them that my lawyer was busy destroying more of her brain cells," says Murphy. "I didn't say how."

"I'm sure they had some interesting theories."

"Lorraine, I wanted to ask you about the suspect we're trying to find, Gabriel Caine. Caine planned and executed the murder of three young people, but he seems to believe he was saving them somehow. How do we deal with judging someone that irrational?"

"From a moral standpoint or a legal one?"

"Either."

"Do you think this man knows the difference between right and wrong?" asks Lorraine.

"Yes, I do. But I think that he has a very mixed-up conception about what's right."

"From a moral standpoint, if this man truly believes that he is doing right, doing good, he could be considered a moral person. But from a legal standpoint, premeditated murder is against the law and is therefore wrong, without ambiguity. If he truly believes otherwise, he might be considered unable to make the distinction. An argument could be made that Caine is legally insane."

"Would you defend such a case?"

"Are you looking for a lawyer for him?"

"No. It's just that I saw this guy, the night that his son died. I looked into the man's eyes. What I saw was someone who was already dead, emotionally. And dead people are far beyond knowing right from wrong. Whatever is driving him is keeping him alive, at least physically. I believe that when Gabriel Caine is finished, he will be ready to die."

"Suicide?"

"In some form."

"What brought this on? Does it have something to do with what happened to Michael?"

"I don't know, it seems that there are so many people out there that need help and don't find any. I don't know."

Landis and Mendez have beaten the bushes for most of Saturday afternoon.

There is no sign of Andre Harris.

Mendez is fatigued. He is not fully recovered from his gunshot wound, having removed himself from the hospital prematurely.

They take one more swing past Vota's house and make plans to pick up the search for Harris again after Michael Murphy's funeral service at the church the next morning.

Mendez feels as if he could easily sleep until then. Landis picks up a Saturday newspaper to check the movie listings.

Rosen bumps into Vota as they both leave the Precinct.

"How is your friend Lorraine doing?" Rosen asks as they walk to the parking lot.

"It went very well. Funny, hearing you refer to Lorraine as my friend. I've been trying to ask Lorraine to marry me since Christmas, but I never seem to be able to get it out. Maybe I'll just ask her tonight."

"Lou."

"Yes?"

"It's none of my business, but I have no self-control so here goes," says Rosen. "It may not be a good time to bring up marriage to Lorraine. She just had what could be considered a life-threatening experience. If Lorraine is dealing with her own mortality, thoughts about her future, marriage, family, whatever, may be difficult for her to address. At least for a while."

"Conventional wisdom?"

"Woman's intuition?"

"Thanks, I'll take that into consideration."

"I could be way off base," says Rosen. "Here's my car."

"I appreciate you stepping up to the plate. Here comes the snow they've been predicting for the past few days," he says as the flurries begin. "Drive safely, Sandra."

"You be careful also, Lou," says Rosen.

She watches Vota walk off as she climbs into her car.

Light snow falling, seeming not to touch him.

You're a blabbermouth, Rosen, she thinks as she turns on the windshield wipers and slowly pulls away.

Andre Harris stands shivering in the claustrophobic entryway between the inner and outer doors of the house.

All of the warmth is beyond the bolted interior door, out of his reach.

When he peeks out from the small window pane in the exterior door, Harris can see that the mild flurries have evolved into a steady fall of heavy, wet flakes.

I hate fucking snow, he mumbles to himself.

Samson pulls into the driveway and rushes into the house, shaking the snow from his coat at the door.

"Are the kids up?" he asks as Alicia takes the coat.

"The girls are up in their room, at the window," says his wife. "They're very excited. Lucy looks as if she's expecting Santa Claus. Maybe we can take them sledding at Lily Pond Park tomorrow."

"I'll have to work for a while in the morning," says Samson. "I'll try to get home early."

"Sit. Relax. The kids left some dinner for you."

"I've been thinking about the man you're looking for, Gabriel Caine," says Lorraine.

"Murphy said he was here to visit earlier today. Did he bend your ear about Caine?" asks Vota.

"I think it was more about Murphy. Tommy's feeling he could have done more to help his brother, should have done more."

"It's understandable. Michael was only twelve when his father died, it was a huge responsibility for Murphy," says Vota. "We've talked about it, and I know that Tommy's mother has spoken with him. I think he'll work through it and realize that there was only so much he could do for his brother, only so much he was qualified to do."

"I'm sure you're right, but I think it goes beyond that. I got the impression that Murphy empathizes with Gabriel Caine. Tommy feels Caine needed help before the accident, at the time of the accident, and even more so since. And there was none to be found. And I believe Tommy feels that the man still needs help."

"Caine may be past the point of accepting help," says Vota.

"It's very sad," says Lorraine.

"Yes, it is," says Vota.

"Tommy said that Caine may be planning to kill again."

"It was something Caine said to the reporter."

"Tommy also said that Gabriel Caine was taking the boy to the hospital when the accident occurred. What was wrong with the boy?"

"I really don't know," says Vota. "His wife told us that the boy was ill and they were on the way to meet the boy's physician."

"So, when you spoke with the boy's doctor, the child's illness never came up?"

"We never spoke with the boy's doctor. We were told that

the pediatrician wasn't at the hospital when the boy died. We didn't feel it was necessary to talk with him."

"Why wasn't the doctor there? Didn't you say he was meeting Caine and the boy."

"Yes, I did. And it's a very good question. Are you thinking that Caine feels he has a score to settle with the boy's doctor?"

"It was a fleeting thought, but I'm sure the doctor must have contacted the Caine family once he learned about what happened," says Lorraine. "To explain his absence and offer condolences."

"I think I'll stop in at Coney Island Hospital in the morning, before the church service," says Vota. "I can find out who the doctor was and arrange to talk with him."

"Lou, look out the window."

"Wow. It's really coming down."

"You'd better get going, before the roads are really bad," says Lorraine.

"Okay. I'll drop by tomorrow."

"Bring me pizza from L & B's."

"Square or round?"

"Why not make it one slice of each," says Lorraine.

"You got it," says Vota, leaning down to kiss her forehead. "I love you, DiMarco."

"I love you, Vota," she says. "Be careful out there."

Murphy drops his mother at her house in Midwood and takes Avenue J heading west.

He stops at a red traffic light on Ocean Parkway.

To the left is Avenue U and another self-medicated hour or two jawing with Augie at Joe's Bar and Grill.

To the right is the Prospect Expressway and another two or three hours having a sober one-sided conversation with Ralph before he can unwind enough to fall sleep.

Murphy turns right when the light turns green.

He shakes off the snow as he walks through the front door

of his house. He swings the door shut and takes a step toward the interior. A sound from behind turns him around. He has time to utter only two words as he reaches for his service revolver.

"God. No."

"God is not here," says Andre Harris, as he squeezes the trigger of his muted weapon three times at chest level.

Batman would later say that he probably died before he hit the floor.

Harris puts the gun into his coat pocket, turns up his collar, and heads out the door and down the front steps. Snow is falling much harder now as Harris hits the sidewalk. He pulls the New York Jets wool cap over his ears, glances quickly in both directions, and he hurries south on foot.

It is the city that never sleeps, and for some the night is still young.

For others, it is the end of days.

TWENTY NINE

The body wasn't discovered until six the next morning, when a sixteen-year-old high school co-ed came to deliver the Sunday *Tribune* to the door.

She dropped her armful of newspapers and ran screaming down the snow-covered front steps to the street.

The large, bold headline across the front page of the *Tribune* read: *Killer Speaks, I Will Redeem Another Child.*

An elderly man walking his miniature poodle nearly let go of the leash as the girl ran crying into his arms. When she was finally able to speak coherently, the man hurried into his house and called the police.

The two officers who responded recognized the victim and quickly found the service revolver and the detective's shield. The younger officer went down to the squad car to call it in.

The older officer, a veteran of twenty-seven years, stood solemnly beside the victim. The fallen detective would be in his custody until the ambulance carried the body away, a responsibility he took very seriously.

The snow had fallen throughout the night, leaving a clean white layer of large shimmering flakes on the sidewalks and streets, sparkling like so many diamonds in a thieves' lair from an *Arabian Nights* tale.

As Murphy runs with Ralph beside him, the sun coming up, the sky clear, the precipitation ended, the sparkling diamonds look to Murphy like snow on the ground.

Literary metaphor is not one of Murphy's strong points.

In two hours, it would be an ugly, dirty slush.

In a few days he and his mother would be walking into Most Precious Blood Church, not far from the home where Murphy grew up.

In Gravesend, a Roman Catholic church was never very far from home.

The funeral service would be attended by scores of friends his parents had accumulated during their long residence in the predominantly Italian neighborhood, before his father had moved the family to Midwood. The animosity between the Italians and the Irish was more myth than reality, particularly when families of police officers were involved.

Patrick Murphy had been well respected and very well liked in the neighborhood, and many Gravesend parents had Patrick Murphy to thank for keeping their children on the straight and narrow.

The tragedy was that he couldn't save his own son, Michael.

There would also be a large police presence at the church—men and women who had worked with Murphy's father during his thirty plus years on the force, and those who had worked with Tommy during his ten years. Not to mention all of the women in his mother's circle, who did work with her at church and played contract bridge on Friday nights. It would be a packed house. SRO.

As Murphy and Ralph come into their last mile on this quiet Sunday morning, the sun is already beginning to turn the snow into soupy puddles in their path.

An hour later, Samson gets the call directly from Chief Stanley Trenton.

"There is no good way to say this, Sam, so I'll just say it. Lou Vota has been killed."

"My God, no," says Samson.

"Ambushed at his door last night, he didn't stand a chance."

There was a long silence on the other end of the line. Trenton broke it.

"I know how you must feel," says Trenton.

"No one should ever have to know how I must feel."

"It was probably Andre Harris. I'm keeping the patrol car outside of your house until we get him. No arguments."

"Sure," says Samson.

"I need a huge favor, Sam," says Trenton. "I don't know who else to ask."

"Talk to Lorraine DiMarco?"

"Yes, please."

"She just made it through brain surgery. Jesus."

"I know. God has no favorites. And Sam, I'm putting detectives from the 76th on this. I want you to stay on the Caine case. You're the only one I trust completely to deal with it and I want you to stay as far away from Harris as possible. Understood?"

"Understood," says Samson.

"That's horrible, Sam. I'm so sorry," says Alicia, kneading her husband's shoulders with her fingers.

"I want you to take the kids to your mother's," says Samson, "and I want you all to stay there until they find this guy."

"What about the funeral service? I wanted to be there for Tommy."

"I would rather you and Jimmy didn't go."

"Who's going to speak to Tommy about Lou?"

"I guess I'll have to, but I want to try putting it off until his brother is buried. Meanwhile, I need to decide how to break it to Lorraine."

"Speak to Lorraine's father, Sam," Alicia suggests. "It might be better if she heard it from him."

"Good idea."

"The man who killed Lou," says Alicia. "Do you really think he might come here?"

"It's possible."

"Can't people feel safe anywhere anymore?"

"I don't know."

"Good morning."

"Mr. DiMarco, I'm sorry to have to call you so early. This is Lieutenant Samson."

"No problem, Lieutenant, how can I help you?"

"I need to speak with you, sir. Alone. Can you get out of the house perhaps? Meet me on the corner, say, of Kings Highway and West 10th?"

"How about West 7th, the small coffee shop next to the subway station?"

"Fine, I can be there at eight," says Samson.

"I'll see you then, Lieutenant," says DiMarco.

When Samson arrives, he finds Salvatore DiMarco at the counter. Sal is holding a heavy mug of coffee, engaged in conversation with the counterman. Samson guesses that these two have been going at it together like this for a number of years. He walks over to greet Lorraine's father.

"Hello, Lieutenant," the older man says, taking his hand. "This is Salvatore Martucci, the proprietor of this fine establishment."

"A pleasure to meet you, sir," says Samson, turning to the man behind the counter.

"I've been having coffee with Signore Martucci for more than forty years, Lieutenant. They call us Sal One and Sal Two around here."

"Could we move to a booth, sir?" Samson asks.

"Certainly, would you care for some coffee?"

"Sure."

"Sal, coffee for the lieutenant, please."

"I'll have Paula bring a pot over."

"Thank you, *paisan*."

Lorraine's father follows Samson to a booth in the rear of the small shop. They take seats facing each other. The waitress drops off a pot of coffee and another heavy mug.

"What is this about, Lieutenant?"

"Lou Vota has been killed, sir."

DiMarco lowers his head and remains silent. Tears well up in his eyes. It is all Samson can do to keep from following suit. Sal DiMarco takes a paper napkin from the table and humbly dries his cheeks. He finally looks up at the lieutenant.

"I apologize for my embarrassing display," he says.

"Not at all, sir," says Samson.

"He was a good man."

"I thought Lorraine would be better hearing it from you, sir."

"Lou has been family since Lorraine completed law school. He was like a son to me. You know we lost a son, years ago."

"Yes, sir, I knew that."

"You know, Lieutenant, I can't say why, but I had the idea that Lou was getting ready to ask Lorraine to marry him. This is a terrible tragedy."

"Yes, it is."

"You'll have to excuse me," DiMarco says solemnly. "I need to be with my daughter now, Lieutenant. Unfortunately this cannot wait. I appreciate your taking the time to see to this personally."

"He was like a brother to me," says Samson.

"A terrible tragedy," DiMarco repeats.

"Thank you for your help, sir," says Samson.

Sal DiMarco rises slowly and moves toward the exit, with a forced smile and a pleasant farewell to Martucci as he passes.

Samson watches him go through the door. The detective is determined to control his own emotions until he is back in his car. Samson leaves a five-dollar bill on the table, rises from his seat, gives Martucci a quick nod, and rushes out to the street. He doesn't quite make it.

Samson leans his hands on the hood of his car and sobs loudly. The sight of a large black man, bent over the hood of the vehicle, stops pedestrians in their tracks.

"Look Mommy, the man is crying," says a five-year-old boy, pointing at Samson.

"Let's go, Joey," his mother says, nearly tearing off his arm as she pulls him along.

Samson rises to a standing position and looks around. People look away and the busy pace of the sidewalk begins again. He sees Martucci watching him from the coffee shop window. Next to him the waitress, Paula, a five-dollar bill clutched in her hand and a sad smile on her face.

Samson climbs into his car and drives away.

. . .

"You're just in time, Dad," says Lorraine, glancing over to the door of her hospital room as Salvatore DiMarco walks in and then looking back up at the TV on the wall. "John Garfield and Lana Turner—it's just beginning."

"Lorraine," he says, as he reaches the foot of the bed.

Lorraine looks down from the television and into her father's eyes.

"My God, Dad," she says. "What's happened?"

Samson had broken the news of Vota's death to Rosen and asked if she would join him to bring the news to Murphy.

Now the three detectives sit in Samson's car in front of Murphy's mother's house. Samson and Murphy talk about Vota. Rosen sits in the back seat, quietly listening.

"I'd better get over to the Precinct, Tommy," Samson says. "We have just about everyone out looking for Harris and Caine, and we need someone to sit in the squad room this afternoon."

"I can help, Sam," Murphy says.

"I don't want to see you back before the burial," says Samson. "That's an order."

"I'll try to stay away," says Murphy as he leaves the car.

They watch Murphy walk into the house as Rosen moves to the front seat.

"How do you think he's doing?" asks Rosen.

"I'll let you know as soon as I figure out how I'm doing," Samson says.

Andre Harris sits in his car on Coney Island Avenue, across from the 61st. Harris sees two cars pull into the parking area. He watches as Samson and a woman, probably another pig, walk into the Precinct.

Harris digs into a paper bag and takes out a sausage, pepper and onion sandwich and a quart bottle of beer.

He is prepared to wait.

. . .

"You really don't need to stay, Rosen," says Samson as she follows him into the Precinct.

"I don't mind keeping you company for a while," Rosen says. "Unless you would really rather be alone."

"What the hell, stick around if you really want to."

Rosen smiles as she follows up the stairs behind him.

Murphy goes up to his brother's room. He sits on Michael's bed and takes out the note his brother left at the Midwood Suites.

When his mother walks into the room looking for him ten minutes later, she finds her oldest son crying.

Murphy stuffs the note into his jacket pocket as he hears her approach the bed.

She sits beside him and silently takes his hand.

Gabriel Caine reads the front page story in the Sunday *Tribune*. Though the piece is far more sensational than he would have preferred, it is at least an attempt to express his mission. Gabriel Caine believes that righteous people will understand.

In any case, he thinks, *it will be finished tomorrow.*

"I need to go, Mom," says Murphy.

"Are you going home, Thomas?"

"Absolutely."

"Will you call me later?"

"I will, Mom."

"I'm going to run across the avenue for some food to take out," Samson says. "Can I bring you anything?"

"Is there anything remotely healthy on the menu?" asks Rosen.

"I think they might do canned peaches with cottage cheese."

"Make it a burger and fries," says Rosen.

Murphy is driving on Avenue J crossing Coney Island Avenue toward home when he unexpectedly turns left without signaling, causing the driver behind him to brake hard and hit his horn. Murphy wonders why he made the turn at all, but decides to continue out toward Gravesend.

Samson stops at the front desk to exchange a few words with Washington and another uniformed officer and to ask if either cared for anything from the diner across the avenue before he walks out of the Precinct.

Harris sees Samson come out of the building, drops the beer bottle, grabs the gun from the seat, and steps out of his car. Samson reaches the corner of Coney Island Avenue at Avenue W just as the traffic light turns green, and he steps off the curb to cross the avenue.

At the intersection of Coney Island Avenue and Gravesend Neck Road, Murphy spots Samson and is about to call out a greeting when Andre Harris appears. Harris moves quickly across the avenue toward Samson with his arm extended.

"Motherfucker," Murphy yells as he puts the gas pedal to the floor and leans on his car horn.

The horn startles Harris who squeezes off a shot and turns toward the sound. Murphy watches Samson go down and plows into Harris at the same moment. Murphy stomps on the brake pedal and watches the gun skip across the avenue.

The collision knocks Harris into the air where his body spins once or twice before landing in the middle of the avenue twenty feet from Murphy's buckled hood.

The commotion has brought Desk Sergeant Washington and another officer running from the Precinct and racing up to the avenue with Rosen not far behind. Murphy hits the gas again and brings the car to within inches of Andre Harris' body before braking abruptly and jumping from the car with his weapon in hand. Washington and the other officer reach the body at the same time.

Murphy looks down at Andre Harris and then quickly over to where Rosen is attending to Samson. She signals that the lieutenant is alright.

"Jesus, Murphy, I think you broke both his legs," says Washington.

"You don't know how close I came to parking on his ugly fucking head," says Murphy. "Get this piece of shit out of my sight before I change my mind again. Call for an ambulance, make it two, and make sure that Samson gets to ride the first one that arrives. Grab that gun and bag it. And be careful with the thing—I'm sure that it's the weapon that killed Sergeant Vota."

Murphy moves toward Samson and Rosen as the others drag a screaming Andre Harris to the sidewalk.

A car slows and the driver honks his horn as Murphy crosses.

"Touch that thing again and I'll shove it up your fucking ass!" Murphy yells.

Rosen is sitting on the street, holding Samson across her lap.

"It's not too bad," she says as Murphy reaches them.

"Not too bad. The fuck got me in the elbow," Samson moans. "It hurts like fucking hell."

"I broke his fucking legs for you, Sam," says Murphy.

"I thought I told you explicitly that you were not to come back here until tomorrow, Detective," Samson says.

"I guess you'll have to write me up, Lieutenant," says Murphy.

A few hours later, Murphy and Rosen stand at Samson's hospital bed. Alicia and Jimmy Samson are also there.

"Where's Harris?" asks Samson.

"He's in recovery. We've got two officers guarding the room. His right leg is broken and the left is mush. He'll probably be screaming police brutality the minute he opens his eyes," says Murphy. "They matched the gun with the bullets that killed Lou. Stump and Junior Jefferson will testify that Harris was gunning for you and Vota."

"So, there shouldn't be a problem getting a conviction for first-degree murder," says Samson.

"Problem? Are you kidding," says Murphy. "When we get that maniac into court he won't have a leg to stand on."

"Are you and Rosen leaving now?" asks Samson.

"What's the rush?" asks Murphy.

"I'd like some time with my wife and son. I'm looking for a little sympathy, and you're here making them laugh."

"Goodnight," says Rosen, grabbing Murphy's arm.

"Tommy," says Samson as they reach the door.

"Don't worry, Sam," says Murphy as they walk out of the room. "I've got you covered."

Back at the 61st, the two detectives sit in silence.

"I think I'll hit the road," says Rosen. "I'll come in to help cover tomorrow."

"You may as well see about a transfer over here."

"That depends."

"Depends on what?" asks Murphy.

"Samson should come out okay," says Rosen, changing the subject.

"He may not be able to pitch for the Precinct softball team this spring, but he'll be fine."

"How is your mother doing?"

"Jesus, I should call her. I told her that I was going home hours ago," says Murphy. "My mother caught me crying in Michael's room earlier today. I told her I was disturbed that Michael had been innocent of taking money from his job and no one had believed him. She told me I was wrong, that she had believed him and my father would have believed him. She said that Michael knew that. She told me that Michael loved me. My mother told me that what happened to Michael wasn't my fault, and that if my father was alive, he would tell me the same."

"Believe her, Tommy," says Rosen.

"That it wasn't my fault?"

"Yes, and that your brother loved you."

"Would you like to go out sometime?" asks Murphy.

"Like to a movie or something?"

"That depends."

"Depends on what?"

"On whether or not I want to look into transferring over here," she says, rising to leave. "Don't forget to call your mom. I'll see you tomorrow."

"It won't be the same around here without Lou," says Murphy.

"I know," says Rosen.

THIRTY

Monday morning. Murphy oversleeps. He decides to skip the morning run.

He takes Ralph with him to his mother's house. He sits watching the *Today Show* while his mother prepares breakfast. It is very quiet.

Without Michael, it will be quiet in the house from now on.

After breakfast, his mother hands him a package.

"This came in the mail for Michael on Saturday," his mother says. "I couldn't bring myself to open it until last night. I remember Michael telling me he had ordered it for you, for your birthday, and there being a problem getting it on time."

Murphy opens the package.

He finds an eight-by-ten inch glossy photograph in a simple black frame.

It is a photograph of Mel Gibson, in a scene from *Lethal Weapon*. It is autographed by the actor.

Murphy looks at the photo and then up at his mother.

"Michael said that it was for your wall. At work," his mother says.

Ripley and Kyle drop Mickey off at preschool and then drive on to the older boy's school where the buses wait to take them to the New York City Aquarium.

"Do you think we should try to free the whales?" asks Kyle as they board the bus.

"Let's play it by ear, son," says his father.

Murphy leaves his mother's house and picks up a radio call

as soon as he climbs into his car.

A shooting homicide at Bedford Avenue and Glenwood Road.

The scene is nearby; Murphy decides to run over to check it out.

When he arrives, he finds that one of the uniformed officers who initially responded to the call has collared a suspect.

"What's the story?" Murphy asks the young officer.

"I saw him standing at the edge of the crowd gathered around the body. I don't know exactly what it was, but he looked wrong to me. I went toward him, as if I was going to question a lady standing next to him, and I saw him make a move. I tackled and cuffed him. The guy had the murder weapon right in his jacket."

"Great instincts. How long have you been on the job?"

"Five months."

"What's your name, I'll put in a good word for you with your captain."

"Davis."

"Michael Davis?"

The kid looked more frightened than he must have been taking down the shooter.

"Yes."

"You were involved in the incident at the Midwood Suites?"

"Yes."

"Do you know who I am?"

"Yes, Detective, sir," says Davis. "I've wanted to look you up, but I couldn't find the courage."

"Well you found it today," says Murphy. "I'll put in a good word for you with your captain."

Gabriel Caine places the gun into the cloth satchel. He places all of the cash that he has onto the table in the back room of the restaurant, with a note for Mitch.

Thank you for your hospitality. I hope this covers what I consumed and will also cover repairs to the back door. I'm sure the gun will be returned.

Gabriel also leaves another note, written in crayon.

Caine picks up the satchel and leaves through the back door. As he walks, Caine digs a bus token from his pocket. In the same pocket is a small plastic bottle, filled with holy water taken from Our Lady of Angels that morning. He heads toward the bus stop for the final trip to Gravesend.

A woman dropping garbage into a dumpster in the alley sees the stranger come out from the back of the restaurant. Knowing that Mitch Dunne is away on vacation, she returns to her apartment to call the police.

Sandra Rosen drives over to the 61st Precinct. She is thinking about her last encounter with Lou Vota. Rosen is trying to decide whether Lorraine DiMarco would be better off hearing or not hearing that Lou Vota had it in mind to ask Lorraine to marry him. Rosen tries to put herself in the other woman's shoes in the hope that it might help her to settle the debate, but the shoes don't fit.

Salvatore DiMarco has taken on the responsibility of arranging for Lou Vota's wake and the church funeral service.

The burial service that follows will be in the hands of the Police Department and would incorporate all of the dignity, protocol and decoration that a detective sergeant killed in the line of duty merited.

Both services were scheduled for Tuesday morning and would draw a large audience; including appearances by the mayor and the commissioner of police.

Lorraine waits for Dr. Barnwell to return from his trip to Maryland, hoping for his consent to attend.

Rosen is admiring the latest addition to Murphy's Wall of Fame when the phone rings.

"61st. Rosen speaking."

"This is Chen, is Lieutenant Samson there?"

"He's not, Detective. Can I help you?"

"I'm at Mitch's Coffee Shop on 5th and 72nd," says Chen. "It's where Gabriel Caine has been hiding out. Caine left another note; it doesn't look as if he's coming back here."

"Make sure nothing is disturbed, Detective," Rosen says. "I'm on my way; I'll call for an evidence team."

Rosen quickly fills Murphy in.

"Let's go to Bay Ridge," says Murphy.

"Why don't I go? You and Mel Gibson can hold the fort. Get a team of crime scene investigators down there," Rosen says. "I'll call you as soon as I see what's doing."

"Be careful," says Murphy, picking up the phone as Rosen runs out.

Gabriel Caine gets off the bus at Stillwell Avenue and Kings Highway. He has some time before the white station wagon will deliver the boy to him.

Caine walks with his hands deep in his coat pockets, his right hand touching the grip of the gun, his left hand touching the bottle of holy water.

Gabriel spots the Del Rio Diner up ahead. He removes his right hand from the gun and glances at his wristwatch. Thirty minutes to go, enough time for a last cup of coffee.

"He's been here," says Rosen. "Would you believe that he left money to pay for what he ate and drank? It looks as if Caine is out there with a firearm, Tommy."

"Great news. Did he happen to leave word of where he was headed?"

"No, just another note in crayon," says Rosen. "Luke, 5:31–32. I don't have a copy of the New Testament handy."

"I've got one here, I'll look it up," says Murphy. "I doubt it will tell us anything. I suppose you should stick around there, on the outside chance Caine comes back."

"I'll stay," says Rosen. "But by the look of how he left this place, I'm sure that Caine is never coming back. I think that Caine is on the way to join his little boy."

. . .

Ripley sits with Kyle's third-grade teacher and one of the other parents behind the children.

The kids sit bundled up like little Eskimos, watching in awe as the dolphins perform.

Ripley feels the cell phone vibrate against his chest.

"This had better be important, Stone," Ripley says, after checking the caller ID.

"I just opened a letter written to Gabriel Caine and his wife, from their son's pediatrician. He wrote that he had attempted to reach them by telephone a number of times, without success. The doctor went on to explain that he had another call that night, shortly after speaking to Caine's wife. A three-year-old girl required emergency surgery at another hospital. When the doctor was finally able to make it over to Coney Island, he heard the news about the Caine boy. He wrote that he was very sorry to learn of the boy's death," Stone says. "Yesterday, the Sunday *Tribune* reported that Caine might have one last victim. This could be it."

"Fax the letter to the 61ˢᵗ Precinct. Make sure that all of the information on the doctor is included," says Ripley. "I'll contact Lieutenant Samson."

Ripley digs Samson's business card from his wallet and calls the Precinct.

Murphy finds the passage in the Gospel of Saint Luke.

They that are whole need not a physician, but they that are sick.

I came not to call the righteous, but sinners to repentance.
So what.

The phone rings; the fax machine begins spitting out pages.

"I've got Agent Ripley of the FBI on the line for Samson," says Kelly.

"Put him through," says Murphy.

"Lieutenant?"

"The lieutenant is not in," says Murphy. "What can I do for you?"

"My assistant, Agent Stone, believes that Caine may be targeting the boy's physician."

"Physician?" says Murphy, looking at the Bible.

"His son's doctor. He was supposed to meet Caine and the boy at the hospital and didn't show. The doctor apparently had good reason, but we don't think that Gabriel Caine is aware of the circumstance."

"You may have something there. Who was the doctor?"

"I don't know. Stone is sending a fax over to you."

"It just arrived," says Murphy, walking over to the machine and taking up the top sheet. "Jesus, I know who this is. I'll try to get hold of him."

"Could you use help?"

"I can always use help. Where are you?"

"At the Aquarium, Coney Island," says Ripley. "With a busload of third-graders."

"I'd hate to drag you away."

"It's quite alright."

"Can you see the roller coaster from where you are?"

"Which one?"

"The biggest one, it should be the nearest."

"The Cyclone?"

"That's it," says Murphy. "Go to the entrance on Surf Avenue; I'll have someone pick you up."

"I'll be there," says Ripley.

Ripley explains to the teachers that he needs to leave on important business, and then he speaks to his son.

"I'll call your Aunt Connie; she'll pick you up when you get back to the school."

"Okay, Dad."

"You're not upset that I have to go, are you son?"

"No. We'll free the whales next time," Kyle says.

Murphy telephones the physician's residence. A woman answers identifying herself as the doctor's mother.

"Charles is at the hospital—his wife has just given birth," says the woman.

"Does he have other children?"

418

"The two girls are here. My husband should be leaving the store anytime now to pick up the boy from school."

"Is the boy the oldest?"

"Yes, he is," says the woman. "What is this about?"

"I don't have time to explain," he says. "I'm very sorry; I don't mean to alarm you. Please remain in the house with the children. It will be alright. Could you give me the number at the store?"

"Detective Murphy," the woman says, after giving him the phone number. "Promise me that you won't let anything happen to my husband or my grandson."

"I promise," says Murphy.

Murphy ends the connection and calls the store.

"Mr. Campo, this is Detective Murphy."

"This is Frank Sullivan. Joe left to pick up his grandson."

"Is he dropping the boy off at home?"

"They usually stop here first—the boy walks home."

"Frank, when they get back have Joe take the boy to his son's house and wait there."

"What's wrong, Detective?"

"I'll explain when I get there, just make sure that they go to the house and stay put," Murphy says.

Murphy starts for the door as the phone rings.

"This is Ivanov; I've got Agent Ripley with me."

"Get over to Avenue S and West 10th," says Murphy.

"That's where the first boy was found, on the roof."

"It is," says Murphy. "Get over to the grocery."

Murphy hangs up and runs out of the squad room.

"So, Frankie," asks Joe Campo, as he turns the white station wagon onto Highlawn Avenue at West 6th Street. "How do you feel about having a new baby brother?"

"I'm glad it's a brother, Grandpa," says the boy. "I have too many sisters already."

"Too many?" says Joe.

"Well, just enough sisters," says Frankie.

"Do you want me to drop you off at the house, with your grandmother and the girls?"

"Can I stay at the store for a while, Grandpa," asks Frankie, "with you and Frank?"

"Sure," says Joe Campo, smiling proudly. "You can hang out for a while with the guys."

Ivanov and Ripley are in her car coming west on 86th Street from Shell Road. Ivanov turns right onto West 6th, heading toward Avenue S.

Gabriel Caine stands on West 10th, on the east side of the street, halfway between the doctor's home and the grocery at the corner of Avenue S. Caine sees the white station wagon turn onto 10th Street from Highlawn Avenue. Gabriel stands watching, waiting to see if the car will stop at the house or continue up to the avenue.

Murphy decides to drive past the doctor's house first. He takes Avenue U to West 9th Street and then heads across 9th toward Highlawn.

When Caine sees that the station wagon is not slowing at the house, he lowers his head and starts moving toward Avenue S. The wagon parks at the corner, on the east side of the street, along the west wall of the grocery store.

Gabriel Caine rushes up to the driver's side, pulling the gun from his pocket as Joe Campo opens the car door.

"Get out of the car, leave the keys," Caine says.

"Sure, relax, I'll do whatever you want," says Campo. "Frankie, get out of the car and walk home, son."

"You get out, sir. Leave the keys," says Caine. "The boy stays in the car."

"Joe, get the boy away from here."

Caine turns to the voice behind him, Frank Sullivan is moving toward him very quickly. Campo starts the engine as the gun in Caine's hand fires involuntarily and Joe tears away across the avenue as Sullivan hits the ground. Murphy hears the gunshot as he turns onto 10th Street and he races to the end of the block. Ivanov and Ripley hear the gunshot as they come over the hill on Avenue S between 7th and 8th. Ivanov

420

speeds to the scene.

Caine stands frozen, looking down at Sully's body.

Murphy reaches the corner and screeches to a stop. As Murphy jumps from his car, Gabriel bolts blindly across the avenue. Ivanov slams her brakes and swerves right to avoid running Caine down.

Joe Campo has come around the block. He sends the boy into the house and runs up to the avenue. Murphy is down on the ground with Sully, on the cell phone calling for an ambulance.

"He ran into the apartment building across Avenue S," says Ivanov, joining them. "Ripley is there, out in front."

"He's on the roof," says Joe Campo.

They all look up to the roof and see Gabriel Caine looking down at them.

An hour later the avenue is jammed.

Cars from the 60th, 61st and 62nd Precincts blockade all through-traffic on West 10th Street and along Avenue S.

Uniformed officers keep onlookers back a good distance from the apartment building. Sal DiMarco and Bobby Hoyle stand among those gathered to the west of the intersection.

A SWAT team is stationed at the fourth floor landing, at the foot of the stairs that lead to the roof. They are told to go no further until otherwise instructed.

Officers have gone door-to-door telling residents to stay in their apartments or to clear out.

Sharpshooters stand out on the street and on a nearby roof, instructed to hold fire unless otherwise ordered.

Print, television and radio reporters have arrived and are still arriving. Serena Huang is only one of them.

Frank Sullivan has been rushed by ambulance to Coney Island Hospital where doctors work on his chest wound.

Rosen has arrived, as have Landis and Mendez. They stand with Joe Campo, Ivanov, Ripley and Murphy in front of the grocery store looking up at the roof.

Occasionally, Caine can be seen peering down at them and at the crowd.

Detective Thomas Murphy finds himself in charge.

It is decided that Murphy and Ripley will go into the building to try talking to Gabriel Caine.

They reach the SWAT team at the fourth-floor landing and can see the door that leads out to the roof.

The door is wide open, but Caine is out of sight.

Murphy and Ripley start up the stairs.

On a Friday afternoon two weeks earlier, at about the same time of day, Joe Campo had led Vota and Samson up to this same roof. To the body of Billy Ventura.

They reach the top of the stairs; neither man has drawn a weapon.

Murphy calls from the doorway, "Gabriel Caine, this is Detective Murphy of the 61st Precinct. I'd like to talk with you."

"Is the man I shot going to be alright?" calls Caine.

"Yes," says Murphy, though he can't be sure.

"I didn't mean to shoot, and I didn't mean to hurt that other boy on Shore Road."

"Unbelievable. This guy has killed three children and he's apologizing for smashing some kid's knee," Murphy whispers to Ripley.

"He won't be easy to talk down," says Ripley, "but I don't think he'll use the gun. Except maybe on himself."

"Mr. Caine, please, we only want to talk."

"Who else is there?" calls Caine.

Just half of the entire Brooklyn force.

"Agent Ripley of the FBI," says Murphy.

"I don't know."

"Please, Mr. Caine," says Murphy. "I have something to show you. It's important."

"What is it?"

"Let us come out," says Murphy.

Murphy and Ripley look at each other. And wait.

"Just you," Caine finally says. "Keep your hands in the

air."

"Jesus, can you believe this?" says Murphy.

"You don't have to go out there," says Ripley.

"But I will. Do me a favor, Sundance," Murphy says, smiling tentatively. "If Caine shoots me, kill the son of a bitch."

"You bet," says Ripley, smiling at Murphy's effort.

"Okay, Mr. Caine, I'm coming out alone." Murphy says. "Wish me luck, Ripley."

"Be careful, Butch," Ripley says.

Murphy takes a deep breath, pulls out the fax copy, raises his arms and steps out onto the roof.

Caine is sitting with his back against the low brick wall that edges the roof on the north side of the building. He is pointing the gun directly at the doorway.

"What do you have to show me?" he asks when Murphy steps into view.

"It's a letter," Murphy says, waving the paper in his hand, "to you and your wife. Can I bring it over?"

"Yes. Slowly."

"Be careful with that thing," says Murphy, staring at the weapon as he moves toward Caine.

Murphy slowly brings his arm down when he reaches the other man. Caine takes the paper. It is the faxed copy of the letter written by his son's doctor.

"Move back to the door," says Caine.

Murphy returns to the doorway.

"Can I lower my arms?" Murphy asks.

"Yes. And sit down there, near the door," says Caine.

Murphy sits. Caine holds the letter in one hand and reads. The other hand holds the gun, pointed in Murphy's direction.

"How is it going out there?" whispers Ripley from inside the doorway.

"Couldn't really tell you," says Murphy.

"The little girl?" says Caine.

"Excuse me?"

"The doctor says here that he needed to operate on a little girl that night, the night my boy died," says Caine. "How is the girl?"

"She's fine," says Murphy, having no idea and having no idea what else he could possibly say. "Dr. Campo saved the girl's life."

"Thank God," says Caine.

Gabriel places the letter on the roof. He takes the bottle of holy water from his pocket and slowly begins to stand.

As Caine rises, Murphy sees the bullets on the ground that had been blocked from view where Gabriel sat. Caine stands with his back to the avenue and extends his arm.

Gabriel waves the unloaded weapon in his hand.

Murphy quickly realizes Caine's intention and jumps to his feet.

"Hold your fire!" Murphy yells.

A shot rings out.

Caine is spun around by the violent impact of the bullet and he topples over the short brick wall as Ripley runs out onto the roof.

Ripley reaches Murphy at the edge of the roof and they look down to the street below.

Gabriel Caine's body lies in the middle of the avenue.

On a nearby roof, a marksman lowers his rifle.

ACKNOWLEDGMENTS

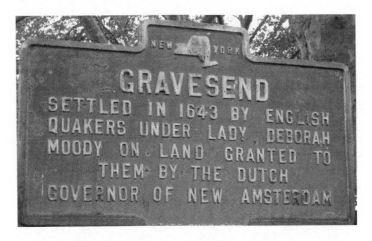

GRAVESEND has gone through a good number of transformations over the course of a dozen years.

The book evolved into its present incarnation when I finally understood what I was humbly attempting to explore...namely how the manner in which human beings handle adversity will ultimately define them as persons...good or evil...weak or strong...fair or unjust...loved or despised...admired or feared.

There are many good and fair and admirable people who helped make it possible for me to complete the long journey...I need to mention a few.

LINDA ABRAMO MICHAELS, for being my most dedicated fan and most effective publicist...and the greatest sister a boy could possibly hope for.

JANIS McWAYNE, for being there at the beginning.

DANIELLA BaRASHEES and SONNY WASINGER, for years of support and encouragement.

STEVEN ALTMAN, for bringing *ART* into the conversation as regularly as possible.

TUPPER CULLUM, for being himself.

ERIC CAMPBELL, for working with me so diligently at getting the novel ready for general consumption.

And finally, for giving me another opportunity to get the words out, I acknowledge my boundless appreciation to DOWN AND OUT BOOKS.

J. L. Abramo, Denver, Colorado

ABOUT THE AUTHOR

J. L. ABRAMO was born in the oceanside paradise of Brooklyn, New York on Raymond Chandler's 59th birthday. Abramo received a BA in Sociology and Education from City College of the City University of New York and an MA in Social Psychology from the University of Cincinnati. He has been a long-time educator, a producer and director of theatre, and an actor on stage and in film; with a number of television credits including roles on *Homicide: Life on the Street* and *Law and Order*. Abramo's first novel, *Catching Water in a Net*, was recipient of the St. Martin's Press/Private Eye Writers of America Award for Best First Private Eye Novel. *Catching Water in a Net* and two follow-up Jake Diamond mysteries, *Clutching at Straws* and *Counting to Infinity*, originally published in hardback, are now available for all eBooks reading devices from Down and Out Books. Abramo is a card-carrying member of the Screen Actors Guild and the Mystery Writers of America.

For more information please visit:

www.jlabramo.com

www.facebook.com/jlabramo

www.downandoutbooks.com

OTHER TITLES FROM DOWN AND OUT BOOKS

By J. L. Abramo
Catching Water in a Net
Clutching at Straws
Counting to Infinity
Gravesend

By Trey R. Barker
2,000 Miles to Open Road
Road Gig: A Novella
Exit Blood (*)

By Richard Barre
The Innocents
Bearing Secrets
Christmas Stories
The Ghosts of Morning
Blackheart Highway
Burning Moon
Echo Bay (*)

By Milton T. Burton
Texas Noir

By Reed Farrel Coleman
The Brooklyn Rules

By Don Herron
Willeford (*)

By Terry Holland
An Ice Cold Paradise
Chicago Shiver
Warm Hands, Cold Heart (*)

By David Housewright & Renée Valois
The Devil and the Diva

By David Housewright
Finders Keepers

By Jon Jordan
Interrogations

By Jon Jordan & Ruth Jordan
Murder and Mayhem in Muskego
(Editors)

By Valester Jones
The Pimp and the Gangster (*)

By Bill Moody
Czechmate: The Spy Who Played Jazz
Fair Trade (*)

By Gary Phillips
The Perpetrators
*Scoundrels: Tales of Greed, Murder
and Financial Crimes* (Editor)

By Lono Waiwaiole
Wiley's Lament
Wiley's Shuffle
Wiley's Refrain
Dark Paradise

(*)—Coming in 2012

63819397R00265

Made in the USA
Charleston, SC
13 November 2016